Born and brought up in Leicester, Lou Wakefield is a writer, director and actor. Highlights of her eclectic career include being in the original cast of *Top Girls* at the Royal Court and the Public Theatre in New York, playing Janet in the *Rocky Horror Show* at the King's Road Theatre in 1975, and Jackie Woodstock in *The Archers*. TV appearances include *Inside Out*, *Morse*, *The Bill* and *Casualty*. Amongst her many television productions, she has directed *Coronation Street* and *Brookside*. She wrote the award winning *Firm Friends* for ITV, and co-writes the highly successful *Ladies of Letters*, for BBC Radio 4, which stars Prunella Scales and Patricia Routledge.

D1516245

Also by Lou Wakefield

Tuscan Soup

Rural Bliss

LOU WAKEFIELD

Sleeping Partners

HODDER

Copyright © 2004 by Lou Wakefield

First published in Great Britain in 2004 by Hodder and Stoughton
A division of Hodder Headline
First published in paperback in 2005 by Hodder and Stoughton
A Hodder paperback

3

A CIP catalogue record for this title is available from the British Library

ISBN 0 340 73513 9

Typeset in Plantin Light by
Phoenix Typesetting, Auldgirth, Dumfriesshire

Printed and bound in Great Britain by
Mackays of Chatham Ltd, Chatham, Kent

Hodder Headline's policy is to use papers that are natural, renewable and recyclable
products and made from wood grown in sustainable forests. The logging and
manufacturing processes are expected to conform to the environmental
regulations of the country of origin

Hodder and Stoughton
A division of Hodder Headline
338 Euston Road
London NW1 3BH

To Avril

I owe a huge debt of gratitude to my good friend Jacki Burgess in Melbourne for answering all my e-mail enquiries about life Down Under, and for her suggestion that I use Black Rock for the location; and to her husband, my good friend Chris, who is the Aussie rep for a home exchange website, www.HomeExchange.com (check it out if you're thinking of house swapping and you're not put off the idea by this book!). Thanks to ten pound Poms, Geoff & Elaine Wareing, and Ella, of the Oldham Exiles web page; to David Quilter for his sailing expertise; to Louise Sherwin-Stark for checking my use of Australian vernacular; to Sue Fletcher for being a brick (and for great lunches!); and as always, to my indefatigable and supportive agents, Clare Alexander and Rochelle Stevens.

I

After the roller-coaster ride of recent events Pauline Watkins should have grown used to seeing the stuff of her wildest fantasies made manifest, but being massaged by the coin-in-the-slot vibrating chair in Kuala Lumpur took the biscuit.

It had been gentle with her at first but now, with a surprisingly single-minded assertiveness, it grabbed the back of her neck between two leather-clad steel balls and reminded her of . . . something she had come away to forget. She felt guilty, heartbroken, aroused – and suddenly extremely anxious that she hadn't left a note out saying where to find the spare linen. Which these days was just par for the course. So why did she feel so close to the edge of hysteria that her toes were curling in her shoes?

Perhaps it was the added stress of having just stepped off a disorienting fourteen-hour flight (or maybe it was the thought of having to step on to another eight-hour flight almost immediately). But being in the grip of these inappropriate dizzying feelings in the middle of a hot and humid crowded airport concourse, with her husband taking photographs and her teenage daughter looking on, was about as bizarre as she could handle.

'Poll. Polly!' Mick called to her, sizing her up in his viewfinder. 'Smile for the birdie! You're supposed to be looking relaxed!'

The whirlpool of emotions that she was sure were reflected

in her facial expression, were instantly replaced by a look of intense irritation. 'Pauline,' she corrected him tersely. God! If he couldn't even cope with *this* change in her, what hope was there for their marriage? She forced herself to smile through gritted teeth for the family album.

Her uncomfortable feelings of guilt having been neatly transmuted into resentment against her husband, she was now free to lie back and enjoy the good vibrations of the chair, and even to wallow defiantly in the sense memories which it awakened. But just as she was remembering a pair of indefatigable hands sensually massaging her body all over, the machine stopped as abruptly as it had started.

'Have you finished now, then?' her daughter Gemma asked her in a nasty accusing tone, which carried with it no respect for post-coital tranquillity, and even less for her mother. 'Can I go and get a Coke now, please?'

'Feel free,' said Pauline, struggling out of the chair with some reluctance. 'I don't know why you felt you had to stay to watch anyway.'

'Dad wouldn't let me go on my own,' Gemma supplied, glowering darkly at her father. 'He thought his likkle girlie might get lost.'

'If only,' was on the tip of Pauline's tongue as she surveyed this fruit of her loins, but she reminded herself sharply that Gemma had reason enough to feel resentful at the moment, so instead she dug around in her handbag for her purse and said, 'The Cokes are on me. Set 'em up!'

Striding over to the self-service cafeteria, followed – or rather, policed, as far as she was concerned – by her parents, Gemma thought she might die of suffocation long before this fortnight was over. She was eighteen for God's sake, nearly nineteen actually – old enough to vote, to drink, to smoke, to marry – and far too old to be on holiday alone with her mum and dad. What *had* she been thinking of? She cursed her stupid brother for not bunking off uni and coming with them, and her heart ached for her boyfriend Stu. If only he'd had more luck in finding work, if only he'd been able to save enough for his airfare . . . Life was horrible. It wasn't fair. Whose idea was it anyway, to go to Australia? Hers and Stu's. They'd been planning it ever since school. Trust her mother to steal their ideas and make them her own. It was daylight bleddy robbery when you thought about it.

And now Dad had uttered his favourite phrase which always made her want to kill, and was wanging on with his precious Facts and Figures. How the hell could she possibly survive fourteen days of this?

'It's a pity,' said Mick, innocently unaware that those three words could turn his daughter's thoughts to patricide, 'that we can't go out and explore Kuala Lumpur. I'd have liked to have seen the Petronas Twin Towers. Designed by the same chap as did the Canary Wharf tower in London. Argentinian. Cesar Pelli. It's 452 metres high, and the two towers are joined by a 58 metre skybridge. Quite a feat. Kuala Lumpur started as a British tin-mining outpost in 1857.' He looked around the cafeteria at his fellow travellers. 'You'll have noticed, even here in the airport, its interesting ethnic mix: 58 per cent of the population are Malay, with 31 per cent Chinese, 8 per cent Indian, and 3 per cent "other", making the Malaysian cuisine one of the most interesting in the world. Average temperature 32 degrees centigrade, 90 degrees Fahrenheit, all year round. Tropical, you see. But very humid: 80 per cent. Of course, they get 2700 millimetres of rainfall a year – or 105 inches – so that's hardly surprising. It's GMT plus 8 hours here, so whereas we left England . . .' he paused to consult his watch '. . . almost fifteen hours ago, it's actually nearly a whole day later already. Weird that, isn't it, when you think about it?

Because by the time we reach Melbourne we'll have lost a whole half-day. Twenty-two hours in the air, but we land thirty-four hours after we took off. Of course, we gain it again on our way back, but . . .'

If he'd held his audience's attention at the outset he had certainly lost it now, but Mick was impervious to such outward signs as heavy sighs and eyes cast heavenward, so interested was he by his inner world of data. Facts were dependable, and reassuringly constant in an ever changing world, and Mick collected them with the same enthusiasm as a child on a beach swoops on shells. Indeed, were he ever to find the courage to answer questions in a television studio rather than from the safety of his own settee, Mick could have been a billionaire – he wouldn't even need to phone a friend. It was feelings that had him confused and all at sea. That, and talking about feelings, as his wife Pauline could testify. With knobs on.

So here they sit now – the Watkins of Leicester – together but alone, in Kuala Lumpur airport, sipping Coke in a country they'll never see, in a time zone that makes no sense to their internal clocks, sweating in temperatures their bodies weren't designed to withstand: the lone representative of the spear side keeping chaos at bay with his hard facts of general knowledge; the two members of the distaff side yearning for the lovers they've left behind. An ordinary family, whose lives are about to change in ways they could not even begin, at this moment, to envisage.

Of course, change was what it was all about. It was the desire for change that had brought them this far already. And all because Pauline Watkins had woken up one morning earlier in the year and discovered she was thirty-nine. Thirty-nine! Next step forty! Halfway to death already, she mused, as her husband arrived in the bedroom with a cup of tea and a card, and what had she achieved? A semi-detached house on the same estate she'd grown up on, her parents up the road, her sister round the corner, her brother a mere stroll away – not to mention the cousins, aunties, uncles, grandparents, friends of the family who went back three generations, all within nodding distance of her own front door; a soul-sapping job in tele-sales; a son away at university, who spent most of his time, she felt sure in her bones, dodging lectures; a daughter who, together with her slacker boyfriend, was doing a gap year which looked to Pauline more like a void; and last but not least, a husband who hadn't touched her in more than a year. Hers was a centre which could not hold. Must not hold. If it did, she might just as well roll over right now and cark it. Such was the darkness of her thoughts at the dawn of her fortieth year.

But Pauline was no quitter and no slouch, and as the weeks went by, rolling over and carking it had slipped way down her agenda of Things To Be Done, and had been completely nudged off her new, more pressing list of Stuff That Needs Doing Urgently. And ironically, it had been her husband's birthday present to her which had occasioned this particular transformation. She supposed now she should be grateful, but at the time it had been all she could do not to throw her morning tea in his stupid placid face and scream like a banshee.

'A *computer* course? *Me?* Have you totally and utterly taken leave of your senses?' A rhetorical question, since clearly he had. Mick just grinned back haplessly, with that irritating mix of affability and embarrassment which was intrinsically his. 'What the hell makes you think I'd be interested in *that*?' she continued mercilessly, waving the receipt from the Adult Education Centre like a weapon beneath his nose. What she wanted from him – what she ached for, if he had but asked – was to be the object of his desire again. A weekend in Paris, a couple of days in London – even, for God's sake, a table for two at the local Harvester – would have gone down better than this.

'It's not a computer course as such,' he explained patiently, as if she cared about the difference. 'It's an Introduction to the Internet. The World Wide Web at your fingertips. I thought you'd find it, you know, interesting. Stimulating. Like you said the other week. About being bored and wanting more stimulation.'

Pauline choked on a bitter laugh which sounded like a sob. Speechless. He had rendered her speechless. He stood there, pathetically vulnerable, his goodness shining from every pore, trying and failing to make her feel better. She'd said her life was empty, and he had tried to give her the world. Did he really not understand, after all she'd said on the subject, that the world she longed for was nestled in his pyjamas bottoms, curled up and sleeping, as was its wont? He'd kissed her affectionately then, and given her a brotherly hug, had slipped back into bed with her and said, 'Fancy a birthday cuddle? We've got half an hour before we need to get up.' And it was in that thirty minutes, as her husband lay sleeping contentedly with her in his arms, that she lay awake, vowing to Change Their Lives or Bust.

In fact, in those few days of her descent into the darkness known as early middle age, 'bust' was the byword which brought her most comfort. Both her kids had left school now. Her son Matt was in his second year of uni, and although he was only over at Nottingham, they rarely saw him between laundry runs. Gemma, though still technically living at home in her gap year, spent most of her time round at her boyfriend Stu's. Apparently – or so they claimed – they were planning their world trip before taking up their places at university. So what was to keep Pauline at home? Wasn't she free now to leave her sexless marriage and strike out on her own, before it was too late, before she got so wrinkled and repulsive that no man, let alone her husband, would spare her a second glance?

Thus she reviewed her life in the dark light of depression. Who needed her? Whose heart went boom-boody-boom when she walked into a room? Nobody's – unless you counted the dog's, and then only at meal times. So what was she *for*, exactly? What point was there in heaving herself out of bed in the mornings, to go to a fluorescent-lit cubicle, to clamp a headset to her ears and work through the phone directory, cold-calling recalcitrant consumers of conservatories? It was no kind of job for a woman who had forgotten that she had a right to be here, that she was a child of the universe, no less than the trees and stars: indeed, these days she laughed hollowly whenever her eye came to rest on the inspiriting text of the Desiderata in the smallest room at home (painstakingly copied in her best calligraphy by Gemma, aged fourteen, as an expression of filial counsel). No, Pauline was buggered if she would go placidly, gracefully surrendering the things of youth. And if Max Ehrmann had had her life, she thought bitterly, she doubted that he would even have had the neck to suggest she try.

Nevertheless, the date arrived when it was time for her inaugural session at night school, and Mick drove her cheerfully, and with enthusiastic words of encouragement, to the local college to take her place behind a computer console, reminding her of the time when her mother had abandoned her on her first day at infant school. Under the cover of hanging her coat on the back of her chair, she dared to squint round the room and saw that, despite her misgivings, there was an upside to this after all. Since most of her fellow pupils were septuagenarians, she was the youngest one there by far.

That first session was unremarkable in every aspect bar one. This is a computer, this switch turns it on, the secret code is www dot, begin. The one remarkable aspect was he who was the keeper of this arcane knowledge. He had a wonderful warmth about him, an engaging kind of certainty that he *did* have a right to be here, and that, moreover, being here was fun: the sort of person who looked as if he felt comfortable in his own skin. She kept sneaking glances at him, sure that she recognised him from somewhere, if only she could put her finger on where.

By the end of the session, though she had learnt what a search engine was and knew how to Ask Jeeves, she was still no closer to answering the question 'Who the bloody hell is he?', but by now it was driving her mad. And though she dallied while collecting her things together, hoping to give him the chance, perhaps, to recognise her and introduce himself, he passed up the opportunity and left the class with a charming smile, assuring them all of his best attentions next week.

It was Mick who put his finger on it when he came to collect her. She was buckling herself into the passenger seat next to him, and answering his excited query, 'How was it?' with a sniffed, 'Not bad,' when he leant over her suddenly, wound down her window, and called out, 'Asheem!', which at first she took for a sneeze. Turning to follow her husband's gaze she saw her tutor approach them. He bent down to peer into their car.

'Mr Watkins!' he said. 'And *Mrs* Watkins. Of course, how silly of me! I thought I knew you from somewhere, but I couldn't quite—'

'Me too,' she assured him. 'How've you been?' It was Dolly and Dinesh's youngest from next door, and it was small wonder she hadn't been able to place him in her mind. Last seen, he had been the irritating, wiry little youth who kept banging his football against their shared garden fence, eventually breaking it. A decade on, the prodigal had returned home, grown up, matured, and filled out in all the right places.

Naturally it made sense to all three parties that, in future, Asheem should give Pauline a lift to and from the classes. Natural, too, that during these short journeys an easy intimacy developed between them – she had, after all, known him since he was a lad, and she was interested to hear what he'd been doing with his life. Less natural, she told herself fiercely, as she censured herself in the bathroom mirror on the evening of week four, for her to be suddenly taking such pains over her hair and make-up. She decided to give week five a miss. But week six was the last session, and calling for her, Asheem wouldn't take no for an answer. To anything, as it so transpired. After the lesson, there was a goodbye drink in the pub with the rest of the class. By the time they left, they both knew they'd be taking the long route home.

That first time, the intensity of her own passion had shocked her. As Asheem had driven them further from home and closer to the point of no return, she had tried to reason herself out of it. It was foolhardy, it was reckless, there was too much at stake. But when he finally brought the car to a halt in Groby Pool car park, she was trembling from head to foot with the anticipation of his touch.

At thirty-nine to his twenty-nine, she was no Mrs Robinson coaching a graduate – if anything it was just the reverse. Whatever else Asheem had been doing in the ten years since he'd left home, he had certainly not neglected his studies in how to make a woman happy. He was inventive and in-exhaustible, it seemed, even in the confined space of his car. And it was so wonderful to feel desired again at last. She felt like Sleeping Beauty, just woken up and raring to go. Driving back afterwards, Pauline knew she would do this again. Didn't they have the perfect excuse for him to be in her home on her afternoons off? If anybody saw him coming and going from her house, he'd been giving her extra computer lessons, hadn't he?

A couple of hours later she was wide awake, lying beside a happily snoozing Mick in their marital bed. At first, the dreadful guilt that was nudging at the corners of her mind was assuaged by her feelings of anger and resentment towards him. This was all his fault anyway – she wouldn't be doing this if Mick had ever taken her complaints seriously. Every time she'd tried to engage him in serious debate over the last twelve months, he'd just agreed, embarrassed and shamefaced, that something needed to be done, and then afterwards done nothing. So if she had been forced to have recourse to infidelity, who in the world could blame her? Herself, apparently.

Tossing and turning, sleep avoiding her like the plague, she finally got up and crept downstairs to make herself a cup of tea and try to think things through. Tempting as it was to blame Mick for her own actions, she was a big girl now and she knew it was specious. She must stop this immediately, nip it in the bud. She didn't like being a liar and a cheat. But if she didn't vent her frustration by sleeping with Asheem, she'd be back being a sexless blob and she already knew she couldn't handle that. And was it cheating, really, when what she was giving away to the boy next door was something her husband couldn't have made plainer that he truly didn't want?

Round and round she went, for hours and hours, locked inside a circular argument, till she thought her head might explode. By 4 a.m., vexed almost to screaming point, she knew she wasn't going to solve her problem tonight any more than she'd been able to solve it before this . . . latest complication . . . had come along to haunt her. But neither could she clock off and go to sleep. Needing distraction from the torture of her thoughts, she sat at the family computer with her third cup of tea, and idly began to surf the web. And so it was, ironically, that at the very moment she stopped seeking the answer, she found it.

Since escape was on her mind – from herself, from her life – she started looking up faraway places. It was soothing to see pictures of the sand and sea and sun in exotic locations, even though she knew she would never be able to afford to visit them in person. But as one site led to another in her desultory, random search, she suddenly found herself staring at the screen and sitting up straight with interest. She had arrived at www.fairexchange.biz, which appeared to offer the impossible. For the modest price of a joining fee, you could be matched up to a family in a far-flung place and swap houses for the duration, with no more money changing hands at all. A free holiday! Or almost. No hotel bills, no expensive eating out in restaurants: all you needed to find was the airfare . . .

She stopped then, and paced about the room wild-eyed, her thoughts leaving the problem of her husband and turning to the problem of her daughter. Wouldn't this solve everything, in one fell swoop, all of them going to Australia together, on a big family holiday? For all Gemma and her boyfriend's talk about taking a year off to see the world before going to university, so far they hadn't taken one step out of Leicester. It wasn't Gemma who was dragging her heels – to Pauline's surprise, her daughter had actually bitten the bullet and was doing the required low-paid, menial work necessary to fund this exercise – it was her boyfriend, Stu. Excuse followed excuse about why he was unable to find profitable employment, and whereas Pauline and Mick had talked abut helping Gemma out with a bit of cash as a reward for all her hard work, there was no way in the world that they had the inclination or the wherewithal to help hopeless Stu. Maybe this could be the answer? Without need for confrontation, they could get her away from his influence for a while. They'd include him in the invitation, of course, but safe in the knowledge that he'd never get his act together to come.

Her mind now racing, Pauline thought too of her absent son, Matt. Since he'd started at Nottingham Uni last year she'd missed him terribly, and though she would never dream of pressuring him, she wished that he'd come home more often. What if she dangled the carrot of a couple of weeks in Australia – would he bite? And could she and Mick ever manage to scrape the price of four airfares together, without having to take out a loan?

Returning to her seat she pictured the rose-tinted scene, coloured by memories of all those happy holidays, long ago, when the kids had been small. Couldn't she recapture that now, remind herself of what she had, rather than what she couldn't have? And wasn't there just the tiniest, remotest possibility that Mick might remember too? If they could just break this cycle, step away from the norm, find a small pocket of space and time where they could breathe again, be together again, perhaps even fall in love again . . . ?

Impulsively, she turned back to the computer and keyed in her credit card details to join the house-swap scheme. Nothing ventured, nothing gained, she thought giddily, as she filled out the online form to offer her three-bedroomed home in exchange for similar, anywhere in Australia. Finally, exhausted and exhilarated, she pressed Send, and dispatched all her hopes to the ether. Now fate would take its turn, and determine whether it would be Sydney or Adelaide, Melbourne or Perth, or a resort on the exotically named Gold Coast. What did she care, so long as they were all together on the other side of the world?

It wasn't until she was back in bed, cuddled up to Mick, trying to get warm, that her high spirits suddenly plummeted. What Australian in their right mind would give up their home in paradise, she asked herself glumly, for a post-War semi on a council estate two miles outside Leicester?

2

Events had conspired recently to make Lorna Mackenzie fear that she might be going off her head. One minute she'd had everything in her life nicely taped down, the next she was staring into a fathomless vortex of chaos. Nothing, not even the death of her father, had unhinged her like this before. Indeed, at the time, everybody had complimented her on how seamlessly she'd coped with that tragedy. Despite the shock of losing her dad to a heart attack when he was still in his early sixties, she had recovered quickly, organised a beautiful funeral, sorted out his affairs, had a granny annexe built in the grounds of her home and moved her mother into it, all within a breathtakingly short time. If anybody could do it, Lorna Mackenzie could.

At thirty-two, she was in the prime of her life: a corporate lawyer in the Melbourne offices of a solid multinational, she had a beautiful home overlooking the bay at Black Rock, a fabulous car and ocean-going boat, a handsome and successful husband, and her widowed mum neat and tidy where she could keep an eye on her, safe in her own back yard. Most of this still held true, of course, but it was cold comfort since the 'husband' part of the equation had suddenly detached itself and spun off out of orbit.

Standing now under a power shower of warm water in the *Lifestyle Centre* in Singapore airport, she shivered at the memory, despite the heat. Finding out about Greg's infidelity had rocked her to her foundation, pushed her to the very edge. After all, there were *some* things in life, surely, that you thought needed organising just the once: which you could safely assume, when you'd done so, that they'd bloody well stay put? And it wasn't as if she was naive or unrealistic. She prided herself on her pragmatism, and she knew what men were like. She had assumed from the outset, as part of her risk assessment, that Greg would continue to get his occasional jollies outside the connubial contract. Which was where she'd made her fatal mistake, of course. She had erroneously presumed that said occasional jollies would be casual.

Well, there was nothing more she could do now, she counselled herself, sighing, as she turned off the water and started to towel herself dry. She'd set all the machinery in motion for the subsequent damage-limitation exercise, and now she'd have to wait and see. Strapping her Cartier watch back on her delicate wrist, she noted with satisfaction that they'd already completed thirty per cent of the journey which would take him with her to the other side of the world, away from the bitch.

Stepping out of the changing room to return her towel, she found her mother already dressed and chatting ten to the dozen to the receptionist.

'All right, darl?' June called loudly, breaking off her conversation as Lorna approached. Not for the first time, Lorna cringed invisibly at her mother's coarse accent. Did she have to sound like an escapee from *Prisoner: Cell Block H*? It wasn't as if she'd been born in her adopted country – Mum had emigrated to Australia as a 'ten pound Pom'.

'That's better, ain't it?' June continued, imperturbably. 'Nice shower. All nice and cool and ready for the next bit of the flight. You'd better enjoy it an' all – we're going to the Land of the Great Untubbed!'

'Ah, England,' offered the Singaporean receptionist, who

was familiar with old Australian jokes about the race who had once ruled over both their lands. 'Yes, they don't like showers, the English. They like their bath. Once a week only.' June obliged her with a raucously appreciative guffaw.

Great, thought Lorna, another thing for Greg to whinge about when they arrived. He hated baths – who wants to lie in their own filth, is what he always said. Still, he of all people knew the answer to that one, now, didn't he? She could barely conceal the complex maelstrom of emotions that was practically tearing her apart as she watched him hove into view from the men's showers and walk over to rejoin them.

It was a testament to Lorna's carefully cultivated sangfroid that neither of her travelling companions – the two people who meant most to her in all the world, the two people she shared her home with – had an inkling of her distress. When she'd opened the letter three weeks ago from 'A Friend' telling her about Greg's latest indiscretion, her face had retained its mask of composure, despite the fact that she'd felt like shoving him head first into his muesli. But she hadn't got where she was today by getting hysterical and not checking the facts. Outwardly showing an unruffled calm, she had driven off to work as usual, and on reaching her office, had closed the door and flipped through the Yellow Pages to P for private investigator. A few days and a thousand bucks later, she was given dates, times and photographic evidence to prove that her relationship was in as much peril as that of her new 'friend' the correspondent, who, it transpired, was the jealous ex-boyfriend of her husband's lover.

Looking at the photographs nearly killed her. It wasn't that the adulterous bastard had been caught in flagrante delicto – these were no soft-port shots taken from behind the wardrobe door or through a mirrored ceiling. It was the ordinariness of them which hurt her the most – a couple snapped as they gazed at each other across a café table; the way Greg's eyes had softened as he smiled at the over-made-up little tart. It looked horribly, to Lorna, like love.

And once she'd been made aware of the seriousness of the affair, she could hardly believe she hadn't seen the signs before. He'd changed his brand of aftershave, he was suddenly sporting silk boxers in preference to his Calvin's, and since when did he keep breath freshener in the glove compartment of his car? Bur worse, much worse than this, he seemed happy. He had a new jauntiness about him: he hummed to himself in the mirror these days as he knotted his tie; his step had a spring in it – the like of which, Lorna was reluctantly forced to admit – she hadn't put there herself since they were courting.

In the days that crawled by after she had eaten of the fruit of the tree of the private investigator's knowledge, she witnessed with new eyes how Greg's mood of joie de vivre grew, and so did her own sense of panic. Her whole world had flipped upside down. Everything seemed strangely surreal. If she'd got *this* so badly wrong, how could she trust her own judgement about anything any more?

Feeling herself sliding out of control, needing some space to reassess and regroup away from the source of her pain and confusion, she had booked herself into the Melbourne Sheraton for a couple of days, telling Greg and her mum she was away at a conference, and her colleagues at work that she was down with the flu. Behind closed curtains in Room 3641, she cried in the darkness for forty-eight hours, eating room-service sandwiches and slugging minibar shots. But on the third day she rose again from the dead and decided to tackle this like the lawyer she was trained to be, dispassionately, and with step-by-step logic. Huddled over a yellow legal pad, she sat up in bed to make a ruthless inventory. Dividing the page with a vertical line, she made two headed columns: What I Do Like About My Life and What I Don't Like About My Life. In her present mood it was no surprise to her that, by the time she had finished, the latter list ran over the course of three sides, whereas the former was totally blank. Well. It was bleak, but at least now she knew where she stood.

In marshalling her thoughts to write them down, she had several revelations, the greatest of which was that Greg was the rock she wanted to cling to, in preference to all the hard places she feared. She allowed her thoughts to roam across the bleak landscape of an imagined life without him, and knew in her bones that she wanted him back. But how? What to do? A mere glance at the incriminating photos told her that if she were to call him to the negotiating table now, she would be operating from an untenably low power base.

And what was it exactly that he got from Diane Lipshitz (naturally, that wasn't *quite* what Lorna called her in her mind) that he didn't feel he could get at home? They were still making love a couple of times a week, early morning meetings permitting. And they spent time together at the weekends, when Lorna wasn't at Pilates and Greg wasn't out playing golf. Perhaps it was something to do with that mystifying phrase 'quality time' which she often saw written in magazines these days. But what quality was it, precisely, that this time was supposed to have? She took an interest in his work. She never failed to ask him how his day had been. What more was she supposed to do? She wished she had a girlfriend she could ask, but the competitive cut and thrust at work didn't encourage sharing confidences with colleagues, and the friendships she'd had, before her job had become her life, were long since gone.

Getting up out of the hotel bed, she surveyed herself in the mirror, comparing her own image to the image of Miss Shitlipz which she held in her hand. Even despite the damage done by her two day cry-athon, she was still fairer of face than Diane – her nose was straighter for starters, her hair sleeker, her skin more clear. And as for their figures, surely it had been years (if ever) since Diane had shrugged herself effortlessly into a size ten frock? So how was it – according to the private investigator's research at least – that this woman had so capti-vated Greg's heart that she was telling all her friends he was seriously considering divorce?

With more questions asked than answered, Lorna checked out of her sanctuary at the Sheraton and drove back home slowly along the coast road to Black Rock, mentally reviewing her yellow-paged notes. She still felt all at sea with her emotions, but worse now was her feeling that in the last couple of days, she had underachieved. She had identified her objective – get Greg back – but not the course of action which would help her accomplish it.

Pulling into her driveway, she glanced over at her mother's granny annexe in the garden, and toyed with the idea of confiding in her, but immediately decided against. Since she'd been widowed, June had enough on her plate without being burdened with her daughter's worries, and hadn't Lorna tear-fully promised her dad on his deathbed that whatever else happened, she'd look after Mum? Putting on a brave smile, she knocked on June's door to see how she'd been while Lorna had been away, and on being invited inside for a cup of tea, found to her amazement that the solution to her problems had been here all along in her own back yard – albeit, in the most alarming of guises.

While her daughter had been in a hotel bedroom reviewing her life and had found it wanting, June had been doing the same thing in the comfort of her own home – or what passed for her own home these days. Two years after her husband had died, she'd had time to recover from the shock of being widowed so young, and now June realised that the biggest mistake she had ever made in her life was to go along with her daughter's idea of moving out of her own nice little flat, and into this granny annexe here. Granny annexe! The very name made her feel as if she was already half dead, and June was a woman who was busting out all over – or at least, she used to be. She was, in the words of the Streisand song, a person who needs people – but since she had moved away from the hustle and bustle of St Kilda and into the quiet, respectable family suburb of Black Rock, it no longer also followed that she was 'the luckiest people in the world'.

In the whole of Melbourne, St Kilda was where June felt spiritually at home. St Kilda buzzed, St Kilda rocked, and every one of its inhabitants had a story to tell. It was bursting to the brim with eccentrics, hippies, prostitutes, druggies, kids hanging out, skateboarders passing through, gays, actors, artists, punks, crusties, drag queens – you name it, if its lifestyle was alternative, it had sent along a representative. And June had known them all. Going shopping down Acland Street, even if it was just a quick nip for a loaf of bread, took her every minute of two hours: nodding and smiling, chatting and waving, getting an update on somebody's current drama, signing a petition for world peace – she'd been *involved*, she'd been at the cutting edge of life in the raw. And she had never, ever, not even for one single solitary moment, felt lonely. Until now.

Now nobody knocked on her door at any time of the day or night, needing a shoulder to cry on or someone to share in a laugh. Though she still kept in close touch with several of her old St Kilda cronies on the phone, and made a point of popping over to Acland Street to see them at least once a month, she didn't encourage them to visit her in her granny annexe. It was bad enough that she had to live here in the quiet of the suburbs. She could do without her colourful friends having to make the journey, only to be stared at by the locals.

Here in Black Rock, folk led tidy lives in their tidy homes and kept their problems behind closed doors. June felt useless and empty, old before her time, a waste of space. Perhaps, she mused, as she reviewed her life, she would have felt differently if Lorna and Greg had some kids for her to look after – maybe then she might have felt useful here, that there was some purpose to all this breathing in and breathing out. But not only were they childless, apparently they were determined to keep it that way. Thinking about her daughter, June could sometimes hardly believe they shared the same gene pool. 'Tight-arsed yuppie' would have been the judgement of June and her Acland Street cronies, if they hadn't known Lorna, and had seen her wandering by.

The thing that had prompted this uncharacteristically maudlin and ungenerous introspection had been propped up on her breakfast bar for a week, taunting her with its promise of a happy fun-filled time, illuminating, like a beacon, the dark shadows of her days. It was an invitation to the wedding of one of her nieces – the sending of which was meant to elicit unbridled joy from its recipient, not melancholia. And indeed, when June had first opened the airmail envelope, her spirits had soared at the thought of being back in the bosom of her family again after so many years. To be back amongst her own kind, to celebrate with people who, like her (and unlike her daughter and son-in-law), knew how to enjoy a knees-up! Fantastic! Just the ticket! And aye, there was the rub.

A quick phone enquiry about airfares to Blighty dashed all hopes of ever revisiting that warm familial bosom again. June knew the state of her bank balance all too well. She had to. The pennies which came into her account from her meagre pension had to be counted one by one, before they flew out again at a frightening speed. And it wouldn't just be the airfare, would it? It'd be hotel bills, and spending money, and eating out all the time, and God alone knew what all else. Her rellies weren't rich – far from it – and she wouldn't feel comfortable bludging off them, or taking up valuable space in their small homes. Besides which, she'd grown used to a bit of privacy over the last couple of years – she wouldn't like living in their pockets, much less sleeping on their sofa for the duration. No, she'd decided, it just couldn't be done. This was her life now – to be carefully counting beans till she died in Black Rock.

Beaten and dispirited, feeling the black gunge of depression starting to lap up around her ankles, she had just sat down at the computer that Lorna and Greg had given her for Christmas to RSVP by e-mail to the invitation in the negative, when mercifully the telephone had rung. It was her downstairs neighbour from her Acland Street days, one Busty Springboard-A-Go-Go – a Chinese Malaysian transvestite who made her/his living singing songs from the sixties in gay pubs and clubs.

'Hello, girlfriend - how *are* you?' s/he asked June now. 'Tell me *every*thing – it's been *ages*! What's been going *down*? Or should I ask – *who's* been going down, you shameless hussy?'

June tried to rally herself enough to join in the camp banter, but the words of cheer seemed to stick in her throat. 'Me,' she said simply, after a brief struggle with her vocal cords. 'Me – I'm going down, Busty – right down to Black Rock bottom.'

'Got those old suburban blues again, darl?' asked Ms Springboard-A-Go-Go sympathetically, and proceeded to get the dirt on June's problems. 'Honey *buns*!' she protested, after she'd heard enough of the doleful monologue about the current strength of the English pound and the relative weakness of the Aussie dollar. 'Be beside yourself no more! We have the technology! A friend of mine has just done a house swap through the Internet – had a month in San Fran, darl, and she'd never have been able to afford it without free accommodation in the US of A. Fire up that computer, girl – I'll find out the website, and be with you toot sweet.'

Such was the depth of her self-pity that, when she opened the door to Busty an hour later, June didn't give a second thought to what the good folk of Black Rock had made of the miniskirted, peroxide-enhanced gender-bender who had arrived on their patch on a moped that morning. But on being scooped up and clasped affectionately between a magnificent pair of falsies, she immediately found herself starting to feel better. As for revisiting the warm familial bosom, she mused wryly, her face crushed in the depths of Busty's perfumed cleavage, if she only made it as far as this one, things wouldn't be half bad.

'Daughter,' pronounced Busty, sensing June's need, 'you should have called me sooner. Clearly, you have not been getting enough hugs.'

'I ain't half missed you, darl,' June smiled. 'But you know what it's like when you're down in the dumps – you just don't feel like seeing anybody.'

'Do I look like *anybody* to you?' Busty demanded, doing a twirl, and taking June by the hand, she led her back into her living room, where they sat together at the computer to wander at will through cyberspace.

With her renewed spirit of optimism, and her friend by her side, June never doubted for an instant that she would find the perfect swap, but when they found that the only Leicester party looking to travel to Melbourne was Pauline Watkins with her semi in New Vistas, she could hardly believe her eyes, or her luck.

'Well, bugger me sideways—' she exclaimed, dropping

back into the East Midlands vernacular of her childhood.

'Girlfriend,' Busty admonished her severely, 'you only have *three* wishes. Use them wisely!'

June laughed happily, and pointed excitedly at the screen. 'That's only the same estate where most of my friends and family live – it couldn't be better!'

It wasn't until they'd keyed in June's details that her earlier doubts and fears started to regroup around her. 'My place is going to be a bit on the small side for a family,' she said, gazing around at her one-bedroom home.

'Let them be the judge of that,' Busty told her firmly, and hit the Send button before June could pike out of the transaction. 'You've got your double bed, and this sofa turns into a double too, doesn't it? They might be a very close family, who don't mind bunking up.'

But that last phrase served merely to increase June's anxiety. 'Christ, I hadn't even thought of that!' she cried in distress.

'The Yuppies,' offered Busty, quickly catching on.

June nodded sadly. 'I can't see either Lorna or Greg liking the idea of having their space invaded by strangers,' she said, deflated.

But it was then that they heard the knock on the front door, and on seeing through the window who it was who had come to call, Busty, with a wicked grin, had beaten June in the race to answer it.

'Dearest girl!' she exclaimed as, flinging open the door, she crushed the speechless Lorna to her manufactured mammaries. 'How *fabulous* to meet you at *last*! I'm your Aunty Busty!'

In Changi airport, Singapore, June caught sight of Lorna's tense expression as she watched Greg walking over to rejoin them, fresh from the shower. What was up now, she wondered, and announced her intention of going off to do a bit more duty-free shopping. She had another couple of presents to buy, she told them, but really she just wanted a little oasis of solitude before she was forced to sit between the two of them for the long, long journey home. *Something* was going on there, she thought to herself, as she debated the purchase of a silk sarong for one of her sisters, but she'd be the last person to be told what it was.

Still, where her daughter was concerned, June was getting used to feeling bemused. You could have knocked her over with a feather when Lorna, still recovering from the shock of taking tea with a flamboyantly feminine blonde Asian transvestite, had not only sanctioned the granny annexe house swap, but had also offered her own home in the package to boot. Since when had Lorna been the least bit interested in her Leicester rellies, and what had provoked her sudden and enthusiastic assertion that she and her husband simply *had* to be there to witness the marriage of a cousin she'd never even met?

When the call finally came to reboard their flight, Lorna saw Greg make a small involuntary movement towards the mobile phone in his jacket pocket, and then think better of it. *Ha!* she thought nastily, in bitter triumph. Now you can't talk to Shitlipz for a whole fourteen hours, and you can't see her for fourteen whole days.

But there was no joy to be had in this Pyrrhic victory. Though it was true that her husband was temporarily defeated, the bloody wounds of battle were all on her own side of the field.

3

Sitting, cramped, between her husband and her daughter in the Economy Class section of the great iron bird which was flying them to the unknown antipodes, Pauline was the only member of the Watkins Expeditionary Force who was still awake when the computer-generated image on the screen in front of her showed that they had just flown over the north coast of Australia. Unable, in her excitement, to keep this news to herself, she shook Mick roughly awake.

'We're here!' she told him. 'Look – at last! Let's get the things down from the lockers!'

Having done his homework on the vast size and scale of the Australian landmass, Mick merely had to half open a sleepy eye to see this was a false alarm and to quell Pauline's excitement. 'We're only just over Queensland,' he told her. 'Melbourne's all the way down at the bottom of the map.'

'Yes I know, but . . .' Pauline protested, unwilling to accept that this long day's journey in a flying battery farm was not now - please, God! – at an end.

'Issanother five hours,' Mick slurred sleepily, and locking his eyelid firmly shut again, abandoned his wife once more to her sleepless solitude.

So what else is new, thought Pauline bitterly, in lurid Leicesterese, as she watched him shrug down in the narrow seat beside her, and roll over to present her with his back. I bring him the other bastard side of the world to rekindle our romance, and he'd still bleddy sooner be sleeping! Why was it always *her* who had to do the worrying, single-handed? Where was it in the marriage contract, in which clause was it writ, that the lifelong maintenance of the emotional health of the relationship fell solely to the bride?

She sighed now, a long, heartfelt expulsion of recycled air, as she pictured their wedding day from two decades' distance. Too young. They'd been far too young. Somebody should have stopped them. But then, who would have thought to have done that when, at seventeen going on eighteen, they'd already been inseparable for two years, and baby Matt was only five months away from bursting out of her belly to join them?

Softened momentarily by her remembered maternal feelings, she turned to look at her second born snoozing at her side. Even with her smudged eyeliner and black lipstick, Gemma still looked like a young angel when she slumbered. Pauline smiled indulgently, and unable to resist the automatic reflex of the loving mother, she reached across to smooth her daughter's hair extensions from her brow. Her reward was a sleepy grunt of angry warning, and an irritable hand shot out of the thin airline blanket to knock her own away. Her indulgent smile withered instantly, its desiccated corpse left trembling on her lips. So this is my life, she thought with lachrymose fervour, and then, butching up, Don't go there. Peering around the darkened cabin for waking help of any kind, but seeing none, she pressed the overhead button to summon reinforcements to her side.

'*Another* whisky and soda?' the arriving Malaysian Airline flight attendant whispered, clearing her empties and unashamedly signalling his disapproval with a sardonically raised brow.

Exhausted, sleepless, desperate, Pauline met his gaze with eyes narrowed to lethal laser points, and toughed it out. 'Seven hundred quid I've paid for this, love,' she hissed back, in a voice deceptively reasonable in tone. 'So, tell you what, save your legs – make it two.'

Chugging back her hard-won nightcap (or should that be 'daycap', she wondered dizzily – she'd lost all track of time) the wife and mother formerly known as Polly Watkins had nothing better to do than to go over and over in her mind the hurried arrangements she'd put in place during the last two weeks for the house guests she would never meet, and to worry about the reciprocal arrangements they had made for her in their own home in Melbourne.

She could still remember, with absolute heart-stopping clarity, the moment she had hurriedly switched on the computer and discovered, out of the blue, June's first e-mail, offering the swap. But that was hardly surprising under the circumstances, was it, she thought, her cheeks ablaze with guilt. Given that, when she'd heard Mick's key in the door that afternoon, and his cheery call announcing his unexpectedly early arrival home, she had been raking the flesh of Asheem's back with her fingernails, clawing her way to her third climax of the day. How else was she to have disguised her shameful secret than to leap from the bed, shoving her lover towards his pile of hastily discarded clothes on the floor, and to urge him in frantic whispers to 'Get your arse covered and parked behind Gemma's computer *now*!'?

After following Pauline's shouted command to make himself a cup of tea and bring her one too, Mick finally tracked them down in Gemma's bedroom, where Pauline, looking flustered, was asking Asheem a series of dumb questions about e-mailing.

'Oh, hiya, Ash,' Mick greeted him, unperturbed. 'Here you are – you have my tea, I'll go and get another one. Been giving Poll a lesson?'

'That's right,' Asheem agreed, grinning back good-naturedly. 'I've been showing her what's what.'

' "Receiving message 1 of 1",' Pauline read incredulously, her eyes glued to the screen, unable as she was to meet her husband's, or her lover's, gaze. How weird. Nobody had ever sent her an e-mail before – besides herself, of course, for practice – and it lent the clandestine post-coital moment an even greater sense of unreality, as the three of them all watched and waited for Gemma's computer to download the mail from the server.

'Who's June Fisher?' Mick asked, bending over Pauline's shoulder to read the sender's name as it popped into the inbox. 'And why is she describing her house to you in such detail?'

'Bleddy hell!' said Pauline, quickly scanning the message. It had been a couple of weeks since she'd left her own details on the house-swap website, and in that time, so much had been happening at home that she'd forgotten all about it. She thought back to that fevered night when, unable to sleep, she had sat in this same spot to surf the web. It had been her firm intention, afterwards, when she'd crept back guiltily into bed with Mick, to finish what she'd started with Asheem the very next day, and never ever eat of that forbidden fruit again. But things hadn't happened like that, of course. On the contrary, she'd been gorging herself ever since like there was no tomorrow.

With June's response coming into Pauline's irregular triangulated life at that particularly charged moment, it seemed to her to be such spooky and uncanny timing as to be a warning from the gods, an imperative which must be acted on forthwith. 'Save yourself,' was the message she took from the screen, 'gather up your husband and your children – all who are precious to you – and run far from temptation.' It was a golden opportunity to get back on the straight and narrow, and Pauline was in the mood for redemption. Before she could weaken and change her mind, she turned from the computer and, in her husband's hearing, thanked Asheem for his kind extracurricular attentions.

'I think I've got the hang of this now, thanks,' she told him, as she ushered him from her daughter's room and down the stairs.

At the back door, Asheem grinned and tried to steal another kiss. 'See you tomorrow,' he whispered.

'No, you won't,' she said firmly. 'It's over. It'll never happen again. Besides, I'm going to Australia.'

Returning upstairs, she sat down with her husband and together they read June's message and started playing with dates and figures on scraps of paper, working out in fine detail how they would finance the upcoming trip. To Mick's credit, he was as enthusiastic as she was to see the other side of the world, but for rather different reasons. 'A family holiday!' he said happily, breaking her heart with his smile. 'The four of us together again, on a great adventure! Fantastic. What a brilliant idea! Well done, Poll.'

It was then that, biting the bullet, she looked him firmly in the eye and laid down the ground rules. 'Two things,' she said. 'One: call me Pauline from now on. I'm too old to be Polly. Polly's a child's name, and I'm a grown-up woman.'

Mick groaned affectionately. 'It's not still this turning thirty-nine thing, is it?'

'No,' Pauline countered fiercely, 'it's this growing up thing. Taking myself seriously thing, taking control. This changing my life thing.'

There was no mistaking her intensity. 'Okay, Pauline,' Mick conceded, none the wiser. 'And two?'

'Two . . .' said Pauline, and drew a deep breath, afraid to give voice to her deepest hopes and fears. 'Two: when we get to Australia, we're going to learn to have sex together again. No more procrastinating, Mick.'

'No, right,' he said, turning bright red and studying his hands. 'Not a problem. Been meaning to get round to that, any road . . .'

Knocking back her whisky in her lonely Mile High Club, Pauline eventually fell asleep about five minutes before they started serving breakfast, so by the time they finally arrived at Melbourne airport she was not only stressed and sleep-deprived, but she was also halfway between being drunk and hungover. Which might have been why she was pulled out of the queue to have her luggage examined so minutely.

'Got any food in here, Pauline?' the Customs officer asked her with a friendly grin, as he unlocked her suitcase.

'No! No food!' Pauline told him, glancing round wildly to see what had happened to Gemma and Mick. To her horror, she saw that they were waiting for her patiently a mere ten feet away. 'There's nothing illegal in there – absolutely nothing!' she averred, turning back to her tormentor and attempting to mirror his smile, watching with dread as he affably and efficiently removed the clothes from the top of her case. This was just her luck! Did she look like a terrorist? Did she have the appearance of a drugs mule? No! She was just an ordinary woman from Leicester. So why her? And why now?

'I'm afraid you'll find I'm just another boring, law-abiding tourist,' she advised the young official, with a desperate laugh.

'Right,' he nodded thoughtfully, as, on the tips of his fingers, he delicately lifted up her new Ann Summers crotchless teddy.

'Embarrassed' is not a large enough word to describe the silence of the Watkins party as they regrouped to leave the Customs area, and to eventually emerge through the Arrivals door to run the gauntlet of meeters and greeters. All around them, their fellow travellers were identified by their friends and relations with whoops of joy or, seeing their names scrawled on bits of cardboard, claimed their cab driver. Soon, only the Watkins stood alone.

Glad to have something practical to discuss, Mick asked, without meeting his wife's eyes, 'What was the arrangement – didn't they say we'd be met?'

'Yes,' said Pauline, scanning the retreating crowds. 'June said she'd arranged for a friend of hers to drive us there and let us in . . .'

Her voice trailed off, her attention now taken by a small hiccup in the general exodus, caused, it seemed, by a tall blonde woman tottering on high heels at speed towards them, struggling to make headway against the flow.

'Watkins!' the creature cried as she neared them, appealing in every direction but theirs. 'Pauline? Gemma? Mick?'

There was a long moment of stunned hesitation from her targeted group, before Pauline, blinking, slowly raised her hand.

'Thank *God*!' said the woman who'd come to claim them as, flinging her arms open, she crushed Pauline's nose against her broad chest. 'Busty Springboard-A-Go-Go, at your service. I'm so *sorry* I'm late, darl,' she winked at Gemma over the top of her mother's head, 'I've been having *such* a bad hair day!' Relinquishing Pauline at last, she bobbed a curtsey to Mick, and glancing down at the new red trainers he was sporting for the trip, she held out her hand to be kissed, and said, 'Welcome, Dorothy, to the Land of Oz!'

Being driven from the airport by Glinda the Good Witch in a brand new Series 5 BMW, Pauline, in her sleep-deprived state, thought that things couldn't have been more out of the ordinary if a great hurricane had come and swept their little house up into the air and flung it somewhere over the rainbow, way up high, to a land that she'd dreamed of once in a lullaby. It was true that the highway connecting the airport to the city was pretty much like any other she'd been on, and that the Australians drove reassuringly on the left, but that was where the similarity ended between this land called Oz and real life. Huge billboards told drivers in a curiously direct way, 'Drink. Drive. Bloody idiot' which, to her English eye, seemed a bit blokeish and rude for a government-sponsored safety campaign. And when the city of Melbourne at last rose on the horizon above its suburban flatlands, it looked to Pauline to be the spitting image of Gotham City. But when, after driving beside the sea for a few miles, they pulled into the landscaped driveway of their holiday home in Black Rock, and parked beside a cute little BMW sports coupé, she realised that any dreams she'd ever had in her lullabies had been remarkably restrained and unambitious.

'This is yours,' said Busty, swinging her legs out of the luxurious saloon and waving a casual hand towards the huge modern glass structure to their left. The Watkins got out and gawped. There before them was a cutting-edge, architect-designed two-storey structure the like of which they had only ever seen courtesy of Kevin McCloud's *Grand Designs* on telly.

Mick, who had chatted affably to Busty throughout the journey, asking her questions, and not appearing to mind that he was now fixed in Busty's mind as 'Dorothy', was the first to recover his wits and the use of his tongue. 'Thought you meant the car was ours,' he joked.

'Oh, yes, did I forget to say?' Busty said, as she unlocked the front door to Paradise. 'The two Beemers are yours too. Come in, come in – I'll explain it all as I go.'

Following her over the threshold, Mick's smile faded, and was replaced with a look of guilty anxiety. Pauline knew what he was thinking. When she'd told him of June's idea to swap cars, as well as the houses, he had at first baulked at the expense of getting comprehensive insurance for their old Datsun. There was no gainsaying that they'd got the better deal. She didn't like to think what was going through the Australian party's minds around now. It was like being caught out at Christmas, having handed over a small box of Quality Street in exchange for a luxury Marks and Sparks hamper. In her mind's eye, Pauline raced back to Leicester, to replace the cushions on the settee with the new ones she'd been meaning to buy off the market.

Inside the house, Gemma was so blown away by everything she saw that she completely forgot about cool. She stood, slack-jawed as a surprised five-year-old, in the middle of the cathedral-sized, minimalist, open-plan living room, and revolved slowly to take it all in. One hundred and eighty degrees of the glass-walled room contained a view of the bay down below them, where the sun shone on boats bobbing on sparkling blue waters. It certainly had a high wow factor.

'Wow,' she said and, turning away from the view, open-mouthed, she caught sight of the fifty-inch plasma screen. 'Wow!' she said again. The built-in DVD brought a similar response, as did the surround-sound home cinema, the Bang and Olufsen hi-fi, the American-style double refrigerator with ice dispenser, and the wall-mounted computerised control panel which bathed the room in a series of pre-set lighting states. Going up what appeared to be a floating stair-case, they were all wowed anew by the walk-in wardrobes, the en suite power showers, the purpose-built gym, the sauna, the remote-controlled blinds, and the swinging seats out on the balconies.

'Where's the swimming pool?' Mick asked, chancing his arm with another joke.

'Outside,' Busty told him, knocking the smile off his face again. 'Next to the hot tub. Come, follow me, Dorothy.' And singing 'Follow, follow, follow, follow, Follow the yellow brick road!' she led them all down the stairs again and out onto a huge tract of land which was apparently their garden.

'Swimming pool,' she announced, gesturing towards twenty-five metres of sunken turquoise mosaic. 'Hot tub,' she said, pointing to a waist-high wooden structure which hung out over terraced beds on a cantilevered platform. 'Isn't it heaven?'

Busty was enjoying herself enormously being the harbinger of such good news. It was particularly satisfying, since she alone shared June's secret of the dirty deal they had struck over the Yuppies. Reading Pauline's e-mail and the description of the house she was offering as a swap, gazing at the attached j-peg photo of the modest semi, jammed in cheek by jowl with its identical neighbours on the post-War estate known as New Vistas, they had at first thought their plan untenable, and then decided on minimal information as being the best course. 'Bring 'em down a peg or two,' June had feistily confided to Busty, after she had unexpectedly sold the scheme to her distracted daughter, sight unseen. 'They're so bloody la-di-dah. Do 'em good to live like the other half for a fortnight!'

'So, now, what else to tell you?' Busty said, turning to the overwhelmed Watkins, and throwing an arm chummily around Mick's shoulders. 'Oh yes,' she said, pointing down the cliffs to the waters below them. 'You've got a thirty-foot ocean-going boat parked down there at the marina; a dinghy; two windsurfers; tickets to various concerts and operas that June's daughter, Lorna, had already pre-booked for this fortnight; and honorary membership of the Royal Melbourne Golf Club for the duration.'

Pauline swallowed hard, her thoughts straying guiltily to what she had reciprocally arranged for their hosts back in Leicester. Suddenly, the guest passes to the New Vistas Working Men's Social Club, which she'd left out with a flourish on the kitchen table, looked a lot less than the exciting surprise she had hoped for.

'But don't worry about all that for now,' Busty said comfortingly, as she led them back towards the house. 'Just get yourselves unpacked and settled in. The deep freeze is heaving, and the fridge is packed to the gills. Anything you don't know or can't work out, just whistle. You know how to whistle, don't you, Dorothy?' she said teasingly to Mick, turning him, haplessly, to face her. 'Just put your lips together and blow. I'm right over here,' she continued, pointing to June's granny annexe, set apart from the main house by the front drive. 'I'll be staying there, in Junie's little palace, to look after her pussy while she's away.'

Of all the extraordinary things that Busty had told them over the last half-hour, this last little nugget of information seemed to strike Pauline particularly hard. 'Shit a brick!' she said, her hand flying to her mouth in horror at what she suddenly remembered had been overlooked in their haste to leave.

'What?' asked Mick, his own heart now skipping a beat. His wife's face was ashen.

'We only went and forgot to take the bleddy dog round to my mum's! I even patted her goodbye, in her basket in the kitchen!'

'Bleddy hell fire!' he responded.

'Whiffy!' cried Gemma.

'Unusual name for a pooch,' Busty offered.

Pauline shot her an apprehensive look. 'Not when you know her,' she warned.

4

As far as Lorna and Greg Mackenzie were concerned, when they vacated their seats in the Singapore Airlines business section at Heathrow, they said goodbye to civilisation. Though both were seasoned travellers, neither of them had been to Europe before, and Greg had certainly never had any previous interest in visiting England. He had a healthy Australian lip-curling disdain for all things concerned with the mother country. For him, all Poms were stuck-up bastards with notions of imperial superiority, and all he had to say on that subject was 'Test Match'.

Quite why his wife had shanghaied him on to this trip was a mystery to him – like his mother-in-law before him, Greg had never heard Lorna be the least bit inquisitive about her English rellies, none of whom she had ever met. But she'd seemed strangely febrile when she'd told him about her cousin's wedding invitation for some reason, and there had been no easy way to quash her determination that they should both attend. Besides which, she had presented it to him as a fait accompli, the air tickets having already been booked, his house swapped from under him, and his suitcase practically packed.

Being of a pragmatic disposition, Greg had shrugged his shoulders and quickly seen the upside. In common with other Australian property developers, he could see the advantage of looking to raise finance in the UK, and he needed to raise a

very big pot of cash for his latest ambitious project, plus . . .
Well. Things had got a little heated back in Melbourne for
reasons he didn't feel quite comfortable thinking about, so all
in all, he'd decided, it wouldn't hurt him one bit to disappear
off O.S. for a while. But that, of course, was before he had
been introduced to the notions of travel and weather, British-
style, and the action of the one on the other.

They had walked for what seemed like miles at Heathrow
airport, first to shuffle through the immigration queue, then
to the scrimmage of their luggage collection, then through
Customs. The whole thing had taken about two hours for
some bizarre reason, and by the time they had been spat out
into the Arrivals hall, Greg had had all the travel he needed
or wanted. It was not, however, all the travel he was going
to get.

Being well-heeled and professional, neither he nor Lorna
had ever arrived at any airport without being met by a chauf-
feured car, so he'd spent quite some wasted minutes scanning
the crowds for a cardboard sign bearing his name, before June
dug him in the ribs and told him to stop dreaming and get a
move on. His wife seemed as surprised as he was.

'Aren't we being met?' she asked her mother in confusion.

'Course we are. Up in Leicester,' June replied briskly.
'We've got a little bit of a train ride first. Come on.'

What she didn't tell them then was that before the little bit
of a train ride began, they would first have to successfully
complete a big bit of travel on the Tube, and that that would
be half a dozen kinds of hell. And Greg had plenty of time to
enumerate them.

When at last they arrived at St Pancras station, much the
worse for wear, the entire concourse was jam-packed with
desolate would-be travellers all staring at a digital notice board,
and all wearing the same placid, long-suffering expression

which put Greg in mind of documentary footage he'd once seen of a queue of cattle waiting their turn at the abattoir. The train announcer having apparently been gagged and muffled, they could make no sense of what she was trying to tell them, and the queue to join the queue at the information kiosk began outside the building by the queue for the taxis. Eventually, June, being an ex-native, struck up a conversation with an Indian family, who explained with patient shrugs that trains were being cancelled or delayed because of a seasonally affective disorder, known here at the hub of the Commonwealth as 'wrong leaves on the line'.

'What's the right bloody sort, then?' asked Greg aggressively, finally blowing his top. 'Cos if some bugger'd give me a sack of 'em, I'd run up the bloody line and replace 'em myself! Christ! England? You can stick it!'

It was then that the train announcer apparently managed to remove enough of the sticky tape on her mouth to make herself understood to most of the crowd around them, and over a crackle of static, they chased towards an exit and were gone.

'What the hell's going on now?' Greg demanded, glad at last to have more elbow room, but worried he was missing out on something crucial.

'Where are you off to, love?' June yelled after her rapidly departing new friends, and received the reply on the hoof of, 'Alternative arrangement – bus outside – hurry – come quick!' Needless to say, being newcomers to the sport of British travel, they weren't quick enough. By the time they were out on the pavement of the frenetically busy Euston Road, the bus was heaving, and leaving.

'Bloody marvellous,' said Greg viciously, drawing his coat around him in a vain attempt to shut out the chill wind. 'Christ, June, I can see why you emigrated, love.' This was by no means the last time he would remark on this. 'So what do we do now? Get ourselves a bloody dog and a bit of cardboard and camp out in a doorway, like those kids over there?'

June was feeling distinctly out of her depth, but there was no way she was going to give her son-in-law the satisfaction of knowing that. But neither did she know how to get back into her depth, so to speak (or rather, so to *think*, since thus far she had just about managed to stop herself from muttering out loud – a worrying habit she'd developed since she'd been living on her own). Out here on the street, everything was so busy, and so loud, it was hard to focus. Reminding herself sharply that not only was she in possession of a British stiff upper lip, she was also a proud battler in the Australian tradition, she concentrated hard on the problem before her: how to get these two whingeing milk-fed yuppie puppies up to Leicester in the quickest possible time, and with the minimum amount of fuss.

If the trains weren't running, they weren't – nothing you could do about that, she decided. And if you'd missed the bus, then you bloody well had to hunker down somewhere warm until another one came by. Information was what they needed, she concluded resolutely – information, and somewhere nice and cosy to sit while they waited it out.

'Okay, follow me,' she commanded her party, loading herself up with her bags, and chivvying them to do the same. 'We're going back in.'

None of them had noticed, during their unsuccessful dash for the bus, the extraordinary Gothic beauty of St Pancras station, and looking up at it now, as they turned back to re-enter it, even Greg was reluctantly impressed. 'God Almighty,' he said, 'shove this bugger up a Transylvanian mountain, and you'd expect to see Christopher bloody Lee coming out with dripping teeth!'

There was no shortage of news at the booth called Information, some of it even coming, hot off the press, onto the computer screen as they stood there, pressed against the waist-high counter, hanging on the Customer Services Supervisor's every word.

'Leaves'll be cleared in the next hour, and trains will then be ready to depart,' she told them, panic-stricken and wild-eyed. 'No – wait!' she cried, looking in despair at the changing picture on her VDU. 'We can't say when the leaves'll be cleared. But there'll be another bus along soon for rescheduled journeys, seats to be allocated on a first-come first-serve basis. Just listen out for announcements over the tannoy.'

At that moment, the train announcer, apparently managing once again to throw off her captors and her gag, screamed something unintelligible to the hundreds of eager listeners who filled the station. Perhaps, by some miracle, some of their fellow would-be travellers had a fluent understanding of strangled tannoyese, or perhaps they were now just operating with all the panicked responses of a herd, but suddenly there was another mass dash for the exit.

'What's she say?' Greg asked, aggressively. 'Where're those buggers off to?'

'No idea,' replied the Customer Services Supervisor sulkily, adding, with seeming irrelevance, 'I've only been working here a week. I should have been sent some relief by now. I'm overdue my lunch break.'

Frustrated and travel-worn, Greg lost the plot completely, and waving his finger in her face, shouted, 'No wonder you lost the bloody Empire, love!' But since he was addressing a twenty-two-year-old English-born Guyanan, he didn't even get the satisfaction of meeting with a spirited defence and a good row. A baleful rolling of the eyes and a kissing of her teeth was the most he could elicit.

Withdrawing from the kiosk for a confab, June caught sight of the pub in the corner of the concourse. 'Come on,' she instructed her charges, leading the way, 'let's go and have a sit down and a drink while we sort out what to do.' Leaving behind the Victorian Gothic splendour of the station, they pushed their way through the crowded pub entrance into twenty-first-century dystopia, to join the inevitable four-deep queue at the bar.

Lorna had been uncharacteristically silent for the last few hours, having apparently lost the will to live, but as soon as they entered the extraordinarily male world of the pub, with its Pokies machines and pool table, she announced that she needed the Ladies urgently. An over-friendly chubby woman at her elbow explained the procedure with a cackle of good-natured laughter.

'You've got to queue to get the key from one of the barmen, duck,' she said. 'And then give it back in when you've finished. I think it's on account of them wanting to stop the homeless using the lavs for washing, and the junkies using them for jacking up. But if you hurry, me mum's in there at the minute, with me little girl, so she can let you in.' Not needing a second invitation, Lorna flew off in the direction that the woman was pointing and gained possession of the key with great relief. What she wanted desperately, even more than a pee, was to sit somewhere quietly for a few minutes to collect her thoughts and calm herself down. But having gained admittance to the cubicle and seeing the graffitied and gouged walls, the wet floor, and the absence of loo paper – and indeed a seat – instead she leant against the wall and wept.

Keeping the lid on her emotions, knowing full well what Greg had been up to recently when he said he'd been kept late at 'meetings', had definitely been taking its toll. Though she had miraculously managed to maintain (she hoped) an outward appearance of calm, inside she was screaming. She hadn't slept well in weeks, more hair seemed to be falling out of her head than growing on it and, since she'd lost all track of when her period should have appeared, she seemed to have been suffering from the symptoms of PMT for a month. She had pinned so much hope on whisking Greg off exotically to the other side of the world away from Shitlipz, but she knew in her bones he had eventually managed to phone her from Singapore airport, and again later from Heathrow. Her fantasy of London had been so different from this reality. She didn't know what she'd been expecting – the Queen to meet them off the plane and invite them to Buckingham Palace to tea? – but it was certainly more romantic than this. How was she ever going to get his undivided attention, make him fall in love with her all over again, when the backdrop to her seduction was so bleak? She was still in shock from seeing the weather outside – never in her life had she been so cold, and never had she seen the sky such a uniform, louring grey.

Her doleful reverie was broken by a desperate woman screaming for admittance on the other side of the door, and startled, Lorna wiped her eyes and ceded the space. Pushing her way back through the pub, dodging beery men, she gave herself a severe mental slap. This was merely a slight hiccup, she told herself sharply, brought on by her own inattention to detail. She should have taken more control of the travel arrangements instead of trusting her mother to get them through. Good grief, if she'd taken the trouble to find out about the potential hassle of transferring from Heathrow to Leicester, she'd have hung the expense and booked a limo to take them the hundred or so miles. Which wasn't, in fact, such a bad idea, she now realised. And she should never have blindly allowed June to bring them into this hellish pit, this Dickensian squalor, when surely to God there must be a perfectly nice hotel somewhere close by, where they could be sitting even now, sipping tea on comfortable couches, while the concierge called them a cab. Thus revivified, and with renewed attack, she returned to the bar to turn their fortunes around, only to discover that she had mislaid the rest of her party.

The earth seemed to slow on its axis as Lorna searched frantically for the familiar shapes of her mother and husband in the crowd. They were nowhere to be seen, and neither was their luggage, and yet she could almost swear that she was standing now on the exact spot where she'd left them. All alone in a foreign land, with only her handbag! She clutched it to her chest, terrified that one of these Hogarthian creatures would snatch away even this scant protection. The scene swam before her, the boisterous men at the bar seeming to grow louder and more dangerous, panic threatening to overwhelm her, when suddenly she was grabbed from behind. With the lightning reflexes of her old karate-class training and without even pausing to think, she delivered a vicious elbow jab to her unseen attacker's diaphragm, and a crushing stamp to his instep. Almost immediately she recognised Greg's tone in the muffled, breathless cry of pain which this elicited. Whipping round to face him, seeing him doubled over in pain at her hands, she felt both mortified and triumphant. She hadn't realised until now just how much she had been wanting to hit him.

'Bloody hell, Lorn! Christ's sake! I think you've broken my bloody foot!' he gasped.

'How was I supposed to know it was you coming at me from behind?' she countered furiously, while feeling strangely elated that it was. 'And where the hell have you been? Where's Mum?'

Just then, June bellowed from the doorway, her distinctive Aussie twang cutting across the blanket of loud English male banter. 'Come on youse two, hurry it up!' she cried. 'Our train's back on, and the bugger's about to pull out!'

The race was on, and by some miracle, all three managed to cover the distance to the platform in record time, and to push and shove their way (they were getting better at this game) into a carriage. Naturally their luck didn't run to them getting a seat, but since they were packed in so tightly with their fellow travellers, they were supported in the upright position by the tight press of other bodies. It doesn't need to be said that the next two hours were not the most comfortable of their lives, but finally, after having left their beautiful home in Black Rock a day and a half earlier, they arrived in Leicester station, crumpled, freezing and exhausted.

All any of them wanted – even the normally ebullient June – was a shower, a cup of tea, and to collapse into a warm bed for the rest of the day. But sadly, that was not to be. As the train pulled out again and other passengers strode purposefully towards the exit, leaving the Australian party counting their cases and looking exposed and lost, a shrill female shriek rent the air.

'Aunty? Aunty June!' it screamed. Turning towards the voice, the three of them saw for the first time one of the treasured English relatives they had travelled so far to see. It was a young woman in her twenties, racing down the stairs towards them on platform shoes, her arms waving and wheeling like a windmill, a massive grin splitting her face from ear to ear. Despite the freezing weather, she was of a mind to disport both her navel ring and her abdominal tattoo on such an auspicious occasion, thus the low-slung trousers and the high-cropped top she had chosen to wear revealed also her swollen and pregnant belly. Fearful, apparently, that they might take her greeting for one of half-hearted enthusiasm, she ran towards them, screaming like a banshee.

'I don't believe it!' she cried (expressing Greg's thoughts precisely) as she skidded to a halt to embrace her aunty June.

'I could of picked you out anywhere! You look so like me mam! I'm Melissa!' And to emphasise her excitement, again she screamed.

Despite her tiredness, June rallied to match her niece's fervour in this mutual exchange of greetings, and screaming back, she introduced Melissa to her cousin Lorna and her cousin-in-law Greg.

To her horror, Lorna, who didn't ordinarily go in much for physical contact (except for the regular kind, between husband and wife) found herself in a long, heartfelt embrace, her back being patted and chubbed, her ribcage being squeezed. 'Okay there?' she felt bound to ask as, still hanging from her neck, Melissa showed no sign of letting her go – on the contrary, she was now planting big wet kisses on her cheeks.

'My Australian cousin!' Melissa marvelled at last, holding Lorna at arm's length, the better to examine her. 'I used to swank about you at school, you know! Used to carry your photo in me pocket and show *everybody*. I had this dream that I'd come over and visit you, and end up staying in Australia!'

Lorna was simultaneously appalled and consumed by a wave of relief that the dream had never come true. Personally, she hadn't ever given her English cousins much thought – indeed, she wasn't even certain how many she had, or what they were called, nor which of her mother's sisters each one belonged to. So why had this Melissa treasured her as a child-hood icon? It was a mystery. Suddenly her new-found relative lunged, grabbing Lorna's face and pressing it against her own, side by side. 'Don't we look alike?' she demanded of June and Greg. 'Can't you tell we're related?'

The honest reply being an unequivocal 'no', June tried to temper this unwelcome assessment with a generous, 'P'raps the nose, love. Yeah, I think I can see it in the nose.' Melissa shrieked her appreciation, which rang in Lorna's ear for a good two days, and did a little war dance on the spot.

Seeing his wife so embarrassed to be the cause of such extraordinary attention, and by now being frozen to his very marrow, Greg stepped in to take control. 'Listen, love,' he said in a commanding tone, 'I don't want to spoil your excitement, but do you think we could do the rest of the ceremonials somewhere warmer?'

'God, yeah, you must be perished!' Melissa realised at last, grabbing Lorna's hand and a case, and hefting them both up the exit stairs. 'Come on, Elroy's waiting in the car. We'll soon have you "Home and Away"!'

Following her out through the small booking hall, whose concourse was large enough to support only one café and a paper shop, Greg started to get the first, faintest inkling that he had crossed the world to a one-horse town. Where was the magnificence of Melbourne's Flinders Street station? Where was the hustle and bustle, the crowds of commuters, the shops and concessions?

Emerging outside into the covered car park, Lorna, still trying politely to free her hand from Melissa's, found herself being led at speed to a customised Ford Escort with smoked-glass windows and alloy wheels, whose sides were positively vibrating with the loudest bass she'd ever heard. Melissa thumped on the driver's window. 'Elroy!' she yelled joyfully. 'Open the boot! Look who I've got here!' The sounds swelled fourfold as a tall black youth flung open his door and emerged smiling from the car. 'Respect,' he told Lorna, offering his hand. 'For real.'

Once Elroy had managed to stow most of the luggage into the boot, the game of stowing the passengers began, and after that, the game of finding the gaps between them to stash the last bags. Greg found himself crammed between his wife and his mother-in-law in the back seat, straddling the transmission and clutching the duty-free gifts, a furry koala tickling his chin.

'Is it far?' he asked desperately, his head jammed at an uncomfortable angle against the roof.

'Nah,' said Elroy, flashing him a grin in the driving mirror. 'Only a couple of mile. Be there before you know it. Been a long journey for you, innit?'

'You can say that again,' said Greg with feeling. He couldn't understand what the lad was waiting for. Everybody was in, why not drive, for God's sake, get him out of this misery? 'So – are we ready?' he prompted. 'Are we off?'

'Just waiting for Parv,' said Melissa, peering anxiously through the darkened windscreen. 'She nipped over the road – wanted to get you some flowers. I hope she's all right crossing,' she added to Elroy in some concern.

'I said I'd take her,' Elroy assured her, smiling, 'but she told me, "I'm a big girl now, Daddy."'

'Did she?' Melissa exclaimed, her voice warm with pleasure. 'Did she call you Daddy?'

'Serious,' nodded Elroy, looking proud.

'Aaaah,' crooned Melissa. 'Int that lovely?' she demanded of the passengers in the back.

Greg and Lorna nodded mutely, mystified, but June who was clearly in the loop, said, 'I told you she'd come round, love, didn't I? She just needed time.'

'Here she is!' announced Elroy, pointing to what appeared to be a small flowering bush moving towards them on long thin brown legs, and he flung open his door and his arms in welcome. 'Here's my girl!'

Another kerfuffle ensued, first fitting the huge floral tribute in the front around Melissa's unborn baby, and then threading the child she had prepared earlier, a giggling nine-year-old half-Indian girl, lengthways across the knees of the Australian party in the back.

'That's your aunty June,' Melissa told her daughter excitedly, as flesh pressed against flesh, 'and that's your aunty Lorna and your uncle Greg. This is Parveen.'

'I'm so glad to meet you at last!' said June happily, who had got the head end and was embracing it with fervour. 'Give us a big kiss, darl!'

'Could you just watch where you're putting your feet?' asked Lorna, struggling to sound reasonable.

'For Christ's sake, let's drive!' barked Greg, juggling a wriggling bottom on his lap.

His word, it transpired, was Elroy's command, and with a shriek of burning rubber, they hit the road at speed. Unperturbed, apparently, by her partner's rally-cross style of driving, Melissa kept up a running commentary of family news, apologising on her mother's behalf for not being there to meet them, but promising that she would pop round to see them that evening as soon as she got home from work. The ten-minute journey passed in a sickening blur, and when the brakes were next applied and Greg and Lorna dared to open their eyes again, they found themselves in a wide suburban street made up of hundreds of identical red-brick semi-detached houses.

'This is where you're staying,' Melissa told them in triumph as they squealed to a halt outside number 236, and she flung open the passenger door. 'Int it amazing – you're just round the corner from us! I'll never understand how you managed that, Aunty June!'

No more would Lorna or Greg, it seemed. Clearly there must be some mistake here, they told each other wordlessly, locked together in an alarmed and stricken gaze, after they had extricated themselves with difficulty from the confines of the car to stare in disbelief at their holiday home. While an excited June and Melissa bustled down the short path of the house next door to get the key from Dolly, and Elroy and Parveen ferried their luggage good-naturedly to their new front door, Greg grasped Lorna's arm and whispered hoarsely, 'She traded *our* house for *this*? What the hell were you thinking of, Lorna? Why didn't you stop her?'

Lorna stared down coldly at his hand, reacting badly both to being grabbed, and to being blamed. Though her feelings had been identical to her husband's a mere micro-second before, now she reminded herself bitterly that if this was anyone's fault, it was his. 'Oh for Christ's sake, grow up,' she snapped, taking him aback with the uncharacteristic nastiness in her tone. 'Where's your spirit of adventure? Don't be such a baby and a snob.'

It was harder, however, for Lorna to maintain her high moral ground once June and Melissa had returned with the key and they all swarmed inside to begin the grand tour. It wasn't that there was anything wrong with Pauline Watkins's home-decorating skills – indeed, most visitors remarked at once on the cosiness of her style. But as a woman who favoured modern minimalism, Lorna, bracing herself to peep into the living room, thought she might asphyxiate in this small space crammed with too much furniture, where the clutter of memorabilia covered every surface and ornamented every wall.

The rest of the party had gone upstairs, and she could hear June and Melissa and Elroy and Parveen deciding on who should sleep where, and dumping the cases appropriately. She didn't know where Greg had gone and, in her present mood, neither did she care, but it didn't much surprise her when she heard his disbelieving roar come from a room apparently directly overhead: 'Bloody *hell*! Can you believe this? There isn't even a bloody shower!' Alone and unobserved, Lorna allowed her mouth to twist into a sardonic smile. Perhaps, on reflection, she decided, this place was nothing short of perfection after all. For what did her discomfort matter when it facilitated such torture of He Who Must Be Punished Without Mercy For The Rest Of His Worthless Days?

His roar had now developed into an abject howl, and though his wife was surprised at the extent of his hitherto un-discovered vocal range, she didn't stop smiling until she arrived in the kitchen, where she learnt that the real source of the high-pitched keening was in fact not her husband but the lonely and forgotten Whiffy, who, due to her long solitary confinement had had a wee bit of an accident.

5

Naturally Pauline had been anxious to sort out the business of her dog, but since that involved speaking to her hosts (who she now regarded as the injured party), she was reluctant to make the call. When she finally braced herself to dial her own home number, the phone was first answered by a chatty young girl who wanted her to know that her name was Parveen, but that she could call her Parv, that she was nine years old, went to Ratby Road School, and that soon she would be having a new baby brother or sister. Conscious of the high cost of long-distance calls, Pauline expressed as much polite interest as she could muster for the child, and then begged to be handed to a grown-up. Elroy came on the line next, pitching straight into a long-winded explanation that the real owners of the phone were currently in Australia, and that there would be little point in leaving a message for them, as they'd be away for a fortnight. Deaf to Pauline's repeated but ineffectual attempts to break into his discourse, after wishing her a nice day, he hung up.

She stood for a moment, bemused, on the balcony of her Black Rock bedroom, the cordless phone now dead in her hand, gazing out across the sea to the impossibly blue sky, feeling completely dislocated from her former life. The sun was warm on her skin, a light breeze teased her hair, and an extraordinarily gaudy red, yellow and blue bird flew across her vision to land in a nearby tree. It was hard, from this distance, to remember the red brick of New Vistas – or indeed ever to want to see it again. Still dizzy from her lack of sleep and surfeit of alcohol, she had a sudden urge to stay here, to lie low and not remake the call, in the hare-brained hope that the rightful owners might never return to this patch of paradise, and that all this would be hers for ever. But the phone started chirping in her hand, breaking her reverie and making her jump, and once Mick had shown her which button to press on the sophisticated digital handset, she found she was speaking to June.

'Sorry about that, love – Elroy didn't realise it was you – we've only just got in, and it's pandemonium here!' June told her cheerfully. 'How are you doing there, darl – got everything you need?'

'It's – fantastic,' Pauline stammered guiltily, wrong-footed by June's generous tone. 'It's amazing. It's like winning the pools. It's . . . I'm . . . We're . . .'

'Glad you like it,' June said comfortably. 'And *your* house is lovely too. Comfy and cosy – I love the cheerful colour scheme. Did I tell you I grew up on New Vistas? I'm so thrilled to be back here, love. I've got me niece round at the minute,' she explained, over a background of screaming and raucous laughter, 'and her boyfriend and her daughter. I've only ever talked to them on the phone before, and seen pictures – never seen 'em in the flesh. I can't tell you what a treat it all is!'

'That's great,' said Pauline, feeling relief sweep over her. 'I was just ringing to apologise for the dog. Has she . . . ?'

'Aah, love, she has, and she's really upset about it, the poor little thing,' June told her, confirming her worst fears. 'What's she called?'

Pauline gagged on her reply, wishing fervently now that she had stamped harder on the joke name the kids had given her as a puppy. 'Whiffy,' she said eventually, in a hard-won level tone.

'Whiffy!' echoed June, apparently speaking directly to the dog. 'Is that your name? Is it? Is it? Well, she's a little treasure. Aren't you, girl? Ay? Yes, Whiff, I've got your mum on the phone just here! Want to hear her voice, pet? Here you go, Pauline, have a quick word with her – I'll put the receiver next to her ear.'

Pauline felt distinctly self-conscious to be talking to her pet long distance. Apart from anything else she couldn't think of a single thing to say after the initial embarrassed hello except, rather stupidly, she now realised, to ask Whiffy to put June back on.

'Listen, I'm really sorry,' she said, as soon as she was sure she was addressing a human, rather than a canine, ear again. 'I'd arranged for her to stay with my mum, but we just totally forgot to take her. I'll call her now, and get her to pop round—'

'Aah, don't do that, darl – not unless your mum really really wants her. I love pooches. She can stay here with us, in the comfort of her own home. You'd like that, wouldn't you, baby?' Down the line, Pauline could hear June laughing gaily, apparently charmed by Whiffy's response. 'She's wagging her tail ten to the dozen, Pauline, and licking me face!'

There was a sudden and explosive increase in the volume of the background noises in New Vistas, which sounded distinctly to Pauline like a door slamming and a man screaming, 'Jesus H. Christ Almighty! What else? Eh? What the buggering bugger else?'

'Is everything all right?' she asked tremulously, frightened to ask what had occasioned such an outburst.

'Oh yeah,' June replied equably, chuckling. 'That's me son-in-law, Greg. Bit overexcited. Just been out to your garage and seen your lovely Datsun. Big surprise for him, that was. I don't think he knew he'd be getting a car.'

Mick, sipping his chilled lager on the swing seat, watched quizzically as his wife closed her eyes in pain, her hand covering her brow. 'What?' he mouthed, but Pauline, listening to the receiver, merely shook her head.

'Anyway, darl,' June continued, 'glad to hear you're settling in okay, but I'd better get on and get meself organised. Me sisters and their families'll be round here before too long, and knowing them, it'll be party party all the way! Say hello to Busty for me, don't worry about Whiffy, and just enjoy yourselves . . . What's that, Elroy? . . . Yeah, that's right, love! . . . Me niece's boyfriend says to tell you to "chill". And I say, don't do anything that I wouldn't do – which gives you a hell of a lot of rope! See youse!'

The phone having gone dead in her hand, Pauline passed it wordlessly over to Mick, unable to work out what it was she should do to terminate the call her end.

'Everything okay there?' he asked, dealing effortlessly with the technology and patting the seat beside him. Bending over to a little fridge conveniently positioned next to the swing, he offered Pauline a can of beer, which she declined with a shake of her head. No need to tell him to chill, evidently – he was lolling there in his vest, shirt off, relaxed as you pleased, as if all this was normal, and he was to the manner born. 'What's wrong?' he asked, seeing her tense expression. 'Had Whiff done a whoopsie?'

'She had, but June didn't seem to mind. She wants to keep her.'

'Great,' said Mick happily. 'So what are you still upset about then?'

Pauline looked at him incredulously. 'Don't you feel guilty that we've got all this?' she demanded with a sweep of her arm, indicating the house behind them, the view in front of them, and ending with the two BMWs parked in the driveway below.

'And all they've got in return is an old banger, our pokey little house, our smelly dog, and Leicester in the coldest November since records began?'

A look of puzzlement passed briefly over his face, but was replaced almost at once with a broad grin. 'Nope,' he said, leaning back expansively and rocking himself on the swing. 'They have this all the time. They'll appreciate it even more when they get back. And in the meantime it's only right that us good guys get to have a turn. Besides, what do you mean, pokey?' he continued more seriously, leaping to his home's defence. 'It's been good to us, that house. It's kept us warm and dry, it's been affordable, we've brought up our kids there. And we've been happy in it, haven't we, Poll?'

Pauline considered the question silently for a moment, a conflict of emotions swirling within her breast. Though she had told Asheem it was over between them on that fateful day when Mick had nearly caught them at it, it hadn't stopped her young lover calling round on the off-chance that he might persuade her to change her mind. And once she'd known definitely that she'd be coming away on holiday, putting herself out of temptation's way in only a few weeks, there didn't seem to be too much harm in having just one more afternoon's entertainment. Then another. And another. They'd even managed to sneak a quickie in his car the evening before she'd left. She felt dirty, she felt ashamed, she felt resentful. But happy . . . ?

Mick, watching her silent struggle, wished now that he had never asked her such a loaded question. He knew what she was thinking (or thought he did): how could she be happy, when her husband couldn't get it up for her? Personally, he didn't like to dwell on that subject overmuch. At the back of his mind – which was the only place he would entertain it – he just assumed it was a temporary setback, something that would sort itself out eventually, that the problem would just disappear as quickly and mysteriously as it had arisen. Or not arisen. Bleddy hell, he thought uncomfortably, squirming in his seat, even ordinary language was booby-trapped if you didn't watch out. And there it was again! Booby. Boobs. He had a sudden, unbidden image of the red and black satin and lace thingy that the Customs officer had pulled out Polly's case, which made him feel extremely nervous. What if she put it on tonight, with no result? His treacherous memory suddenly slung up other images for his inspection: of him curled up in bed in his striped pyjamas, pretending to be asleep, and Poll lying there behind him, crying in the dark; of her on her knees on the bedroom floor, begging him to explain why she didn't turn him on; of their unexpressed mutual embarrassment, watching telly, when the onscreen action started to get hot.

He shuddered, despite the heat of the Melbourne afternoon. There was just too much pressure on him, that was the problem. On the rare occasions recently that he had felt a slight stirring, enough to contemplate at least having a go at it, he'd been frozen into inaction by the mere thought of possible failure. 'In the main, I meant,' he prompted her quickly, wanting the subject closed. 'We're generally happy, as opposed to unhappy, Poll?'

'Pauline,' she said automatically, her brain fusing around the complexity of her own myriad unspoken thoughts. What was the point, she asked herself bitterly – of anything? Here she was in paradise, and she was still unhappy. Much as she despised Mick for making her feel like this, she hated the fact that she'd been doing the dirty on him with Asheem. She felt permanently weighed down by guilt these days. Crippled by it. Bored by it. She wanted it over. She wanted to like herself again. She'd even been on the brink of spilling the beans, before he'd interrupted her train of thought, just for the relief of having a different type of feeling.

She pulled herself up sharply. No way. She couldn't possibly tell him. It would be the point of no return for Mick – he'd never get over the betrayal. No, she had to give this holiday a chance. A last ditch attempt, just for a fortnight. And if that didn't work, then . . .

'You look knackered,' Mick supplied softly, getting up to put his arms round her, and suddenly acknowledging her exhaustion in the familiar anchorage of his embrace, she slumped against his chest, her head nestled in his neck. He kissed her hair and stroked her back, his heart swelling with an almost unbearable feeling of tenderness. He loved the woman to bits, for God's sake – he couldn't bear to see her so unhappy and it all to be his fault. He'd make it up to her, he vowed, holding her gently – he would, he would. And soon. Not now, obviously, not while she was so tired and jet-lagged. But tonight, maybe . . . He felt himself getting anxious all over again. Well, if not tonight, then tomorrow, or at the very latest, possibly, the day after that. No, no, he shouldn't give himself an ultimatum – that was the trouble, it just didn't help . . . Sometime over the next two weeks any road, he vowed to himself sternly, when they were both feeling nice and relaxed.

A now familiar, and unmistakably transgender voice floated up from somewhere down below them. 'Aah – love's young dream!' it trilled. They both started and broke from their embrace like guilty adolescents, their most intimate moment of the last twelve months fractured by this unwelcome interruption. Mick peeped over the edge of the balcony in time to see Busty hitching up her skirt to straddle her moped, a crash helmet perched ineffectually on top of her blonde wig. She waved, and held up an empty shopping bag.

'Just off to rehearse some new tunes for a couple of hours,' she called up exuberantly. 'Thought I might get a few things in for a little barbie after – save you cooking on your first night.'

'Very nice. Thanks,' said Mick, digging in his trouser pocket for his small roll of Aussie dollars. 'Do you want some cash?'

'Oh!' cried Busty, her hand flying to her chest in a theatrical display of astonished appreciation. 'What I'd give to have a husband like you – you're so lucky, Pauline!' Two pasty English faces peered down at her, looking confused. 'I'm so touched,' she continued. 'No man's ever offered me money before. At least, not to do the shopping!' Her merry peal of laughter was drowned out suddenly by the thrum of the moped's engine starting up, and waving, she roared off down the drive.

'Think I might have a lie down for a bit,' Pauline volunteered, swaying on her feet. 'Have forty winks. I hardly got any sleep on the plane.'

'Come on then, cobber,' Mick said, in an appallingly bad attempt at an Australian accent, as he helped her back inside. Pauline couldn't remember when she had felt so tired. She was dizzy with it. Another sign of her advanced age, she supposed. Her head was full of cotton wool, and everything seemed strangely surreal. But then again, given the circumstances . . .

'You've got to admit, it's pretty weird, though,' she mumbled, slurring her words and staggering against Mick on leaden legs.

He smiled as he steadied her and helped her over the threshold. 'Yeah? What's weird?'

'Everything,' she said, with a limp wave of her hand. 'All of it. I keep thinking we're on reality TV. Keep expecting to see a camera following me around.' Her knees crumpled as soon as she reached the bed, and solicitously, Mick drew the sheet over her and stroked her hair.

'Need anything?' he asked her softly.

'Ngah,' was her reply, which had turned into a snore before he'd tiptoed out of the room.

Ever since its acquisition by the British in the eighteenth century, and even after the sun had set on the Empire and the Commonwealth had risen in its place, Australia has been the satisfyingly far-off place for the English to send their troublesome children, to make them or to break them – but in any event, to get them completely out of one's hair when they've become an embarrassment at home. For generations, packing off the adolescent recidivist to the antipodes has been the exasperated parent's ultimate weapon, when sending them to their room has proved to be simply not far enough. And though she had not been banished here by her parents, but accompanied by them, Gemma – who had been resident on the continent for a mere two hours – had already started to show signs of self-improvement.

After following Busty round on the grand tour of the house, she had banished herself to her bedroom and shut the door firmly behind her to keep her parents out. Having been in their company non-stop for what seemed like for ever, she needed to get some head space, and to chill. Surveying her new room, she was struck at first by how spartanly it was furnished, and how much space there was, compared to her own few square feet of chaos back home. Where she had painted her walls black and then lined them with stacks of books, boxes, clothes, bin bags, CDs, vinyl, bits of furniture and household items she was collecting for the glorious day when she could finally leave home, childhood games, teddy bears, cuddly toys, magazines, papers, folders of old school work – this room was all white, with a high ceiling, a huge wide window, and was completely bare save for a bed, a bedside table, and a bank of blank cupboard doors. It was both daunting and exciting, full of a sense of unfathomable potential and gravitas, as if it were an empty stage, or a blank canvas, awaiting her presence to bring it to life. This was all hers! She felt herself swelling to rise to its challenge, to prove herself, to be somebody, to show them all just who she was, what she was made of. And then almost immediately she felt herself deflate again, overawed and uncertain of her capabilities, daunted by the mocking, silent dare of the room to deliver the goods or get the hell out; as if it had slapped her cheek with an invisible gauntlet and flung it down, taunting her arrogantly to have the guts to pick it up.

Well, she'd soon fix that, she thought sulkily. No way was she going to be seduced by its smug, understated Sunday-supplement values. It could take her as she was, or lump it. Throwing open her suitcase and ransacking it on the floor, spraying a wide arc of disordered jumble across the quiet white expanse, she chucked most of her clothes over her shoulder until she'd located both pieces of her bikini, meaning merely to change, and to hike straight out to the pool. But when she started pulling open the doors of empty, pristine cupboards in search of a towel, she was stopped in her tracks by the sudden discovery of any amount of them, white and soft and springy, stacked on a gleaming chrome rack in her very own private bathroom, a Japanese silk kimono hanging from a solitary peg waiting to welcome her into its embrace. Wicked! Deadly!

On further investigation, this was a bathroom completely outside her experience. For a start off, there was no bath. There was a loo, and next to it a matching low basin for washing your feet (weird or what?), then another huge sink at normal height, a vast mirror surrounded by lights, and, sticking out of the wall, a shower head. No curtain though, which just went to show you that these fashion victims could take minimalism too far. Stupid gits, she thought sneeringly, feeling comforted by a return to her normal sense of superiority – everything would get wet, and where would the water go? But what did she care? If it flooded – tough. It wouldn't be her fault. She hadn't designed the stupid thing.

Now she was in here, though, she might as well try it out, she decided, peeling off her travel-worn clothes – yekk, they were minging! She turned on the wall-mounted tap, and was astonished at the power of the deluge she had provoked. The only shower she'd experienced previously was the one at Stu's bed-sit, which he had to share with the four others who lived on the same floor, and that was a lukewarm drizzle. Getting under it gingerly at first, she soon found herself luxuriating in a wonderfully warm cascade, and shoving her soaked hair extensions behind her shoulders she breathed a sigh of pure pleasure, welcoming the clean water onto her grimy upturned face. Ah! She could get used to this. Pity she hadn't thought to bring her soap and shampoo in here though (God! she admonished herself, censoring her thoughts – she was starting to sound like her bloody dad with his 'it's a pity this' and 'it's a pity that'!). But just as she was about to stomp back into the bedroom to fetch her toiletries bag, already out of sorts again, she noticed the two matching chrome plunger bottles in the little recess by the tap, one discreetly labelled 'Shampoo', the other labelled 'Soap'. Spooky business! Magic or what? It seemed to her uncanny, as if the room were enchanted and it could anticipate her every wish, and fulfil it, before she even had to ask. She began almost immediately to feel more kindly disposed towards it.

Her churlish thoughts about the inadequacy of the drainage proved to be unfounded too, she noted, as she finally switched off the water and began to towel her hair dry. The tiled floor had been cunningly laid at a slight angle to direct the flow of waste towards a small grate in its centre – the whole room was a shower. Cool! Chucking her towel on the floor and shimmying into her bikini she went back into the bedroom and was about to leave directly for the pool outside when, remembering to fetch a fresh towel and her shades, she turned in the doorway and saw the mess she'd made of the once proud room.

Quite what made this occasion different from the countless times she had left a room in a worse condition than she had found it, she couldn't, if challenged, have said. It might have been something to do with what psychologists call 'enlightened self-interest', or perhaps it had a connection to what campaigning socialists know as 'enfranchisement' and 'inclusion'. Whatever, she just suddenly thought that it wouldn't be as nice to return here, with the room in this state, as it had been when she had first arrived. There was something stately about the room when it was stripped down to its bare elegance which had all been spoilt by the fine spray of her hastily flung clothes. It was almost as if she had desecrated a beautiful sculpture or vandalised a gallery, she thought guiltily, as she started to retrieve the contents of her suitcase from the bed and the floor. And once they were in her hands, it really seemed no extra effort at all to hang them in the closets rather than to cram them back into the case. Returning to the bathroom to dump her wash bag, she noticed some drawers by the sink and decided to stow her make-up and hair stuff in them, filed in different compartments by category. The wet towel on the floor was duly picked up, wrung out, and hung up to dry, and before she knew it, she was wiping down the mirror and the walls.

Battle-hardened parents everywhere will understand the mental tussle Mick experienced when, arriving in the doorway, he found his normally domestically challenged daughter on her hands and knees in the middle of the bathroom floor, picking her hairs out of the plughole and tidying them into a bin. Pithy, laconic phrases like, 'Bleddy hell, I never thought I'd live to see the day . . . !' rose automatically to his lips, but were firmly fought down by his *own* sense of enlightened self-interest. And neither did he fall for the temptation of going over the top with the reward of praise, knowing deep in his bones that, at this stage in her development, if Gemma even suspected for one moment that what she was doing pleased him, she would never attempt it again.

'Knock knock,' he said cheerfully instead. 'Hiya! Fancy an explore?'

She leapt to her feet with a frown on her face, as he knew she would, embarrassed and cross to be found in such a compromising position, and in a tone so sarcastic even Anne Robinson might envy it, she pointed to her bikini-clad form and said, 'I'm going for a swim? Du-uh!'

'Oh, okay,' her father responded equably. With all the sangfroid of a conjuror who has something up his sleeve, he jingled a set of keys in the air before turning to go. 'I'm off to put that little deuce coupé through its paces. See you later.'

She was in her shorts and halter top and pounding down the stairs after him before the grin had left her face.

As the miles stacked up behind them, Mick and his daughter settled into a comfortable and companionable silence which had become unfamiliar to them now for almost a year – or to put it more accurately, ever since Stu had become the major influence in Gemma's life. In that time, they had come to know brooding silence and seething silence, despairing silence and silence meted out as punishment, but had become strangers to this easy familiarity of being in each other's company with nothing much to say. For once there was nothing for Mick to nag her about, and nothing for Gemma to wind him up over – there was just the car, the road, the sun on their faces, and their shared enjoyment of same.

When they'd first got in the car, of course, their excitement had been voluble – apart from anything else because of the brand spanking newness of it, the impressive array of instruments, the neat little steering wheel which looked so dinky between Mick's large hands. They sat there in the driveway for a while, the leather seats embracing their semi-recumbent forms, marvelling at the engine's gorgeously throaty voice, while Mick familiarised himself with the layout of the cockpit and they both got used to the fact that they had a legitimate claim to be here, and that anytime they wanted to, they could just take off in any direction they chose.

'Okay then?' asked Mick, turning to Gemma with a huge and naughty grin once he had thoroughly investigated the tight gate of the shift and was confident he'd selected first gear.

'Hit it,' she agreed, and neither could contain their shout of disbelieving laughter or whoops of excited delight, as they found themselves out on the road with the wind in their hair and all heads turning their way.

After a while of driving aimlessly between one suburb and the next, mopping up all the attention and envious glances of other less fortunate travellers, Gemma found a Melway tucked behind the seat, and navigated them to a wide highway, where they burned serious rubber for a glorious half-hour, and covered forty miles.

'Best start back,' Mick said, glancing at the clock, and he turned off at an intersection. Gemma groaned, threatening to break the good mood between them.

'Already?' she complained, mentally condemning her father for the sad old fart he'd become. 'What for – where's the hurry?'

'Busty's doing us a barbecue tonight,' he explained. 'Come on – see if you can find us a way to the coast road in that book – we'll drive back next to the sea.'

'But it's still early!' she whinged, having apparently already forgotten that going home, these days, meant having the opportunity to swim in the pool, or play in the gym, or just watch a DVD on the fifty-inch plasma screen, your feet up on the plush settee, a can of cold beer in your hand. 'We'll just be sat there waiting, with nothing to do!'

Mick smiled enigmatically, not rising to the bait. But then, why would he, when in his new role of conjuror he had previously secreted his final trump card in his breast pocket, to be produced out of thin air with a flourish? He patted his chest now, producing a small chink of metal against metal, and said, 'Hello, what's this? Could it be the key to your heart?'

'Unlikely,' she replied sulkily, a myth-debunking sceptic of the possibility of magic.

'Oh well, in that case,' he said, striving for nonchalance while fishing in his shirt pocket, 'they must be the keys to our yacht. Still, if you'd prefer to just keep driving . . .'

His reward was an excited scream, a mock angry thump on the arm, and the satisfaction that never before had his daughter called him 'you bleddy bastard' with such affection.

Finding the coast road back – indeed, finding their way to the marina – was the easy bit, it transpired. But once they parked the car and got out to walk towards the ranks of moored boats, they also left behind the expansive new feelings of confidence and status that went with it. Neither of them knew one end of a yacht from the other, the only sailing they'd ever done having been on the car ferry between Dover and Calais when they'd been on a cheap booze run to France, and as they walked nervously towards the *Lovelorn*, past people who seemed to know what they were doing with these large and expensive-looking craft, they began to feel self-consciously like trespassing landlubbers.

'This is it, then,' Mick said doubtfully, checking the name on the hull against the name on the key ring in his hand, and staring up with awe at the fourteen metres of mast that towered above them.

'Go on then,' said Gemma, nudging him forward and glancing round apprehensively to make sure they were not being observed. 'You first.'

His initial attempt to get aboard – by grabbing hold of the rail and trying athletically to fling himself across – proved almost fatal, his left foot somehow missing the deck and getting stuck between the hull and the concrete quay. There was a tense and sweaty moment of desperate twisting and wrenching, and then suddenly he was on board but on his back, his limbs waving limply in the air like a dying insect's.

'All right there?' a concerned male voice called out, from somewhere above him and over to the right. Still prone, and red-faced now from exertion and embarrassment, Mick shaded his eyes against the bright sun, and peering up into the sky, saw the shape of a man hanging nonchalantly from the mast of the neighbouring yacht.

'Yeah,' he said, managing a strangled attempt at a laugh as he heaved himself back onto his feet, which mercifully were both still present and correct and attached to the end of his legs. 'Don't know what happened there!'

'Easily done,' said the man graciously, effortlessly shinning down from his perch and landing lightly back on his own deck. Now that they were on the same level, Mick could see that in fact he was little more than a lad, about the same age as his own son. 'You'll be the Poms, then,' he told them, and joining Gemma on the quay, he offered his hand to help her board the *Lovelorn* in a shipshape and ladylike fashion.

'My name's Todd, by the way,' he continued, following her on deck.

Gemma's father was interested to see the change that Todd's attentions wrought in her. He had never seen his daughter simper before, let alone bat her lashes.

'I'm Gemma,' she informed him with a girlish giggle, and then, remembering her cool, she tossed back her hair extensions and looked him brazenly in the eye. 'And that's my dad, Mick.'

'G'day,' said Todd, momentarily spellbound by this display. He grinned back at her for what seemed like an age, then blushing unexpectedly, he turned back to Mick. 'Junie came down and told me to keep a look-out for you. So. Here you are. Good journey? How're you finding us so far?'

'Great,' said Mick. 'Fantastic.' He was uncomfortably aware that his daughter's answer was a silent, and perhaps unconscious – but nevertheless lascivious – licking of her lips, and he was glad that young Todd's back was turned towards her. He was used to seeing her around Stu, but in the twelve months they'd been an item, he'd never seen her so much as hold his hand, let alone kiss him. Certainly, never before had he seen his little girl as he saw her now, as a woman, as a sexual being. It made him feel quite uncomfortable, not to say queasy. Or maybe that was just the motion of the boat.

'Thinking of taking her out?' asked Todd, surprising Mick, as if the boy had stolen the words right out of his own head.

'Oh, the boat,' said Mick recovering quickly, and trying to look as if he knew what he was doing as he fitted the key into the cabin door lock. 'No, I don't think so. Just thought we'd have a look round today, familiarise myself with the layout and so forth, grab the manuals – that kind of thing.' The door gave way to his fumbling fingers, and gratefully he disappeared inside.

'Sailed much before?' asked Todd, politely standing aside for Gemma to precede him before following them into the cabin.

'Not so's you'd notice,' said Gemma. She made herself at home at once in the salon, draping herself full length across one of its two fitted seats in what, to her father, seemed to be a most uncalled-for and provocative manner. 'Is it hard?'

Mick wandered off alone, unnoticed by either of them, despite a thorough clearing of his throat before he left.

'Nah, not really,' Todd told her. 'Can be dangerous, though. You need to know what you're doing with the sea – she can be a bit wild and unpredictable at times.'

It sounded to Mick, who was currently staring vacuously at a bank of instruments in what he would later learn to call the nav station, that the two young people were speaking entirely in sexually loaded double entendres, and in these cramped quarters, being an unwilling eavesdropper to their inter-course (bleddy hell fire – now he was doing it himself!), he started to feel uncomfortably like a huge and hairy goosegog. Unused as he was to examining his feelings, even Mick was uncomfortably aware that his spirits had taken a dive. Only minutes ago he'd had more than he'd ever thought to wish for, and been happy. Now suddenly he felt disenfranchised and dispossessed. What was going on? Surely he wasn't jealous of this boy, was he? That would be daft. It was only natural that kids that age would flirt together, wasn't it? And hadn't he himself been willing Gemma silently this whole last year to lift her eyes up from the dreaded slothful Stu, with his Anarchy UK badges and his unwashed jeans and his know-it-all attitude, and spot somebody different, somebody with a bit of get-up-and-go, somebody clean cut and wholesome; somebody, in short, like this lad Todd? So what was the problem?

Discomfited by this unfamiliar bout of introspective self-enquiry, Mick found a renewed interest in the instrument panel before him, and he bent forward to peer at the dials and displays, trying to work out their functions. A more thorough sweep of the area revealed the longed-for manual, and once his nose was buried in it and his mind was satisfactorily distracted from the bigger question, the answer sneaked in sideways. He had been looking forward to getting to know his daughter again, to being the prime focus of her attentions for a while, to sharing some quality time together like they had when she was younger – like they'd been having in the car.

The tight feeling in his chest and throat, of which he now became aware, reminded him somehow of when his mum had died, and quickly adding two and two, he was suddenly over-come by a huge wave of anxiety that his time had come, that his heart was giving out early, just like hers had. Certainly it was pounding ten to the dozen, filling his ears with the noise, and his hands were sweaty, his breathing laboured, his vision darkening . . . Could it happen like this, then, on board some-body else's boat, on the wrong side of the world, with no Polly by his side to comfort him in his last moments . . . ?

'All right, mate?' asked Todd, unexpectedly appearing at his side and putting a warm hand on Mick's back. 'Want to sit a minute? You took quite a fall back there. Bang your head?'

'No, no, I'm fine,' said Mick, but he gratefully allowed the boy to help him down into the chair. 'It's probably just jet lag,' he continued, attempting a smile, now his breathing had grown more regular and his pulse had steadied. It was calming to feel another human's touch, even though it was provided by a stranger. 'Panic over,' he said, unwittingly but accurately diagnosing his trouble, and stood to test out his legs. 'Right then. Better get back. It's been a long day. I've probably been trying to fit too much in.'

'Yeah, it's a bloody long journey, so I'm told,' Todd grinned, and Mick found himself smiling back at the youth's friendly open face.

'So, is that your boat next door?' he asked him, replaying their earlier meeting in his mind. God, if that had been Stu who'd witnessed his embarrassing tumble onto the deck, he'd have heard a cruel shout of laughter as he landed, not a concerned enquiry about his health. He'd only known this boy five minutes, and already the lad had twice expressed interest in his condition. As rivals went, he realised, he could grow to like this one given half a chance.

'In my dreams,' said Todd. 'Nah, I just help out around here where I can.' He grinned again broadly, revealing a full set of fine white teeth. 'Try to ingratiate myself, you know, doing the jobs that the owners can't be bothered with. That way they often ask me to crew.' His grin grew half self-mocking, half cheeky. 'I've sailed this lady a good few times,' he said, with the rising Australian inflection at the end of the sentence, making the statement sound like a question.

'Ah,' said Mick, catching on, but still smiling, still charmed by the boy. 'I see now why you've been so kind. And there was me thinking you were a good Samaritan.'

Todd slapped him chummily on the back, enjoying the joke against himself. 'Ah no, mate, you're all right, that was for free.' The cheeky grin returned as he continued, 'But if you *wanted* me to, well now – I could show you the ropes any time, that'd be my pleasure.'

'Deal,' said Mick, offering his hand.

'You little beauty!' Todd exclaimed, as he enthusiastically pumped Mick's arm. Fishing in his back pocket, he pulled out a card. 'Here you go – that's me – Todd Cameron. And there's my mobile number. Just give me a call, and I'll be there!'

They were outside on the deck before Mick realised that

there had been no sign of Gemma in the salon, and turning from relocking the door, he finally spied her standing moodily on the quay, impatient, it seemed, to be off. Now what the bleddy hell was up with her?

'Are you coming, Dad?' she called crossly, as Todd tactfully helped him across to dry land. 'I thought you said we shouldn't be late?'

'Plenty of time,' he said, embarrassed by her rudeness. 'See you then, Todd. I'll be in touch.'

'Good on you, mate,' said Todd, giving Mick a final matey slap on the back. 'Look forward to it. See you, Gemma.'

'Yeah – whatever,' she muttered, throwing him what seemed to be a dismissive wave, and she stomped back towards the car.

'Nice lad,' Mick offered tentatively, as he buckled himself into his seat and they set off to go back home, in a rather less friendly atmosphere than when they'd arrived.

Gemma snorted derisively. 'You would think that,' she said.

'Why? What do you mean?' Mick shot her an anxious sideways glance, now the protective father. 'What did he do? Did he say something to upset you?'

'Course not!' she scoffed. 'Him? He's so bleddy clean cut he'd squeak if you squeezed him. God, what a boring git!'

'I see,' said her father, mystified by the depth of her feeling. 'Well, you're going to have to get used to him. He's going to teach us to sail.'

'So long as you don't leave me with him like just now,' she said with an accusing glare, 'and expect me to make nicey-nicey polite conversation. Just because we're both youth doesn't mean we've got anything in common, you know.'

'I just went to find the manual,' Mick said in a small hurt voice, feeling rather silly now about his earlier misreading of the situation. 'I thought as you didn't follow me you were happy where you were.'

'Huh,' said Gemma, but after a horribly familiar sulky silence which lasted the rest of the way home, she appeared to rally as they pulled into the drive. 'What time's the barbecue?' she called in a pleasant enough tone to Busty, who was unloading bags from the panniers of her moped.

'About an hour, darl,' was the reply, delivered on the trot, as Busty ferried the food into June's house. 'Sorry, I'm running late as always, but these things can't be rushed, and these babies have to be marinated.'

'Yum,' said Gemma, turning to her father with a twinkle in her eye. 'Marinated babies for tea. My favourite.' Mick laughed, too relieved that her bad mood had lifted to be suspicious about the cause. 'What would we be doing now if we were in England? What's the time difference?' she continued, unexpectedly slipping her arm through Mick's, as the two of them stood together looking out at their sea view.

'Eleven hours at this time of year.' Mick glanced at his watch, always glad to be asked a factual question. 'So I'd be about to get up, and you'd still be snuggled down in bed.' He chubbed her arm, and chanced a joke. 'Or just getting in from one of your clubs as it's Saturday, knowing you.'

Gemma obliged him with an unoffended laugh, and still arm in arm, she steered him towards the house. 'Wonder if Mum's awake yet,' she prompted him.

'I'll go and have a look,' he said. 'Better not let her sleep through – her body clock'll be all over the shop if she does.' They parted at the top of the stairs. 'What are you going to do?' he asked, not wanting her to feel left out while she was in such an amenable frame of mind.

'I'm just going to read for a bit,' she said, as if butter wouldn't melt. 'Or maybe start my Australian journal.'

'Good for you!' Mick congratulated her. Reading was

another thing that seemed to have gone out of the window since Stu. 'See you in a bit, then.'

'Yeah, see you.' Gemma smiled as she watched him go into his room. Locking her own door behind her, she crossed the room and made herself comfortable on a nest of pillows, picked up the bedside phone, and keyed in Stu's mobile number.

When they all reconvened an hour later, Pauline was rested (and now sober), Gemma was happy, Mick was relaxed, and Busty was a man called Chin. Not surprisingly, hearing their new friend's voice emanating from this flat-chested, trouser-wearing stranger caused a moment of stupefied bewilderment from the party from New Vistas who, since their initial surprise at meeting Busty at the airport, had taken her persona in their stride. But once he had controlled his attack of the giggles ('You look like stunned mullets!' being his first reaction, hopping up and down and clapping his hands), Chin explained his transmogrification.

'I had a dress rehearsal and photo call for my new show today, darl-a-darls,' he told them. ' "Busty Springboard-A-Go-Go Goes Ga-Ga". It takes *hours* to get her made up and frocked up, so I had to get changed before I met you to bring you here.' Mick's expression still being in the dropped jaw position, Chin affectionately closed it with a delicately outstretched finger. 'You'll get used to it, Dorothy,' he assured him with a smile, and conjuring a bottle of Australian fizz from an esky, he continued mischievously, 'Now which of you big spenders is going to pop my cork?'

Pauline being the first to recover her wits and her manners thanked him for his hospitality and, after a brief tussle with wire and stopper, produced a gushing fountain of sparkling foam, earning herself no less appreciative applause than if she had just won the Melbourne Grand Prix by a mile.

Suffice it to say that, once toasts had been proposed and drunk to, and their glasses had been replenished and emptied again, the Leicester contingent's first evening in Oz proved to be an hilarious and unqualified success. We could, of course, linger here a little longer. We could watch and admire the warm camaraderie which developed amongst them. We could envy them the green-lipped mussels which had been marinated in lemon grass and garlic, drool over the lamb steaks seasoned with ginger and soy, and frankly want to kill for the succulent mangoes, cooked in foil with palm sugar and rum.

But why endure the torture of covetousness, when with a mere flick of the globe, we could be back in dear old Blighty enjoying Schadenfreude?

6

Unlike June, neither Lorna nor Greg could be accurately described as party animals. In the normal run of things, their preferred form of socialising was dinner and shop talk with two or three other professional couples in one of Melbourne's many excellent restaurants, or making up a small group to meet for drinks before taking in a concert. Of course, in their upwardly mobile twenties they had worked hard and played hard, but now they were in their thirties, they worked even harder and therefore played less. Which is one of the reasons that they had poured so much energy into their beautiful home – it was important to both of them, after a hard day, to have a place where they could just kick off their shoes and relax. Needless to say, that place was not 236 New Vistas Boulevard.

After enduring a gruelling hour of screeching and guffawing, of feet pounding up and down stairs, of clattering teacups and overexcited laughter, of back slapping, of bad jokes, of the bloody dog barking like it was fit to be tied, Melissa, Elroy and Parveen had at last reluctantly left (with heartfelt reassurances that they would see them again later), and June had taken Whiffy for a walk round the block, or as she put it 'down Memory Lane'. Quite whether that was for the benefit of enhancing June's recall of the streets of her childhood or to remind the bastard mongrel where it was supposed to take its bloody dump, Greg couldn't say – although he posed the question most forcefully to Lorna once they were alone.

'What?' he challenged her, as he was met with a cold and silent critical gaze. He was still in search of the relief that a bloody good row might offer, which Midland Mainline Customer Services had earlier denied him. 'Don't tell me you're happy to be here in this bloody hovel, stepping round dog crap?'

'No, I was just thinking,' Lorna returned archly, her voice a couple of degrees frostier than the weather outside, 'you're obviously going to fit in here better than you think.' And with an insouciance that made him want to shake her, she returned to her unpacking, trying to wedge her unsuitably flimsy clothing around Pauline's woolly jumpers in the drawers.

'Yeah? And what makes you think that?' Greg barked aggressively.

'Well, you've only been here five minutes,' said Lorna briskly, as one might speak to a fractious child, 'and already you sound like a whingeing Pom.'

No criticism could have been harsher. The wind now out of his sails, Greg blustered a denial and regarded her with puzzlement. This was so unlike her. Normally when he was in a bad mood she backed him up or calmed him down, so what the bloody hell was going on? After all, it was she who'd got them into this fix. She should be feeling guilty, should be trying to appease him, to cheer him up. Moodily he flung himself full length on the bed, where he found that his body all but disappeared into its softness. 'Christ Al-bloody-mighty!' he complained, fighting his way back to the surface. 'Will you look at the state of this bloody mattress! I'm going to be crippled in here with my back!'

'I rest my case,' said his wife the lawyer, turning with a frigid smile. 'Well, I think the bath'll be run by now. Okay with you if I go first?' she continued, evidently not caring if it was or not, since she was already armed with a towel and on her way out.

Greg dismissed her with a wave, his head sinking back on the pillow. 'Be my bloody guest, Lorn. You know how I feel about bloody baths.'

She stopped for a moment in the doorway, unable to resist. 'Not sure that I do these days,' she said provocatively. 'It used to be something about not wanting to wallow in your own muck, didn't it? Don't know if that still applies.'

By the time Greg managed to struggle back up out of the bed's embrace to check her expression, she was gone. What the hell had she meant by that? He knew that Diane had been blabbing to her friends about him. Was it possible that Lorna had got wind of the affair? Cos if she had, it was best out in the open and denied sharpish. Affecting an air of injured innocence, he followed her into the bathroom, where she was already stripped off and testing the water's temperature with her toe.

'You all right, love?' Greg asked her in a softer tone, his hand straying to stroke the smooth skin of her naked back. Bloody oath, she was lovely. At times like this, he didn't know why he bothered with the likes of Diane Lipshitz. It occurred to him now that if he couldn't have the satisfaction of a good row, a good rut might cheer him up.

'I'm fine,' she replied crisply, hopping into the bath and submerging herself up to her chin to avoid his touch. Not having had a minute to herself since she'd arrived, Lorna had been looking forward to some quiet reflective time alone. She felt she was dangerously close to being out of control – more interested now in punishing Greg than in adhering to her original plan of bringing him to England to seduce him. She needed to order her thoughts, to work out her priorities. Did she want revenge, or did she want her husband back? To kiss him or to kill him – which? The way she'd been behaving towards him recently made her realise that she just wasn't clear on that point any more.

Peeking through half-closed eyes, she was disconcerted to see him so near her, perched on the edge of the tub, gazing down at her with that affectionate smile which only ever meant one thing. She closed her eyes quickly again and, holding her breath, dunked her head down under the water, blocking him out. On the one hand she couldn't imagine life without him – just the thought of it brought an icy grip of terror to her heart. But on the other, presuming she did succeed in getting him back this time, how would she feel when the next Shitlipz inevitably came along?

Well that one was easy: merely posing the question in her mind produced an overwhelming rush of rage which raced through her body like a lit fuse. And talking of explosive feelings, how the hell was she supposed to concentrate on life and death issues when his hand had gone deep-sea fishing in the bath? Didn't he realise the danger he was in? Didn't he know that she was a woman on the verge of homicide? Gasping, she plunged back to the surface with a kick of her legs, causing a tidal wave to swell and soak his shirt. Good. Serve the bugger right, she thought viciously, rubbing water from her eyes. But instead of the expected outburst of anger or whingeing, a wry chuckle met her ears.

'Well, I couldn't get much wetter. 'Less I was in there with you,' he said, and proceeded to strip off his clothes.

'Greg—' she began.

'Lorn,' he replied, stopped in his tracks by the warning note in her voice. Her coldness and sarcasm over the last few hours had unsettled him, prompting an unfamiliar rush of fear and longing. Kneeling by the bath in his boxers, he took her hand tenderly in his. 'I don't say it often enough I know, but have I told you today how much I love you?' he asked.

'No,' said Lorna warily, eyes narrowed. 'I don't believe that subject has been broached.'

'Well I do,' he said, and pressed her hand chastely to his lips. 'And, you know, sorry for being a whingeing bastard. You've got to admit all this here's a bit of a shock, but – I shouldn't take it out on you and it won't happen again.'

Lorna thanked him nicely, willing to be disarmed by his apology – after all, wasn't that why she was here, to remind him how important she was to him? – and when he offered to wash her back, she obligingly sat forward and handed him the soap.

Students of the courtship rituals of primates will, of course, be unsurprised to hear that, once the grooming had started and the attentions of the alpha male had been secured, the mating began swiftly thereafter. Not normally aquatic creatures, however, there was a certain amount of jostling and repositioning to be done to ward off drowning the female and, given the size of the watering hole – a good two feet shorter than the dominant partner – there was also a certain amount of folding of limbs to be done and unnatural contortions to be effected. The unusual choice of habitat for this activity added great excitement for both animals but, sad to say, seconds before the moment of what might have brought them mutual satisfaction, a howl of pain from the male signalled that the fun was now over for both of them.

'What?' cried Lorna.

'My – bloody – back!' gasped Greg.

'Jeez,' she said, her frustration outweighing her concern. 'Well, *move* for God's sake – you're crushing me!'

His lower legs being in the air, his elbows struggling to take his weight, jammed in against the slippery sides of the bath, he was in no position to obey her, or to alleviate his distress. 'Can't,' he sobbed, after a Herculean effort that contributed nothing to change their circumstances except to bring him more pain. By now he was crying real tears. 'I'm stuffed,' he moaned.

'Yeah, well that makes two of us,' said Lorna drily – or rather, wetly, since trapped beneath him she was locked in her own battle against gravity to stay topside of the water. 'Maybe if I try to wriggle out from under,' she suggested, pushing against his chest and managing to fling one leg out over the edge of the bath.

'No-o-o!' he cried. He gripped her shoulders in a spasm of pure agony, thus sharing it generously with her. 'Just stay still a minute,' he begged, 'till it passes.'

A minute passed, but not the pain. 'May I remind you,' said Lorna eventually, in a long-suffering voice, 'that last time, that took a fortnight?'

Rescue came half an hour later from an unexpected source, when Whiffy the Wonderdog returned from her perambulations with June. Her mood had changed swiftly since this new mum had appeared to take charge of her, and having recovered somewhat from the anxiety of being abandoned by her real family for a day and a half, she was now of a more cheerful and optimistic frame of mind. Since things had already improved so much, her doggy logic told her, maybe Mum and Dad and Gemma had also come back home while she was out. Thus it was that, let off the leash in the hallway, she decided against June's invitation to join her in the kitchen for something to eat and instead, tail wagging, trotted off to explore upstairs.

There are worse things that can happen to a man in Greg's position than being discovered on top of his wife in the bath, bum in air, by his mother-in-law – and having his nether regions investigated by an overexcited, curious dog must certainly rank high amongst them. Naturally, his howl of outrage – not to mention his scream of agony when he tried to escape the thorough research currently being undertaken by

Whiffy to establish the olfactory difference, once and for all, between scrotum and anus – was enough to bring June pounding up the stairs, where she stood, open-mouthed, in the doorway. Being a broad-minded woman, however, once she had collected her wits (and believed her own eyes), she took the extraordinary tableau vivant in her stride and set about their rescue – although it goes without saying that Greg and Lorna would have been happier if she'd done it without rushing to the phone to recruit outside help, and without getting a fit of the giggles.

If Lorna thought that nothing worse could happen to a woman in her position than being introduced by her mother to her two aunties for the first time ever, then that was because she had yet to experience the trio of sisters' retelling of the tale, with actions, to other previously unknown extended family members at the New Vistas Social Club in the lull between songs on Karaoke Nite.

Being the butt of a joke (oh yes, make no mistake, this pun, amongst others, was used to hilarious effect several times that evening) had never been Lorna's idea of having a good time. Her sense of well-being, ever since a child and to the present day, depended on a self-image of competence, dignity and style, and none of these qualities was to be discerned in Aunty Mo's impersonation of her as she lay on her back beneath Aunty Jo's Greg on the leatherette bench in the Albert Lumb Functions Room, June having already bagged the part of the Wonderdog Whiffy. The performance proving popular, and the various factions of the family arriving at staggered intervals over a period of two hours, there was every opportunity for the reunited siblings to perfect their roles, and indeed to expand them. By the time the last second-cousin-once-removed's mother's new boyfriend had watched and applauded, fake orgasms had been added, and Whiffy, although female, had learnt to cock her leg by way of an encore.

Greg had elected, through teeth gritted with pain, to stay home for the evening, flat on his back on the floor, but noting his absence, the irrepressible Melissa had urged Elroy to go and pick him up in the car and bring him along, lest he miss out on all the fun. Annoyed as she was with him for making her the focus of all this unwelcome attention, Lorna still put up an unsuccessful but spirited attempt to intercede on her husband's behalf, knowing he'd be happier to suffer alone, but Elroy was not to be dissuaded from his mission, and after a couple of calls on his mobile he left in high spirits, promising to sort him out and return with his man forthwith. No one was more surprised than she was when, an hour later, and to a huge roar of approval from the crowd, Greg duly arrived on Elroy's arm wearing a vacuous grin, his back pain apparently forgotten.

Though Lorna's smile, starved as it had been of humour, had grown extremely thin throughout the evening's display of family bonding, she had to concede that the whole sorry episode had doubtless ensured their popularity amongst the rellies. Naturally, Greg was hailed with enthusiasm by one and all as a valiant hero wounded in action, but she too was welcomed by the womenfolk as one of them, and admired by the men. She was a 'chip off the old block' apparently – or as Aunty Jo offered to wild applause, 'We've always been a randy lot, us Hibberts!'

Karaoke Nite was well supported, and the smoke was getting to Lorna, stinging her eyes and burning her throat. Of the two dozen or so kinsfolk who'd turned up for the welcome party, barely a handful were not seriously addicted to the noxious weed – and none seemed as concerned as she was that around their tables oxygen had become a scarce resource. They were all too busy shouting and laughing and drinking like fish. Even Greg, who was normally the first one to complain when anyone dared to light up within a five-metre radius of him, didn't seem to notice or to care. But then again, he was being anaesthetised at regular intervals by his new male friends, who were determined to turn him against that 'bleddy Australian four x-ing froth' and convert him to the joys of a good English pint. Thus, within a startlingly short period of time, he had already tried all three of the hand-pumped beers on offer at the well-stocked bar, and was now working his way through the speciality bottled ales, Old Peculier currently going neck and neck with the Bishop's Finger in the competition for his favour.

At the beginning of the evening, when invited to order a drink, Lorna had asked for a glass of white wine, but one sip of the stuff was enough to convince her that here in Leicester, viniculture was an unknown art. She was used to the rounded tropical flavours of Australian chardonnays, the nose bursting with suggestions of orange-fleshed melons, of ripe bananas, of sun-blushed peaches. Rolling the thin acidic house wine over her discerning palate and swallowing it quickly with a moue of distaste, she was reminded more of rancid acetone with a twist of lemon, and she had parked her glass back on the table, refusing the increasingly pressing offers to repeat the experience as round followed round, until Uncle Vince, concerned by this deviation from proper Hibbert behaviour, insisted on her trying something else.

'You don't want to drink that, duck, it's rat's piss,' he told her amiably, draining her glass in one quaff and earning the approval of the crowd with his subsequent colourful impression of a man dying from poisoning, clutching his throat and rolling on the floor. Springing back to his feet with a bow and a grin he gave due deliberation to the volley of suggested favoured tipples from the womenfolk, finally narrowing it down to a selection of four, with which he returned triumphant from the bar.

'That's your brandy and Babycham,' he announced, plucking it from the tray and setting it before her with a flourish.

'Can't go wrong!' yelled cousin Sharon on smoking breath, lifting her own glass of the lethal cocktail in salutation. 'Guzz straight to yer 'ead! Guzz straight to mine, any road,' she guffawed. Well, that would certainly go some way to explaining *your* behaviour, thought Lorna primly. Certainly nobody in her acquaintance sat with her knees wide open in a miniskirt.

'Here's your Dubonnet and lemonade,' continued Vince, and hearing no champion's voice in support of that choice, he looked around the table. 'Who picked that?'

'Velma,' screeched Aunty Mo, jabbing with a pointed thumb at her mother-in-law at her side, who had temporarily, it seemed, lost consciousness. 'You've got to admit she's a good advert!'

'Nuff said,' Vince twinkled, setting down the third. 'Rum and black.'

'That's mine, ta,' claimed Jo, and jokingly tried to take it, earning slapped hands and catcalls for her pains.

'And last but not least,' began Vince, but he was beaten to the line by Melissa.

'Southern Comfort and Coke!' she cried excitedly, grabbing Lorna's narrow shoulders in a crushingly affectionate embrace. 'I picked that for you, that's my drink, Lorna. Go on, have a taste – you'll love it!'

Not normally much of a drinker, Lorna looked askance at the four glasses lined up before her, but it was clear from the cries of 'Neck it!' and the countdown which was now being chanted, that she would find no clemency here. Even her own mother was counting with the rest of them, and Greg was no help whatsoever on account of already being three-quarters of the way to legless. Reluctantly taking the glass from Melissa, who was about to administer it personally – and in that pursuit already had her in a friendly neck lock – she took a conservative sip of the Southern Comfort and Coke, and found that actually it wasn't so bad. She didn't care a fig about the alcoholic content – like many women in extremis, it was the sugar which her body craved to calm her jangling nerves, and that was there in scads. She drained the glass so quickly she even beat the countdown, earning warm applause. Her popularity soared to new heights with the similarly quick dispatch of the Dubonnet and lemonade followed straight away by the rum and black, so much so that her new family relented when she said she'd sit and nurse the brandy and Babycham for a while if it was all the same to them, on account of her needing to catch her breath. Only Melissa wanted reassurance that her drink had found most favour, keen as she was for her intense feelings of kinship to be reciprocated and, softened by the alcohol, or the sugar, or perhaps just by being loved so unexpectedly and unconditionally by this young pregnant woman who was herself more like an overgrown puppy, Lorna magnanimously put her mind at rest.

'Definitely liked yours the best,' she confided over the music to Melissa's pierced ear, 'but don't let on, or they'll try me with some more.'

Unable to contain her gratitude and glee at being chosen above the herd, Melissa's answer was a big sloppy wet one on Lorna's cheek. 'I've waited all my life for us to meet,' she told her flattered but puzzled cousin, 'and I always knew we'd be best mates when we did.'

'Why?' Lorna felt prompted to ask, her usual inhibition now being three drinks in the past. 'I don't mean why would we be best mates,' she hurried to explain, Melissa's smile having disappeared as if she herself had slapped it off her face. 'I mean why have you waited all your life to meet *me*? Why me?'

For once in her life rendered speechless, Melissa's mind fused at the enormity of trying to explain the obvious. 'Just cos,' she shrugged finally.

'Because . . . ?' Lorna pursued her.

'Well, like, you know – when I was a kiddie,' Melissa explained, 'getting your letters and your cards and stuff. It was exciting – foreign stamps and that, and that thin paper, when you have to tear round the edge really careful so's you don't rip the words up inside – you know, them whatthey-called thingies.'

'Aerogrammes,' Lorna supplied, now more bewildered than before. '*My* letters and cards?'

'Well, Aunty June's I s'pose,' Melissa conceded. 'She used to write to me mam regular, before e-mails and that – but you always signed them. I've still got them indoors – I could show you, if you like.'

'Right,' said Lorna, her memory supplying no details to substantiate this claim. It was possible, of course, that June could have got her to add her childish moniker to the missives sent back home, but if so it had certainly not made as much of an impression on her as it seemed to have done to this recipient.

Melissa suddenly looked excited and mysterious. 'You still haven't noticed, have you?' she challenged her, with one eyebrow raised and a strange little wiggle of her head.

'Noticed,' echoed Lorna, playing for time. 'Give us a clue.'

This was the kind of game that Melissa enjoyed. 'I spy with my little eye something beginning with E,' she teased, and turned her head to one side for Lorna's inspection.

'Eye?' she offered, examining Melissa's make-up. 'Eyebrow? Eyeshadow – you've changed your eyeshadow?'

Melissa yelped with laughter, delivering a swift and rather painful jab to her ribs with her elbow. 'No, you daft bastard, look!' she said, again with the head wiggling. 'Don't tell me you need another clue? Come on, Lornie, you're looking right at it! E-A!'

'Ear? Your ear?' Lorna suggested doubtfully, glancing at the vast array of metal hardware which decorated its entire rim and vied for space in the lobe.

'Ring, ear*ring*,' Melissa said in frustration, selecting one by feel and ruthlessly pushing it towards Lorna, despite the fact that it was still attached to her head.

'Very nice,' said Lorna, at last identifying a tiny silver kangaroo with an even tinier joey peeking out of its pouch.

'It should be – you chose it!' she was informed to her surprise. 'When I were a baby! Don't tell me you've forgot?'

'No, no, of course not,' she lied. She knew now that, though she seemed so much younger, Melissa was in fact twenty-seven, so Lorna would have been five when she was born. Trying to imagine herself at that age, a faint childhood memory stirred, of being taken by June to a jeweller's shop to pick a lucky charm. She could see the ornaments in her mind's eye now, dozens of them, mounted on card, and could remember being particularly excited over the ones that did something: the helicopter whose rotor blades really turned; a cat sitting on a dustbin, and when you lifted the lid, there inside was the skeleton of a fish; and a kangaroo – of course! 'You can take the joey out of its pouch,' she remembered now with enthusiasm, but attendant on this memory was a feeling of having been cheated. When Mum had told her to pick one, she'd thought she was being invited to choose it for herself, and had sulked for days when it had been wrapped in a box and sent off to some new baby she'd never even met.

'Yeah, well you could,' said Melissa. 'But me mam had it soldered in before she'd let me wear it as an earring. It fell out once and I nearly lost it. I were that upset – I had the whole family out on their hands and knees in the garden, and in the end it were in me bed! Not surprising really – I used to sleep with it under me pillow. It was the most precious thing I had,' she confided happily, tucking her arm through Lorna's and snuggling up closer to her on the bench. 'I had this Catholic friend at school who wore a gold cross round her neck, and she told me she held it when she prayed to Jesus every night. So then I started to whisper all me secrets to Kanga here, and pretend I was telling them to you.'

Looking at Melissa, whose face was suffused with affection for her, Lorna's head reeled at the power she'd been given. The discovery that she had been deified by somebody she had never met – or come to that, not ever given a thought to – would have been heady stuff for her even if she hadn't been three sheets to the wind and suffering from jet lag. As it was, it was just plain spooky. She felt like the legendary butterfly who, innocently flapping its wings on one side of the world, provokes a tidal wave on the other. She knew that ignorance was no defence in law, but surely she couldn't be held responsible for having been the stuff of this person's childhood dreams, or for being the object of her love now? She felt overwhelmed by Melissa's gushing affection, invaded by it, claustrophobic. She preferred things to be measured and contained.

The irony was not lost on her that only a couple of weeks before, when she'd been at her lowest ebb in the room at the Sheraton, she had wished she had a best girlfriend with whom she could talk things over. Bloody hell. It just went to show the wisdom of the old Chinese adage, 'Be careful what you wish for: you might just get it and more.' How much more could you get than bloody Melissa?

As if in answer, a screeching howl of feedback filled the room, swiftly echoed by a screeching howl of hysteria from her new best friend at her side. 'They're going to do it now!' Melissa screamed, turning to her with eyes fizzing with excitement and dragging Lorna to her feet. In front of them, everybody was getting up for a better view of whatever it was that had provoked the dreadful noise from the microphone on stage, so even when she was standing, all Lorna could see was the backs of people's heads. No worries for Melissa, apparently. Using Lorna's shoulder (and then Lorna's head) to steady herself, she climbed onto the bench they'd been sitting on only a moment ago. 'Come on, Lornie, get up here with me!' she yelled over the continuing howlback, and pulled her up with a surprising strength to join her.

'We can't stand on the furniture!' Lorna protested, her spike heels sinking into the upholstery and threatening to topple her, but, giggling, Melissa merely spun her round to face the front and propped her against the wall, snaking her arm through Lorna's with her usual iron grip. And now she had a clear view of the stage, Lorna realised that the least of her problems was staying upright, for there, waving away the karaoke DJ, each armed with a mike, were the three sisters Hibbert. For crying out loud, she thought wretchedly, closing her eyes in dread. If they were going to perform the epic bloody saga of sex in the bath with Whiffy again – for all these strangers to see this time, not just the two dozen rellies – she would never, ever, speak to her mother or aunties again.

Suddenly, Aunty Mo's voice boomed from the speakers. 'He int got the music – he says it's too old,' she told the audience. 'So we're going to do it wi'out.'

'Unless there's a penis in the 'ouse?' Aunty Jo added, and was inexplicably answered by several cries of 'Betty!'

Unable to believe her ears, Lorna's eyes flew open again, in time to see a seventy-something woman being helped to the stage by willing hands from all sides and settling herself at a piano. Well, thank Christ she'd misheard – although she realised with a jolt that it was small comfort to acknowledge that it was her own imagination which was now supplying the double entendres.

While Jo briefed Betty, Mo continued to brief the audience. 'You all know us, Mo and Jo,' she told them, and obligingly they cheered and sang back at her, 'Got my mojo working . . .' She grinned back, waving them to settle down. 'Yeah, well, we'll probably get round to doing that later. Any road, where was I? Oh yeah. But most of you won't remember our big sister, June, who emigrated to Australia. This is the first time we've seen her in thirty-five year!' There was warm applause and whistles as June took a bow.

Having primed Betty, whose fingers now hovered over the ivories ready for action in a heartbeat, Jo rejoined her co-stars at the mikes. 'This is the first time we've sung this in thirty-five year an' all,' she informed them, signalling Betty to begin the introduction. 'So if we've forgot the words, you'll all have to la la along. Anybody remember the Beverleys?' she asked over the opening chords, and as the older half of the audience sighed with pleasure and started to clap, the trio joined hands and gave voice to, 'Sisters, sisters, never were there such devoted sisters'.

Watching them from her vantage point at the back of the hall, what struck Lorna most was the shared history between her mum and her aunts, of which she herself was ignorant, and the easy intimacy which had been so effortlessly re-established after half a lifetime of being apart. It was extraordinary too to see her mother's features echoed in the faces of these two women who flanked her. Like three peas in a pod, they were slightly different from each other in shape and size, but clearly from the same mould. Lorna tried to imagine what they would have been like all those years ago, when they had first performed this song. They must have cut quite a dash, three young women nudging twenty, rehearsing in their bedroom perhaps, using hairbrushes for mikes, working on the routine that, miraculously (and barring a couple of hastily glossed over mistakes), they all remembered so well now. Had they bickered over make-up, had they borrowed each other's clothes? When they'd walked down the street together arm in arm, coats swinging, strutting their stuff, had people stopped to stare? There go the Hibberts, three fine-looking girls.

An only child herself (and married to one), Lorna had no direct experience of having siblings, and so she'd never placed any importance on this missing part of June's life. And clearly it was a huge part. Her mother was radiant with the joy of reunion, it was really quite moving to watch. Though the song was meant to be humorous (at least, the way the Hibbert Sisters were performing it), a tear leaked out of the corner of Lorna's eye, and she felt a stab of guilt that it had never occurred to her before now to treat Mum to the airfare home. Well, that much she could change, she thought, brushing away the tear only to find another one taking its place. From now on she would see to it that June got to visit every year if she wanted to – twice a year if she liked.

Rather irritatingly Melissa had started to sway with the music, and though at first Lorna tried to stand firm and hold her ground, locked as she was in her pregnant cousin's embrace, she was out-matched in weight and in number and forced to go with the flow. Though initially she was stiff with resentment, after a couple of verses (and the rest of her brandy and Babycham), her body seemed to soften of its own accord and before she knew it she was singing along with her dancing partner, smiling, eyes sparkling, the two of them joined at shoulder and hip.

At the piano, Betty's chords were rolling extravagantly towards the big finish and at the front of the stage, Mo and June and Jo, arms around each other's waists, scaled the heights of the final harmony. The applause was deafening as they took their jubilant bows, but since Lorna was enthusiastically adding to it herself, she didn't even mind when Melissa demonstrated her startling ability to whistle through her fingers.

As their mothers left the stage with their aunt, the cousins turned to grin at each other, their eyes shining with sentimental tears.

'Weren't they great, Lornie?' Melissa demanded excitedly. 'Int it lovely to see them together?'

Lorna nodded, torn between laughing and weeping, and rooted ineffectually in her pockets for a tissue.

'Aah,' said Melissa approvingly, grabbing her shoulders and lifting her face. 'Are you crying? Come here, you big softie – you're just like me!' However inaccurate this assessment, Lorna gratefully allowed herself to be gathered in her cousin's arms, her body bending round Melissa's swollen belly, her head tucked into her neck, the silver kangaroo and joey pressing into the soft flesh of her cheek.

Returning to their table, June and Mo witnessed their daughters' embrace with huge pleasure, and in June's case, great surprise. She couldn't remember a time when she had seen the habitually self-contained Lorna display such affection, or look so vulnerable.

'Aah,' said Mo, slipping her arm round her sister's shoulders, unconsciously echoing her daughter's sentiments.

'Int it lovely to see them together at last? Our Melissa's really been looking forward to meeting her in the flesh.' Conspiratorially she drew June closer. 'She's going to ask her to be the godmum, you know.'

Her heart swelling in her breast, June didn't think she could be happier until, glancing over at her son-in-law, she saw Greg cracking up at something that Elroy had just said, slapping him on the thigh in evident enjoyment, pulling him closer to yell a riposte in his ear. She felt like Alice must have felt after falling through the looking glass, everything she thought she knew about her daughter and her husband turned upside down and back to front. Clearly she should have brought them here years ago if, in just one short evening, their personalities could be so transformed. But after a moment, with all her experience of life on Acland Street, a suspicious thought nudged at the corners of her mind.

'What did Elroy give our Greg to get him looking so relaxed?' she asked Mo, her accent having already lurched into a strange hybrid of Aussie and Leicesterese. 'Were it a joint, or sommat stronger?'

'Don't worry, it weren't nothing illegal,' her sister reassured her. 'He took him round his mam's to get him some of her Valium.'

The party finally broke up an hour later, Elroy driving them back, and fish and chips being bought from the Chinese take-away and consumed en route. The magic bubble of bonhomie was still unbroken when Melissa and Elroy drove off into the night and the Australian party-goers were left alone in their humble holiday home, the overexcited Whiffy jumping up and dancing round them.

'Bloody good impression of the mutt earlier, Mum,' Greg congratulated June generously, bending down pain-free, it seemed, to scratch Whiffy's ear. 'Well, I'm bushed. Ready for bed, Lorn?' he asked his wife and, taking her by the hand, he led her towards the stairs.

'Hang on,' said Lorna, happy enough to go with him, but dropping his hand to go back to June. 'Night, Mum,' she said with an affectionate grin, and to June's surprise, she took her in her arms and kissed her. 'I'm so happy you're so happy,' she told her, the earlier mix of cocktails having down-sized the range of her vocabulary. 'And I was so proud to see you up there on the stage.'

June returned her embrace and her kiss and they stood there for a moment, swaying gently with tiredness and the enjoyment of holding each other close. 'Thanks, darl,' she said. 'Thanks for the ticket, and for giving up your home. This is the best present I've ever had.'

'Every year from now on, Mum,' Lorna told her with a final squeeze. 'And I'm just sorry I never thought of it before.'

June watched her daughter follow her husband upstairs, a lump in her throat, and turning to Whiffy she said, 'How's about it, Whiff? Fancy a cuddle tonight?' Whiffy's wuff was an unequivocal yes, and after a quick scamper round the garden, the two of them retired to June's bed in Gemma's room, to snuggle up together in heartfelt contentment.

That night, Pauline and Mick Watkins's bed saw more marital action than it had seen in a year, and snuggling up happily afterwards, Lorna and Greg drifted off into their dreams in a tangle of limbs and sleepy, whispered reassurances of undying affection.

7

It would be wonderful indeed to report that, back in Black Rock on that same night, Lorna and Greg Mackenzie's bed had similarly witnessed such exuberance of passion, but alas that had not been the case. As they mounted the stairs to their bedroom after a wonderfully convivial evening round the barbie, each step that took them away from that location of gustatory pleasure and towards the ubiquitous site of their deep-seated problems, both Pauline and Mick felt ever more anxious, the warm intimacy of the last few hours slipping from their shoulders like a disappearing magic cloak. By the time the mystified and impatient Gemma shut her own bedroom door in their faces, finally cutting off their unusually protracted goodnights, their exhortations to sleep well, to dream sweetly, to lie in as long as she liked, her parents, at last left alone in each other's company, were as full of naked terror as Adam and Eve had been after scarfing their first apple.

If some tactless fool had been present at that moment to offer a penny for their thoughts (and if that same fictional entity had ensured their honest response by previously administering a truth serum), he or she might have had the satisfaction of getting two for the price of one. For, as husband and wife shuffled their reluctant steps towards the Mackenzies' master bedroom, echoing loudly in both their minds were the words of Pauline's second new ground rule: 'When we get to Australia, we're going to learn to have sex together again. No more procrastinating.' Well, here they were in Melbourne, and as they stepped over the threshold of their personal Room 101, their eyes lighting at the same time on the horror of their shared worst fear – the double bed – the desire to procrastinate had never been so urgent.

'Want first go in the bathroom, Poll . . . ine?' Mick asked awkwardly, hurrying to correct his breach of his wife's first new ground rule, pertaining to her name.

'No, you're all right,' she said, trying to sound casual. 'You go first. I'm going to unpack my case.'

Mick started as if he'd been shot, now as acutely aware as his wife of the red and black time bomb which ticked silently in her suitcase, waiting to blow their fragile status quo apart. 'I was going to do that for you earlier, when I did mine,' he lied quickly, edging towards the bathroom. 'But I thought if I did, you wouldn't know where anything was.'

'That's right,' she agreed, eager to be rid of him, and she gestured towards the en suite door to hurry him on his way. 'Go on then, off you go. Chop chop.'

'I – might be a while,' Mick added unromantically. 'I haven't been since we left home, and that chilli pickle's knocking.'

Pauline was more than happy to be generous. 'Take your time,' she encouraged him expansively. 'Here – want your book?'

Mick relaxed at once, cheered to think that he might be allowed to distract his mind from the inevitable. 'Good idea,' he said gratefully, and he disappeared into the haven of the bathroom, the yacht's manual tucked beneath his arm.

Left alone at last, Pauline twisted the combination lock's tumblers to the year of her birth, and with a quick nervous glance to make sure that this time there was no witness to her folly, she lifted the lid of her case. There, brazenly straddling the rest of her clothes, lay the crotchless teddy, its sequined suspenders winking shamelessly in the light. Red-faced at the memory of its last airing, she wondered now how she'd ever had the guts (or foolish optimism) to buy the blasted thing. She'd sooner ride naked on horseback through the teeming streets of Coventry than strut her stuff for her husband in this lewd lingerie tonight, with her bits framed by its split lace frills. Shuddering at the thought, she crammed the offending item deep beneath a pile of her sensible knickers in one of the drawers that Lorna had cleared for her use.

It wasn't that her desire to heal the sexual side of her marriage was any less now than when she'd impulsively ordered this siren's suit from her workmate Beth (who moon-lighted most Friday nights as an Ann Summers rep). It was rather that she couldn't bear to make the attempt on her own. Let's face it, she thought bitterly, if she'd wanted that, she would have followed the lead of the majority of the female party-goers that evening, and gone for the more pragmatic option of the vibrator with the six interchangeable heads. No, she still yearned more than anything for Mick to want her, but her heart quailed at the thought of the almost certain failure and rejection that would come her way instead. And having witnessed, as she had, his look of horror at airport Customs, who could blame her?

While her husband sat in the adjacent room, lost in his own world of sea and wind, greedily increasing his knowledge of sailing while gratefully decreasing his body weight, Pauline hung the rest of her clothes in the vast walk-in wardrobe, admiring as she did so the quality and quantity of Lorna Mackenzie's collection. Bugger me, she thought, distracted from her gloomy thoughts despite herself, if this is what she's left behind, what the bleddy hell has she taken with her on holiday? She'd be wearing more money on her back than New Vistas had ever seen, that was for sure – even counting the stuff that fell off the back of lorries and landed in the homes of the estate's usual suspects.

Her mind having taken her homeward, her thoughts strayed inevitably to Asheem, sending a tingling frisson down to the pit of her stomach. God, he was good at it. He was like an Olympic athlete. Never seemed to get tired. Her pleasure was his pleasure, apparently. Sensuous. That was the word for him. The things he'd taught her . . . !

Closing the wardrobe doors, she sat down heavily on the bed, her head in her hands. What was she supposed to do now, with this knowledge? She knew it was wrong to compare, but she couldn't even begin to imagine Mick getting up to half the stuff that was basic routine to Asheem. And then again, it wasn't so much *what* he did, as how he did it. Sometimes he came on overwhelmingly strong, at other times gentle and teasing. He played her body like an instrument. Made her feel like she was all woman, full of a power which astonished her. She'd heard of multiple orgasms before, of course, but she'd thought they were an urban myth. And now she'd had them, how was she to do without them? To her horror, she suddenly caught herself counting on her fingers how many nights were left before she went back home. Outrageous! What was she thinking of? She'd only just arrived. And she hadn't endured that bleddy awful plane ride to wish her time away so soon.

She didn't kid herself that Asheem would remain faithful to her for the whole fortnight. Come to that, she reminded herself, she was pretty certain he hadn't restricted his attentions just to her while she'd been right next door. A lad like him, with his lusty appetite, was sure to hedge his bets, have several women on the go at once. She didn't know whether she felt jealous or not. Well, she did. And she did. But it was silly to feel like that when in all honesty (at least, on most days) she only wanted him for one thing herself.

Again her thoughts turned back to making love with Mick, and she chewed anxiously at a hangnail. She'd been desperate for his attentions all this time, but now that something might actually happen in the bed department, it made her feel really nervous. It had been bad enough dealing with her frustration over the last twelve months, with him only wanting cuddles. But now, say he did get over . . . whatever his problem was – what then? He didn't exactly have Asheem's breadth of experience or skill. So how was her body going to react, if and when Mick did get started? Would it be able to respond, would she get turned on? Or would she just lie there feeling disappointed, cold and critical – untouched, as it were, by his touch?

The sound of the loo flushing next door jolted her to her feet, and for a moment she looked about her in panic, as if she might flee from the bedroom like a virgin bride protecting her honour. Now this was just plain daft, she thought, catching onto herself. He was her husband, for goodness sake, the father of her children, the man she'd loved and lived with for more than twenty years. Of course they could sort this out. Given time. And patience. After all, there was no rush to get it perfect straight away. Rome wasn't built in a day. She'd just have to downscale her expectations, if necessary. And not expect the fireworks.

On the other side of the bathroom door, Mick was in a bit of a pother himself. One minute he'd been sitting there, pleasantly lost amongst spinnaker winches and triple-line organisers, and the next, an unwelcome thought had come nudging at the corners of his mind and was refusing to budge. And it wasn't the usual, confidence-sapping thought of his failure as a husband, the one that made him feel permanently drained and a waste of space. No, he was so used to feeling like that now, it was second nature to him. It was like some people describe having a headache – you only notice it when it stops. Fat chance of that happening, he mused glumly. But again, the sharp new thought prodded at the inside of his skull, pricking his conscience like a red-hot needle, suddenly making him blush with guilt. Before, he'd felt like a powerless victim of this . . . business downstairs. But now . . . He needed more time alone, to think this through.

'I'm going to have a shower, if that's all right with you?' he called through the inch-thick wood which separated him from the nemesis known as Pauline.

'You carry on,' she shouted back, with what sounded to him like an edge to her voice. 'I'm off to use the one in the spare room.'

Hearing the bedroom door click shut behind her, Mick let out his tension with a sigh of relief and stepped into the shower to turn it on full blast. The last thing he needed at the moment was for her to come in wearing that . . . lacy article, he thought – offering to soap his back for him, and God alone knew what else. If he tried to rush his fences now, while this internal critic was so loud in his ear, he was bound to fail, wasn't he? It stood to reason that if it had the power to pull his thoughts away from learning about yachting – an interesting, but not exactly emotionally loaded subject – it would certainly get in his way if he were to try . . . anything more demanding. No, he needed time and space to be alone with his thoughts, to meet his mental tormentor head on, to listen to this voice of criticism and to answer it as honestly as he could. Even if it did sound so accusing. And a bit like his dad. Judgemental. Critical. Rejecting.

Mick shivered and adjusted the water temperature. Glancing up at the shower head, he noticed a lever and several icons, and instantly intrigued, he played with the settings. Oh!

Blimey! You could have it on spray, on needle-like jets, or this chunky thrumming massage-type thing that pummelled your neck and shoulders just where they ached. Oh, God, that was good! Bloody Nora, he should cocoa – right on the spot. Must have been carrying the suitcases. Or being cramped up on the plane. Or maybe the tumble he'd taken on the boat.

'*There you go again*,' said his dad in his ear, loud enough to make Mick jump and hit his elbow on the tap. '*Mind like a butterfly. Can't concentrate on the stuff that really matters for a minute. Worse than useless.*'

Mick leant into the corner of the tiled wall, his knees turned to jelly, and for the second time that day his hand flew to his chest to check his racing heart. It was banging like it was fit to bust, beating at his ribcage like a trapped and terrified bird. How long could it keep going at this break-neck speed? How many times a day could this happen – and for how many days? – before it collapsed exhausted, getting feebler and feebler, and gave up the ghost?

'*Big cissy*,' said his dad with a sneer. '*Bleddy nance.*'

Was he losing his grip, hearing voices?

'*Be wearing suede shoes next, you great fairy.*'

No. He wouldn't listen. After all, he knew it wasn't really his dad speaking. It was his own mind playing tricks. He could choose to ignore it if he wanted to. Drown it out with the noise of the shower. Or whistling. Or humming. Or distract himself with a vigorous activity. Like soaping his armpits, or scrubbing his back with this loofah . . .

'*Here we go again – what did I tell you? But you – you never listen to a word.*'

Okay, fine, so tell me again now! Mick instructed his thoughts angrily, viciously turning the water off and throwing down the loofah; finally giving up on his usual displacement activities, which had never failed him before, to stand naked before his unseen tormentor, hands on hips. And thus it was that, like Archimedes before him, Mick Watkins had his eureka moment in the bathroom. For suddenly, in the silence, the answer struck him like a gong. He knew *exactly* what he had to do to begin to turn things around.

It was so simple. So obvious. So unthreatening, actually, when you stopped being scared and just listened. And it was nothing that he didn't already do, in other situations – that was the daft thing. So what had stopped him from knowing the answer all this time?

My fear of guilt stopped me from listening to myself, came the clear-headed reply.

He was at once struck that, this time, the response had come in the first person, in his own voice rather than his dad's carping tones. He considered this carefully from every angle. What a curious instrument the mind was, what tricks it played! He ought to read up a bit more on psychology while he was about it – borrow one of Gemma's books, maybe, when they got back home. He seemed to have a mental habit of giving himself advice by making himself feel bad. He should watch that.

Going over to the sink to brush his teeth, he felt almost euphoric with the excitement of discovery, of finally being within sight of changing things. Nothing was so bad when you knew what action to take, he acknowledged to himself cheerfully in the mirror. Here he'd been all this time, feeling terrible about feeling terrible, and doing nothing about it to help himself, or to help poor old Polly – Pauline, rather, as he should say now. He'd been so scared of being inadequate that he'd just stuck his head in the sand and tried to ignore it. Cowardly. No wonder the penny had finally dropped while he'd been reading up on yachting, and no wonder it had been prompted by feelings of guilt. He'd been pouring so much energy into distracting himself from his problem, and none at all into solving it.

Well, all that was set to change now. Starting tomorrow, he'd tackle it head on. So there was only tonight to be got through before things improved.

With a stomach-churning dip in his spirits, he turned from his reflection and willed himself to go back into the bedroom, where, finding Pauline had not yet returned, he slipped into the double bed, and fell instantly asleep.

When Pauline returned to their room, she was no less relieved to find Mick out for the count than he had been to find her absent. She'd got herself into quite a state while doing her nightly ablutions in the guest bathroom, and she'd started to regret her 'Sex Now' ultimatum. It put too much pressure on both of them. Well, on her, if she was honest – she hadn't been thinking overmuch about Mick's side of things. She'd been too busy trying to banish remembered images of Asheem, glimpsed in the afternoon light of her bedroom back home: of him gazing down at her through half-closed, smiling eyes while he . . . Of the feel of the lovely ridge of muscles down his back, of his long slim thighs, of his hands on her naked skin, his fleshy lips pressed . . .

Yes, well, no need to torment herself with that all over again, she admonished herself, slipping quietly between the sheets so as not to wake Mick, and lying tidily on her own side of the bed, her hands folded over her tummy. What she'd feared most was that these images might come into her mind while she and Mick were attempting to go at it – or worse, more shameful, that she'd have to call them up to get herself in the mood. Standing outside the bedroom in her nightie, trying to summon up the courage to turn the doorknob and join her husband, she'd felt completely self-conscious and edgy, and less like having sex than she'd ever felt in her life. She hadn't even felt like this when she'd been a virgin. She and Mick had been together for ever. They'd learnt on each other, everything coming in a slow and natural progression, as and when they'd been ready. He'd been her first boyfriend, and she'd been his first girlfriend. And only, as far as she was aware.

She tried to imagine Mick having an affair, and rejected it out of hand. He'd have ample opportunity, of course, meeting housewives in their homes every day as he did. And that's what repairmen got up to in mucky movies, wasn't it? Swaggered in in their overalls, started off examining their appliances, and then crash bang wallop – he's got her pressed up against the washing machine while he's trying out the spin cycle. But Mick would never do that, not even if his urges were stronger and he was all in working order. Wouldn't be able to carry it off. He was a lousy liar. Unlike her. His mouth went all funny and he couldn't look you in the eye. And that was just when he was trying to keep the secret of what he'd got her for Christmas.

Her heart lurched with guilt-tinged affection, and she turned over to look at him sleeping, and gently smoothed his hair off his face. He was breathing softly and evenly, his eyelids serenely still, his lips slightly parted, like an innocent child. He was a good man. A lovely man. Everybody always said as much. Kind and generous, always supportive, great with the kids. And the things they'd been through together. Like the time he'd borrowed his mate's motorbike and sidecar when she'd had her first pains with Matt, driving like mad to get her to the Infirmary fast. Pauline smiled at the memory. They'd been so young and inexperienced, so green. He'd torn up and down the hospital corridors shouting for help, and he'd got a right rollicking from that dragon of a Sister. He'd been told in no uncertain terms to take her back home and sit it out; that if he really wanted to be a hero, he could make her a cup of tea and help her practise her breathing till she was a lot further on. And that's exactly what he'd done. Hadn't kicked off and caused a fuss like most lads his age would have done, embarrassed by being in the wrong. He'd just driven her back nice and slow, made her comfy on the sofa, and held her hand while they counted and breathed. And the expression on his face, a day and a half later, when he first saw Matt, when he first held his son in his arms. She felt all choked up now at the memory. Such love there had been in it, such wonder. He just couldn't get over the tiny little fingernails. He'd kissed each one. Perfect, he'd said, in an awestruck whisper – he's perfect, Poll. Like his mum.

If only, she thought now, lying beside him, full of remorse – if only she was half as good as he supposed her to be. And if he ever knew how she'd betrayed him . . . The hurt she'd cause him, the terrible grief. It would split him in two. His family was everything to him. Her and the kids. His whole life.

Sighing with regret, she snuggled down next to him and put her arm across his chest to hug him close, stroking his side and burying her face in his pyjamas to breathe him in. He went 'Mmmm,' contentedly in his sleep, and without waking, his legs sought hers out and twined them in his. So natural, it felt. They fitted each other so well. Two halves of a whole. If only it could be like this when they were both bleddy awake! What was it that had gone so terribly wrong? Was it familiarity breeding contempt? Did he know her too well now to make him feel randy – saw her more as a sister after all these years, more like a mate? Or had he lost the urge completely? Did that happen to men? Could it have been Melinda Messenger lying here now instead of her, and still he'd just be snoozing?

As was their wont these days, her thoughts turned quickly from remorse to resentment, and she unlaced her body from his, sliding back over to the cool side of the bed. Given her own anxiety tonight, it had been all very well him dropping off so quick. But what if she'd been hot to trot? How dare he just nod off like that on their first night away, as if she'd never said anything about what this holiday was supposed to be for? So was this it? Was this as far as he was prepared to go to put things right? Nowhere? Zilch? Sweet FA?

She caught onto herself again as she was starting to curl away from him in an angry foetal shape, all sharp edges and elbows and furrowed brow. Very neat, Pauline, she congratulated herself contemptuously – you just carry on and blame the victim, you make yourself feel better, whatever you do. Again she sighed, but this time with resignation. If only she didn't feel so wide awake. This was like being at home – him sleeping, her thinking. What a waste, to come all this way and bring their problems with them. But what had she expected? Had she really thought that, just by travelling thousands of miles, the trouble would disappear?

She lay now in the darkness, trying to calm her breathing which had become rapid and shallow with her feelings of anger, and tried to distract herself by replaying the events of the evening. It'd been weird seeing Busty in trousers and no make-up. His voice had been the same, and his gestures, so it had been really confusing, seeing him as a bloke. She had nothing against gays, she just hadn't had that much contact. Well, none really. She liked Julian Clary, what she knew of him from TV. And Lily Savage. Transvestites. Were they gay? You read about wives who'd suddenly discovered their husband's secret hobby – found their stash of women's clothes in the top of the wardrobe, or came home and caught them in front of the mirror, all togged up and wearing pancake. They seemed to say that it was nothing to do with sex though, didn't they – that they still fancied women, they just liked dressing up in their clothes? But Chin *must* be gay, mustn't he? He was so camp. And look at the way he flirted with Mick, batting his eyelashes and touching his arm – he was all over him like a rash. He wouldn't do that, would he, if he wasn't a . . .

Her body stiffened, her eyes flying open with a crazy new line of thought. Did it take one to know one? Did Chin see something in Mick that she hadn't? Could somebody you thought you'd known for twenty-five years suddenly turn gay? Or been gay all along, but suppressed it? Could that be what the matter was with him? That he couldn't control his secret desires any longer? That Pauline just wasn't man enough to turn him on?

When she finally awoke late the next morning, it was to find herself alone in bed after a night of strange and troubling dreams. Mick with breasts, snogging Busty. Herself with a penis and a goatee beard. Asheem in drag, making love to Mick. She was only too glad that her husband wasn't lying there next to her as she struggled to banish the disturbing images from her waking mind.

She was less glad, however, when she ventured downstairs and found his note propped up against the kettle.

'Didn't want to wake you,' he'd written. 'Popped out shopping with Chin. Back soon.'

Mick was not a happy shopper. He was already feeling self-conscious enough about tracking down what he wanted, without Chin glued to his side trying to be helpful. But when he'd gone down to the car first thing and bumped into Chin, who was about to mount his moped in the driveway, he'd foolishly told him he was going shopping, and before he knew it, his trip had been hijacked.

'What kind of shopping?' Chin had asked him.

Mick cleared his throat and looked shifty. 'Oh, you know. Bits and bobs,' he said, hoping that might be an end to it.

'Food? Clothes?'

'Just – stuff,' said Mick, struggling now. 'This and that. I'll need to browse.'

'I can take you to lots of big stores,' Chin had told him decisively, jumping off the bike and taking his arm to lead him to the Beemer coupé. 'In Melbourne.'

'That's all right,' Mick assured him, wild-eyed. 'I'll find them.'

'No, no, I'll show you – it's too complicated to explain,' said Chin, who was already in the passenger seat, buckling his seat belt with one hand and waving Mick to join him with the other. 'Get in-*lah*. It's no trouble. I've got a few errands to do in the city myself this morning, and I was just starting to wonder how I was going to carry things back on the little phut-phut. Much nicer to travel in style.'

As it turned out, Mick was greatly relieved to have a guide at his side as he drove for the first time into Melbourne. There seemed to be so many rules he was unfamiliar with, not least of which was the mind-boggling hook turn.

'Now get over to the left, because we're going to turn right,' Chin told him confusingly as they were approaching a large and busy intersection.

'You mean the right lane, surely, where the trams are?' Mick countered, frozen with indecision as busy Melburnians honked all around him. He'd been charmed to see the trams at first, but had been less and less so as he'd come to realise that he had to share the road with them.

'Trust me, Dorothy,' said Chin firmly. 'Don't ever even think of getting in a tram lane – unless you want to be shunted from here to eternity.' Hanging out of the window to smile and wave ingratiatingly at the angry morning commuters, he suddenly squealed and started blowing kisses at the woman in the car next to them. 'Oh, a miracle! She's going to let you in! *Merci beaucoup, cherie!* Go, go, Michaela! I take back everything I was thinking about her dress sense,' he continued, settling back into his seat as Mick performed the unlikely snaking manoeuvre as instructed. 'Who would have thought that beneath all that day-glo acrylic beat a heart of gold? Don't you love it when people surprise you?'

Not much, thought Mick glumly a few minutes later, after they'd finally found a parking spot and Chin had announced his intention of being his personal shopper.

'We'll go into David Jones first,' Chin told him, linking his arm chummily to guide him through the streets. 'It's a department store, darl. Perfect for browsing. Then when I've got a feel for your taste . . .' In the pause, Mick felt himself being scrutinised critically, and for the first time in his life, he felt self-conscious about what he was wearing. '. . . I can take you to other shops. More cutting edge-*lah*. You need to raise your profile a bit, you know – show off the goods, strut your stuff. A spunk like you doesn't want to be hiding his assets in a shell suit.'

Mick's eyes widened in alarm. 'A what?'

'A shell suit? Isn't that what they call that daggy thing you're wearing? Actually, I didn't even know they still made them. It's practically retro.'

'No, the other word,' Mick said uncomfortably. It was all very well Chin calling him Dorothy in fun, but he didn't like to think that he might have got the wrong idea about him.

'Spunk?' said Chin, not lowering his voice at all as they threaded their way through the crowds. Mick winced. He had nothing against gays, but he didn't want to be mistaken for one – particularly when he had a flamboyant one hanging off his arm. 'That's what we Australians call a handsome hunk like you, love.'

'Oh,' said Mick, too busy feeling relieved to be flattered. 'That's what we English call . . . something different altogether.'

They had arrived outside David Jones, where Mick's attention was immediately taken by the sound of buskers playing didgeridoos, and where for the second time in less than an hour, pulling him back from stepping off the pavement into what he'd thought was a pedestrianised street, Chin saved him from death by tram. 'Pay attention, Dorothy,' he chided, firmly steering Mick away from danger and towards the store entrance. 'These things are lethal, unless you're in them.'

'I was listening to the music,' Mick protested, trying to drag his heels so he could stay to listen to the bunch of youths opposite, who were playing all kinds of native instruments, the like of which he'd never seen. They were all dressed in the garb favoured by his own kids – mostly faded black stuff, torn jeans, holey T-shirts with political slogans – and one of them reminded him strongly of Matt. It was such a pity that Matt wasn't here with them – he'd have loved this. A pity too that he didn't dress more nicely, he thought, frowning. He was going to have to shape up and change all that after he graduated. Couldn't have a lawyer going round in scruffy clothes, with his hair all anyhow.

'Whitey wannabes,' Chin sniffed damningly, and without a backward glance he propelled Mick through the shop door. 'You want to listen to aboriginal music, I'll take you to a club where you can hear the real thing-*lah*. Now,' he continued, beaming broadly and surveying the merchandise with relish as they entered the cosmetics department, 'we might as well start here.'

Mick's protestations were quickly curtailed when it became evident, while looking at lipsticks, that they were shopping for

Chin. Or for Busty, to be more accurate, since her new show was due to open soon, and she needed a complete change of make-up.

'Her costumes mainly have a pink theme this time,' Chin explained, speaking in the third person and opposite gender about himself, as he tried different testers on his hand. 'Except for the torch song at the beginning, where she will be in a sheath of shimmering scarlet. What do you think of this – Sugar Plum? Too mauve, would you say?'

It had been years since Mick had been out shopping with Polly (Pauline, *Pauline*, he reminded himself irritably). Not since they were courting, probably. These days, she just whizzed round town on her own to get her stuff – said he held her up with his agonising over items, while she just saw it, tried it, bought it, or didn't. Chin was very thorough – more like himself – and the two of them were soon deeply immersed in a serious consideration of the relative merits of Dreamy Cream as opposed to Sunset Surprise, with Mick reading the small print of the list of ingredients on the box to further their research. Was hypo-allergy a concern of Busty's, he wanted to know, because if so, she should really be thinking of . . .

He was silenced so completely when the glamorous Estée Lauder consultant, Shirlee, joined them, to welcome Chin warmly and to offer her help, that to the naked eye he appeared to have been freeze-dried, and when his opinion was sought and he finally found his voice again, it was to answer her friendly query with a gruff and manly, 'I dunno, it isn't for me. It's up to him. Her. Me wife'd know better.'

Chin rolled his eyes. 'Oh dear,' he teased. 'He's worried that you might think he's a queen, darl.'

Shirlee beamed broadly and chubbed Mick's arm. 'What – in that daggy outfit, love? You have got to be kidding!'

Even after visiting just that one department, this shopping

expedition was proving to be an instructive and salutary experience, Mick mused, as they were on their way to women's wear, a small carrier bag containing men's moisturiser and a bottle of scent dangling from his wrist. He always liked to think of himself as being completely without prejudice of any sort, but compared to Shirlee he was still a narrow-minded bigot, just like his dear old dad. She'd been so natural with them. Hadn't cared less about serving two blokes with lip gloss and foundation stuff, even before he'd embarrassed himself by making the point he was married. He felt ashamed of himself now, distancing himself from Chin like that, letting him down. It had been no skin off Shirlee's nose either way, so why should it be any off his?

'She's fabulous, isn't she?' Chin demanded, turning back from waving goodbye to her.

'Lovely,' Mick agreed, and as a gesture of solidarity, and by way of an apology, he slipped his arm companionably through Chin's. So what if people thought he was gay by association? If they were that small-minded, let them, he thought pugnaciously, as they stepped off the escalator into Lingerie, his head held proud and high. Bring it on, as Gemma might say.

His wish was Pauline's command, it transpired, when she grilled him in the kitchen four hours later. He'd returned in irritatingly high spirits, laden down with bags and bubbling over with stories, while she'd just been stooging round the house, haunted by her dreams and worrying about her fears of the night before. With every hour that passed and brought no sign of Mick or Chin, her anxiety had increased, and when she finally heard the car stop outside in the drive and ran to the balcony to peer over, it was to see them both hugging and kissing goodbye outside Chin's door.

She was standing now in a defensive posture to listen to his debrief, her back against the sink, her arms folded. Nothing she was hearing was doing anything to put her mind at rest about her suspicions concerning his possible change of sexual orientation.

'Shirlee was a man?' she echoed dully.

'Yes, incredible!' Mick agreed, excitedly putting down his shopping bags to root through them. 'Chin told me afterwards, when we were looking at the bras. You could have knocked me down with a feather! You'd never have guessed it, Poll. She is gorgeous. Fabulous bone structure.'

Now where the bleddy hell had he got that from? What did the Mick that she was married to know about bone structure, fabulous or otherwise? But still he burbled on.

'She had the chop last year, apparently. You don't like to think, do you?' he shuddered. 'But she just never felt like a man, not even when she was a kid. Always felt like a woman, trapped in a man's body. Transsexual, you see, whereas Chin's a transvestite. Well, not full time. Only for his shows. And except for the occasional party.'

'Right,' said Pauline, eyes narrowed, nodding towards the bags. 'So – you've been spending up then, I see. Not like you. What have you got in there?'

'This,' said Mick, finally finding what he was after, and he crossed the kitchen with a happy smile to hand her a small box. 'Bought you some scent.'

'What did you do that for?' Pauline demanded, accepting it ungraciously. 'It's a waste of money.'

'No, it's not,' Mick returned gallantly, pecking her on the cheek. 'You deserve a treat. Don't spoil you enough, probably.'

'But I was going to get some in duty free on the way back, if we had any spare cash. Would have been half the price.'

'But Shirlee gave me a discount,' he said defensively, producing more goodies from the David Jones carrier bag. 'And loads of freebies. Look here, what she's sent you. Nice make-up bag, with loads of bits in. Here you are – mascara, lipsticks, eyeshadows . . .'

'What's that you've got in that box there?'

'Oh, that's for me,' said Mick, colouring slightly.

'Yeah? Got you wearing make-up, has she?' Pauline joked, with a tight smile which didn't quite make it all the way up to her eyes.

'No, it's moisturiser,' he admitted, and hastened to explain. 'Apparently a lot of men are using this now. Helps counteract dryness from shaving. And this particular one has got a UV screening agent in it. That's crucially important here, you know. The ozone layer is really thin over Australia, so you can get burned dead easy – they've got a high incidence of skin cancer. There's posters up everywhere by the beach – "Slip, Slop, Slap". Before you go out, you're supposed to slip on a long-sleeved shirt, slop on the sunscreen and slap on a hat. I think I've got that right. Anyway, Chin reckons we need factor thirty lotion, so I bought some of that as well.'

'So you and Chin went to the beach, did you, after you'd finished shopping?' Pauline queried, in what was meant to sound like an off-hand manner, as she turned to busy herself with the kettle. 'That's nice. Cup of tea?'

'No, thanks,' said Mick. Though he could no longer see her expression, he could hear from her voice she was in a dangerous mood. What a pity, when he was feeling so cheerful himself, having had a great time being out with Chin and meeting some of his friends. And, more especially, having managed to shake Chin off for long enough in one particular shop to achieve his own secret objective of tracking down the article he hoped would at last improve things in the bedroom department. 'No, we didn't go to the beach as such,' he explained. 'But we walked beside it for a bit, in a place called St Kilda, after we left town, when we went to see Sukie for a final fitting. She's been making Busty's costumes for the show.'

'So what's Sukie – fish or fowl?' asked Pauline tartly, spooning half a bowl of sugar into her tea and stirring it viciously.

'Ay? Oh,' he said, getting her drift. 'No, Sukie's a real woman.'

'A *real* woman?' Pauline challenged, turning on him with glittering eyes. 'Not like me, then. So what's she like? All big tits and pouty lips and legs that go all the way up to her arse?'

'Don't be daft,' said Mick, and bravely dispossessed her of her tea to put his arms awkwardly around her. 'Come on, give us a kiss and a cuddle. I'm sorry I was away for so long, duck – I never meant to be. And I'm back now. What do you fancy doing? Ay? Have you had any dinner? I hope not, cos I've bought some stuff for us to have a picnic outdoors. Where's Gem? I thought we might go and find a nice beach and park ourselves on it this afto. Chill out, you know, take a few beers. Maybe have a swim first. What do you say?'

'What's in them other bags?' is what she said, eyeing them over his shoulder. 'Can't all be food, surely?'

'Oh, you know – bits and bobs,' Mick told her evasively. 'Bought meself a couple of books—'

'What a surprise,' Pauline said drily. Mick and his books. It was where all his spare cash always went. She wouldn't mind if he bought novels, something she'd be interested in reading after he'd finished. But they were always dry dull things, full of facts about stuff she couldn't care less about, let alone understand. 'Your head'll burst one of these days if you don't watch out. What else?' Releasing herself from his embrace in a deceptively gentle way, she made a surprise move towards the pile of carrier bags and grabbed one before Mick could stop her.

'What's this?' she asked accusingly, as she pulled out a length of flimsy floral material.

'It's from Sukie,' Mick told her, unperturbed. His secret lay in a different bag altogether.

'Going to run you up a frock, then, is she?' said Pauline nastily, shaking out the fabric to examine it in the light. 'Not really your colour, sweetie.'

Mick laughed. 'No, it's for you. There's one in there for Gemma as well.'

'What's in there for Gemma?' his daughter demanded, as she joined them from upstairs. 'Thank God you're back. I'm bored to tears. Are we ever going to go out?'

'Yeah, we're going off for a picnic in a minute,' said Mick. 'And you'll both be able to take these. They're called mew-mews, I think she said.' Taking one from Pauline's hands, he wrapped it around his hips. 'You tie them like this, and wear them on the beach. Sukie sent them over as a present. She runs them up out of leftover material. Nice, aren't they?'

While Pauline assimilated the image of her husband model-ling a skirt, Gemma eyed the two muu-muus with an expression of the unimpressed. 'Bit bleddy bright, aren't they?' she said damningly. 'Didn't she have no black?'

'Don't be so ungrateful,' Pauline admonished her auto-matically. 'Anyway, you wear them on the beach, not to a funeral. Very nice, Mick. You'll have to thank your friend Sukie when you see her again.'

'You can do that yourself at Busty's first night,' Mick said, divesting himself of his flowered wrap. 'She'll be there. And so will Shirlee.' Reminded of her unfavourable comments about his own outfit, he picked up another bulging bag and held it tightly closed, as if it might contain a dangerous snake. 'Do you think I look . . . daggy – in this tracksuit?' he asked them self-consciously, nodding down at his clothes.

'What's daggy when it's at home?' asked Pauline. 'And who told you you did?'

'Chin. And Shirlee,' said Mick uncomfortably. He wasn't used to talking about his appearance, nor to drawing attention to himself like this. 'I don't know what it means exactly, but I know it's not good. I thought maybe you might know, Gem?'

'Probably means sad old bastard, and if so, then yes,' Gemma told him, with a frankness all her own. 'Don't tell me they persuaded you to buy some new clothes?' she continued, making a sudden lunge for the shopping bag in his hand and gaining possession.

'Yeah,' her father admitted shiftily, watching her as she pulled out a shirt. 'What do you reckon?'

'Coo-ool!' said Gemma admiringly, holding it up. 'Well deadly, Dad! Can I swap you for my mew-mew?'

'Give it here,' said Pauline, grabbing it from her daughter to examine it and turning back to Mick with surprise. 'This is nice, this is, Mick. Did you choose it, or did Chin?'

'Chin.' Mick squirmed at the recent memory of being made to parade up and down in the shop like a clothes horse. 'Had me trying on everything. And his mate, Robert, whose boutique we were in.'

'Boutique,' sneered Gemma, now shaking a pair of trousers from the bag. 'You big poof!' Pauline shot her a look of alarm. 'Hey!' Gemma continued, impressed by her father at last. 'These are seriously nifty! What else have you got in here?' She up-ended the bag and riffled through its contents. 'Another shirt – nice one! T-shirt. Shorts. Bleddy hell, Dad, thank God for that! I was dreading being with you in them baggy maroon things you've been wearing ever since I was born. Does that mean we can burn them now? Hey, come on, let's have a fashion show! Put them on!'

'I'll put them on in private, if you don't mind,' Mick said bashfully, reclaiming his new wardrobe and his bag of books and heading for the stairs. 'You two get yourselves in your swimmers and your mew-mews,' he called back. 'Last one in the sea's a cissy!'

Left alone in the kitchen, Gemma and Pauline exchanged a wide-eyed look of shock, but for rather different reasons.

'Well, well,' Gemma laughed, firmly nabbing the less floral of the two beach wraps and claiming it as her own. 'My dad, a fashion victim. Whatever next?'

What indeed, thought Pauline apprehensively, her eyes settling on the jar of moisturiser he'd forgotten to take with him in his rush to try on his new clothes. As bizarre and unlikely as her dreams had appeared to be in the light of day, they now seemed to have been downright prophetic.

By the time Mick had finished faffing about in front of the bedroom mirror, Pauline had changed into her beachwear, slopped on her factor thirty, packed up the food and filled the esky with beers, and had lugged the picnic out to the open-topped Beemer, where she sat in the driving seat looking at her watch, drumming her fingers on the wheel and eventually, in her frustration, leaning on the horn. Even Gemma, who always kept everybody waiting while she redid her make-up a thousand times and agonised over her outfit, had been ensconced in the back seat for a good five minutes before he reappeared. It was the first time ever in the Watkins family history that the girls team had finished first in the race to get ready to go out.

But when Mick finally did emerge from the house, his new shirt and shorts topped off by a rather rakish cowboy-style hat (never before seen and worn at a jaunty angle), even Pauline had to admit it had been worth the wait. Moreover, she felt dowdy by comparison.

'Look at *you*!' said Gemma, after giving her father an appreciative wolf whistle as he walked towards them, grinning self-consciously. 'Aren't you the business! Well fit! Ay – you want to watch him on the beach, Mum. You'll have to fight 'em off to keep him!'

'Very nice,' said Pauline tersely. 'Get in then, Mick! The sun'll have gone in before we get on the beach at this rate.'

Mick settled himself in the passenger seat next to her, flipping down the sunshade and catching sight of himself in the vanity mirror. 'This is an Akubra,' he said, adjusting his hat by a few millimetres and turning his head to admire the result. 'Genuine Aussie, this is. They come in all shapes and sizes. You two should get one before we go. I couldn't decide between this one here and another one with a sort of chunkier, kind of squarer, crown. But Chin said that this one looked—'

'Very nice,' said Pauline again, putting her foot down hard on the accelerator to turn at speed towards the gates, jerking Mick back in his seat and causing him to clutch onto his carefully positioned new Akubra with both hands.

'Are you all right to drive, Poll?' he asked, glancing at her nervously as he recovered himself, and checking the road for traffic. She could be a dangerous weapon in a car when she'd got one on her. There had been an incident in the Asda car park last year that had set them back a couple of hundred quid, and it had been a mercy that the indecisive woman in the Ford Fiesta had survived it at all, let alone with her limbs intact.

'Pauline,' she replied tartly. 'Yes, thank you. Are you all right to navigate?'

'Course, sorry – go left here, then straight over at the junction,' he said, and inwardly kicked himself for forgetting the new rule about her name yet again, particularly now, when he should be doing everything in his power to appease her. What the bleddy hell was up with her? Was she still pissed off that he'd been out with Chin for so long? She never normally minded if he was a bit late, so long as she knew where he was. Maybe she was just still tetchy because of the jetlag and the time difference. Or did she think he'd been selfish, spending so much money on his new clothes? He must explain to her about the fantastic exchange rate, about how cheap everything was, and offer to take her out shopping tomorrow. But then again, he thought in his own defence, if you added up all the money *she'd* spent on clothes over the years, compared to what he'd spent on himself . . . Still, he knew from experience that discretion was the better part of valour when she was in this kind of mood. 'You look nice in your new mew-mew,' he told her now. 'Colour suits you. Brings out your eyes.'

But those same eyes never left the road, and she merely said, 'Mm,' through tightened lips.

'Nice car, isn't it?' he tried again, after a long silence which had only been punctuated by more road directions from him, and during which time she had appeared to relax a little. As evidence, she was now sitting back comfortably in her seat, instead of leaning forward aggressively with her nose almost touching the windscreen.

'Lovely,' she said, finally smiling, and patted the steering wheel admiringly. 'I couldn't half get used to this.' She'd been giving herself a bit of a talking-to as she drove, and had reminded herself that a man was innocent until proven guilty. There was nothing inherently poofy about him buying himself some new clothes, and let's face it, she thought, he didn't half need some. And wasn't it just possible that he'd got himself all togged up for her benefit, as a way of getting himself (and her) in the mood to rekindle their romance? She should be encouraging him, not punishing him, she decided. Her hand slipped off the gear stick to caress his naked thigh, and to her surprise and pleasure, instead of jumping like a scalded cat as he was wont to do these days at the slightest sign of intimacy, he answered by giving her an affectionate look and slipping his arm around the back of her seat to play with her hair.

Watching this rare display of touchy-feely affection between her parents from the back seat, Gemma thought that she might puke. The last thing she needed from this ill-advised family holiday was to watch these two old wrinklies do the nasty. Yekk – the very idea! There should be a law against people getting up to that kind of thing after they'd passed a certain age, and when it was your own mum and dad, for God's sake – double yekk – it didn't bear thinking about. And it was all very well for the two of them, coming away together and getting all sexy in the sun – what about her, on her Jack Jones, thousands of miles away from her boyfriend, and without even her brother to keep her company? She already felt lonely enough and desperate for people of her own age, without having to witness the pensioners getting all lovey-dovey and shagging each other all over the shop.

Things didn't improve much when they got themselves camped on the beach to have their picnic either, although even she had to admit that Dad had brought them to a good spot. Nice sand, and what looked to be some very fit lads wind-surfing down at the sea. But once they'd finished fussing with getting the big umbrella up, and going on about everybody having to squash up together to sit in the shade (God – with all this space, and all this sun!), the crumblies were still all over each other. Kept offering each other bits to eat and going 'ooh' and 'aah', and tasty as it was, it was only bread and cheese and bits of cold meat, for Christ's sake. Her mother looked like she was going to have a bleddy orgasm when it came to the fruit, and when they'd finally finished fiddling with the food and her dad told her mum to lie on her front so he could rub her all over in sun cream, Gemma could stand it no more.

'I'm going in the sea,' she said shortly, getting up and re-arranging her muu-muu. 'It's too hot here.'

Her dad looked up from squeezing lotion on his hands. 'Don't go swimming yet for a while, Gem,' he said, like she was a kid and he still had some say in the matter. 'You need to let your food go down first, for at least a couple of hours. You might get cramp else.'

'I'm not going swimming,' she retorted, already walking away from them, without a backward glance. 'I'm just going to paddle.'

'Well let me put some of this stuff on you then,' he called after her. 'You don't want to go getting burned! Gem! Gemma, stop a minute!'

She did exactly that, wheeling round on the hot sand to fix him with a piercing look. He drove her absolutely mental with his 'you don't want this, you don't want that'. What the bleddy hell did he know about what she wanted? It was her own bleddy business anyway, the nosey git. 'I have got some of my *own* on, Father,' she told him, in a dangerously measured and patronising tone. 'I don't want your fàctor five hundred and three, thank you very much. I haven't come all the way to bleddy Australia to use total block and go home without getting a tan.'

'Yes, but it's—' Mick started to protest.

'Let her go,' said Pauline, squinting lazily at her daughter as she stomped away from them again. 'You know what she's like when you tell her what to do. And if she gets burned, it's her own stupid fault – maybe then she'll learn. Anyway,' she continued coquettishly, 'I thought you were going to put some of that stuff on me?'

Mick gave up on Gemma and returned his wife's smile. 'Yes, I was, wasn't I?' he said, kneeling down again by her side, and spreading the now sun-warmed lotion up the length of her back with both hands.

'Mmm,' said Pauline.

'Is that nice?'

'It's lovely.'

Emboldened by her improved mood, Mick decided he'd stick his neck out even further. '*You're* lovely,' he said awkwardly. Complimenting her at every opportunity was stage one of the new master plan that he'd been turning over in his mind in the few spare moments that he'd had since his epiphany in the bathroom the night before: focus all his attention on Pauline, and concentrate his efforts full-scale on rebuilding the damaged part of their relationship. *Forget learning about sailing,* his inner voice had told him when he'd been sitting on the pot reading the yacht manual, *you haven't got time to bother with this kind of frippery! You need to start revising your relationship skills. Or don't you care that your marriage is about to go bung?*

Of course he cared! He cared like mad. Pauline was everything to him. Everything. If she were to leave him because of his . . . difficulties . . . down there – which she'd be quite within her rights to do, given that he hadn't been honouring one of the most sacred vows in his marriage contract for the last twelve months – well, then he didn't know what he'd do. Go mad, probably. Become an alcoholic. Start shuffling around on street corners in smelly clothes with a can of cider in his hand . . .

'That's too hard now, Mick,' Pauline complained, squirming away from him, conscious of the irony in her choice of words. Too hard – him? If only! 'I think you've done that spot, thank you.'

Realising he'd disappeared inside his own head, Mick

apologised and inwardly chastised himself. Concentrate, Watkins, for God's sake! If you can't even put lotion on her without getting it wrong, there's no hope for you, I give up!

'What are you suddenly so wound up about anyway?' Pauline asked crossly. He'd completely spoiled her mood now.

'Nothing,' he said. 'Sorry. This better?'

'Mm,' she conceded grudgingly. 'Not bad.'

Down at the water's edge, Gemma had never felt more isolated and lonely in her entire life. All she wanted was to talk to somebody of her own generation with whom she had something in common – was that too much to ask? But now she was closer to the windsurfing lads who were pratting around in the sea, she could tell at a glance that they weren't her type. They all looked like that Todd idiot, all hard muscles and tanned skin, and watching them dance across the waves on their stupid bleddy boards just made her miss Stu all the more. Wouldn't catch him doing outdoor bleddy pursuits or working out in a gym like this load of goody-goody daddy's boys obviously did – that was just falling for the media hype in the mainstream zines, buying into body fascism. And what was so great about having a toned six-pack and big biceps when half the world was starving? For the thousandth time in the two days since she'd been here, she wished she hadn't come – or rather, she wished she'd come with Stu and not the smooching geriatrics. How bleddy embarrassing was that?

A load of Sharons and Tracies had swanned down to the shore in their bikinis just after she'd parked herself there, and they'd made camp right in front of her, waving at the lads, giggling and chatting – she knew they were laughing at her. Well, fuck them if they didn't like the look of her. Who wanted bleached streaks and big bazookas anyway? Daft bleddy bimbos. They'd be lost in Leicester – they'd look like right bleddy knobs. Anyway, she'd be buggered if she'd move just cos they were trying to make her feel self-conscious. She'd just lie back and ignore them, block their stupid girlie voices out with her Walkman, think about Stu and what he'd say now if he was here. He'd have a really great put-down for them – he was always brilliant at that. Call them Barbie dolls or some-such. Ask them where Ken was. She wished they'd bog off though. It was so bleddy hot, she couldn't half do with going in the sea, but she'd sooner cut her throat than walk in front of them while they gawped at her and made rude comments about her bum. Conscious of its size now, and of the cellulite she'd caught sight of in the bedroom mirror, she turned over and lay on her back feeling resentful. She felt a bit torn about doing this sun-bathing lark. She agreed one hundred per cent with Stu when he said how ironic it was that it was the white middle-class supremacist racists who paid a fortune to get themselves brown while oppressing real dark-skinned people, but then again being this white did tend to make you look even fatter than you were. Would he be pissed off with her when she went back home with strap marks? She could tell him that it wasn't her fault, that she hadn't been trying to get a tan as such, but that she'd just happened to fall asleep in the sun after she'd been swimming. Which was only the truth after all, when you thought about it. Or it would have been if the Barbies'd just bugger off and let her get in the bleddy sea . . .

The trick was to not get himself in a panic, Mick had counselled himself eventually: he must neither leap ahead in his imagination to the anxiety-making final stage of the clause about worshipping his wife with his body, nor dwell on his past failures pertaining to that act. He must just concentrate his mind on the moment he was in, work through things thoroughly and methodically, step by step. That was, after all, how he approached problems at work as a matter of course, and even the most intractable mechanical challenges were overcome by this method. Slow and steady wins the race, Watkins. It was practically his mantra.

Suddenly becoming guiltily aware that he had again become mentally side-tracked from his plan of attack, he refocused his attention on his hands and what they were supposed to be doing: giving pleasure. Actually, he mused, unable to stop his lifetime's habit of analysing progress as he went, *giving pleasure was very pleasurable in itself*, when you just concentrated on that and only that. *So how about giving her another compliment?* the voice inside his head suggested now, in a helpful and reasonable tone. Good idea. He cleared his throat to prepare the way for something really nice to say. But what, exactly? He didn't want to sound false. So tell her the *truth*, he told himself severely – tell her what you're thinking about her *right now*. How did her skin feel beneath his hands? Lovely. No – he couldn't use that again, he'd only just said it. What did she look like, then, lying there in the sun in her bikini? Gorgeous. Beautiful. How did he *feel* about that? Choked, as it turned out. 'You're the most beautiful girl on the beach, Pauline,' he said, in a voice thick with emotion.

'Ah, that's nice,' she murmured with some surprise. She raised her head a little to look at him. 'Are you starting a cold?'

'No, no,' he said, blinking rapidly to dispel the tears which were threatening to gather, and he coughed to clear his throat again. 'No, I was . . . ahem . . . I was just thinking, you know – about how . . . about how . . .'

He'd got her worried now, and tense. He only ever did all this coughing and spluttering when he had something difficult to say. She raised herself up on her elbows and turned her head to look him in the eyes. They were all sparkly, like he'd been crying. 'About how what?' she prompted him, fearing the worst. How sad he was to admit at last that he was gay?

'About how gorgeous you are,' he said in a rush, 'and about how much I love you.' Awkwardly, he bent forward to kiss her gently on the lips, and when he drew away, Pauline's anxious expression had melted into a relieved and happy smile. How daft she was being about him going out shopping with Chin, she told herself – it was all perfectly innocent, if a bit unusual. And he had looked cute in his new clothes in the car. He looked pretty damned cute now, in his trunks. He had a lovely bod, she had to give him that – kept himself nice and trim. If she'd been cross with him last night for chickening out and going to sleep, he was certainly making up for it this afternoon, she thought. She'd been really enjoying this attention, his hands gliding smoothly over her skin, and now him saying sweet things. It reminded her of when they'd been younger, when they'd had all the time in the world just to love each other, before Matt and Gem had come along, and the nights had somehow seemed to get shorter.

'Go on then,' she said flirtatiously, looking like the teenaged girl she'd been. '*How* much?'

'As much as there's stars in the sky,' he said, with an urgency fuelled by sincerity, and to calm himself down, he started to stroke her again. 'As big and as deep as that ocean out there. If you was to count all these grains of sand, and then add them to all the other grains of sand in the entire world, and then cubed it, you still wouldn't be anywhere near. I love you so much, Pauline.'

'And I love you, Mick,' she said. 'I really, really, really do.' Now both of them had sparkling eyes, and they hugged, enjoying the familiarity of each other's bodies, the unusualness of showing each other affection these days, and the warmth of naked flesh on naked flesh. Pauline kissed his neck and chuckled. 'This is like finally having that honeymoon we dreamed of when we were kids, but couldn't afford, isn't it?'

'Can't afford it now,' Mick laughed, 'but bugger it. Anyway, you, get back on your tummy,' he instructed her, and when she'd done so, he started on her legs.

Pauline moaned with pleasure. 'Ooooooh, that's nice, Mick.'

A grin started to spread from ear to ear, infecting his whole body. He felt so happy, he thought he might burst. *There you are, you see*, his inner voice whispered encouragingly in his ear. *That wasn't so hard, was it? Now come on, old son, more of the same, follow it up . . .*

'I could give you a foot massage, if you like,' he offered shyly.

Lying there in the sun being spoiled rotten, Pauline gave herself up entirely to the pleasure of being so much putty in her husband's hands. All her fears of the night before began to evaporate in the warmth of this marital intimacy. What did it matter that Asheem was a sexual gymnast? Nothing he'd ever done with her came anywhere close to this kind of bliss. How her body had missed her husband's touch!

Ohhh.

Aaaah.

'Fabulous,' she murmured, aware that she'd started to drool onto the towel. 'Ohhhh, Mick, I am absolutely and utterly—'

'Burned to buggery!' screamed Gemma, at surprisingly close quarters, making both her parents jump guiltily. She was standing over them, flapping her arms like an injured toddler, tears streaming down her carmine face. She looked like a boiled lobster.

'What the bleddy hell did I say?' Mick demanded, unable to stop his parental 'told you so' as he sprang to his feet to examine her, his anger fuelled by concern.

'Why didn't you come and wake me up?' Gemma countered, adept as always at blaming somebody else. 'It isn't my fault I fell a-bleddy-sleep! Don't touch me! It hu-hu-hurts!'

'Right, let's get her back home and sort her out,' said Pauline tightly, starting to gather up the picnic things.

So much for romance, she thought bitterly, as they trooped back up the beach to the car. This was more like the demanding early days of motherhood than any second sodding honeymoon.

After baby had finally been cooled down, calmed down, covered in calamine and put to bed in a darkened room, Mum and Dad regrouped on the swing seat of their bedroom balcony to have a beer and watch the stars replace the sun in the sky. Now that Gemma's drama was over and they were alone again they both started to feel rather self-conscious and anxious, and not a bit like continuing where they'd left off. It had been all very well on a public beach where nothing much could happen except a bit of kissing and touching, but now they were on their own, in private, and they could do anything they liked, any move on either part seemed frighteningly fraught with potential danger. What if Mick couldn't get it up again after all? What if, in the heat of the moment, Pauline did something she'd learnt from Asheem, something she'd never done with Mick, and what if he asked her where she'd got that from? What if they started kissing and cuddling and neither one got turned on? Or what if one of them got turned on and the other one didn't? What if—

'Mum!' Gemma shouted from her room. 'Can I have another drink of water?'

Pauline sighed, pretending she wasn't relieved at this welcome interruption, and stood and stretched. 'Coming,' she called back. 'Blimey, I'm tired,' she yawned, as she left to play nurse, preparing the way for an excuse, should she need one, on her return.

'I'll have first go in the bathroom, then,' Mick told her, preparing the way for his own excuse. He needed a bit of privacy just now to calm his rising panic, and also to take another look at the secret weapon he'd bought that day. 'Might take me book in,' he called after her, and as soon as she was out of the room, he did exactly that. Seating himself on the loo, he turned to Chapter Two of his new purchase, *Trouble Down Below* by Dr Ed Neuberger MD, and was comforted to read, 'Now that you've started paying her some quality attention with the compliments and the massages, don't make the mistake of thinking you can plunge right back in again straight away . . . Make a game of the fact that you are *not allowed* to have full sexual intercourse . . . Rediscover each other's bodies . . . find out what drives her – and you – wild with desire . . .'

'I've been thinking,' he said tentatively, when he and Pauline met again in bed half an hour later and she'd presented him with her back to cuddle. 'What with it being so long since we've . . . you know . . . maybe we should start again by doing more of that like we did on the beach? Touching, sort of thing. Playing. Make more of a game, really, of not . . . You know, like maybe even making it a rule that we can't . . . go the whole hog. Kind of give ourselves the opportunity of rediscovering each other's bodies, without the pressure of . . . you know . . . What do you think?'

'Sounds like it could be a good idea,' said Pauline, interested, turning to face him. She actually did feel quite tired after nursing her fractious daughter, but since Mick was prepared to talk about the problem after all this time, she certainly wasn't too tired to listen. And taking the pressure off sounded fine by her. 'So,' she continued, invitingly, she hoped, 'what kind of thing did you have in mind?'

Mick had been wondering that too. 'Well, I was thinking I

could start off by giving you a back massage, p'raps, if you fancied it. See how we go from there. I found some nice-smelling oil in the bathroom.'

'Oil, eh?' she smiled, now fully awake. 'Kinky. Shall I take my nightie off then?'

'No, I'll take it off for you,' Mick said, entering into the play-fulness he'd promised.

'One condition, though,' said Pauline, as he pushed her nightdress up and slipped it off over her head.

'Name it, oh Queen.'

'I get to take your 'jamas off as well. If you're offering your-self as a love slave, I want you naked.'

'O-kay,' said Mick. He felt a bit vulnerable at the thought of having his little man out on display, and possibly, therefore, within grabbing range. 'Remember the rule, though.'

'I am your Queen, and I *make* the rules,' she replied, sliding his pyjama bottoms down his legs and looking at him appreciatively. 'Don't worry,' she continued, seeing his look of anxiety and his defensive posture. 'You're safe from attack. I won't do anything sudden. Mm. You've got a lovely bod, Micky. I was thinking that on the beach.'

Mick grinned self-consciously, willing himself to relax. 'D'you think so?'

'I do,' she said, and kissed his chest. 'Now fetch me that oil, and rub me down.'

Over the course of the next hour, having given themselves permission to play in an unpressured, goalless way, they had the best time together that they'd had in years. It was fun to play, and they had a real good giggle sticking to the parts that Pauline had assigned them ('Slave – you are being very cheeky!' 'I am, Madam?' 'What shall I do as punishment? Shall I – smack your bottom, perhaps?' 'No, oh Queen, not

smacking my bottom! Anything but smacking my bottom!'
'Very well, slave – I shall bite it. Turn over.'). Once they'd
discovered how sensual the oil felt, how it made their skin feel
pleasurably slick and slippery as their bodies rubbed together,
they applied it to each other with liberal abandon, and what
had started as a back massage for one quickly turned into an
(almost) full body massage for two. Indeed, by the end of that
halcyon hour, things were going so well and they were both
feeling so relaxed and confident, that Mick's little man, who'd
been watching shyly from the sidelines, safe in the knowledge
that he was out of bounds, began to feel the faint stirrings of
actually wanting to come out and play with them – if not today,
perhaps, then almost certainly at some time in the near future.

Pauline's anxiety that she might compare her husband's
unpractised skills unfavourably with her lover's expertise, also
proved to be unfounded. Given permission to experiment and
a naughty character to hide behind, Mick became emboldened,
and thus more inventive and adventurous. There was something in particular that he had never done to her – something
which Asheem did often and with relish – and to which she had
discovered she was extremely partial. Never in her wildest
dreams had she ever thought that Mick would even contemplate such an act, but here she was now, lying half on, half off
the bed, clutching at the sheets with outspread hands, and there
he was, kneeling at her feet on the floor, and actually starting
to do it. Oh my God, she whispered, relinquishing her grip on
the sheets to caress Mick's hair. Ohhh – my – G-o-o-o—

The impassioned scream that rent the air was from the lips
of neither the doer nor the done by, but the effect on both of
them was immediate and electrifying, impelling them to fling
covers over their nakedness at lightning speed, to cease their
activities at once, and in Mick's case, to gaze wild-eyed at an
improbably small place in which to hide his head in shame.

Gemma was standing in the doorway, back-lit by the landing light.

'Can't you two leave each other alone for one minute?' she cried, in horrified disgust, before she ran back, sobbing, to her room.

A frozen silence reigned in her absence for what seemed like an age, before the rigor of tension left the bodies of her stricken parents and they collapsed, deflated, with pounding hearts.

'Shall I go in and see her?' Mick offered after a while, with doom in his voice, once his breathing had started to steady.

'No, I'll go,' said Pauline resignedly. She struggled to her feet and drew on her gown with difficulty over her oil-slicked skin, rearranging her hair as she crossed to the door. 'Bleddy hell, Mick, talk about bad timing,' she commented with a dry laugh, pausing for a moment to turn to address him. He was still crouched on the floor, his whole body bent over protectively to shield the bashful little man from view.

'We've done nothing we should feel ashamed of, though,' he suggested tentatively.

'No, we haven't,' she concurred, and went back to give him a reassuring hug and kiss. It was one of the nicest kisses either of them could ever remember, intimate and loving and profound. 'Bit bleddy ironic, isn't it? Her thinking we're at each other all the time,' she murmured into his neck, and they both giggled.

'We'll have to prove her right, then, won't we?' Mick said shamelessly, as Pauline set off once again to calm her outraged and hysterical daughter.

She turned in the open doorway to look him brazenly in the eye. 'Hold that thought, slave,' she commanded him firmly. 'I'll be back.'

8

Some things are inevitable and, however much we may rail against them, inescapable. As sure as day follows night, as ineluctably as the sun replaces the moon and stars in the morning sky, so too does sobriety succeed drunkenness. But where the transition between darkness and light is etymologically enshrined in the lovely word 'dawn', which also suggests 'new beginnings', the passage between giddy inebriation and clear-headed soberness is known by an altogether uglier name, a name which carries with it the dwindling influence of yesterday's baggage. 'Hangover' is that accursed term, and on that morning after the night before her visit to New Vistas Social Club, Lorna Mackenzie woke to the worst that it could do.

Last seen cuddled up in an affectionate post-coital embrace with her husband, Greg – last heard, as you may remember, whispering endearments to him before sliding from conscious to comatose in one fell swoop – by ten o'clock the next morning they were as far from each other as their bed would allow, their heads empty of everything except pain and re-crimination. Drifting unwillingly towards sentience, they needed water and plenty of it, but both of them were buggered if they'd be the one to fetch it. Racked with pain, they were locked in a wordless competition to prove which of them was the more indisposed, in pursuit of which they were conducting early sound experiments, where 'ngaaah' meant 'I am very ill.

Please be so kind as to look after me,' and 'ngaaw' meant 'Shove it up your arse. I am dying here.' In a nutshell, they were not at their most empathic.

It is true to say that, in addition to the deleterious after-effects of a surfeit of alcohol, Greg had his excruciating back pain to deal with. The effects of the Valium having worn off some time during the night, and the effects of the soft mattress having been hard at work all through it, he was in a paroxysm of agony as he lay there on the edge of the bed, gingerly fingering his afflicted vertebrae, and silently comparing the feeling in his mouth to the bottom of a cocky's cage. But in the whole of her well-ordered life, Lorna had never had the merest whisper of a headache after taking drink, let alone this tortured throbbing, this depression of spirits, this longing for the kind of peace that only death could bring. Neck and neck in the invalid stakes therefore, it was a close-run thing as to whose suffering was greater, but one thing was certain: neither could look to the other for support. Thus chronically afflicted, having almost lost the will to live, they were in urgent need of the miracle of rescue from an outside source.

And there are those who may say they got it, when Whiffy the Wonderdog launched herself onto their bed to cover their faces in affectionate licks, while enthusiastically bounding over their bodies. It goes without saying, of course, that Lorna and Greg Mackenzie would not be among their number.

Whiff had been dispatched with news, news, important news! Melissa and Elroy had arrived to see them, as arranged the previous night, and were waiting for them downstairs even now as she barked! The two Australians having temporarily lost all recall, and neither of them being fluent in Canine, they nevertheless both howled loudly in response – though it has to be said, this was done instinctively, and more due to pain than a desire to communicate with the wretched creature. But moments later, when Melissa thundered into their bedroom with tea and toast and shared the hilarity of their situation with them in a raucous whoop of screeched laughter, a screamed invitation to Elroy to come up here and see what she could see, and a bellow of something that sounded like delight at their discomfort – but which was apparently an expression of sympathy, Leicester-style – the power of memory returned to them at a stroke, and they knew they were in the hell also known as New Vistas.

Normally so assertive, Lorna had no weapon in her arsenal to repel Melissa's determined assay to drag her off into town. She had given her solemn promise (apparently) to go with her cousin to look at wedding paraphernalia this morning, and she was being held to it by all the methods at Melissa's disposal: loud protestations, face stroking, a jovial shaking of her by the shoulders, bed stripping, whining, and threatened tears. In the end, it was less painful to get out of bed and go with the flow than to try and withstand the attack – and that thought was fully endorsed by Greg's imprecation for her to 'Humour the cow and leave me in peace!' There being no peace, however, for the wicked (this being Melissa's immediate witty response), he too was hauled out of bed and helped to dress by Elroy, who'd been deputed by his bride-to-be to take him to Casualty for more Valium, since his mother's generosity concerning her prescription drugs was now exhausted.

Though June was pressed strongly to join either party rather than stay at home and endure the tragedy of being left all on her lonesome, which Melissa felt would be an unbearable and miserable fate, she politely declined on the grounds that, at her age, she'd had enough excitement in the last couple of days to last her for a goodly while, and that she just needed to rest and potter about with Whiffy.

Wild-eyed and desperate as she was dragged out through the

front door and down the garden path, Lorna looked back over
her shoulder, all the way to Elroy's Escort, begging her waving
mother to come with her. And though June's sense of relief at
the blessed quiet was intense as the sound of Elroy's
customised engine receded to a mere dull roar in the distance,
she was left with the haunting image of her daughter's white
and tortured face staring accusingly at her.

But, as she remarked to the grinning Whiff as they returned
indoors, though she felt a little bit guilty about leaving Lorna
unprotected in Melissa's hands, it was nothing that another
nice cup of tea in bed wouldn't put paid to.

Elroy was justly proud of his new state-of-the-art, five-
speaker, in-car entertainment system, so he was more than a
little disappointed when the Mackenzies first asked, then
begged, then screamed for him to switch it off. Listening to it
had been, as Lorna was the first to aver through gritted teeth
in the resulting hush, like being *in* the bloody amplifier with
Sean Paul – a comment designed to be damning, but which
the good-natured Elroy took as a compliment of the highest
order. And so they continued on their way in as near
companionable silence as was possible with somebody as
loquacious and ebullient as Melissa in the car, and with
another who was as generous in sharing his distress over his
misaligned spine as Greg.

Being by nature both stoic and benevolent (and by circum-
stance merely eight and a half months pregnant with the
attendant inconvenience of swollen ankles and lower-back
pain), Melissa immediately identified Greg's discomfort to be
far greater than her own and selflessly elected to be dropped
off at some distance from the city's shopping centre so that he
could be transported to the Royal Infirmary with all due
dispatch. Feeling the damp and chill November air as she got

out of the car, however, Lorna rather less selflessly demanded Greg's overcoat in addition to her own, arguing that he'd be inside in the bloody warm being bloody cosseted, while she was clearly destined for a morning of orienteering in the great bloody outdoors. Though he put up a vigorous defence against this course of action, contending that to remove said article of clothing would cost him more pain than it would give her relief, he was soon disabused of the notion when Lorna, teeth already chattering in the wind, started to tear it off him with her own bare hands. As she donned the captured trophy with an air of bitter triumph and they eyed each other malevolently before she slammed the car door, both husband and wife were aware that this altercation marked the lowest point ever in their connubial bliss.

'He'll be all right,' Melissa reassured her, mistaking the look of venom on her cousin's face for concern as they watched their men speed away, and she hooked her arm through Lorna's to guide her towards a pedestrian crossing, thus distributing the extra weight she was carrying evenly between them.

'Course he will,' said Lorna dismissively. And if he wasn't, what did she care? After the shocking nightmare she'd half-remembered on waking, the lurid details of which had been coming back to her on the drive into town, a teeny bit of back pain was the very least she could have wished on him right now. For, in her dream, she'd been sitting up in bed at home, reading some material from work and making notes, while next to her, Greg was making enthusiastic love to Shitlipz. When she'd realised what was happening and asked them what the *hell* they thought they were doing, they had both looked up at her with self-satisfied smiles, and told her they were 'doing what came naturally'. The bastards. Reliving it now, she stifled a sob.

'Are you all right?' Melissa asked her, as they battled against the keen headwind which was sweeping unhindered up Charles Street.

Lorna pulled Greg's overcoat around her for warmth, for once in her life not giving a hoot that her costume wasn't fully coordinated. 'Just dandy,' she said grimly, as much to persuade herself as Melissa. 'No worries whatsoever.'

'We'll just nip and get the serviettes and stuff for the reception, then maybe have a bit of brekkie,' Melissa said comfortingly, observing her favourite cousin's pale, pinched face with motherly concern as she pushed her through the doors of the inappropriately named *Celebrate in Style!* 'You look like you could do with a nice cup of coffee to bring you round.'

Lorna attempted a smile, but found that either her features, or her heart, were too frozen for anything warmer than a grimace. 'That'd be nice,' she said, forcing herself to focus on the tawdry tinsel anniversary banners, and the giant day-glo balloons which urged the recipient to *Smile! You're forty today!*

Melissa's concept of 'just nipping' into a shop, however, transpired to be what Lorna would have classed as moving in and setting up camp. After half an hour of traipsing up and down the aisles with not one purchase yet in their possession, Lorna began to wonder how long a woman *could* agonise over the minuscule decision of buying white paper napkins embossed with wedding bells in silver, or white paper napkins embossed with wedding bells in gold.

The trouble, in her critical assessment, was that Melissa had absolutely no method whatsoever. Just as she seemed to be on the brink of coming down decisively on one side or the other, her magpie instincts and her butterfly mind had her racing across to the other side of the store, distracted by another product altogether. At last, desperate for the promised caffeine, Lorna wrenched a life-sized blow-up model of a bride and groom out of her cousin's hands and *forced* her to focus, by grabbing her by the face and staring deeply into her eyes with a frightening intensity.

'Lorn!' Melissa protested, looking rather like a surprised fish, since Lorna's firm grip had her mouth pinched together from both sides. 'Oo hur'hin' ngee!'

'I don't know what you're trying to say, and I don't care,' her captor warned her viciously. 'Now concentrate, Melissa, as if your life depended on it, which right now it does: napkins – silver or gold?'

'Goh?' Melissa offered, pop-eyed with uncertainty.

Lorna rewarded her by letting go of her lips and dragging her back to the napery section by her elbow instead. 'Gold it is, good decision,' she said, stuffing two packets into their wire basket in a business-like fashion. 'Will a hundred be enough?'

'Dunno,' said Melissa, massaging her cheeks into their proper place, her roving eyes already straying back to the inflatable novelties. 'I'm hopeless at maths.'

A desperate woman, Lorna grabbed her by the kisser again. 'How many guests?' she demanded.

'I uh-oh,' said Melissa, eyes bulging. 'Ee ih-hens oh iph El-loysh ngang cang cung o'her.'

'You're giving me words, I want numbers,' her mentor instructed her.

'Ngay-gee . . . hay-ee?'

'I understood you to say "maybe eighty". Nod if I got that right.'

Melissa nodded.

'Then two packs is good,' Lorna confirmed, and pulled her over to the other side of the aisle for the next big decision. 'Plastic knives and forks. Ten to a pack, how many packs?'

Melissa struggled to reply through her giggles and the constricting influence of Lorna's firm grip. 'Ah uh-oh,' she said. As one might expect of such a fun-loving girl, she was taking this as an amusing game rather than as a serious threat to her life. 'Or-ee?'

'No, not forty, Melissa,' Lorna corrected her, in a dangerously controlled voice. 'What do we do when we divide by ten?'

By way of an answer, Melissa's eyes first blinked, then glazed. 'Huh-hoh,' she shrugged happily.

'We take off a nought,' Lorna informed her forcefully. Aware that she was attracting the attention of the store's uniformed security guard, she let go of Melissa's face but continued to pin her with her laser-like gaze. 'Tens into eighty, take off a nought . . . ?'

After a rather long silence, uncertainty cleared from Melissa's features like a cloud passing over the sun. 'That's a trick question!' she squealed, wagging her finger excitedly in her cousin's face, and hopping up and down on the spot. 'You nearly had me there, Lorn!'

Lorna's brow furrowed as she strained to identify any sense at all in this assertion. 'No, it's a perfectly straightforward piece of easy, first-base mental arithmetic, Melissa. Where's the trick?'

'The trick is, there int no nought in "eighty", otherwise it'd be "oughty",' she giggled.

Reminding herself that she was here as a teacher of shopping efficiency and not as a maths coach, Lorna sighed and counted eight packs of cutlery into the basket. 'Need plastic glasses?' she asked tersely.

But before Melissa could even begin to focus her mind on that question, a loud chirruping of 'Advance Australia Fair' came from Greg's purloined overcoat, galvanising Lorna's attention as if she'd been stung.

'What's that?' asked Melissa, adept as always at giving her full attention to any distraction on offer.

'Greg's mobile,' her cousin responded, heart pounding, as she pulled it out of her husband's coat pocket to stare in horror at the digital display.

'No, you daft bugger!' Melissa chortled. 'What's the tune?'

Lorna's world having flipped over on seeing the name 'Diane' filling the miniature screen, it was a good few moments before she responded distractedly, 'Australia's national anthem.' Her brain was in overdrive, flicking between the two powerful responses of her gut: to answer the bitch's call and face her out, or to upchuck. But before she could do either, the phone diverted to its answering service.

'You know what, Lorn?' Melissa said, her cousin's stricken expression not evading her notice at last. 'I think we'd better go for that brekkie now. You look like you're going to flake out.'

'Not till we've got everything from here that you need,' Lorna said hollowly, grabbing a box of a dozen champagne flutes and focusing her entire mental faculties on the problem of dividing eighty by twelve. At this moment, in a public place, and with an educationally challenged companion to care for, she knew she needed to keep her mind occupied in order to calm down. There would be plenty of time later – once her hands had stopped trembling, for instance – to break her own rules about privacy and access her husband's lover's message from his mobile.

Besides which, she reminded herself sternly, squaring her shoulders to the task in hand, even in extremis, half-poisoned by alcohol and with her marriage fast disappearing down the tubes, nobody could point the finger and accuse her of shirking her organisational duties.

The same could not be said, alas, of the overworked triage staff in the crowded A&E department of Leicester Royal Infirmary,

as Greg was finding out to his cost. Ignorant of the trouble he
was in with his significant other on the opposite side of town,
he was under the mistaken impression that the worst that
could happen to him was that he'd had to limp painfully and
bravely all the way to the reception desk from the car park,
where he'd abandoned Elroy to the hopeless quest of finding
a vacant space.

Now standing impatiently at the reception cubicle, he was
struck once again by the complete and utter inability of the
bastard Poms to run anything efficiently – or even at all. For
starters, these idiot arseholes here seemed to be pathologically
incapable of appreciating the urgency of his situation, insisting
that he fill out a form and wait for an unspecified amount of
time (though not for more than four hours, apparently, by
Government edict – Christ!) before anybody even vaguely
medical would assess him.

'I don't need assessing, dear,' he loftily informed the
implacable back of the receptionist, who'd returned to her
filing after furnishing him with a clipboard and pen, thereby
forcing him to raise his voice and bang on the thick wall of
shatter-proof glass which kept her at bay from the pain-
maddened public. 'This is a recurrent problem that has been
pre-diagnosed by my own chiropractor back home.'

'Can you *not* bang on my window, please,' she instructed
him sternly, not even bothering to look up. 'You'll be seen in
due course when you've waited your turn. Just watch for your
number.'

Greg heaved a sigh of frustration and banged on the desk
instead. 'I'm trying to save your resources here, love. I've
already *been* diagnosed by Melbourne's finest, is my point. L3
and L4 – that's two of the vertebrae in the lumbar region to
you – get out of alignment at the slightest bloody—'

Now he had her full attention. 'If you don't step away from

the window and take a seat immediately, I shall be forced to call a member of Security,' she warned him edgily. In her defence, had Greg but known it, today was her first day back at work after having been lunged at by a desperate diabetic a fortnight before. 'Next!'

Having thus dismissed him, she immediately switched to a more sympathetic tone, smiling past him at the elderly man whose head wound was still oozing fresh blood. 'Ay up, me duck, what's happened to you?'

'Can't remember now,' the man said vaguely, pressing a sodden handkerchief to his lacerated scalp as he attempted to circumvent Greg. 'Oh ar – fell down and banged me head, was it?'

Adopting an assertive stance to defend his place in the queue, feet apart, clenched fists on hips, Greg accidentally elbowed the older man in the chest. 'Ah, sorry about that, mate,' he said reflexively, righting the elderly bleeder while inwardly cursing him for being in the bloody way in the first place. The receptionist fixed him with a meaningful glare, her hand moving threateningly to the phone to call up reinforcements. Fucking marvellous! All he needed now was to be thrown out of Casualty without the relief of the medication he'd come for. Making a supreme effort for a renewed attempt at detente, he smiled ingratiatingly and modified his volume to a more acceptable level. 'Look, love,' he confided desperately, 'all I need is a few more Valium just to get me through this. Then I'll be gone, and out of your hair.'

Confident at last in his ability to self-diagnose, a slow smile of recognition spread across the receptionist's face. A prescription drug junkie, just as she'd thought. Well, she'd soon scare him off from taking up scant National Health resources and her valuable time. 'I'll page the psychs,' she offered, sounding deceptively sympathetic. 'But you'll still have to sit over there quietly till your number comes up.'

'The *psychs* – are you *mad*?' he replied, practically speechless with rage as, at one and the same time, he lost both the plot and his place in the queue. 'It's my bloody *back* that needs seeing to, sweetheart, not my *head*!' But meeting the receptionist's baleful gaze, and mindful of her threat to bring in the shrinks, he retreated as instructed to the seating area, where he remained on his feet in a conspicuous but futile act of rebellion.

'Ha ha!' he laughed humourlessly to nobody in particular, but nevertheless attracting the attention of every bastard and his dog. 'Bloody pointless hanging around here, that's for sure, waiting to be carted off by the men in white coats!' Enraged and in agony as he was, however, he was also aware that his current behaviour might lead his fellow cripples to believe that such carting off might make them all feel better, so striving for a look of devil-may-care insouciance he began to side-step, in a strangely random and pain-peppered pattern, towards the exit doors. And, as it transpired, towards his wife's cousin's fiancé, who was just coming through them.

'Ay up, bro, where's the music?' Elroy joshed him, witness as he was to Greg's curious dance of egression.

'Don't know what you're talking about, as per fucking usual, Elroy, but we're leaving,' Greg snapped ungenerously as he limped towards him, forgetting now the bond they'd forged over Bishop's Fingers the evening before. Twirling his outstretched hand to signal that Elroy should turn around and go back from whence he'd come, he continued his shuffled progress in his wake.

'Fucking mother country?' he called back to his bemused spectators, unable to resist having the final word from the relative safety of the double doors. 'Fucking useless!' And having satisfied himself that at last he'd won his argument, he left his fellow patients in a worse state than he'd found them, having added his insult to their injuries.

Outside in the newly-sprung sleet storm Elroy was found sheltering under the canopy of the ambulance bay, warming himself round a freshly lit spliff which, forgiving as ever, he immediately offered to Greg. 'Brass fucking monkeys,' being the antipodean's only response as he availed himself of this generosity, Elroy replied cheerfully, 'Innit?' and there being little more to say on the subject, they tacitly agreed to suspend further conversation until they'd finished the joint, at which point Greg's next comment was, 'Bastard.'

'Ay! It were finished, man – it were down to the bleddy cardboard, if you don't mind!' Elroy protested, refusing to feel guilty as he stubbed out the roach underfoot.

Naturally Greg hastened to put right the unintended insult. 'Not you, dickbrain, the fucking cow on reception, you twat.'

'S'all right then,' sniffed Elroy, duly mollified. 'So wha'ppen in dere den?' he continued, the effects of the Jamaican herb, apparently, having gone straight to his speech to play havoc with his native Leicester accent. 'Wouldn't she give you no Valium?'

'She gave me nothing but fucking abuse,' Greg informed him sourly.

Another small silence fell upon them as they watched the weather and willed it to turn, and in that respect at least they had some small measure of success, when the driving sleet suddenly changed direction from vertical to a gravity-defying horizontal. As Elroy exclaimed, it were awesome, but perhaps you had to be there to appreciate the wonder of it, and most certainly you had to be stoned.

Greg, who was chilled to the very marrow of his displaced bones, had been hoping the marijuana might make his agony more bearable – and in a way it had, insomuch as it was now difficult to focus his attention on anything very clearly. 'We could wait here till bloody doomsday for this to bloody stop,' he complained to Elroy, hugging his arms to his shivering chest.

Elroy nodded. 'You know what I *mean*?' he agreed buoyantly.

'Right then,' said Greg decisively, gritting his teeth, and leaving their shelter he set off at a brisk hobble.

After an ill-advised joke about giving Greg a piggy-back to the car was taken seriously, Elroy's second mistake was to ask his cargo where he wanted to go now.

'Gotta be your mum's, hasn't it?' said Greg, levering himself painfully into the Escort. 'Get her to change her mind about giving me the drugs.'

'No way!' cried Elroy, looking askance. 'When that woman has said no, she means *no*!'

Greg smiled knowingly. 'You just drive, mate, and leave the rest to me,' he said immodestly. 'I've never met the female yet who can resist my kind of sweet-talk.'

Half an hour later, however, as he found himself getting back into the car, he was forced to agree that meeting Mrs Williams had been an education.

'What did I say when you hahks me the first time?' the spirited lady had challenged her son through her unopened front window.

'No?' offered Elroy.

'Bel*ieve*,' she'd said, and had swished the blinds shut.

'She might at least have lent us her phone book,' Greg complained, as he wondered aloud where the hell one might find a good chiropractor in this godforsaken hole.

'Chiropractor,' mused Elroy who, though vindicated in respect of his mother's response, was not one to bear malice. 'I've heard of that somewhere.'

Greg's eyes raised themselves to heaven in a silent appeal.

'Wait a minute!' Elroy said. 'That's the one spelt funny, with a cee haitch, innit?'

'C, H, I, R, O, P—' Greg began wearily, unwittingly echoing his wife's simultaneous attempt to bring their young cousins up to educational snuff.

'Yessss! I seen a sign for one, man, up Stoneygate way,' exclaimed Elroy, and he turned on the engine to roar down the street. Clutching the dashboard to steady himself against the resultant G-force, Greg only hoped he wouldn't be dead before they got there.

Life and death issues were on Lorna's mind too. 'What would you do if you found out Elroy was cheating on you?' she asked, occasioning Melissa to choke on her all-day breakfast in the greasy spoon café.

'Bleddy hell, Lorn!' she spluttered through regurgitated egg. 'Give us a chance, we int even married yet!'

'Course not,' said Lorna, who shouldn't have needed reminding, surrounded as she was by seven carrier bags of wedding accoutrements. 'But say if you were, and he was?'

Uncharacteristically, Melissa regarded her life-long heroine with something approaching coolness. 'Why, what have you heard?'

'Nothing!' Lorna was quick to reassure her. 'Elroy's too nice to do anything like that to you,' she suggested after an uncomfortable silence. 'He'd never cheat.'

'That's what you think,' said Melissa unexpectedly.

Now this was more like it. Information on how to keep an unfaithful man on the straight and narrow, it appeared, was about to come Lorna's way. 'What happened?' she asked, all ears.

'He only went off and bonked Yvonne Beasley,' Melissa spat. 'The tart.'

'And you found out?'

'Every bugger knew,' said Melissa, outraged all over again. 'It were practically front page of the bleddy *Mercury*.'

'So what did you do? Confront him?'

'First off,' said Melissa, relishing the memory, 'I poured glue in his shoes.'

'Glue?' Lorna asked, sure she'd missed something. 'In his shoes?'

'His favourite hundred quid Nikes,' Melissa qualified. 'Got him where it really hurt.'

'I see.' Clearly that wouldn't work on Greg, thought Lorna. He could easily afford to just go out and buy another pair.

'Second off, I writ BASTARD in green felt tip on his forehead while he were asleep,' she offered, her eyes narrowing as she got into the swing of things vengeful. 'He had to live with that for a week.'

'Was it indelible?'

Melissa grinned and nodded. 'You're not bleddy kidding, Lorn.'

'O-kay,' said Lorna, wishing she'd never bothered to ask. So far, she couldn't see herself doing any of these things to Greg. 'Then what?'

'I told him if he ever did that again, I'd string him up by his goolies.'

'My God!' said Lorna, satisfied at last by the picture of her own errant husband dangling painfully in mid-air. 'What did he say to that?'

'He asked me to marry him!' Melissa chortled.

Now Lorna was very puzzled indeed. 'He asked you to marry him after you'd threatened to hang him up by his balls?' she checked dubiously.

'No, he asked me to marry him *because* I threatened to hang him by his balls,' Melissa explained patiently. 'He suddenly cottoned on to what he might be losing, see.'

'His testicles?' Lorna suggested.

'No, *me*, you great wazzock!' Melissa corrected her, thumping the table in her mirth. 'And Parv, of course,' she continued more soberly.

'Parv,' mused Lorna. 'Oh Parveen – his daughter.'

'Parv int Elroy's! I had her with a lad called Gurdip, when I were still at school. That's how come I didn't go to college,' she added irrelevantly. Lorna pursed her lips into silence. Getting pregnant might have been one reason why Melissa hadn't achieved a tertiary education, but she suspected that having the concentration of a gnat might have had more to do with it. 'But Elroy's known her since she were a toddler,' she continued, 'and he loves her like mad. Mind you, it's took her a lot longer to come round to loving him. That's why I couldn't marry him till she did.'

'But she has now,' said Lorna.

Melissa nodded happily. 'You saw how choked he were the other day when she called him daddy.'

Lorna smiled weakly. So no clues here, then, for her. Without the loss of a child with which to threaten Greg, she was evidently powerless to keep him. 'That's good,' she said, without enthusiasm.

'Good, Lorn?' Melissa exclaimed, disappointed by her cousin's cool reaction. 'It's abso-bleddy-lutely *indelible*! She couldn't stand the sight of him at the start.' Chortling to herself, she returned her attention to the remains of her breakfast, and Lorna tried another sip of what had been described in the menu as a cappuccino, but which reminded her of dishwater in every respect. God, how could people live here, she wondered, and how could they get it so wrong when Italy was just down the road? At this moment she longed to be back home in Melbourne – at least she'd have the comfort of a good cup of coffee, Shitlipz or no Shitlipz. And thinking of whom . . . She looked down at her hands. Yes, they appeared to have stopped shaking at last. So. Time to snoop into her husband's affairs.

'I'm just popping to the Ladies,' she told Melissa, 'back in a tick.'

Melissa's reply was a loud belch followed by a groan. 'Might follow you in a minute,' she called after her, putting down her knife and fork for a moment to rub her huge belly. 'I've got terrible wind now, after all that.'

Small wonder, thought Lorna distastefully, as she threaded her way through the crowded café to the privacy of the ladies' loos – she was feeling quite bilious herself. She was familiar with the expression 'eating for two', but at the grotesque rate Melissa had been shovelling fried food into her mouth over the last ten minutes, she must have an army to feed in there. However much she was dreading hearing what Shitlipz had to say, she comforted herself, it would be a blessed relief to get away from feeding time at the zoo.

Locking herself into the small cubicle, she fished Greg's mobile from his overcoat pocket, and with fingers which had annoyingly started to tremble again, flicked through the complex menu. As with all his boy's toys, Greg naturally had to have the top of the range, most cutting-edge of systems, with countless features including picture messaging, blue tooth, global satellite tracking, access to the web, and God alone knew what all else. After a few tense and sweaty moments and a liberal use of profanity, Lorna finally accessed recent messages, and scrolling through them, her stomach churned as she saw just how many times Diane's name appeared on the list. It was worse than she'd feared, even in her darkest hours – the woman was clearly obsessed with him. The image of Glenn Close and boiled bunnies flashed into Lorna's mind, but just as she was mastering the impulse to upchuck, she started as though stung when the phone suddenly beeped in her hand. Was the bitch actually texting him even at this moment? Christ almighty! Heart pounding, vision greying, Lorna leant back queasily against the thin partition wall to steady herself. Her legs had turned to jelly, her head was spinning sickeningly, and she feared that she would pass out there and then. Willing herself to butch up, she forced herself to press OK, despite the fact that she felt anything but, and right there before here unfocused eyes, instead of the expected text message, Shitlipz herself started to swim into view. Lorna peered in disbelief at the photo-image which filled the small screen: stripped to the buff, a breast cupped in each hand as if offering them to the viewer, Diane was winking and pouting a kiss.

Sinking to her knees in an unwilling but urgent embrace of the porcelain, Lorna threw up the small amount of coffee she'd been unwise enough to swallow earlier. But if she thought at that moment that things couldn't get any worse, she was soon disabused of the notion by the sudden arrival of an hysterically overexcited waitress, an insistent banging on the cubicle door, and the shouted imprecation, 'Are you the lady with the pregnant friend? You'd better come quick! Her waters have broke!'

When Lorna rejoined her stricken cousin at a run, still mopping her face with a paper towel and trying to banish images of breasts from her mind, she found that for once in her life, Melissa was not seeing the funny side. In fact, she was crying, in between her grunts of pain.

'I can't believe it's come this early!' she was sobbing to the galvanised crowd. 'I'm getting married in a few days, to the dad. Why couldn't it have waited? I wanted this one to be properly illegitimate! Call Elroy on his mobile, Lorn – see if he can get hold of a preacher to meet us at the Infirmary!'

But, rising as always to an organisational challenge, Lorna was already otherwise engaged on the phone. As was the cab company she was trying to call. 'What's the number for the emergency services in England?' she demanded of all at large, raising her voice to cut across the clamour. 'I need to get her to a hospital!'

A couple of women near her laughed hollowly. 'You won't get an ambulance to come out just for a woman giving birth, duck,' one counselled her. 'You have to be dying to get one.'

'And even if you could, you'd be quicker tekking the bleddy bus,' said her friend.

'My mate had her last one on the 271,' another wit volunteered above the hubbub. 'When it came to filling out "Place of Birth" on its certificate, she put "Fare Stage 3, Saffron Lane"!'

The crowd laughed appreciatively, and Lorna felt dangerously as if she were losing control. 'Give me another cab number, then,' she instructed the café owner, Greasy Joe, as she grabbed him by the lapels to emphasise her seriousness.

'Don't worry, me duck,' said a male customer at the counter, who was now waiting for his takeaway bacon butty in vain. 'I've got me van outside. I'll run you down there. So long as you don't mind the smell of fish.'

Lorna did mind, as it transpired, but there was little point in complaining, she told herself, as she crouched in the back of his van between crates of deep-frozen haddock, her hand clamped over her nose. And, given that their rescuer had scant regard for red lights or give way signs, at least the journey time was mercifully short.

'Good luck wi' it, then,' he called after them cheerfully, watching their slow progress through the hospital's main doors, which was made all the slower by Lorna having to struggle single-handed with the seven carrier bags of wedding paraphernalia, and by Melissa's insistence on keeping her thighs clamped together as she walked. She was still entertaining the vain hope of keeping the baby in place until Elroy could be found, preferably in the company of a registrar and a valid certificate of marriage.

'Try him again, Lorn,' she begged, for the seventeenth time since they had begun their journey. 'He can't still be engaged.'

'He is, though,' Lorna said grimly, tucking Greg's mobile back into her pocket, as the lift doors at last mercifully opened outside the Maternity Unit. If anything, she was even keener than Melissa to track Elroy down, having absolutely no desire whatsoever to usurp his position of birthing partner. The very idea of seeing the miracle of reproduction at such close quarters made her feel queasy all over again.

Happily, they were better organised for birth that day at the Infirmary than they had been for emergency admissions, and with a speed and efficiency which would have improved Greg's low opinion of the National Health Service no end, they were soon ensconced in a birthing suite, where Melissa was checked over and calmed down by an unflappable midwife.

After assessing the dilation of Melissa's uterus (while Lorna kept her eyes averted and struggled anew with her now familiar feelings of nausea), she made for the door. 'Pace yourself, it'll be a while yet,' she advised. 'I'm needed next door. Just remember your breathing, and save all your energy for the big push later. Your friend here'll keep you company, and you can ring the bell if you need me.'

Left alone in sole charge of a woman in the advanced

stages of labour who was now, due to the administering of a strategically placed suppository, liable to explode from at least two of her orifices at any moment, Lorna's anxiety rose to an unmanageable level. Already stressed by her earlier sighting of Shitlipz's breasts, she felt unequal to this challenge, and when Melissa instructed her to 'Pass us that bedpan, quick!' she heaved and filled it with her own bodily wastes.

'Blimey!' chortled Melissa, valiantly clenching her buttocks as Lorna sank back onto the bed before rallying herself to set off for fresh supplies. 'Don't tell me you're pregnant and all!'

If Lorna's journey to the hospital in the back of the van hadn't already taught her how it felt to be smacked around the face with a wet fish, she would have learnt it in that moment, such was the force of her shock.

'Don't be silly, that's *morning* sickness. It's three o'clock in the afternoon now,' she said slowly, her mind racing feverishly to recall the exact date of her last period. When the hell had it been? She knew she was late, but she'd put it down to the emotional state she'd been in since she'd found out about Shitlipz and Greg. She couldn't possibly be . . . Could she? . . . No . . . Impossible.

Melissa snorted. 'That means nothing,' she said confidently. 'I were throwing up 24/7 for the first three month with both of mine. Oh, but wouldn't it be great, Lornie, if you was? We'd be mums together!'

To her huge satisfaction, tears started to roll down her cousin's cheeks. 'Aah,' she crooned happily, 'you great soppy date. Mind you, that can be another sign that you're up the duff. I were crying non-stop this time, even though I were really happy to be having El's baby – they say it's your hormones. Have your tits been sore and all?'

With a feeling of cold dread and sudden certainty, Lorna nodded through her tears. She'd thought up to now that the tenderness in her breasts had been a sure sign that her period was on its way. Of all the times this could happen! She couldn't deal with this now, on top of everything else – not when she was just making up her mind to leave Greg.

'Do you feel up to getting me that new bedpan now?' asked Melissa, urgency replacing sympathy in her tone. 'Cos I don't think I can hold it in no longer.'

Nothing she could possibly have said at that moment could have made Lorna recover more quickly, nor move any faster than she did. And having returned in a trice with the new receptacle, she had excused herself again even before Melissa had finished expressing her gratitude over receipt of same. 'I'll go and find us a cup of tea,' she called back through the door, once she had achieved the sanctuary of being on the other side of it. 'Give you a bit of privacy.'

'Don't be long, Lorn,' Melissa grunted back anxiously, and glancing at her wristwatch as she strode away, Lorna decided she would give her at least a good half-hour. She had already been the reluctant witness of as much practical biology as she could take in one day, and besides which, there was now a certain item that she needed to get her hands on without delay, the purchase of which would necessitate finding a pharmacy.

When the two cousins were at last reunited, both women had been productive with their time. Lorna had managed, after following several false trails, to get hold of a pregnancy predictor kit, to find some privacy in a public lavatory, and to have her worst fears confirmed; and Melissa, still unable to raise Elroy on the phone, had at least managed to get hold of her mum, Mo, who arrived in the birthing suite together with June only seconds before Lorna returned, weeping, with her news.

'I'm pregnant,' she said, with the gravitas normally reserved for announcements of death.

Recovering swiftly from her shock and surprise, June embraced her daughter joyfully. 'But that's fantastic, darl – that's wonderful!' she said.

'No, it's not,' sobbed Lorna.

'No, it bleddy well int,' echoed Melissa in a stunned voice, lifting her head from Greg's mobile after another fruitless attempt at calling her fiancé. She offered the phone for the others' inspection. 'Who's that bitch?' she demanded of her stricken cousin, as June and Mo inspected the still life of Shitlipz And Breasts which was displayed on the small VDU. 'And what the bleddy hell does Greg think he's doing, getting pictures of her bazookas?'

'It's his lover,' Lorna admitted on quivering lips. 'His mistress. The woman he's going to divorce me for. The reason that we're here.' Despite her lifetime's observance of keeping a lid on her feelings and of rigid self-control, all this and more tumbled out in a torrent of raw emotion now, her usual defences swept away by the crashing waves of hormones which were currently coursing through her newly pregnant body. They talk about the miracle of birth, and here it was, in all its glory, in all its mystery and power. For here, in this headily intense female atmosphere of a birthing suite, in the company of her mother and her mother's sister and her mother's sister's daughter, with her new baby first-cousin-once-removed even now readying herself for the white-knuckle ride of her nativity, Lorna at last learnt how to let go.

In the company of this monstrous regiment of women, in the bosom of this feminine cabal, she wept, she chucked up, was comforted, and supported; her deepest fears were shared, her terrors soothed, her rage encouraged, her desire for vengeance given wings. Bold plots were hatched, rejected, then taken up anew and redefined. Melissa's first impulse to text back, 'Die, bitch,' to Shitlipz, for example – though none could fault the direct nature of its appeal – was massaged, primped, and finally transmuted into a cleverer and more subtle ruse. Once Lorna's tears were dried, her make-up repaired, and everybody had agreed that the most flattering light was to be found over by the window, she was posed and photographed, smiling serenely, using the tiny camera in Greg's phone, and the resultant image was relayed at once to Diane Lipshitz in Melbourne by the magic of satellite, together with his last words on the subject of their former affair: 'Lorna is pregnant. I'm over the moon. Don't call me again. G.' Better safe than sorry, it was unanimously decided once the message was sent to expunge the recipient's number from the mobile's memory (if not from its owner's), but for good measure, and on sudden impulse, Melissa had the bright idea of drowning the whole thing in the bedpan of effluence she'd prepared earlier. It goes without saying that, once the connection was made between the vanquished mistress's name and her subsequent grisly fate, great giddiness ensued from one and all.

Satisfied as they all were by the ingenuity of their initial sally in this bloody battle to control hearts and minds, however, the assembled company's appetite for revenge and retribution was yet to be assuaged. Something had to be done to Greg to change his errant ways. Some effective form of correction must be found, some punishment meted out, some potent curse brought down around his ears so that he would never, ever, not ever as long as he lived, be temped again to stray from the path of marital bliss, nor slink away from his new responsibilities of fatherhood. But what could that be, and where would they find it?

Such was the intensity of the four women's focus on this question that they had quite forgotten the real reason they were here in this room until Melissa's body, caught up as it was at the very epicentre of the machinations of the mysteries of the universe, unequivocally demanded her complete and total attention.

'Shit a brick!' she cried suddenly, inadvertently but accurately describing the acuteness of her pain. 'Get the midwife! Find Elroy! The baby's on its way out!'

It is hard to find the words to describe the feelings of the two men – and they had certainly given up trying – after Elroy finally managed to grab his phone out of Greg's greedy grasp to answer Lorna's subsequent call. An intense, red-blooded silence reigned between them, an atmosphere of barely contained antagonism that you could have cut clean through with a knife. Fuelled by his untreated back pain, frustrated by Elroy's bone-headed stupidity, disdainful of everything Pom, Greg was lip-curlingly surly and grim. As for poor Elroy, having never in his whole life met anybody as selfish, as bossy, as just plain *rude* as Greg, he was struggling against his heart-felt desire to stick one on the bugger.

'How was I supposed to know there's a difference between a chiropodist and a chiropractor?' were his first words on the matter, once he had joined the women at break-neck speed to witness the birth of his child. He was wild-eyed and frantic when he burst through their door, terrified he had missed Melissa's great moment, which, mercifully, he had not. He explained in a rush that, on discovering the problem of his dyslexia outside the Stoneygate foot clinic, Greg had cussed him out, smacked him round the head, and commandeered his mobile, which was why Lorna had kept getting the engaged signal. 'He even wanted me to drive him home first, before I come to the hospital, if you can believe that!' he expostulated, still shaking with rage. 'I just took off, man, left him in the street, still shaking his fist and bad-mouthing me!'

'Calm down,' Mo chastised him, relinquishing her post at her daughter's side to her overheated future son-in-law. 'She don't need you in this state while she's struggling to make you a dad.'

Tears streamed from Elroy's cheeks to Melissa's sweating brow, as he sank down to sit at her side and embrace her. 'My kitten,' he sobbed, 'my baby-cakes. I am just so sorry I weren't here for you earlier.'

'You're here now,' Melissa comforted him, hugging him tight in the brief lull before another contraction tried to tear her body in two. But turning from Jekyll to Hyde as a fresh wave of pain overwhelmed her, she suddenly pushed him away screaming, 'Don't you dare ever fucking do this to me again, you bastard!'

'And pant, pant, pant,' said her midwife pragmatically, having heard all this before, and worse.

Looking on askance as Melissa laboured to go forth and multiply, Lorna felt unequal to the challenge that she would face herself in a few short months. Would she too be reduced to this red-faced wreck, this miserable wretch racked with pain, at the mercy of forces too great, surely, for any woman to bear? And where would Greg be then, while she struggled alone to give life to his progeny? In Shitlipz's arms? Hiding his head in her cleavage? For there was no way that he'd be at her side, as Elroy was with Melissa, stroking her forehead, holding her hand, whispering encouragement, calling on God to let *him* bear this pain, let him be the one to suffer, instead of his princess, his goddess, his queen.

Feeling a warm hand on her arm, Lorna turned to find June looking at her in some concern. 'Come and have a bit of a sit, darl,' her mother said, steering her carefully towards a chair. 'You look like you're going to pass out.'

From her seated position, head down between her ankles, Lorna heard rather than saw her new baby cousin's loud arrival to the world. Another screamed oath from Melissa, a triumphant shout from Elroy, the sharp sound of a slap delivered by the midwife, all presaged the heartfelt cry of protest which sprang from the tiny, gunk-covered bundle of joy as she took her first lungful of air.

'It's a girl!' said the midwife.

'My daughter!' cried Elroy.

'Thank the fuck that she's out,' wept Melissa. 'Give her here.'

After the post-partum flurry that followed – the snipping and knotting, the cleaning and weighing, the stitching and crying – rapture reigned unconfined. Even Lorna, who had never been big on babies, was filled with a sense of wonder and awe as all twenty of her little cousin's perfectly formed digits were proudly counted and displayed by Dad, and when it came to be her turn to 'have a go on her', as urged by Melissa, she found, to her huge surprise, her heart swelling in her breast and the tenderest of smiles softening her features as she gazed down at this brand new baby nestling in her arms, and the little girl gazing back.

'We're going to call her Lornetta, after you – aren't we, El?' said Melissa, regarding her cousin fondly. 'If it'd been a boy we'd have called him Lorne.'

'Yeah, that's right,' Elroy confirmed. 'Lornetta Beverly, after you and me mum.'

'What about me?' Mo demanded, half joking.

'Lornetta Beverly Maureen June Melissa . . .' Elroy began, but at that moment the door opened and Parveen galloped in to meet her new baby sister, having been picked up from her extra-curricular ballet class by her Aunty Jo.

'. . . Parveen Josephine Williams,' Elroy concluded

decisively, generously including all the women in the room.

'Let's hope nobody else visits you tonight,' joked Mo. 'Or the poor little bugger'll murder you when she has to start filling out bleddy forms.'

It was the word 'murder' which prompted Lorna to remember her husband as the laughter died down, and suddenly looking much graver than a moment before, she reluctantly returned Lornetta to Melissa's arms and announced her intention of going home, which in turn provoked Elroy's high spirits to plummet.

'Yeah, you'd better,' he told her, unhappy at being the bearer of bad tidings. 'Forgot to tell you. That's where he said he were going when I left him frothing at the mouth in the street.'

'Back to New Vistas?' asked Lorna, sounding deceptively casual as, with hammering heartbeat, she gathered her things.

Elroy shook his head dolefully. 'Back to Melbourne,' he said. 'Cos he says everything here's crap.'

Returning by taxi Chez Watkins, expressions of encouragement and solidarity still ringing in her ears from June ('Be strong, love. And remember, whatever else happens, *I'll* always be here for you'), from thrice-divorced Aunty Mo ('The men come and go, me duck, but your kids never leave you. Sometimes you wish they bleddy would!') and Melissa ('If he gives you any trouble, just tell the bastard I'll be after his balls'), Lorna tried to calm her rising panic and decide on her plan of attack. Never before had she confronted Greg about his infidelity, but now, without doubt, this had to be done. Come to that, never before had she had occasion to tell him she was expecting his baby, and this subject too must surely be broached. But how? And in which order? She knew she didn't want to blackmail him into staying; knew for certain that she didn't want to feel in the years to come that he had only grudgingly stuck with her for the sake of the kid.

So what did she want, she asked herself morosely, as the cab swung into New Vistas Boulevard and her holiday home (huh!) hove into view. What reaction was Greg capable of under these circumstances, which didn't require him to have a complete change of character? For hadn't she kept him by her side all these years by letting him know that his leash was long? And hadn't he been quite clear, from the very start, on the question of them having babies? 'No way, no day' had always been his refrain – with which, hitherto, she had gladly agreed.

A hollow laugh was her reply to the taxi driver as she paid him off and he told her to have a nice night. Swallowing hard to quell her feeling of a sickening sense of dread (not to mention her dreadful sense of feeling sick), she advanced on shaky legs to the door of 236. She would remain calm at all costs, she promised herself, as she willed her fingers to have the courage to turn the key in the lock. She would talk this over reasonably and logically, lay her cards on the table, let him decide freely on what he would do. For one thing had become quite clear to her in these last hours in the birthing suite, she now realised: she was going to have this baby, with him or without him. She was going to be a mother come what may.

Calling his name, she followed his answering angry shout up the stairs to share this news with him. If he was prepared to be penitent, if he vowed to change his ways, if he promised his future fidelity, then she in her turn would magnanimously forgive him and welcome him gladly to join her on the path to parenthood. If, however, he was fool enough to leave her, to choose Shitlipz's tired old tits over her own nurturing nipples, then let the devil take the hindmost, and let Melissa have his balls.

With this, then, as her battle cry, Lorna entered the bedroom to find Greg flinging clothes one-handed into his suitcase, his other hand clamped to his lower back.

'What did you say?' he asked in astonishment, as he straightened up with difficulty to face her, the ferocity of her attack having taken him quite by surprise.

'I said,' she stammered, wrong-footed, being fairly surprised herself that the words in her head had made themselves manifest at such an early stage in negotiations. 'I said,' she repeated more firmly, 'that if you leave now, Melissa's sworn she'll castrate you.' So much for reason and logic and keeping calm at all costs then, she admonished herself ruefully. But now there was no turning back.

'Is that a fact?' Greg replied dismissively, recovering sufficiently to return to his packing. 'Well, in that case, she'll have to save up the airfare to Oz first, won't she? And I can't see those couple of losers managing to do that in a hurry. Jesus! What a waste of space that boyfriend of hers is!'

'He's tried to help you to the best of his ability,' Lorna snapped back hotly. 'He's been at your beck and call ever since you got here, running round after you like a blue-arsed fly.'

'Yeah, and a fat lot of use that's been,' Greg sneered, pushing past her in the doorway to retrieve his wash bag from the bathroom next door. 'I suppose he told you that he took me to a bloody *chiropodist*?' he called back to her, raising his voice unnecessarily since she was following hot on his heels. 'I've been driving round all bloody day in that souped-up sewing machine of his, and all I got is worse back ache.'

'And while you'd got him doing that, Greg, his fiancée was giving birth to his baby! We couldn't even get through to tell him, because you were hogging his mobile, trying to sort out your pathetic bad back!'

'If you call this pathetic, Lorna,' said Greg with cold dignity, 'then you've never suffered from misalignment of the lumbar vertebrae. And if we're talking about who was at fault, I only had to use his phone because *you'd* got my mobile in the overcoat you insisted on snagging from me.' He held out his hand imperiously. 'So I'll have it back now, thanks.'

'You want your phone?' Lorna challenged him triumphantly, after she'd recovered from a puzzling outburst of maniacal laughter. 'Then you'll have to go swimming in shit.'

One thing Greg couldn't stand was a foul-mouthed woman, and in that respect at least, his wife had rarely let him down. Examining her critically now, it was quite clear to him that she was overwrought, but what had got her into this state was a complete and utter mystery. 'Darl, come here,' he said, changing tack and drawing her to him in an attempt to calm her down. 'I thought you'd be as pleased as me to be going back home early.' But to his horrified surprise, she roughly shook herself free to stand apart and glare at him, pinning him with eyes brightly glittering with rage.

'And why would I be pleased about that?' she confronted him venomously, reckless now in her heady descent to get down to the nitty gritty. 'What *pleasure* do you think I get exactly, from watching you slink off to shag your girlfriend?'

A look of alarm flashed across Greg's eyes, but was replaced almost instantly by one of hastily mustered incomprehension. 'What do you mean by that?' he blustered. 'I haven't got a girlfriend.'

Lorna sighed irritably. 'Don't take me for an idiot, Greg. You've been having an affair with a woman called Diane Lipshitz for at least the last two months, and according to my information, she's been telling all her mates that you intend to divorce me and marry her.'

'That's utter rubbish!'

'Be very careful what you say,' Lorna warned him icily. 'I'm not bluffing. Unless you start telling the truth and we sort this out now, tonight, then you'll have your divorce quicker than you bargained for. Or is that what you want?'

'No!' Greg exclaimed fervently. 'No, I don't. I've never said anything of the sort! Ever. I never would—'

'Don't lie, Greg, I *know* what's been going on! Why the hell do you think I brought you here, to the other side of the world, for Pete's sake?' she demanded, gesturing around the small cramped room. 'To get you away from her!'

Taking a breath to deliver a rebuttal, Greg stopped unexpectedly and merely exhaled, the fight apparently going out of him. 'Yeah, well,' he said finally, his head lowered. 'That's the same reason as I agreed to come here.'

Expecting a more spirited defence, Lorna was rendered speechless for a moment, before checking, 'So you'll give her up?'

'I'll be glad to,' he said with sincerity, daring to meet her eyes again. 'What can I say? She . . . she got me in a weak moment and I apologise, Lorna. The woman means nothing to me, nothing. She was just an itch I scratched – a couple of times. Not proud of myself, but there you are. To be honest, it's a relief it's out in the open at last. She's been coming on really strong and I can't shake her off. What happened – did she contact you? I'll bloody kill her if she's been hassling you!'

'Her ex wrote to tell me,' Lorna said shortly, deciding against telling him about hiring the private detective and the lost days at the Sheraton. 'But if he hadn't, I'd have found out today when she sent a photo of her tits to your mobile.'

Greg had the grace to look embarrassed. 'Jesus, love, I'm sorry. Christ. What a mess. I don't know why I did it. I'm a bloody idiot.'

'But this isn't the first time, is it?' Lorna pursued him. 'All our married life I have turned a blind eye to your affairs – and for that I blame myself, I got it wrong. I let you get away with it, I pretended it didn't hurt me, but it *does*, Greg, it does.'

'I'm sorry, love,' he said again.

'How would *you* like it if the boot was on the other foot? How would you feel if you knew I was lying to you and having affairs?'

'I wouldn't like it a bit,' he said briskly. 'Point taken. It won't happen again.'

She regarded him coolly, trying to decide if she could believe him. 'It had better not, Greg, because I promise you, if it ever does, that's it. Finito. I'm just not prepared to tolerate it any more. As far as I'm concerned, you're on probation, and I'll be watching you like a hawk.'

'Fair enough. I'll go and see her as soon as we get back home if that's okay with you, and tell her not to contact me again.'

'No need to do that. You've already done it,' said Lorna, realising as she did so that it was now her turn to come clean. 'You texted her back after she sent you the photo.'

Greg laughed, relieved that his dirty work had been done for him. And he had to admit it was a bit of a turn-on to see Lorna doing her jealous tigress act, chasing off marauding females so she could keep him all to herself. 'Good on you, love,' he grinned admiringly. 'So what did I say?'

'You told her I was pregnant and that you're over the moon.'

It took a moment for it to sink in, and Lorna watched in dismay as her husband's smile slowly faded. 'You're pregnant? For real?'

Lorna nodded. 'And you're over the moon,' she prompted him.

'Are *you*?' he asked doubtfully. 'I thought we didn't want kids?'

'Changed my mind, apparently.'

A flicker of suspicion crossed his face. 'Did you plan this, because of Diane?'

'Give me some credit,' she snapped. 'I'm not the one who does things behind people's backs.'

'Right,' he said, too distracted to rise to the bait. 'So – do you want it?'

'Yes, I do.'

He sat down heavily on the bed, for the moment his back pain forgotten. 'Shit, Lorna, this is all so sudden. Are you sure?'

'Surer than you, it seems,' she said, with a sinking heart.

'Well, I mean, love – it's a big decision. And we always said that . . . It'll change everything. Our lifestyle, our freedom. I just don't know if . . . I need some time to think about this.'

'You do that,' she said hollowly, and retired to the bathroom to upchuck again.

Thereafter things went from bad to worse, and by the time June returned home, it was to find Lorna crying in the living room, and Greg, having finished his packing, already asleep upstairs.

'But he can't go back to Melbourne now,' June said practically, as she and her distraught daughter sat in the kitchen drinking tea. 'Apart from anything else, Mick and Pauline are in your house, and they've got every right to be there.'

'Says he's going to ask one of his mates to put him up, or he'll stay in a hotel,' sniffed Lorna.

'Think he'll go and stay with that woman?'

Lorna shrugged. 'He says not. I've told him what'll happen if he sees her again.'

'He does love you,' said June thoughtfully. 'You can see that in his eyes when he looks at you. Maybe this was just the warning he needed.'

'But if he doesn't want this baby . . .' Lorna protested morosely.

'Doesn't want the competition,' her mother diagnosed. 'Too much of a spoiled brat himself.'

Lorna looked at her sharply. 'Don't you like him, Mum?'

'I do, as a matter of fact,' said June. 'He's always been very good to me. He just needs taking down a peg or two, in my opinion. Bit full of himself since he started to make all that money with his property deals. And normally he's pretty easy-going – not like the whinger he's turned into since we've been here.'

'To be fair,' said Lorna, 'I think he has been genuinely suffering with his back pain.'

June laughed and got up to put the kettle on again. 'Pain in the neck, more like. Another cuppa?'

'Yes, please.' Watching her mother going through the re-assuring routine of making tea, Lorna had to admit that it was an ill wind. She couldn't remember the last time she'd sought June's opinion, or sat in a kitchen with her late at night to chew the fat. Probably not since her teenage years. And why was that? Maybe she, too, had become a bit full of herself of late. Thought that with her eduction, with her high-powered job, she knew best – that her mother's homespun wisdom wasn't worth seeking.

'But then, of course,' June was saying, clattering cups in the sink, 'here he's nobody, is he? Hasn't got his big car and his big house and his big job. People here don't know he's "Greg Mackenzie", with all that means to folk in Melbourne. They don't glad-hand him and give him the hero's welcome like they do back home. Off his patch here, and probably feeling inse-cure. Men can be funny buggers, love,' she concluded, as she brought fresh tea back to the small table. 'Specially when they're nearing forty, like Greg. Can start to do all kinds of stupid things to prove to themselves they're still young.'

'Did Dad?' asked Lorna, genuinely curious. Here was another first. She'd never had a woman-to-woman talk with her mother about her own married life before.

'Well now, your dad—' June began slowly, but as the phone rang at that moment, this conversation didn't get finished until several days later, and when it did, Lorna had cause to wish she'd never tried to prise the lid off this particular can of worms. But for now, she had enough on her hands with Melissa calling from the maternity unit to find out how things had gone.

'What the bleddy hell's the bastard on about?' demanded her cousin down the phone, furious on Lorna's behalf as she retold the Greg story. 'There's no thinking involved now – he's having a baby and that's that.'

'Well, I am,' said Lorna. 'As for him, we'll just have to see.'

'But you're not going back to Melbourne with him, are you, Lornie?' Melissa pleaded. 'Now I've got Lornetta I need you more than ever to help me organise the wedding. And you've got to be here for her christening – you're her godmum!'

'No, I'm not going back with him,' Lorna said dully. She needed time apart from her husband to think things over every bit as much as he did at this moment. Did she want him to stick around after all this? And if she decided that she did, could she trust him again? Come to that, why, having never entertained a single maternal thought hitherto, was she herself so suddenly determined to have this baby? All this needed to be sifted through, without the distraction of hearing Greg's fears on the subject, she'd decided.

By the time she put the phone down, June was coming back in from the garden with Whiffy, looking bushed.

'Think us two'll toddle of to bed now, love, if it's all the same with you,' said June, giving her daughter a goodnight kiss. 'Will you be able to sleep?'

'I will,' said Lorna ruefully, 'if I can just keep this tea down. I'm shattered.'

'It's been a big day,' said her mum, and she gave her a heart-felt hug. 'It'll all turn out for the best, love, you just wait and see. He'll come round, I'm sure of it. I mean, let's face it,' she joked softly as they made their way upstairs, 'how can he fail to fall in love with a little miniature of himself? He'll have twice as much to brag about!'

Lorna smiled weakly. 'I hope so. I think.'

But as the two women settled down to sleep in New Vistas Boulevard to await what fate would bring them, plots were being hatched in the birthing suite of the Royal Infirmary to ensure that June's prediction would come true.

'He needs teaching a lesson,' Melissa said grimly to Elroy, who was still holding his baby girl with a soppy expression on his face, unable to bring himself to leave. 'I mean, look at you. You come round to liking babies, didn't you?'

'Yeah,' said Elroy, 'but I've been exposed to them, haven't I? There was both me sisters' kiddies, and Parv, and now little Lornetta. It's different when you get to know them, when you have to look after them.'

'We should kidnap him, then, and lock him up with one,' Melissa threatened idly. 'Make him take responsibility for somebody else for a change. Teach him some discipline, the spoiled stuck-up brat. Give him a short sharp shock.'

'He isn't coming near my baby to practise on!' Elroy countered protectively. 'So you needn't even start thinking about that!'

'Oh – my – God!' Melissa said slowly, a wicked smile

spreading from ear to ear. 'That's it – I've got it! Give us your mobile here, quick!'

'What are you up to?' Elroy asked suspiciously, watching her key in a number from memory. 'Who're you phoning now?'

'Somebody who's got babies, who specialises in correcting naughty boys' behaviour, and whose main client's away at the minute,' said Melissa with glee, her eyes shining with mischief as her call was connected. 'Hi, Sheil! It's Mel. I think I might have some good news . . .'

Elroy's features froze in horror as the penny finally dropped.

Bleddy hell fire!

Not Sheila Strict!

9

Having left Mick holding a certain thought after Gemma had seen him getting down and dirty with her mum, there are those among us will no doubt be gagging to know what else he'd been holding in the meantime. To those people I say, patience is a virtue – the truth of which wisdom Pauline Watkins would be the first to confirm. The only trouble was, having finally had her fancy tickled the poor woman had no time for patience and she was feeling anything but virtuous.

Nothing Pauline could say on that fateful, interrupted night of connubial bliss would persuade Gemma to stay in what she rudely referred to as 'the knocking shop', and she had gathered her things and flounced across the garden to take refuge with Chin, who, despite the lateness of the hour, had graciously agreed to accommodate her.

Returning to the marital bedroom to share this latest development with Mick, Pauline felt insouciant and rebellious, like a recidivist schoolgirl who had been caught getting up to no good behind the bike sheds. She practically skipped back down the corridor after her dressing down from the humourless headmistress (otherwise known as her daughter), and jumping on the bed to straddle Mick, she bounced up and down excitedly. If she had been chewing gum, she would have blown a bubble and popped it.

'Alone at last,' she told him, looking as gleeful as he was rueful.

'How's Gemma?' Mick asked her guiltily, having already forgotten that only half an hour earlier he had averred that they'd done nothing to be ashamed of, and he shrank from the touch of his wife's wilfully wandering hands. 'What did she say?'

'She said we were disgusting old perverts,' said Pauline, in a tone more fitting to one who had just been awarded a gold star for good behaviour, rather than the good earbashing she had in fact received. 'She's thinking of ringing up Childline, but in the meantime she's gone to live with Chin. Now where were we? Oh yes . . .'

Sitting up quickly, just as Pauline was adjusting her own position to continue where they'd left off, Mick's head collided painfully with hers, putting them both momentarily off their stroke as they stopped to rub their bruises.

'Sorry,' he winced, 'but – staying with Chin? What will she say to him? What will he think?'

Pauline's effervescence had been quite knocked out of her by the cracking of skulls, by Mick's sudden squeamishness about being touched, and by his reaction to Chin's part in their little drama, and when she replied, she no longer sounded as gay as she had so recently been. In fact she sounded quite bitchy.

'What's a bloke who dresses up as a woman going to say about a married couple having consenting sex?' she sniffed nastily. 'Ooh now, let me think . . .'

'No, but I mean—' said Mick, eyes lowered.

'What?' said Pauline, eyes narrowed.

'It's—'

'What?' she repeated accusingly. 'And why would you care?' Her own theories on that subject were now developing wildly.

'Embarrassing,' he ended lamely.

She regarded him coldly – his arms folded primly across his

chest, his legs crossed – and her hopes of his finishing the business he had started evaporated like a cloud of steam. (Mick could almost see it coming out of her ears.) Back to square one, then, she thought bitterly – me frustrated, and him neither use nor ornament. He'll tell me in a minute that he's tired now, and that he wants to go to sleep.

As proof of the pudding, Mick yawned.

'I suppose you're tired now,' she suggested with barely concealed aggression.

'Well, I am feeling . . . a bit jangled,' he said apologetically. 'It was a bit of a shock.'

'So you'll be wanting to go to sleep,' she offered sardonically.

Choosing to be oblivious to her tone, he smiled weakly in gratitude for the cue. 'Just use the bathroom,' he said, sliding out of bed to cross the room.

'Don't forget your book,' Pauline snapped, seizing his yacht manual from the bedside cabinet and flinging it towards the bathroom door. When it hit Mick in the back of the knees, both of them were brought up short.

'Sorry,' she said curtly, when she met his injured gaze.

'We'll . . . do some more tomorrow,' he promised, full of guilt, as he returned the book to its previous resting place, and he bent to kiss her chastely on top of her head. 'I just don't think I can get back in the mood tonight, Poll, what with Gemma and everything.'

Pauline's lips tightened. 'Right,' she said. 'Fair enough.' As she watched him go back to the bathroom again, she suddenly decided that Asheem's bum was nicer than Mick's by far. If only he were here now, she thought bleakly, or if only I were back at home. Then I'd see some action.

There had been no rekindling of the fires of passion that night, then, and with few further words passing between them after Mick returned to bed from his ablutions, they eventually settled down under the covers a chaste – and in Pauline's case, a resentful – distance apart, to sleep. It helped her mood improve not one jot when, from the whiff of fragrance wafting from Mick's face as he snuggled down under the covers, she correctly inferred that he'd been in the en suite slopping on his new bleddy moisturiser.

Waking early the next morning, Pauline knew at once that she was in a bad mood, and after a few seconds of reflection, she remembered why. Her dreams had once again been vividly transgender, featuring Mick with shoulder-length blonde tresses and stilettos, dancing a fandango for a circle of admiring men. Turning to look at him, innocently sleeping, she felt venom exuding from her every pore, and though she tried to remind herself that her fears about the possibility of him being gay were more than likely all of her own making, nevertheless she felt rejected and betrayed. Why the bleddy hell was Chin's opinion so important to him? He'd recovered soon enough from the embarrassment of his daughter having seen what no child, even one who'd recently achieved her majority, ought to see her father do. He'd been the one who'd immediately said they shouldn't feel guilty. So what had stopped him carrying on where they'd left off once the cuckoo had flapped furiously out of the nest?

She turned again sharply to view her husband, her body stiff with umbrage, meaning to wake him roughly and demand an answer, when she saw, with utter astonishment, a projectile shape under the sheets which told her that she wasn't alone in her feelings of rigidity. It was the first time she had seen his wedding tackle ready for action in twelve months. Since their differing working hours always afforded her two hours longer in bed than Mick, who rose most days (and in most senses, had she known it) around six, the thought didn't occur to her for one second that what she was witnessing was the normal physiological phenomenon of the healthy male's morning erection and, shameless opportunist that she was, before you could say 'knife', she was at it.

To say that this was a rude awakening for Mick may be to understate his case: one minute he had been, in his dreams, at the helm of the Mackenzies' yacht, seamlessly steering a perfect course across the dancing waves and issuing the order to hoist that mainsail higher, and the next, he woke to the nightmare of being eaten alive. At least, that was what his sleep-befuddled mind told him, as it scrambled to awareness in flat panic.

Was it his fault, therefore, that his knee-jerk reaction was to fling the owner of the masticating mandibles three feet in the air and clear over to the other side of the room? Was it fair, as he pleaded later in his own defence, that he be held accountable for his first response being an ear-splitting scream of terror and repugnance? But there was no placating the feral monster in the sleep-tossed fright-wig, who rose menacingly on all fours from the place where she'd landed, and who stormed down the stairs in a huff. And wouldn't he have gladly followed her to iron out their misunderstanding if only shock, and the painful palpitations of his heart, hadn't kept him welded to the sheets? Surely anybody could understand that all he could manage in the circumstances was to call out 'Pauline' in a weak and placatory voice?

Not his wife, though, apparently. She was too busy banging things about in the kitchen.

He knew he'd disappointed her the night before, and he didn't feel good about it. But neither had he felt good about the world and its wife (or in this case, his daughter and his transvestite friend) knowing the ins and outs of his sex life. Although it was true that he'd managed to make a brave show of it in the immediate aftermath of their discovery, in the half-hour he'd had to himself while Pauline had been talking to Gemma his insecurities had eaten away at his self-confidence, and his father's criticising voice had been loud in his ear. What if Pauline wanted to have full sex when she returned, he'd started to worry. He'd wilfully put her in the mood for it, and she might just assume that everything was better now. He'd been following the advice of Ed Neuberger MD by the book, and had been glad to find that the good doctor's directives in Chapter Two, *Taking the Pressure Off*, really seemed to work. Once he had granted himself permission not to even attempt to go all the way, things had been a whole lot easier. Well, witness last night, before Gemma had burst in. But though Pauline had agreed to this new tactic in principle, say if she got overheated and hurried things along too fast, and then say if he failed – or his thing failed – to come up to scratch? That was when his dad had kicked in, reminding him that he was useless.

But even then, he'd tried to rally. He'd told the old pater-familias where to get off, and had turned to Dr Neuberger for comfort. He'd been reading the book systematically so far, but in his increasing panic he riffled through the chapters in search of words of wisdom about what worried him most: why was this happening to him, did it happen to other men or was he abnormal?

Turning to Chapter Five of *Trouble Down Below* he at last found his concerns addressed, but the two main physical reasons – alcoholism and drug addiction – had no resonance for him. Mick favoured a quieter life, evidently, than many of his fellow sufferers. Which only left Psychological Factors – Stress. Was he stressed? He turned this over in his mind. Well, of course, he must be. Why else would he be attacking his own confidence in the shape of his father's carping voice? But if so, what was he stressed about? More to the point, what had started stressing him out a year ago, and was continuing to stress him out now? None of the big traumatic events suggested by Dr Neuberger had come to challenge him: no divorce (although, at this rate, that would come sooner rather than later if he didn't buck his ideas up), he hadn't been recently bereaved nor lost his job, hadn't had a life-threatening illness (but then again, these heart flutters kept giving him the jitters). So what the bleddy hell was up with him? '*Nowt*,' his father cackled cruelly in his ear, '*that's the problem, you can't get it up, you big nance. You're a failure in bed, just like you've been a failure at everything the whole of your life.*'

And that had been when he'd heard Pauline galloping back up the stairs – he'd only just managed to shove his copy of *Trouble Down Below* under the bed in the nick of time – and what had she done? Only made his worst fears manifest, that was all. Come back in with a wicked gleam in her eye, wanting to recapture the mood. Well, he couldn't. He just plain couldn't. He knew it made no logical sense, but when she'd told him Gemma had gone to stay with Chin, he'd felt exposed, felt as if everybody – not just Pauline and his father and himself – knew that he was rubbish through and through.

Just thinking about it now made him flush with shame, and he threw off the bedclothes, feeling hot and out of sorts. 'Get a grip,' he told his accursed appendage accusingly. 'Stop bleddy monkeying about. You know that you can do it first thing in the morning, so it's obviously not physical – it's all in your head.' But *what* was in his head – what what *what*? He was no closer to cracking that than he was to satisfying his wife. He heaved a sigh and fished Ed Neuberger out from underneath the bed again. Maybe Chapter Six of the American sex guru's tome would hold the answer. But glancing at the heading – *Help Yourself: Beat Your Meat and Beat the Problem* – he seriously had his doubts.

*

Downstairs, Pauline was so angry that she was talking to herself out loud. But then she had to, otherwise she'd never have heard herself over the din of the cupboards she was slamming and the pots she was crashing. She was in such a strop that everything was getting on her nerves, and just now her chief bugbear was Lorna Mackenzie's bleddy streamlined kitchen. 'You can take bastard minimalism too bleddy far!' she cried, as she tried and failed to find the toaster behind any of the dozens of brushed stainless-steel doors. Having finally located it, she proceeded to make burned toast whilst also managing to burn herself on the kettle. 'I hate it here!' she screamed to the ceiling, as she hopped from foot to foot in pain and ran her injured hand under the cold tap.

This whole stupid idea had been a disaster from day one, thinking that Mick would change just because of a change of venue. She passionately wanted to be home – at least she knew where she kept things in her own kitchen – and now spite was fuelling her frustration, she didn't feel a bit guilty at this moment about her affair with Ash – Mick owed it to her to let her get her satisfaction elsewhere if he couldn't be bothered to do it. In fact, yes, she thought vengefully, she would bleddy well tell him about it if he didn't shape up. If she didn't get laid by the time they went home, she would give him an ultimatum: sort yourself out, or get used to the idea that I have a lover next door.

Too cross to go searching for the discreetly hidden waste bin, she scraped charcoal into the sink, and slammed what was left of the toast straight onto the granite work top, where she plastered it with too much butter and sank her teeth into it as if it were her bitterest foe. That's what she'd do all right, she vowed angrily – she'd bleddy well have her cake and eat it: live with Mick and shag Asheem. She could just see it, though. 'I'm off next door for a good rut then, love,' she'd tell him. He'd probably hardly glance up from one of his stupid bastard books: 'All right then, duck – will you be back in time for tea?'

What was it with him, why didn't he want her, she demanded of a mug as she slammed it down to scald its insides with hot tea. Why, amongst other things, was he being such a bleddy poofter with his face cream? And back she came to the question of his now questionable sexuality. Why had the thought of Chin knowing what they'd been up to upset him so much? Was Chin her rival, and if so, what was she supposed to do about that? Start wearing wigs and too much foundation? Pad her bra with falsies and mince about in four-inch heels?

Despite her anger she laughed at the image, and her mood lightened a little as she sipped her tea. Maybe she was over-reacting just a bit, she suggested to herself as she started to calm down. All this banging and crashing about in the kitchen reminded her of Gemma's hysterical displays, which was rather chastening. It was childish to have a temper tantrum when you couldn't have what you wanted. In fact, she thought, make that toddlerish – she was behaving like a very small person in their Terrible Twos who was being denied chocolate at the check-out.

In her own defence, however, she reminded herself that it had been a bit of a bastard shock, not to mention extremely rejecting, when Mick had kicked her off his whatsit just now. But then, replaying it in her mind, even that image made her suddenly giggle into her mug of tea. Looking at it from his point of view, she could see that she might have had a similar reaction if she'd woken up to somebody playing with her bits. Then again, she mused, these days, maybe not. Thinking about their attempts at love-making last night, it had been wonderful to receive Mick's best attentions, even without the satisfaction of a climactic release. It had been completely different from doing it with Ash – that was sex, not making love. Last night, there had been a wonderful sense of intimacy between them, which couldn't be matched by her randy boy lover. What she had been missing most, she started to realise, was her husband's desire for her, much more than just the physical act itself. It had made her feel attractive and wanted, loved and cherished, and she could certainly do with a bit more of that.

Now that she was feeling calmer she decided she'd apologise, take him some tea, talk things over more reasonably. This time, having already found the makings for breakfast, she managed to get the bread to toast to perfection, and she loaded it with strawberry jam from Lorna's vast fridge. She'd been silly about this place too – how could she hate it? It was like a show house for third-millennium living, was she mad? How great would it be to wake up every morning to this, to look out of the kitchen window and see this huge, beautifully planted garden, the Beemers waiting outside to whisk her to wherever she chose to go, the turquoise water of the swimming pool winking at her in the sun, and . . . wouldn't you just bleddy know it? Bleddy Chin waltzing across the driveway in her direction. What the hell did he want?

Stomping back upstairs, her new-found tolerance already having failed its first test, she yelled Mick's name – which was just as well since it gave him due warning of her return. In her current mood who knew what she'd have done if she had seen her husband, so soon after he'd rejected her own advances, with his hand down his pyjamas trying to commit self-abuse at Dr Neuberger's prompting? Killed him, probably. As it was, however, Mick had just enough time to hastily return the good doctor's manual to its hiding place under the bed, and to give up, with some relief, his unsuccessful attempt to 'beat his problem', which he had been doing joylessly and with a grim sense of duty to leave no stone unturned.

'Your friend's at the back door,' she told him. 'And there's some breakfast downstairs if you want it.' No way had she been going to bring it up for him now.

'Chin?' asked Mick, blushing at the idea of having to see him after Gemma had no doubt spared no details in the telling of her tale. 'Wonder what he wants?'

'You'd better go down and find out,' Pauline replied tersely. 'He's probably coming to beg us to take Gemma back, knowing what she's like when she's got one on her.'

But in the event, when Mick went down to see, Chin had come over for permission to borrow one of the cars. 'I'll get this girl of yours out of the way,' he said, winking suggestively.

'Is she all right then?' asked Mick bashfully as he handed him a set of keys.

Chin rolled his eyes. 'We're working on it. She thinks she's suffering from post-traumatic stress disorder. Honestly, darl, as a drama queen, she almost out-queens *me*! But it'll do you all good to get a bit of space. I can take her around and show her some of the sights.'

'Are you sure you don't mind?' Mick checked. 'Don't you need to rehearse for your show?'

'I do, but I can't-*lah*. Not without Linda Loveless, my "co-star" as she calls herself – really she's hardly more than a stooge!' Chin said with feeling. 'I mean, all she has to do most of the time is just stand there and look beautiful, while I have to do all the hard work, singing and dancing and strutting my stuff. We're supposed to be rehearsing her into the show today, and she's just called me from Sydney to say she isn't coming now until the day after tomorrow! She's met this man and it's *lurve*, apparently, and she can't tear herself away. I told her, if she isn't on that plane I shall fly up there myself and *whip* her all the way back to Melbourne on foot. Amateur! Anyway, I'll keep Miss Gemma out all day, so you and Pauline can have some quality time together. Have fun.' He looked him over appraisingly, hands on hips, and licked his lips. 'But from what I hear, you don't need any encouragement from me, you naughty little muff diver. See you.'

Feeling abashed about having done nothing to warrant his apparent new status of demon lover, Mick watched Chin sashay back across the garden and suddenly felt panicky about being left alone with Pauline for the day, once she knew they couldn't be interrupted by Gem. It cleared the way for renewed attempts at Doing It, and he still felt too demoralised for that – even more so now, in fact, since he'd got no result at all from his bash at a hand-job, except for an aching wrist and a sore whatsit.

'Wanted to borrow a car,' he called to her shouted query as he made his way slowly back upstairs. 'He's taking her out for a drive. Shall we do that?' he asked, suddenly inspired. If he could get her out of the house for a bit he might avoid potential humiliation, and maybe he'd be in the mood for it later, when he was feeling more relaxed.

'Fine,' said Pauline, biting back the impulse to suggest that instead, they went back to bed. What would be the point, after all? More rejection? No thanks.

The rather tense day of sightseeing which resulted brought neither of them any joy, although Mick's love of facts sustained him a little as he read her interesting bits from the guide book. Frankly Pauline couldn't have given a toss about Captain Cook's cottage having been brought stone by stone all the way across the world to be re-erected here. There was only one re-erection she was interested in, and she'd even gone off that now.

'He was probably homesick,' she said dismissively. At least she could relate to that. Personally she was as sick as a parrot to be stuck here instead of in her own home in Leicester, getting a good seeing-to from Asheem.

'No, it wasn't done till relatively recently, way after he'd died,' said Mick, ever the student.

Pauline laughed hollowly. 'Not in his lifetime, then. Quite a few of us have to get used to that.'

After dragging her round Fitzroy Gardens, South Melbourne market and the Maritime Museum, the day was almost gone, and Mick was in no doubt that he'd failed to distract her from their little problem (*'Very little,'* his father sniggered from his hiding place in Mick's head). Moreover, as the daylight started to fade and they were driving back to Black Rock, his own feelings of panic grew stronger. He'd promised Polly (Pauline, *Pauline*, get it right!) that they'd make another attempt at It today, and man of principle that he was, there was no getting away from the fact that he had to honour that. He only hoped that the wine might help relax him, and he poured a glass and drank liberally while Pauline angrily burned chops on the barbecue.

'I'm . . . sorry about this morning,' he finally ventured hesitantly, after they'd eaten the sacrificial lamb and he'd wiped the charcoal from his mouth and slugged more wine to take the taste away. 'It was just – I was asleep, and it was a bit of a shock.'

'Yeah, I'd worked that out, thanks,' said Pauline, unwilling to reciprocate the apology. 'So what should I do in future – make an appointment?' She knew she was being a bitch, but she couldn't help herself.

Mick laughed uncomfortably. 'I was wondering more if I could keep an appointment I'd made with you? I did say last night, didn't I, that we'd try to do some more today?'

'Well, that's a romantic way of putting it,' she sniffed, not in the least bit tempted. 'In fact, I was thinking of going for a swim.'

'Not straight after your meal, surely?' he called after her in alarm. She stopped short on her way to the house to get her swimming costume, and turned to give him a contemptuous glare. 'Who'd care if I drowned?' she challenged him, and not waiting for an answer, she disappeared inside. Mick could have kicked himself for being such a knob, but instead he downed the rest of the wine straight out of the bottle. What to do now? Follow her and get more abuse? Stay here to make sure she didn't do anything silly when she came back down? He was still debating the question when she returned in her bathers and jumped into the pool. There was no doubt about it, his marriage was on the line and drastic measures were called for, he decided, as he watched her cleave angrily through the water. Casting caution and his clothes to the wind, he stripped to the buff and followed her in.

'I'm being a prat, sorry,' he panted, as he resurfaced to see the astonishment on her face. 'I didn't mean to make it sound like a chore. I want things to get better between us just as much as you do, Poll, honestly – Pauline. Sorry.'

She was disarmed as much by his rash act of swimming on a full stomach as she was by his evident discomfort with her now. It didn't make her feel good to be seen as an ogre who had to be approached with such care. 'Oh, call me what you want,' she conceded, meaning to sound more gracious than she did. 'I've been a right tetchy cow lately.'

'And you've been well within your rights,' he assured her.

'Not entirely,' she admitted, thinking of Ash and her recent thoughts in that direction.

'The thing is,' Mick started bravely, having been resisting Dr Neuberger's advice to discuss his insecurities with his partner, 'this – trouble of mine – has been going on so long now, that when we do get round to doing something I get nervous and panicky when things go too fast. That's why I suggested taking the pressure off me by not trying to go all the way. It's not that I don't want to make love to you – I would if I could. But I'm trying to get my confidence back by degrees. I know that must be frustrating for you but, last night, before Gem came in, I thought we were doing quite well.'

He sounded so vulnerable that a feeling of shame was now added to Pauline's burden of guilt. 'We were doing well, Mick. It was very nice. Very adventurous and exciting. And nice for me to feel wanted by you. That's what I've been missing.'

'And that's what you're going to get more of,' he averred, and so saying, he dived underwater again.

Ironically, it was in the course of his ensuing demonstration of how much he wanted her, which involved a good deal of treading water on Pauline's part and an impressive display of breath control from Mick, that Pauline finally saw things from her husband's point of view. By the time he was on his ninth dive, she grabbed him by the ears and hauled him back up to the surface. 'It's no good, I can't concentrate,' she gasped, wiping water from her eyes. 'I keep just getting into it and then I start worrying one of us is going to drown. I can't relax enough.'

Mick nodded. 'Too much pressure?' he said sympathetically, and suddenly seeing the irony of their reversed roles at the same moment, they both laughed and hugged each other, bobbing up and down in the water to stay afloat.

'I do love you, Mick,' she said suddenly, with a catch in her throat.

'And I love you, Poll,' he returned, enjoying the closeness and the feel of wet flesh on wet flesh.

'I feel like I've just swum the Channel,' she said after a while, gently disengaging herself from his embrace. 'My legs are bleddy knackered.'

'Shall we go indoors, then?' he offered, and emboldened by the fact that it wasn't he who'd stopped things this time, he added playfully, 'As my queen and mistress knows, her word is my command.'

In the event, though, once they'd showered and washed the chlorine out of their hair, all his queen wanted was to snuggle up and go to sleep. It was all very nice that he wanted to give her pleasure, and she was touched that he was really trying to make things better, but once they were in bed and he was carrying on where he'd left off, she found she could no sooner relax properly on dry land than she could in the pool. 'It's hard for me to get into it, knowing I can't just let myself go,' she said apologetically. 'I don't trust myself not to get too excited and do something that might scare you, so I keep holding myself back.'

Mick was instantly cast down. 'I'm sorry,' he said. 'It's like a contagious disease. I've infected you with it now.'

'Not your fault, love,' she was quick to reassure him. 'And I suppose the upside is that at least I know what it's like for you now. Anyway, practice makes perfect. Like you said today, we'll do some more tomorrow.'

Mick was fully aware now, too, how unromantic that sounded. He propped himself up on his elbow, remembering then what he'd been planning in the romance stakes. 'I was having a look through those theatre and concert tickets earlier, that the Mackenzies had already booked for themselves in advance and left out for us to use while they're away. There are some tickets to the opera tomorrow night if we fancy it.'

'The *opera*?' said Pauline in a disappointed tone. Her taste in musical dramas leant more towards Andrew Lloyd Webber.

'It'd be a bit different, though, wouldn't it, Poll?' Mick said, trying to whip up her enthusiasm. 'We've never been to one of them, have we? It'll be an education.'

'Suppose so.'

'And now I know why we've never seen one,' Mick continued, still awestruck since looking properly at the tickets. 'It cost the Mackenzies three hundred dollars apiece – I think it's some charity do. Anyway, at that price our seats should be so close, we'll be practically on the stage! *And* we get to have free drinks at a reception! We'll get all dressed up, and have a proper date. Cos it's not all about sex, is it? It's about romance and enjoying quality time together. Getting in the mood.'

'You're right,' she said, smiling at his excitement.

'So how do you fancy this for a cracking day out tomorrow? We'll take the yacht out in the morning, and then finish off with champagne and opera. Ay? How much more romantic can you get than that?'

'That's brilliant, Micky,' she said, pulling him to her to hug him again so he wouldn't see her eyes sparkling with tears. How different they were, she thought guiltily. Posed with the same problem, she went off and shagged the boy next door, whereas Mick came up with inventive and adventurous ideas on how to improve things. She didn't deserve his goodness, and she knew it. 'You're the best,' she whispered.

'I will be, Polly,' he vowed, holding her tight. 'Don't give up on me yet. We'll get there eventually.'

'Or drown trying,' she joked, and grinning, they cuddled up to sleep.

The next morning, having seen neither hide nor hair of Gemma since she had stormed out two nights and a day ago, they both decided it was time for a rapprochement, and braving her own embarrassment and the thought of her daughter's continued hostility, Pauline crossed the gulf that separated them to knock on Chin's door, where she found to her huge surprise that she and Mick weren't the only ones to have been attempting change.

'Oh, we decided it was time she got that dead cat off her head and went for a different look,' Chin said airily, when her mother had sufficiently recovered from her surprise and dared to offer a compliment about her daughter's appearance. Gone were the tatty black hair extensions and instead a short crop in natural brown framed Gemma's newly revealed elfin face. Gone too was the white foundation, most of the facial metal ware and, miracle of miracles, the black lipstick. She looked healthier than Pauline had seen her in a long time. Since before Stu, in fact, but that insight she kept tactfully to herself.

'We thought we'd have a day out on the boat,' she said. 'Do you fancy coming along?'

'Fabulous!' exclaimed Chin, clapping his hands together. 'I love seamen!'

Falling back into her old ways in her mother's company, Gemma's smile faded and turned into a scowl. 'Depends if you're going to behave yourselves,' she warned pejoratively.

Before Pauline could leap to her own defence, Chin had done it for her. 'Now, darl, what have we said? Mummy and Daddy were just playing mummies and daddies. It's perfectly natural and we *all* do it.' He gave Gemma a meaningful look, at which she smiled back lecherously, telling Pauline more than she wanted to know about what she got up to with Stu, and making her feel deeply envious of this easy intimacy between her daughter and this relative stranger. And left out. Her new, more relaxed mood began to sour as she watched them, and she could almost feel her lip start to curl. In a few days, Chin had apparently managed to have more influence over Gemma than her own mother had had in years. Not to mention the effect he'd had on Mick and his wardrobe. What was it about him that was so seductive? Because personally, she just couldn't see it. And now he'd only gone and invited himself along with them on the bleddy boat ride.

'And what did we say last night, about what doors are for?' Chin continued to Gemma, in what sounded to Pauline like a rather smug tone.

'Knocking on,' Gemma replied dutifully, with a shocking absence of resentment.

Chin smiled indulgently. 'That's right, daughter. Boundaries, and space. We all need them – even elderly parents.' Gemma laughed.

Are they doing this on purpose, Pauline asked herself irritably, are they trying to make me feel jealous and excluded? But rearranging her features, she said instead, 'So shall we see you out front in about forty-five minutes?'

'Perfect,' said Chin, returning the car keys to her. 'That'll give us plenty of time to decide on our costumes. We shopped till we dropped yesterday, didn't we, Gemma? All that depressing old black just looked so wrong with her new image.'

On her way out, Pauline paused in the doorway and eyeballed him. 'You seem to have a way with making over members of my family, don't you?' she said, and despite the accusatory nature of her tone, Chin laughed with delight.

'Well, thank you. But then, they are such good clay to work with. I'll do you too, Pauline, any time you like,' he offered good-naturedly, scrutinising her with a professional air.

'Can't wait,' said Pauline, biting her tongue behind a terse smile, and feeling redundant and usurped, she left them to it.

Taking their maiden voyage on their own private yacht would have been adventure enough for anyone, even if Chin hadn't decided to come as Busty and Gemma hadn't fallen overboard. But as the day unfolded – which later came to include

Pauline and Mick involved in theft, deception and bondage, and ended with all three Watkins having to re-evaluate all that was dear to them – it became apparent that these events were merely a foretaste of the high drama in which they were about to be caught up, and a fitting prelude to the passion of the Australian Opera Company's gala performance of *Carmen* which Pauline and Mick attended later that evening. But to begin at the beguine . . .

Despite the short notice, Todd had swiftly reorganised his day after Mick phoned to tell him they were going to be putting the *Lovelorn* through her paces, and the lad was already there on deck doing efficient things with ropes by the time they finally managed to get themselves down to the quay – naturally Gemma and Busty kept everybody waiting while they messed about dressing up for the occasion, and then Gemma caused a further delay by insisting on dashing back to her room in the big house before she would allow them to leave.

Drumming her fingers impatiently on the steering wheel of the Beemer while she waited in the drive, Pauline was feeling no more kindly disposed towards Chin than ever, even before he eventually appeared as Busty, weighed down with bags, wearing a chiffon frock, espadrille wedges and a turban, and greeted Mick with an appreciatively drawled, '*Bonjour, matelot!*' But even she had to acknowledge that it was worth the wait to see Gemma emerge in her new linen slacks and dinky little voile top and with her hair and make-up done beautifully, *au naturel*. And Mick, who was less prepared for this transformation than her mother, had been absolutely gobsmacked.

'Gem, you look beautiful!' he'd exclaimed, giving her a gawping once-over as she joined them at the car. 'What have you done to your hair? It looks lovely.'

'Duh – cut it?' said Gemma sarcastically, her bad manners, alas, having remained untouched by her makeover. Although she rather liked the compliment, she was feeling out of sorts after having been prevented by Chin from calling Stu on June's phone. ('Greg and Lorna can afford it-*lah*, Junie can't,' he'd told her firmly yesterday, taking the receiver from her hand. 'If you want to talk to him, go back to the big house.') So for the last thirty-six hours she'd been unable to speak to him, and now she couldn't last another moment longer. 'You'll have to wait,' she told the assembled sailing party imperiously, and she strode over to Lorna and Greg's residence to abuse their hospitality some more.

Re-entering the beautiful bedroom which the randy, out-of-order behaviour of her parents had forced her to forsake, she felt doubly resentful towards them as she flopped down on her bed and dialled Stu's mobile. It wasn't fair that she had to miss out on staying here just because the crumblies couldn't control their baser instincts, and fun though it was to bunk up with Chin/Busty, the sofa-bed in June's cluttered granny annexe was certainly no match for all this.

'Stu? Hi!' she said into the receiver, a happy grin at last transforming her face as she heard her boyfriend's voice. 'It's me!'

'Oh – hiya,' he said, sounding inappropriately under-whelmed.

Gemma's grin vanished as quickly as it had appeared. 'What's the matter?' she asked.

'Nothing. Hang on a minute.'

Though she pressed her ear hard into the handset, she couldn't make out what he said next, but it was clear he was talking to somebody over the thumping background music. At last the line cleared a little, although when he spoke again he sounded all echoey.

'Where are you?' she asked, her suspicions aroused.

'In the bog,' he replied shortly. 'What's up?'

She'd been longing to tell him all about the over-aged sex she'd been forced to witness and to broach the subject of her new haircut, but now, she decided, was not the time. 'Nothing. I just haven't spoken to you for a bit, that's all,' she said, striving to echo Stu's offhand tone. 'In the bog where?'

'Party,' he said.

'Yeah?' she offered, hoping to encourage him to give more information, but, 'Yeah,' was all he replied.

'Good?'

'Not bad.'

'Nice one,' she said, with false enthusiasm. 'So what's the time over there?'

'Duh – I dunno, I don't wear a watch, remember?' he said, using the kind of sarcasm which Gemma herself reserved solely for use on her parents.

'Right. So,' she responded, as hurt by this, if she had bothered to reflect on it, as her father had been only minutes before at her own hands. 'Who's there then?' she said, knowing full well that she was starting to sound like a loser.

'Usual suspects.'

'Yeah?'

'Yeah.'

'Cool.' After dying to speak to him for so long, she was now bitterly regretting having made the effort. 'Well, anyway, I'd better get off,' she continued, at least having the nous to be the one who had something better to do than have this stilted conversation. 'A few of us are going out on the yacht.' No need to specify that the few of whom she spoke comprised her parents, and a drag queen who'd decided to come as Greta Garbo.

'Yeah, right,' he responded, unimpressed. 'Better not be late for that.'

It was just possible, she thought optimistically, that he was miffed with her for not calling him sooner. 'So have you been missing me?' she asked coyly, unable to resist.

'I'm surviving,' he said wryly. 'See ya later.'

Returning the receiver to its cradle, Gemma almost lost the will to live, but catching sight of herself slumped in the mirror on the opposite wall she was disgusted at how like a victim she looked, despite her new image (which actually, she thought, as she was drawn to examine her reflection more closely, wasn't half bad, considering), and posing with her shoulders pulled back and her cheeks sucked in, she stalked outside to the car with the backward-leaning gait of a supermodel. Stu could be a moody bugger sometimes, and he was probably just feeling jealous not to be here with her, enjoying all this.

Well, let him feel jealous, she thought feistily, as Mum drove them down the hill and she gazed out of the car window at the sun sparkling on the blue, blue sea below. He should. Do him good not to take her for granted. And if he'd thought she wouldn't come to Australia just because he couldn't afford it, she'd shown him different. It was well wicked here, and he could have been enjoying it with her if he'd just stuck at any one of the half-dozen temp jobs he'd tried for a day and walked out of. She'd done her bit, waiting tables, cleaning offices.

But they'd arrived at the marina, and these uncharacteristically critical thoughts towards Stu were chased away by the sight of their very own yacht, the *Lovelorn*. And there was Toddy boy, busy doing boy things on deck. Glancing at him, and conscious of her own attractiveness and striking change of image, she suddenly felt well wicked herself. She had to admit he was fit. *Well* fit, as it happened.

So, anyway – Stu, she thought, shaking herself as Mum parked and they all got out of the car. Yes, Stu. Well, basically, he was out enjoying himself at a party without her, wasn't he?

So why shouldn't she enjoy herself without him? It wasn't as if she was going to *do* anything anyway, but it might be nice to have a bit of a flirt. Knowing Stu, he was more than likely doing exactly the same right now. Or worse, she acknowledged, with a sudden spasm of horror, if Jacqui bleddy Reeves was at the party, who they'd had words about before. Could that have been who he'd been talking to before he'd gone into the bogs? Well, bugger that. If that was what he was up to, she'd soon show him.

Ignorant of his daughter's reasons for her vamping progress across the quay, Mick was happily surprised to note Gemma's more than friendly greeting of Todd as he welcomed them aboard, and pleased too when he saw the lad's amazed reaction to her new image. For today of all days, Mick was in the mood for romance, and if that included Gem being attracted to a nice lad like Todd instead of that waste of space back home, all the better.

'Well,' said Todd, turning to Mick with a smile, visibly forcing himself to stop ogling Gemma. 'Are we right then, skipper?'

Flattered and terrified in equal measure to be identified as the man in charge, Mick agreed that they were indeed right then, and went off with Todd to address the business of getting under way. Though he was nervous about his first time out on a boat, he had been studying the yacht manual with the same assiduousness as he'd been applying himself to Dr Neuberger's teachings, and before too long, Pauline – who was not much of a sailor herself either – was relieved to see that his diffidence was replaced by an air of determined concentration and quiet confidence. Her face softened as she watched him move about the deck and man the helm. This was her Mick at his best, she thought – competent and sure of himself with the complexity of practical things. She sighed, sad to think that this self-confidence didn't carry over into the bedroom. Oh well, no use brooding, she told herself sharply, and noting that Busty and Gemma had gone into a huddle together over the bags of clothes and wigs that Busty had insisted on bringing for some strange reason known only to their little club of two, she resentfully comforted herself with being the martyr who had thought to bring the makings for lunch, and went below decks in search of the galley to stow things away sensibly in the fridge.

And sod it, yes, to change into her bikini, to cover herself in factor thirty, and to take a glossy mag and a glass of white wine back up on deck to sunbathe. For wasn't she on the biggest, most expensive, most exotic holiday she was ever likely to have in her life? Wasn't she supposed to be having quality time, she asked herself crossly, as she spread out her lonely towel and laid herself on it, trying to remain deaf to Gemma and Busty's irritating giggles – what the hell were they up to? She peered at them covertly over the top of her magazine and finally understood why Busty had brought all the changes of frocks. They were organising a photo session for publicity shots for Busty's show, with Gemma doing her David Bailey (with the outrageously expensive SLR camera that *she*, Pauline, the vilified and unappreciated mother, had saved up to buy for her when she'd insisted on doing photography A level), and Busty going over the top with daft poses and trilling, 'I am Qveen Christina and I am lookink enikmatic, because I vant to be alone,' which Gemma, inexplicably, found to be the funniest thing she'd ever heard.

But despite feeling excluded from the girls' gang, it was impossible to remain in a huff with the boat skipping merrily over the waves, with the sun warming her skin, the salt breeze on her face, and the nice drop of chardonnay finding its mark. Pauline settled down more comfortably, abandoning her attempts to focus on the magazine, and drifted into a long and pleasant doze which wasn't disturbed until the sounds of screams and urgent shouting alerted her to the fact that there was a man overboard, and that that man was her daughter.

If the gods had set themselves the task of looking after Gemma's welfare personally and protecting her from all harm, they couldn't have done better than to have dispatched a guardian angel like Busty to oversee her transformation from ugly duckling to beautiful swan, for it meant that all human eyes were on her – and particularly Todd's.

It was true that he had already found her appearance eye-catching enough at their last meeting, pre-makeover, but that was because Todd was good at seeing beneath people's surface presentation. He had never been big on grunge or goth, and had been surprised to have found himself thinking about Gemma quite a bit since she'd blown hot and cold at him the other day. Surprised too to find himself longing for Mick's call. When it had finally come, early this morning, his first excited thought had been about how to get her to come out with him this evening to the party he'd been invited to, and his second thought had been about what his friends would say if she did.

So when he'd caught sight of her crossing the quay and coming towards the *Lovelorn*, completely and utterly transfigured into a creature of unsurpassable beauty and grace, he had been buffeted by a mixture of emotions which ranged from incredulity and anxiety that his eyesight was failing him, through to wonder, awe, and aaah, sweet mystery of love, hope that maybe, just maybe, this metamorphosis had been wrought with him in mind.

And though sailing was his absolute first love – and sailing Greg Mackenzie's *Lovelorn* in particular was always an eagerly anticipated treat – he had found the usually exciting procedures of putting out to sea to be little more than an unwelcome distraction from his primary aim, which was to engage Gemma on her own in conversation, to impress her with his charm and wit, and to invite her out this very night. Thus, though his industriousness and diligence in showing Mick the ropes could not have been faulted, not once was Gemma out of his thoughts while he set to to trim the sails, and rarely was she out of his sight.

He had watched the accident in the making through every heart-stopping moment while he'd been working the Genoa winch. Gemma had been setting up a shot of Busty who was posing in the companionway, and in order to avoid her dad at the wheel, she had stepped down onto the bathing platform in the stern which was a mere foot above water, its surface depth being barely more.

It had been like watching the old gag when the photographic subject keeps being instructed to back up until they fall off the edge of the cliff, but in reverse. In this case it was the photographer who, absorbed in framing the shot through her lens, had forgotten her relationship between dry deck and sea, and had stepped back into the fathomless abyss. But though Todd had clearly seen it coming, when it happened it was like in a dream, where despite everything being in slow motion, the outcome was inevitable, the distance to be covered between rescuer and rescued an impossible chasm, a bridge too far. Even his attempt at calling out a timely warning seemed to him to be like trying to shout through treacle, and his eventual cry of alarm came too late to alert Gemma to the danger, but merely accompanied her on her journey into the deep.

Thereafter, however, everything happened so fast it was a blur. In one huge and daring swallow dive taken at a run, Todd cleared the gunnels by a whisker, swam aft with strokes super-charged by the adrenalin which was surging through his veins, found her, grabbed her, and threw her back up from whence she'd come. By the time he'd heaved himself up to join her on the bathing platform, fully prepared to administer the kiss of life, he could see from the look in her mercifully open eyes that no plan he could have hatched in his wildest dreams could ever have been as effective as this in getting her to notice him.

After that, he was sure that various people did various sensible and practical things to make them both more comfortable, like finding towels and improvising coverings while their own clothes dried out in sun and wind, but all Todd was aware of was being close to Gemma, and being in a warm and happy daze.

Since their progress had been arrested by Gemma's near-death experience and they were already at anchor, once everything was shipshape again and hearts were out of mouths and back in chests where they belonged, Pauline suggested lunch. There was a general giddiness in the air due to everyone's relief that disaster had been averted, and even Gemma chose, atypically, not to sulk about her accident, but to laugh about it. All in all the picnic was a relaxed and happy affair and proof, thought Mick, noting Gemma's new warmth towards Todd, of the truth of the old saying about ill winds. Well, if that was the case, he would put it to the test again immediately.

'Are you really feeling okay now, Gem?' he asked her unnecessarily, since the sparkle in her eyes said it all, and receiving her answer in the affirmative, he continued, 'Cos Mum and I were thinking of using some of the tickets, tonight, that the Mackenzies left out for us and there's only two. Would you be okay on your own if we went?' Short of taking Todd to one side and commanding him to date his daughter, this was as far as he could go, he felt, in helping to prepare the lad's way.

'Sure,' said Gemma with a smile. She glanced cheekily at Todd before mimicking him. 'No worries,' and both kiddies laughed like drains.

Really, thought Pauline in surprise, having already written off the possibility of her and Mick leaving Gemma that evening, if she's this amenable after being snatched from the jaws of death we should have tried drowning her years ago and at regular intervals.

'You could come out with me, if you like,' Todd offered, striving for the right balance between sounding offhand and welcoming. 'A few of my mates are having a party. They've rented a warehouse – it'll be pretty cool.'

'Wicked,' said Gemma. That'd be one in the eye for Stu, she thought, when she told him she'd been out partying too. Hey Mr Gander, meet Ms Goose.

'So what are you going to see tonight?' Busty asked conversationally, and when Mick said, '*Carmen*,' she screamed. Naturally she had everybody's undivided attention.

'What?' said Mick uncertainly. 'Isn't it any good?'

'Good, darl? *Good?* Quite apart from it being my absolute favourite . . .' Here, Busty interrupted herself to give unexpectedly full and fine voice to the first few lines of '*L'amour est un oiseau rebelle*', and graciously acknowledging the spontaneous applause this occasioned, she continued, '. . . tonight's gala performance is also the social event of the *year*! The tickets are like gold dust! Trust Greg Mackenzie to have got some. And I bet his include the VIP reception?'

'We do get to have champagne and nibbles,' Mick affirmed, feeling rather guilty now, since Busty would clearly have given anything to be in their place.

Busty started to hyperventilate theatrically, flapping her hands in a paroxysm of hysteria. 'Oh, oh, oh, oh,' was all she could currently say.

Here it comes, thought Pauline sourly, she's going to try and blag our tickets off us and Mick'll give in, just watch.

But not for the first time, and certainly not for the last, Busty confounded her expectations. 'You have *got* to let me make you over for it, darl,' she said, grabbing Pauline's arm in her excitement. 'You said yourself earlier that you just couldn't wait, and now you won't have to!'

Back at Black Rock, the party repaired to the big house – all except Todd, whose day's deferred commitments now had to be met before calling for Gemma at ten. They would be out all night at the party, he told Mick and Pauline, if that was okay with them? He'd have Gemma back in time for breakfast, and they could call him any time on his mobile if they were worried. How nice to be asked, they both thought, as they agreed that would be fine, and how unusual for them to feel that she would be in safe hands.

Mick was given first go in the bathroom, and he repaired there as usual carrying a book.

'Not more sailing study?' Pauline asked him affectionately. 'Surely you don't need it – you did really well today, Mick.'

'Thanks,' he said, hiding the title of Ed Neuberger's manual behind his back as he stood in the open doorway, his egress impeded by Pauline wanting to give him a hug and a kiss. 'Well, you know – there's always more to learn.' He so wanted the day to end perfectly once they'd returned home from the opera, that he thought he'd revise the chapter on psychological stress in the hope of heading off more trouble down below. He was already getting nervous and regretful that, once again, he had set himself up to be under pressure later, with all his talk the night before of this day of romance, and getting themselves in the mood.

He was spared the need for further duplicity about the

nature of his study by Busty tapping on their bedroom door, impatient to inspect Pauline's limited holiday wardrobe for anything remotely suitable for the gala, and gratefully he retired into the en suite, locking the door behind him.

'I haven't brought much,' Pauline told Busty defensively, as she directed her to the small portion of Lorna Mackenzie's wardrobe where she'd hung her few going-out garments.

'Hmm,' said Busty, critically flicking through the rail. 'I wonder if I might have something you could borrow.'

Looking at her current costume, on the tip of Pauline's tongue was, 'Only if I want to look like a man in drag,' but instead she said, 'I'll leave you to it for a bit then. I'm just going to check on Gem.'

To her surprise she found Gemma hugging her knees on her bed and close to tears.

'What's the matter, love?' she asked her, and dared to take her in her arms, which mostly these days wasn't allowed, except for occasions like this.

'I was just thinking about Stu,' Gemma told her on trembling lips.

'Yes?' said Pauline. Her heart sank. Like Mick, she had taken a shine to Todd, and having watched Gemma after he'd rescued her from drowning, she had high hopes that she had too. Not that it could go anywhere, she'd reminded herself, what with him being in Australia and Gemma returning to Leicester before too long, but a little holiday fling with him might just open Gemma's eyes to possibilities other than Stu. 'What were you thinking?'

'It's just sunk in that I could have died today,' said Gemma dramatically, hiccuping on a sob. 'And how would he have coped if I had, all alone?'

'Right,' said Pauline, wondering privately if what Gemma wasn't actually suffering from was the pre-emptive guilt of knowing she was attracted to Todd and feeling bad about putting herself in temptation's way at tonight's party. Though it was her daughter who had the A level in psychology, Pauline's own experience of the shame which can result from sexual misconduct had been learnt literally hands on. 'Well, Gem, you've had a big shock,' she said practically, rocking her daughter gently in her arms. 'And it's shaken you up. But you didn't die, and even if Todd hadn't rescued you' – no harm, she thought, in reminding Gemma which of her beaus was the life-saver, and which the life-denier – 'I'm sure you'd still have been okay. You're a strong swimmer, and a resourceful girl.'

'Do you think so?' asked Gemma, pleasantly surprised to receive praise from her mother, and going fishing for more.

'Course you are, you're clever, like your dad,' said Pauline, suddenly conscious too that these days she tended to dole out more criticism to Gemma than compliments. It was nice to find this little oasis of calm between themselves, away from the pressures of everyday life.

'I'm really sorry about drowning the camera,' Gemma said in a small voice. 'I know it cost a lot.'

'Ah, love,' said Pauline, hugging her tight, quite choked herself now. 'The camera's nothing, compared to having you safe. We can always save up for a replacement, but I'd never have another one like you.'

'Well, that'd be a bonus,' Gemma laughed, her maudlin thoughts on her own mortality lifting. 'So anyway – what do you really think about my hair?'

Pauline could hardly believe her ears. It had been a long time since her daughter had asked her opinion on anything, least of all her appearance. She was struck, as she was invited to examine her now, that she was looking at the face of the beautiful young woman Gemma was becoming, rather than the gauche young girl who had been hiding behind a curtain of rats' tails. 'It's great,' she told her carefully, conscious that, despite their current closeness, it was still fragile enough for any comment she made now to be construed as criticism. 'It really suits you, Gem. Brings out your features. You look really striking. Amazing.'

Gemma grinned self-consciously. 'I just hope Stu thinks so when I get back home,' she said. 'One minute Busty was playing with my hair, the next she's got these big scissors out, and it's all on the floor. She's bleddy bossy. Makes you seem like a pussy cat by comparison.'

Pauline almost purred. How nice it was to be complimented on her mothering skills, albeit by default. She only hoped this new mood of Gemma's would last.

'Actually,' Gemma continued, glancing round the beautiful room, 'I might move back in here now.'

'Really?' said Pauline, trying to sound pleasantly surprised.

'Yeah,' said Gemma. 'It's been great being with Busty. But I didn't half miss all this.'

'Right,' said Pauline, wondering if now would be the moment to reiterate Busty's lesson about space and boundaries concerning old married couples. But even as she thought this, Busty herself was calling for Pauline outside the door.

'You go, I'm all right now. Thanks for cheering me up,' said Gemma. 'I'm going to have a nice long wash. I've been missing this power shower and all.'

Heavens, thought Pauline, as she got up to open the door. Even if Gemma did resist the temptation of having a flirtation with Todd, the change of hairstyle wasn't all Stu was going to have to get used to on her return. Betrayal of the working class and the embrace of consumer culture was going to take some swallowing down too.

On the landing outside, Busty Springboard-A-Go-Go was agog with excitement. 'I have found the most perfect thing for you-*lah*!' she said, holding up a frock which Pauline at first took doubtfully, and then, as she examined it more closely, handled reverently. It was the quintessential little black number of every woman's dreams, which she was sure had once had a price tag to match.

'Is this one of yours?' she asked doubtfully, for nothing she had seen of Busty's wardrobe so far had ever hinted at such understated restraint.

'Isn't it yours?' asked Busty. 'I found it in your closet.'

'Must be one of Lorna Mackenzie's,' Pauline said, handing it back regretfully.

'So borrow it,' said Busty shamelessly.

'I can't do that!'

'Yes you can, Mum,' insisted Gemma, who had joined them to exclaim about the quality of the cut and the gorgeous weight of the material. 'She won't know, and you'll look deadly in this! Come on, just slip it on and have a look at yourself,' she tempted, leading her mother back into her bedroom by the hand.

Against her better judgement but in tune with her desires, Pauline did as she was instructed and the three of them crowded excitedly round the mirror. There was no question about it – it was fabulous. 'No, I couldn't,' she said slowly, but nevertheless admiring herself from every angle.

'But you *must*, darl – it was made for you!' insisted Busty.

'You could have it dry-cleaned after,' coaxed Gemma.

Pauline's resolve wavered, lust overcoming circumspection. 'Hand finished,' she asserted, and with that codicil on laundering agreed, the deal was done.

Emerging unsuspecting from the bathroom, Mick proved to be a tougher nut to crack in the matter of wearing Greg Mackenzie's tuxedo, but with two women and a transvestite working on him in concert, cracked he was, and wear it he did.

'But it's stealing,' he protested, as his arms were being shoved down the sleeves.

'It's only borrowing,' his daughter corrected him. 'And you wouldn't mind if he wanted to wear any of your stuff.' Not that that was likely, she thought, judging by the quality of these clothes – unless Greg had a hidden fetish for baggy polyester mix.

'And June told us to make ourselves at home,' Pauline reminded him, there being no more fervent believer than a recent convert. 'It was in her note – "Use anything," she said.'

'Besides which, Dorothy,' said Busty, stepping back to admire her handiwork and pushing husband and wife together in front of the mirror, 'just take a look at that and then tell me what you think.'

Gazing awestruck at his own reflection, side by side with his stunning wife, Mick had to admit that they looked the absolute bees' knees – like a couple from a film. But the clincher for him was Pauline's pleading, questioning look. How could he deny her the pleasure of wearing that frock when she looked so beautiful in it? And if she did wear it, how could he escort her in anything of his own that he'd brought over in his case? Or anything he'd ever owned, come to that.

'We'll just have to be very, very careful,' he relented, under the hypnotic sway of the three pairs of eyes which were willing him to yield. 'And no choc ices in the interval,' he warned Pauline severely.

So great was the buzz that night at the Sydney Myers Music Bowl that it radiated out down all the roads which led to it, as lucky gala-goers queued up patiently to park their cars for Melbourne's charity event of the year. But Mick and Pauline Watkins were spared even this minor inconvenience, since Mick had spotted in the swanky folder which accompanied their top whack tickets that they should make for Car Park 'A', where their complimentary parking voucher was politely examined, and their convertible BMW coupé was waved in quickly and efficiently by a smartly uniformed official. From there, it was a short and pleasant stroll to the conveniently sited Star Bar, where a champagne reception awaited them. By the time they entered those hallowed portals and joined their fellow gold-pass holders, any guilt they might still have been suffering in respect of stolen clothes was replaced with an overwhelming sense of relief that they had allowed themselves to be persuaded to wear appropriate costume.

'Bleddy hell fire,' whispered Pauline, glancing round at the assembled throng after she had effusively thanked a passing waiter for being so kind as to give them their glasses of bubbly. 'Talk about posh, Mick! They all look like they're famous, don't they? I bet you if we lived here we'd know all these faces. Oh my God – isn't that the bloke off *Neighbours* over there?'

'Could be,' said Mick, lifting his head from his perusal of the programme. He wasn't much of a soap aficionado, outside the bathroom. He grinned at Pauline, neither of them able to believe their luck, and they clinked glasses. 'Better than a poke in the eye with a sharp stick, isn't it, Mother?'

'Not half,' she agreed, and in the lingua franca of Leicester they could not have bestowed higher praise.

Liveried waiters circulated the crowd with silver trays bearing tiny tempting morsels, of which the Watkins enthusiastically availed themselves (and under Mick's instruction, ate very carefully and with napkins tucked in their necklines, in order to avoid accidents), and it seemed to them that no matter how much champagne they sipped, their glasses were seamlessly and invisibly replenished. They were already feeling quite mellow when a general shushing presaged 'A message from our President', and after being congratulated by him for giving so generously to the charity he headed, they were encouraged to take their seats, and to enjoy the performance.

Following the glittering exodus towards the auditorium, Mick and Pauline found to their surprise that they emerged once more into the warm night air, and were directed to the VIP section of a vast outdoor arena, already thronged by eager opera lovers. Above them, the first stars started to twinkle in the darkening evening sky, and as they settled themselves comfortably in their well-placed seats, the stage lights went up, the orchestra stood to welcome the presence of their august conductor, and taking their cue from their neighbours, the Watkins joined in the applause.

Pauline had not been looking forward to the actual performance – particularly since Mick had told her it would be sung in French and had felt it necessary to brief her on the plot from the programme notes so she could follow the story, which she had thought sounded a bit overblown. But from the very first crashing opening chords of the Prélude she was on the edge of her seat with excitement, and delighted to find some of the songs so familiar. And Carmen herself was so passionate. The shameless way she seduced the upright Don José and got the poor man to fall hopelessly in love with her, to turn his back on all that was dear to him and allow her to escape arrest, was about the sexiest thing Pauline had ever seen.

'What a minx!' she said excitedly to Mick, as they made their way back to the Star Bar in the interval.

'She's no better than she ought to be,' agreed Mick.

'And I didn't realise I'd know so many of the tunes,' she said, grabbing a glass of champagne from a touring waiter, as if now to the manner born.

'Me neither,' said Mick. Avid student that he was, he had decided to do something when they got home about filling the huge void in his knowledge about opera. 'If anybody asks what I want for my birthday, I wouldn't mind a CD of this. Wouldn't mind going to some more operas after this, either. Might see what's on at the De Mont,' he offered, speaking of Leicester's touring concert venue.

But before Pauline could manage to endorse this sentiment with enthusiasm of her own, two strange hands had clamped them both by the shoulders from behind, and turning with a start, she recognised their owner as the man in the seat next to theirs.

'You've got to be Lorna and Greg's guests from England,' he told them jovially. 'I'm their mate Bryce, and this is my wife, Fern.'

A beady-eyed woman popped out from behind him and smiled at them tightly. 'We'd booked tonight as a foursome, before they decided to go haring off O.S.,' she explained, 'so we guessed it must be you sitting next to us, once we'd heard your accents.'

'Oh, right, hello there!' said Mick, stammering guiltily. He eased his shoulder out of Bryce's grasp, terrified lest he recognise the feel of his friend's evening suit.

'Pauline and Mick,' said Pauline, equally on edge but with more reason, for didn't the men's tuxedos all look pretty much the same, whereas she might just as well have had an arrow above her, pointing down at Lorna Mackenzie's designer frock. 'Pleased to meet you,' she said, looking anything but, as she folded her arms across her chest in a vain attempt to hide any distinguishing couturier features from Fern's look of quizzical scrutiny.

'So you've done a house swap over the Internet,' Lorna's friend said to her now, in what seemed to Pauline to be a loaded tone. 'That okay? I said to Lorna that personally I wouldn't really like it, somebody I didn't know being in my home. Not that I mean to suggest that you two aren't looking after everything for them beautifully over at Black Rock.' She gave a brittle and humourless laugh, and Pauline's heart sank. She knew. 'Didn't you feel like that, Pauline? You know, worried that strangers, people you'd never met, would be wandering round your home without you there, and maybe abusing your trust?'

'No, not at all,' said Pauline with conviction, for that much at least was true. She hadn't given a thought to the possible abuse of her things, for what was there to abuse? Nothing they owned was new or expensive, and it certainly hadn't occurred to her to lock up her wardrobe. 'We dealt mainly with June – Lorna's mother?'

Fern nodded, saying nothing, waiting, Pauline felt, for her to hang herself.

'She seemed really nice in her e-mails, and I spoke to her a couple of times on the phone,' she continued, praying for the interval to be over and this awkward conversation to be at an end. 'I just hope they're having such a great time in our house as we're having in theirs.'

To her huge relief, the bell sounded for the return to their seats. 'Oh dear, better get back,' she smiled apologetically, and downed her champagne to take Mick's arm and lead him away. After all, she knew she was as good at lying as Carmen the gypsy, but her nice husband would crack immediately under the slightest interrogation and blab the truth, the whole truth, and nothing but the truth – so help them God.

'We'll come back with you,' said Bryce genially, interposing himself between them, and added conversationally, 'I'm working with Greg at the moment, Mick. We're both in property development, got a big office block project we're working on together in the CBD. You might have seen it going up if you've been over that way – the Swan Tower?'

'Oh,' said Mick, feeling completely out of his depth. 'No, but – very nice.'

'So what line are you in, then?' Bryce inevitably asked as a follow-up, and as her husband's lips were preparing themselves to damn them with the words 'plumbing repairs', Pauline butted in quickly, 'Washing machines mostly, Bryce.' For how could a repair man's missus afford this dress, which she was going to have to claim as her own if bleddy Fern didn't stop being so suspicious?

'Oh right, retail,' said Bryce, more easily duped than his wife. 'White goods. Quite a small profit margin in them, I gather, Mick. I guess you have to be pretty competitive?'

'Well, you know,' Mick faltered, feeling the pressure of Pauline's hand tightening on his bicep. 'We get by.'

Bryce laughed heartily, clapping Mick across the back. 'You Poms and your understatement,' he said amicably. 'Well, if you are doing okay and you find you've got a bit of spare cash at some time in the future, Greg and I are always looking for investment, Mick. Melbourne's where it's happening these days, mate.'

'Right,' said Mick, thinking of the two hundred and seventy-six pounds forty-three pee which was currently accruing two point five per cent interest in his savings account at the Woolwich. 'Well, not at the moment, but I'll bear it in mind.'

Pauline relaxed her grip on his arm, feeling safer now as they had arrived at their row and she could see the orchestra filing back in. She was quite proud of Mick that he was carrying this off so well, and privately she was starting to see the funny side of their duplicity, already framing it in her mind as a good story to entertain the folks back home. Rather too soon for the dogged Fern, however.

'It's an amazing coincidence that you and Lorna go for the same designer,' she said disingenuously, pinning Pauline with her accusatory gaze as they reclaimed their seats. 'She's got that exact same dress. Bought it quite recently as a matter of fact.'

'Really?' said Pauline, in a creditable attempt at incredulity. 'I've had this old thing ages. Mick bought it for me when he was over in Paris on business – how long ago would you say that was now, Mick – five years? Six?'

'Getting on for that,' her husband muttered supportively from his hiding place behind his programme. He cleared his throat and studied the notes for Act II in what he hoped would seem to be a preoccupied manner.

To Pauline's delight Fern looked quite put out as she continued. 'Yes, I keep meaning to sling it out – I've had so many new ones since there's hardly room in my wardrobe – but as Mick chose it himself for one of my birthdays, it's got sentimental value for me. I'm surprised Lorna could still get hold of one after all this time. But maybe she's got a copy?' she concluded wickedly as she watched the conductor take his place at the podium.

Enthusiastically applauding his return – as much for him saving her from further inquisition as for his performance – Pauline settled down to listen to the Entr'acte, but couldn't resist taking a quick glance at Fern first. Now it was she who had her arms folded across her chest in defensive posture, and from the bitter set of her mouth you'd have thought she'd been sucking lemons. Pauline grinned wickedly in the darkness, her hand straying to squeeze Mick's thigh. She was grateful and gleefully surprised that he had backed her up in her mendacity – he was normally such a stickler for honesty – or a stick-in-the-mud, as she sometimes thought unflatteringly. Perhaps, as much as she was feeling emboldened by the proud and wilful spirit of the opera's eponymous heroine, he had been similarly influenced by Don José's rejection of the straight and narrow path. The thought made her feel powerful and sexy, an archetypal temptress, capable of seducing a duty-bound man away from the correctitude of his moral high ground and off into the bushes for a little bit of what he fancied and a lot of rumpy-pumpy. Giddy with champagne, she squirmed in her seat with anticipation. Much as she wanted to watch the rest of Carmen's story, she could hardly wait to get her hands on Mick at home. After all, hadn't he spoken of this evening being about getting themselves in the mood? Job done, as far as she was concerned. And hadn't he already shown signs of wicked rebellion, of a willingness to be led astray by her?

Driving back in the open-topped sports car after what they both agreed wholeheartedly had been the best and most exciting evening of their lives, they giggled like naughty school-children about their near discovery and how they'd so skilfully avoided detection.

'The look on her face! And when Bryce gave you his card at the end,' Pauline chortled, 'and reminded you about investing in his company. He must have thought we were loaded!'

'Serve them right,' said Mick unashamedly. 'Couple of snobs.'

'So when are you going back to Paris to get me another new frock?' asked Pauline playfully, stroking his knee.

'Well, you heard Bryce,' Mick laughed in return. 'Not much profit margin in white goods. We might even have to cancel our Christmas cruise.'

'God, it was brilliant, though, wasn't it, Mick?' Pauline sighed, leaning back luxuriously in her leather seat and stretching out her legs. Witnessing Carmen's waywardness, her fickle treatment of the soldier who had given up his career for her, followed by her whirlwind affair with the cocksure, strutting toreador, had inevitably drawn her thoughts to her own situation – married to Don José and shagging Escamillo next door. It was undeniably exciting, but it was dangerous, and although she couldn't imagine Mick ever stabbing her in a jealous rage, it reminded her again of how hurt he would be if he were to discover her infidelity, and how much she was therefore putting at risk: the security and stability of her married relationship, not to mention a friendship which had spanned two and a half decades. But watching the opera had also inspired her to hope again that Mick might be persuaded to change, just as Don José had. It was up to her to inflame him with desire like the shameless Carmen, to make him feel as if she danced for him alone, to tickle his appetite, to tease him beyond endurance – to take a much more pro-active sexual role in fact, she now admitted to herself, than had ever previously been her wont.

'Fancy some more bubbly?' she suggested as they let themselves in through the kitchen, hoping to disinhibit him. She turned to fix a smouldering gaze on him, pouting, doing a take-off of Carmen. 'We can have it upstairs in my room, if you like, señor.'

'Si,' Mick readily agreed, entering the game. 'You go. I bring.' He watched her exit all the way up the open-plan stairs as she wiggled her bum provocatively for his benefit, and at the very top she turned back to him to wink and crook her finger, inviting him to follow, before disappearing from his view.

She was not alone, as it happened, in having been influenced by the opera's story. Given the choice of the two male roles, Mick wanted more than anything to be the swaggering, potent Escamillo rather than the tortured Don José. And why shouldn't he be? He was as aware as Pauline that the holiday was ticking away with things as yet unresolved, and if he wasn't in the mood after a night like tonight when you could practically smell the pheromones wafting off the stage, then surely he never would be.

Besides which, he was nursing a truly amazing secret: a major miracle had occurred under cover of darkness while he was watching Carmen strut her stuff. The old wedding tackle had at last sat up and taken an interest during the second act, shortly after he and Pauline had got away with duping Bryce and Fern – perhaps as a result of it? He'd acted out of character in lying to them about what he did for a living, but instead of feeling guilty he'd felt reckless, unfettered, devil-may-care. Of course, the champagne had probably helped. But – he'd had a stiffy! He hadn't been as chuffed and astonished as this since he was pubescent. When he'd realised what was happening it had been all he could do to remain in his seat and keep this news to himself – he'd felt like standing up and crowing and telling the whole auditorium, had felt like grabbing Pauline by the hand and dragging her home quick sharp to give her a right good seeing-to.

Even now they were home this feeling of excitement and euphoria hadn't gone away, although naturally the whim whams had started to set in a bit. What if, when the moment came, the miracle stopped happening? What if he led her on, got her all excited, and then couldn't manage to . . . ?

Don't go there, he counselled himself quickly, tearing the foil and wire off the champagne bottle and popping the cork. Have another drink or two to distract your mind. He poured himself a glass and swallowed it straight down. The mistress and slave thing had almost done the magic the other night, he reminded himself, so stick with this role-playing business. Concentrate on the images from the performance. Be that toreador. Strut that stuff. Follow that wild gypsy, whose love is like a rebellious bird.

Swaggering upstairs with the bottle and glasses, he boldly made his entrance into the bedroom pelvis first, singing the toreador song, but the effort was wasted – Pauline was nowhere to be seen. The bathroom door was shut, however, and on closer examination turned out to be locked. Now here was an interesting reversal. Normally it was him taking refuge in the loo.

'Carmencita!' he called imperiously, rattling the door handle. 'Where are you? You cannot escape me now. Come out, and face your Escamillo!'

'Your Carmen prepares herself for you, señor,' Pauline called from the bathroom, where she was struggling recklessly into the Ann Summers crotchless teddy. In the few moments she'd been alone, she'd been racking her brains abut how to ensure Mick's courage didn't fail him now. He'd made it patently clear already that the pressure to perform put him off his stroke, that he needed to take things slowly, but the way she was feeling tonight, there was no *Slow* setting at her disposal – there was just *Fast, Hot To Trot,* and *Get Your Bleddy Kit Off Now!* There was only one possible answer, she'd concluded wildly. She would take the upper hand. She would forbid him to touch her, use reverse psychology – it always worked with the kids. Tell them not to do something and it was done before you knew it. And if he disobeyed . . . well then, she'd tie him up, she'd decided, and had ransacked Lorna's scarf drawer to that end. Make him feel he had no say in the matter, that this was going to happen anyway, whether he liked it or not (it was a fantasy that certainly worked for her). Tease him beyond endurance, then ravage him.

'Please, make yourself more comfortable,' she called through coquettishly, as feverishly she tried to figure out what went where with the red and black teddy. 'The more you wait, the more you want – is that not so, señor?' At least, she bleddy well hoped so – otherwise, the muck state she was in, she might well explode.

But had she known it, her reverse psychology idea was

already doing its magic on the other side of the door. As he released the doorknob with a grin, Mick was experiencing a stirring in a different kind of knob altogether. There was no false pelvic strutting now as he crossed the room to put the champagne on the bedside table – it was like doing the three-legged race solo. Blimey O'Reilly, he thought, looking down with pride and amazement, it didn't half do the business, this pretending to be different characters. If she didn't come out here soon, he'd be breaking the door down next. And if this was what the opera did to him, he'd be buying them both season tickets to Covent Garden when they got back home, and bugger the expense.

Catching sight of himself in the mirror, he decided he looked more like 007 than a toreador in Greg's tuxedo, and although James Bond wasn't half bad as a sexual role model, it might get a bit confusing to be playing two parts at once. Taking off his jacket he struck a swaggering pose, unable to tear his eyes off the bulge in his pants. Just wait till Polly saw this! O-bleddy-lé or what? He tore off his bow tie and opened his shirt buttons down to the waist, rolling up his trousers to the knee. Hmm. Not so like a toreador that you couldn't tell the difference – the black socks and dress shoes made him look like some sad English bugger at the seaside. Off with them too, then, and look sharp about it, he concluded – it wouldn't do to be presenting a passion-killing costume when she came through the door, and judging by the tra-la-la-ing that had suddenly started up in the bathroom, that would be any time now.

Frantically ripping off the offending socks, he just had time to make it back to the bedside table to dim the lights and pour the champagne, when the en suite door was flung open and there was Pauline in all Ann Summers's glory, her naughty bits barely concealed behind a teasingly improvised skirt of silk scarves which hung from a narrow belt at her waist, her arms held high, clicking her fingers like castanets, dancing slowly and sexily towards him on four-inch heels, humming Carmen's insolent song of Don José's seduction.

For a moment, Mick was nonplussed. This wasn't quite what he'd had in mind. Apart from anything else, he was all braced to play the part of the assertive Escamillo and seduce *her* rather than the other way about, and here she was casting him in the role of the boring dutiful soldier who had to be persuaded. Then again, there was no denying that she didn't half look sexy. And whereas only a week or so ago, at the airport, this costume had terrified the life out of him, he now found to his huge relief that the little man downstairs was not only all a-quiver at the sight, but was positively eager to climb out of his drawers – a fact duly noted by Pauline, judging by the astonished gleam in her eye.

Feeling more pleased and proud of himself than he could ever remember, he sucked his tummy in and puffed out his chest to display the goods, offering a glass of champagne in his trembling outstretched hand, which she snatched and emptied, her eyes boring holes into his.

'You are my prisoner,' she announced, tossing the empty glass back to him, and she plucked one of the four strategically placed scarves from her waist, revealing a tantalising flash of buttock as she did so, and advanced towards him. 'Are you going to come quietly?'

'No, I will not!' Mick protested, standing his ground, getting quite in the swing of it now. 'I prefer to come loudly, I will roar like a bull!'

Catching each other's eyes, they both had to suppress a fit of the giggles before Pauline recovered enough of her earlier hauteur to push him over backwards, and he fell on the bed. She was on him like a flash, straddling his chest, and tying one hand to the bedpost. 'There is no escape, señor. You can roar all you like, but no one will hear.' Whipping another scarf off her nether regions, she tied his other hand. 'And Carmen will show you no mercy,' she breathed in his ear.

Already dizzy with testosterone and champagne, in his prone position with its worm's eye view of her lace-encased breasts, mercy was the furthest thing from Mick's mind. They'd never done anything like this before, with her on top and being so assertive, and he'd had no idea until now that he'd like it. A groan escaped his lips as she roughly pulled back his shirt and licked him from navel to nipple. Like it? He loved it! May it never stop! Nevertheless, a corner of his mind was still concerned about niceties.

'Better take Greg's trousers off,' he whispered hoarsely, unable to stop himself. 'Wouldn't want to make a mess.'

'Hey!' joked Pauline, sitting up straight to look down at him dominantly. 'Who this Greg, and where he? How many men you think Carmen want in her bed at one time? I see only you, señor,' she continued seductively, slithering off him. 'And it is *your* trousers that is coming down, right now.' She was immediately as good as her word. 'What this?' she cried in mock alarm, caressing the bulge in his Y-fronts in her cupped hand. Halle-bleddy-lujah, this was going better than she'd dared to hope! 'You have weapon? You hide huge sword?'

Not unnaturally, Mick was thrilled by her choice of adjective and felt himself growing huger by the moment as she frisked him thoroughly below the belt. 'It is a present, Carmencita. I bring for you,' he boasted.

'Maybe you did, maybe you didn't,' said Pauline, licking her lips as she plucked the third scarf from her belt. She couldn't remember when she'd last seen him in this state. If she'd only known twelve months ago that a bit of badinage and bondage could produce this effect, she'd have had him trussed up like a turkey and acting out roles all year. 'But now I think maybe I cannot trust you not to try to escape,' she said, tying his right leg to the end of the bed.

Mick moaned in anticipation, straining against his bonds to lift his head and keep her in view through passion-clouded eyes. Only one last scarf now impeded his vision of the worst Ann Summers could do and he was champing at the bit to see it, but Pauline was just as determined to keep the tease in her strip.

'You want Carmen to remove this?' she asked unnecessarily, wafting the scarf with one hand while the other strayed up his still free leg.

'Si,' Mick moaned.

'And you realise that when she does, she will use it to tie up this other leg? That then you will be completely in Carmencita's power?'

Mick panted his fervent assent.

'So be it,' pouted Pauline at length, and pulling the scarf off with a flourish so that Mick could feast his hungry eyes, she was in the act of anchoring his last free limb to the bed when the door was flung open, their weeping daughter crashed in, and the air turned blue with screamed expletives.

10

When Greg Mackenzie woke for the second time that day he found himself in a darkened room, straining to peer at a strange ceiling, and completely unable to move. His first sleepy thought, that he was dreaming, was swiftly replaced by the far more urgent terror, that he was paralysed. But after some frantic experimentation he discovered that he was lying spreadeagled and bound hand and foot. His mind reeled. There was no correlation between this and anything that he could remember.

Fighting against an inexplicable muzzy-headedness he tried to recall exactly his last conscious memories. He'd been on his way to the airport – yes, that was right – being driven by Elroy, who had called up first thing to offer him a lift. He'd been going back home to Melbourne, unable to stand Leicester for another moment longer – mainly, as he now understood it, because he couldn't find a chiropractor for love nor money. With that thought came the familiar nagging awareness of the excruciating pain in his lumbar region. Could an emergency situation have developed in Elroy's car? Had he been driven to a hospital and operated on? The way his head felt, maybe he was recovering from an anaesthetic – that seemed a possibility. But why then was he tied up? Was he in traction perhaps? He tried calling, 'Nurse!' but nobody answered, and in the ensuing silence his anxiety increased tenfold with the sudden idea that perhaps he'd been kidnapped and was being held for ransom.

Unlikely, he concluded. He shook his head to try to clear it. No sense in getting paranoid, that wouldn't help him. Better to stick to the known facts. Fact – he'd woken up this morning beside Lorna, who, he'd learnt last night, was pregnant. Shit, yes, what with everything going on now he'd forgotten all about that! And she had found out about Diane – they'd had a row about it. This couldn't be . . . could it? . . . Could this be Lorna getting her revenge? Had *she* arranged for him to be kidnapped? Or taken a contract out against him? And Elroy was in on the deal? Panic seized him, his heart beating wildly, and he tugged frantically against his bonds, achieving nothing but sore wrists and ankles.

No, that was crazy – more paranoia. Since when was the Lorna he knew capable of being an accessory to murder? Ridiculous. There had to be a simple and logical explanation, if only he could concentrate on what was known. They'd said goodbye – she'd been a bit tearful as he remembered – but they'd both agreed they needed a few days apart to think things through, and she was determined to stay for Melissa's ruddy wedding. He'd hobbled downstairs with his suitcase, had taken some paracetamol with his tea, before Elroy arrived to drive him the hundred or so miles to Heathrow. Now, that hadn't happened, he could swear it – he had absolutely no memory of hours spent on motorways. So the clue lay some time after he'd got in the car.

He remembered Elroy handing him a spliff for his back pain, and the almost instant relaxation of his muscles as he'd smoked it – remembered feeling grateful and thanking the bloke. But then – yes, that was it! – then El, looking sheepish, had dug around in his pocket and produced half a dozen

Valium. Said Melissa had begged them from a friend so Greg could get some shut-eye on the plane. Told him they were only low dosage, so he could take two now. Remembered swallowing them down with a can of Coke, and . . . nothing. Nothing else till he woke up here.

Jesus! He *had* been kidnapped and Elroy *was* implicated, there could be no other logical explanation. But why? And how had such a loser ever managed to find either the guts or the gumption to bring it off? All he knew about the bloke was that he couldn't organise a bloody fart in a bean factory, let alone single-handedly mastermind an abduction. What was he, a bouncer in a nightclub? How much grey matter did you need to do that? Unless . . . Christ, who was being thick now? Nightclub bouncer – he could have contacts in organised crime! Had he blabbed to a mate about Greg being loaded? Had they hatched a plot together, and if so, with what end in view? It was hardly likely, was it, that Melissa would allow him to fleece her favourite cousin for ransom? She was crazy about Lorna – had even named her stupid baby after her, apparently. She'd be more likely to protect her than hurt her, for Pete's sake.

A cold creeping terror slowly inched through Greg's veins, as a scene from yesterday floated, unwelcome, into his mind. Had he been a little bit rough on Elroy perhaps, when he'd demanded to be driven back to the hovel in New Vistas before he'd allow the bugger to go and see Melissa give birth to their baby in hospital? Could he have pushed him too far? He'd certainly looked murderous when he'd driven off and left Greg marooned outside the chiropodist somewhere beyond the black stump. Was it possible that it was revenge Elroy was after? And if so, what kind? Was he going to come back to torture him, or leave him here to slowly starve to death? And where on earth was 'here' exactly? Was it somewhere remote or – please, God! – were there neighbours who might hear if he shouted for help?

'Help!' he shouted, putting to the test immediately his last forlorn hope. 'Help! Murder! Kidnap! Call the police!'

He froze as he heard the door to his prison bang open.

'Pack it in!' said a female voice in a stentorian tone.

Straining to lift his head, he could just make out a woman's figure silhouetted against the light of a corridor behind her, tapping what appeared to be a cane against her thigh.

'I can see that somebody here needs teaching a bit of discipline,' she said, as she approached him with menacing tread.

'Who are you? What do you want?' Greg cried, struggling in vain to free himself.

'You will call me Miss Strict,' came the bizarre reply. 'And what I want is your total obedience.'

Lorna had been using her time since Greg had gone, to review their relationship – an audit, she thought in her businesslike fashion, which was certainly long overdue – and she was surprising herself with some of the conclusions she'd been drawing. She had stayed in bed when he'd got up early to drive to the airport with Elroy, and when she heard the front door close behind him she felt suddenly bereft and rather weepy. Already she missed his physical presence beside her, the re-assuring warmth and bulk of him. But being by nature efficient and pragmatic, she decided to use the situation to test out how she would feel if they were to part permanently.

In her experience there were always pros and cons to every argument, and as she stretched out luxuriously across the Watkins' double bed to consider them in this instance, she had to acknowledge that the upside of his leaving was having more room to herself. An intelligent woman, she was, of course, alert to the metaphorical implications of this. It wasn't merely that his absence would give her more physical space to enjoy (or not), she would also have more mental space. There would be no shared decisions (the thought of which felt rather worrying and burdensome), but then neither would she have his solo decisions foisted upon her. Like having the boat, for instance – a purchase which he'd made entirely off his own bat without a single word of consultation with her, and which furthermore, in calling it the *Lovelorn*, he had thought to pass off as her Christmas present two years before.

Never in a million years would she have blown that amount of money on a toy – and that was what it was for Greg (apart from the obvious status symbol, she thought, with an uncharitable twist of her lips). And it wasn't as if either of them was a natural born sailor – every time they took the dratted thing out there was tension, fighting with lines and sails and each other. Indeed most of the time – except when the boy Todd came out with them, whose skill could make the boat dance over the waves rather than plough into them – Greg was content to motor along using the engine rather than do battle with the sails. She had started to think that they were a bit of a joke down at the marina, being seen as landlubberly yuppies with more money than sense, and if it had been a project she had initiated herself, she would have started by learning the ropes at sailing class, by reading up on the subject (she had more in common with the man whose bed she was lying in than she could possibly have known).

Thinking about the *Lovelorn* (the current irony of the name was not lost on her) led her to ponder the question of their joint finances – or rather, the lack of them. They had been married eight years, and still they held separate bank accounts, with not even a joint one for household expenses. Again, they had never talked about this. It had sort of fallen out that she paid for the day-to-day regular outgoings – food, utility bills, etc. – and Greg shelled out for the big splashy one-offs, like the plasma screen, for instance, or the gym equipment – neither of which had been put to much use once the initial thrill of owning them had worn off. So what did she think about this arrangement, she now asked herself frankly – was she happy with it? (No.) Was it something she felt resentful about? (To be perfectly honest – yes.) Therefore they should talk about it if they intended to stay together, she concluded. And particularly now, with a baby on the way.

It was this new development which was sharpening her mind to what was wrong with her marriage, of course, every bit as much as the Shitlipz fandango and Greg's serial infidelity. Here she suddenly had the astonishing opportunity and huge responsibility of shaping a new young life, to be the major influence on another human being, and already she felt protective of the little person she was carrying. When she had selected Greg as a mate she hadn't thought about his suitability as a father, rather it was his suitability as her partner which had influenced her decision. She had admired what she considered to be his ease of passage through the world, the way he dealt seamlessly with people, always finding something to say to them in any situation, where she often found herself to be stiff and uncommunicative. It was a skill that she'd admired and hoped to learn by example, but, instead, that had remained his thing, and she had just coasted along lazily in his wake. If she were to find herself in the position of bringing up this baby on her own, that must change. She'd have to get used to making friends with other mothers, to welcoming the children of strangers into her home – in short, to being a much less private person. And how would she feel about that?

To her surprise, she found that as much as the thought frightened her, it also quietly excited her. She decided she would like to be the kind of person who had good friends with whom she could kick off her shoes and let down her hair. Having less privacy would also mean having less of a sense of isolation from her fellows and more of a sense of belonging, of acceptance. Who knew – it might even rub off enough for her to accept *herself* as who she was, without her usual self-critical feelings that she wasn't good enough. 'For what?' she suddenly felt sufficiently emboldened to demand. To live, to breathe, to take up space in the world? It was quite a shock to realise that, at her core, she lacked such self-confidence. This too must be addressed if she was to be a positive role model for her growing child. As for Greg, she concluded, if he was going to stick around, he'd have to do some growing up himself. Learn to be less selfish. Her mum had been right when she'd said that he behaved like a spoiled brat these days, and it did seem to be getting worse since he'd become so successful, and the closer he got to middle age. Maybe he did need taking down a peg or two – but quite how that was to be achieved, Lorna couldn't conceive. If he couldn't see it himself, then nothing she might say would make any difference. But, of course, in his absence her heart grew fonder, as the hours, then the day, rolled by. He did have his good points, and those she missed. She missed his companionship, his body in her bed when at last she retired alone that night, his sense of humour . . . not that that had been much in evidence on this holiday. June had been right about that too – he'd turned into such a ruddy whinger! The one compensating factor for not having him around was getting to spend more time in her mother's company, just the two of them together, which was great, but even that turned her thoughts to what her life might become if her marriage did prove to be over – living as a single woman with her mother and her child. Much as she was learning to appreciate June, she didn't see her as her primary relationship. She wanted a man, and she wanted that man to be Greg. She wanted to believe him when he'd told her he wouldn't cheat on her again.

But she was still anxious about him being back in Melbourne alone – would he be able to resist Ms Shitlipz's (sizeable) charms? He'd said as he'd left that he would buy a mobile phone at duty free since Melissa had drowned his last one, and that he'd call her with the new number, but that hadn't happened, and surely he must be home now? Thirty-six hours had elapsed since their parting, when he'd held her so sweetly, had apologised again so sincerely, had sworn his allegiance and his fidelity from this point on. Until he called her she didn't know how to get hold of him – he hadn't been sure where he'd stay, and she didn't want to muddy the waters by desperately phoning round his mates to see if he was with them, or worse, try to trace him at work, admit to his secretary that she didn't know where her husband was. What kind of a sad idiot would that make her sound?

So the longer he was gone, and the greater his silence, the more she was becoming convinced that wherever he was holed up, he was up to no good.

Greg was in a tight corner and desperate. He had no idea who this Miss Strict was, nor who was paying her to keep him prisoner, nor why. Once he'd recovered from his initial terror, anger took its place and he'd tried to threaten her. Did she realise what serious charges would be brought against her once he regained his liberty? Did she know how long she'd rot in jail for kidnapping and falsely imprisoning him? Who was behind this? But his normal bullying tactics cut absolutely no ice from his bound and prone position, and she refused to answer his questions, even when he bit his tongue in an effort to appease her, and tried to put them more politely. Moreover, she punished him for his impertinence of speaking when not spoken to by leaving him in the dark room for hours at a time completely alone. Then the creeping terrors returned and he began to wonder if he'd ever get out of there alive.

Periodically she would return to lift his head and feed him water, and she would ask him if he was ready to be a good boy yet, but so far – even in a weak moment when he'd sworn that he was and begged for her forgiveness – she hadn't believed him. All he'd managed to make out in the gloom was her silhouetted figure, and she appeared to be wearing a cloak or a gown with wide-sleeved arms, which made him wonder, with all this talk of good and bad, if he'd been abducted by some kind of wacko religious sect. Why else wouldn't she succumb to his offer of a substantial bribe to set him free? What had happened to her good old-fashioned sense of greed, for Christ's sake, he asked himself in deepest puzzlement, unless it was that old ascetic killjoy Christ himself. Never before in the whole of his experience had he encountered anyone who took the offer of half a million Australian bucks as an insult, and walked away.

His lowest point came when he finally lost control of his overfull bladder and peed himself on the bed where he lay. His spirit entirely crushed, and fearful of the consequences (Hadn't he warned her and warned her that this very thing might happen if she didn't let him visit the dunny? It just wasn't bloody fair!), he gave up all hope of rescue and wept. That was how Miss Strict found him on her next visit to his cell. And that was when, at last, things started to go a little bit easier on poor Greg Mackenzie.

Lorna was beginning to learn the benefits of having a hot bath instead of a shower. Like most Australians she'd never seen the attraction of lying there in your own muck, and apart from the fateful dip she'd taken with Greg in this very bath a few days ago, she'd never been the least bit tempted to think there might be any advantage to be found. So since she'd been at New Vistas she'd been making do with the pathetic trickle from the hand attachment which could be fitted to the bath taps with a rubber hose. But this afternoon, when she'd admitted to June how upset she was not to have heard from Greg yet, she allowed herself to be persuaded into having a good long soak, the efficacious and restorative properties of which, her English-born mother assured her, had to be experienced to be believed. A hot deep bath was drawn for her, bubbles were added, candles were lit, and a tape was selected from the Watkins' collection (*Twenty Popular Chill-Out Anthems*) and left on auto-play just outside the bathroom door. It was, as Mum had promised, sheer bliss, and so relaxing that she drifted off into a brief and pleasant doze.

When she woke she felt like a different woman, ready to cope with anything – and this despite the fact that what had woken her was the sound of Melissa's braying laughter coming from downstairs. She smiled at the prospect of seeing baby Lornetta again. Rising from the now lukewarm water and patting herself dry, she baulked at the thought of wearing any of her constraining tailored clothes, and feeling chilled out enough not to bother about niceties, she raided Pauline's wardrobe for the lilac velour leisure suit she'd spotted there earlier. As she snuggled into the warmth of its soft loose folds she wondered now at her initial disdain when she'd first laid eyes on it, and vowed to buy herself one for occasions such as this.

Padding downstairs in Pauline's borrowed woolly slippers, she found June and Mo in an excited huddle, Elroy cradling the baby in his arms, and Melissa conducting a lively – not to say hysterical – chat with somebody on Elroy's mobile phone. At her entrance, everybody suddenly looked unaccountably shifty and stopped talking (about Greg not having called yet, Lorna assumed), except for Melissa, who waved cheerfully at her while giggling manically into the phone to whoever it was who was tickling her funnybone.

'Here she is!' said June, recovering quickly and sounding falsely jovial.

Clearly, thought Lorna, they'd been talking about her. 'Hi, Aunty Mo – what are you two plotting?' Lorna asked, to cover her own embarrassment.

'Oh,' said June evasively. 'Nothing much. Mo ran into an old mate of mine earlier, and we're going to meet up later. You'll be right for a couple of hours on your own, won't you, love? It'd be boring for you – it'll be just us yakking about the old times.'

'Sure, no problem,' said Lorna, not taken in for a minute by her mother's obvious dissembling. She'd probably have to get used to this for a while if Greg and she did split. She could just imagine the gossip spreading like a bush fire when she got back home – 'She got pregnant and he left her!' 'What a bastard!' 'Yeah, but it makes you wonder – was it his?' 'Oops – watch out – here she comes!'

But these gloomy thoughts were interrupted by Melissa who, having finished her call, came to embrace her with her usual enthusiasm, squeezing her till she squeaked.

'I was just on the phone to my mate Sheila,' Melissa explained, still trying to control her fit of the giggles. 'She is absolutely hilarious!'

'Ah,' said Lorna. What did she care? And anyway, there were more important things to discuss with her cousin, for naturally she was still taking her organisational duties seriously and the wedding was looming ever closer. 'Did you decide who was going to pick up the cake?'

'Me,' said Elroy uncomfortably, unable to meet her eyes.

Lorna felt sorry for him, thinking that he must be feeling bad about having driven Greg to the airport, which was ridiculous. The amazing thing as far as she was concerned was that he had forgiven Greg so quickly as to offer him a lift at all.

But Melissa was not to be put off her track. 'She's a single mum, right?' she chortled. 'Got two kids, but both dads buggered off soon as they'd popped out, and neither of them don't send no money. But you know – what else is new?' She rolled her eyes. 'Any road, Sheila, my mate, she's dead clever see, and she's aiming to be one of them who takes the pictures in hospital – what's it called?'

'X-rayer?' offered Mo.

'Radiographer? Radiologist?' suggested Lorna.

'Yeah, one of them,' agreed Melissa. 'But, that means studying, right, and how's she going to afford that when she's got to go out to work to feed her kiddies, yeah?'

'Yeah,' said Lorna. The same worry had occurred to her about her own situation, although not because of financial fears. What was exercising her mind was who would look after the baby when she was out at work. She hadn't yet broached the subject with June, but she knew that without her mother's help, she'd be stuffed. At her firm, if you couldn't give one hundred and twenty per cent, you quickly found yourself side-lined, and she hadn't worked this hard for so many years to have that happen.

'So first off, she does phone sex,' Melissa continued, pulling Lorna from her reverie.

'I'm sorry?'

'You know, blokes phone up and you have to talk rude to them for so much a minute,' Melissa explained. 'That's quite popular with single mums – you can work from home, like. You could be "Bored Housewife", or "Big and Busty", but my mate found herself specialising in "Strict Teacher", see?'

'I could go now, if you like,' Elroy suddenly said, edging furtively towards the door.

'Where?' demanded Melissa with a frown, cross to be interrupted when she was on such a good conversational roll.

'Get the cake,' Elroy muttered self-consciously.

'Don't be daft, El, it won't be ready till tomorrow. Park your arse,' his fiancée advised him shortly. 'So anyway, Lorn, my mate Sheil ends up meeting this old judge, right? He was one of her regular callers and they're not supposed to make dates with the clients, but her and the judge managed to talk in code and arrange a meet, yeah? And it turns out that all he wants is to come round her house once a week for discipline.'

'I'm just going to take little Lornie out for a walk round the garden,' said Elroy, and was jumped on immediately by all the mothers in the room who judged it to be far too cold out there for a newborn baby. Reluctantly, with all eyes upon him again, he sat down.

'What sort of discipline?' asked Lorna appalled, thinking of the two kiddie witnesses to this weekly arrangement of Sheila's. 'Not S and M?'

'No, this is why it's so good, see?' Melissa guffawed. 'He just wants to be her slave and be bossed about – wash the floors, scrub out the lav and everything – and all she has to do is be horrible to him and tell him he int doing it good enough. She's in her last year at uni now, and she's earned enough off him to keep her and the kids, *and* she's had her housework done!'

'Sounds like a good arrangement then,' said Lorna, wondering quite when she would be allowed to bring the conversation round to more practical matters, like had the hire of the wedding car been taped down yet.

'It's a bleddy cracking arrangement,' agreed Melissa through a renewed bout of giggles. 'Cos like, sometimes he has to go off round the country, right – what's it for, El – circuit training or some such?'

Elroy stopped in his tracks, his progress towards the door arrested once more. 'Er,' he said, wild-eyed.

'He's a circuit judge?' Lorna posited.

'Whatever,' said Mel airily, returning to her theme with gusto. 'So anyway, he's away now, right, so she's taken on a new pupil, just for a few days. She was just filling me in on his progress . . .' She stopped to bend double, the better to deal with a fresh attack of mirth. 'And for a very, very naughty boy, he's been doing quite well recently.'

'I'll wait for you in the car then,' said Elroy hurriedly, sliding out of the room with his baby. 'I've heard this one before.'

'You haven't heard the latest!' Melissa called after him, but apparently he didn't want to since he was already hotfooting it down the front path. 'She's had him on nappy changing duties today, with her youngest,' she told the remaining all-female party with glee. 'This is a bloke who don't like babies, see, so she's training him up for his wife, who's expecting. She says he's taking to it like a duck to water!'

Lorna joined in the laughter with her mother and aunt. 'You ought to have given her number to me, before Greg left,' she joked bleakly. 'I'd have paid her good money for that!'

And for some strange reason, Melissa found this funnier than anything she had heard so far.

I I

It had looked as if things couldn't get any worse for the Watkins, but after the dust had settled, and after Mick had quite literally gnawed his way out of his bondage (Pauline, hurriedly throwing on a robe, had rushed out after Gemma, unintentionally leaving him tied to the bed), it turned out that not only could things get worse, they could get catastrophic.

If the rude shock of having been discovered for the second time in so compromising a tableau hadn't been bad enough, Gemma had then delivered a piece of unimaginable, life-changing news to her parents in the brief lull between screaming obscenities and slamming out of Mick and Pauline's bedroom, so for a moment they were so stunned as to doubt their own ears. The main thrust of her speech, doctored for those of a sensitive disposition, was, 'While you have been heedlessly enjoying your depravity, I, your beloved daughter have been text-dumped by my boyfriend, and by the way, your son and heir has dropped out of university.'

Naturally, once her parents' hearts had started pumping blood to their brains again, it was the latter part of her colourful oration which provoked their worst distress. For even had they loved Stu to bits and thought him the most wonderful future son-in-law they could ever hope to meet (which they categor-ically did not), they would have been sorry, but not devastated for Gemma that he'd dumped her. She was an attractive young girl, and at eighteen she had the whole of her adult life ahead of her to find her perfect partner. But Matt dropping out of uni? Unthinkable, a total tragedy! The first Watkins ever to aim for a white-collar profession, and here he was throwing the chance away! Why? What terrible thing could have happened to him that he would even consider turning his back on all the years of grinding slog and hard work that had got him into university?

It was his mother's terrified imaginings about the possible answers to this question which impelled her to race after Gemma and leave poor Mick to liberate himself as best he could from the ties that bound him (or rather, the silk scarves), so by the time he had liberated his right hand with his teeth, used his right hand to free his left, both hands to tackle his feet, pulled some clothes on and then staggered unsteadily after her, Gemma was already calmer and merely weeping under Pauline's patient but incisive interrogation.

'I *was* out with Todd at the party,' was her sobbed reply to Pauline's puzzled probing as he finally entered her room. 'But I was thinking about Stu and what a shame it was he wasn't there, so I used Todd's mobile to text him. And then he texted me back.'

'Why?' was out of Mick's mouth before he could stop himself. 'Why on earth would you think about Stu when you were out with Todd?'

'Because Stu is my boyfriend!' Gemma spat, eyes narrowed spitefully at her father. 'Or he was. Now he's Jacqui bleddy Reeves's – the cow!' More tears. 'Are you happy now? You've always hated him!'

Immediately regretting his gaffe, Mick would have kicked himself except his ankles were still too numb, but Pauline came to his rescue.

'No, we don't hate him, Gemma, that's unfair,' she said. 'We've never said a bad word about him, except to back you up when you have, and he's always been welcome in our house. It's just that neither of us thought he made you very happy, and that's all we want, love. Isn't it, Mick?'

'That's right,' he agreed, joining them both on the bed to take his turn at cuddling Gemma, and to his immense relief his daughter accepted his embrace. 'Poor you,' he continued sympathetically as he rocked her in his arms. 'What a horrible shock. Jacqui bleddy Reeves, ay? Bleddy typical. Now, *her* I've never liked, not since she tried to get off with him that first time. He must be mad. But he'll regret it – you can be sure she'll see to that.' He was rewarded with a thin and watery smile.

'Yes,' said Pauline, shamelessly taking the opportunity to try to turn her daughter's head away from seeing her life as a half-empty glass, and towards perceiving it as half-full. 'You should go out with Todd and his mates more while you're here, to get back at Stu. Really enjoy yourself in the time you've got left.'

'I might just do that,' Gemma sniffed, freeing herself from Mick's embrace and drifting towards her en suite bathroom. 'I might even phone him now and get him to come and pick me up again, take me back to the party. He said I should if I felt like it later.'

'That's the spirit,' said Mick following her, desperate to get back to news of his son. 'But before you do, Gem, just fill us in on Matt. Did you talk to him? What did he say? Why's he thinking of dropping out of uni?'

'More than thinking – he's done it,' she said offhandedly, her attention riveted to her own image in the mirror. 'God, look at the state of my eyes – look what that two-timing bastard's done to my make-up – I look like a panda! I'm going to have to take all this off and start again.'

Never having raised a hand to his daughter, Mick now fought down the impulse to shake her till her teeth rattled.

How on earth had he and Pauline managed to raise a child so shallow and so self-obsessed? He just hoped it was a hormonal stage she was going through and that it would soon pass. He seemed to have to spend the whole of his life these days dancing round her dark moods. He took a deep breath to steady himself. 'So – Matt?'

'Yeah, I called him earlier, before I went out,' Gemma said, cleaning mascara off her cheeks. 'He's had enough. He doesn't like it there, says it doesn't feel right, so he's packed it in. I just caught him at his flat as he was moving out.'

'Doesn't *feel* right?' Mick expostulated, and he felt Pauline's calming hand slip round his waist.

'Did something happen, Gem?' she asked her daughter. 'What was it that upset him?'

'He said it wasn't anything specific, he's just decided he doesn't want to be a pen-pusher all his life, cooped up inside. He's always been practical. He likes being out and about, doing stuff with his hands.'

'There's hobbies,' Mick shouted. 'He could make model aeroplanes in his spare time, or do origami if that's what turns him on! But if he gives up this chance of an education, what's he going to do to put food in his mouth? Be a bus driver? A dustman?'

'Steady,' said Pauline, rather affronted. 'My dad drove buses, as you well know, and we were none the worse for it. And Julie at work, her husband Ken's a dustman. Suits him. He loves it. Likes the hours, likes working in a gang, feels he's doing something useful for the community. So long as Matt's happy, Mick.'

'Yeah,' sneered Gemma, 'since when were you such a snob? You mend washing machines. Are you saying you're not as good as some bloke who wears a collar and tie behind a desk in some lousy office?' She paused in her make-up ritual to eyeball her father in the mirror. 'Dad, read my lips: he doesn't want to be a lawyer any more. He reckons he never ever wanted it really, he was just doing it for you.'

'For . . . ?' said Mick. His brain had fused. He felt as if she'd just kicked him in his gut. 'Doing it for *me* . . . ? He never . . . I didn't . . . He always wanted . . . I can't believe it! What's his mobile number, Pauline?' he asked, rushing back into Gemma's bedroom to the phone. 'I've got to talk to him before it's too late!'

'His credit's run out on his mobile,' Gemma called after him. 'I told you – I got him on the land line at his flat, but he was just going out the door and that was hours ago, so you won't find him there now.'

'We'll have to go back home, then,' said Mick decisively. 'I'll call the airline, tell them it's an emergency, see if we can get an earlier flight. You better not be too late back tonight, Gemma, you might need to pack.'

'What's the point?' she said. 'You won't be able to get hold of him any better from home than you can here – you don't know where he'll be. He didn't even know himself where he was going for definite. Thought he might go walkabout, stay a few days here and there with different friends. He wants some time on his own to chill out and think.'

'But he's thinking the wrong things!' Mick cried. 'I need to talk to him to put him straight! Why didn't he call me?'

'Maybe because he knew exactly what you'd say,' said Gemma, abandoning her make-up now, the better to defend her brother. 'It was talking to you that got him into this in the first place, Dad. You're the one who's always been going on about him doing a law degree. He'd never have thought that up for himself in a million years. He just plain doesn't like it. He's miserable, has been since he got there. Doesn't like the course, and doesn't get on with the people on his course. He's got nothing in common with them, says they're all stuck-up and obsessed with earning shed loads of money.'

'He could be a defence lawyer, stand up for people's rights!' Mick expostulated desperately. 'Bleddy hell, if he's worried about making too much money, for God's sake, he could be one of them who only take on legal aid stuff. Or he could use his expertise working for a charity, like Liberty or Amnesty. Come to that, he could just *give* all his money to charity if it made him feel better!'

Gemma shrugged and turned her attention back to the mirror. She'd done what she could to help Matt, and personally she didn't really get what was up with him either. Living here in this wicked house, she'd been starting to wonder what was so wrong about making shed loads of money if it could buy you all this. Beat the bleddy socks off New Vistas, that was for sure. 'Anyway, he said he'd get in touch with you when you're back,' she said, pushing past her father to get to the phone, eager now to conclude this episode of parental drama and call Todd. 'So like I said, there's no point rushing off home early to try to force him to go back. Just chill, Dad. It's his life, not yours.'

With Mick in his current state of mind there was clearly going to be no return to the wildly abandoned champagne-stoked sex session which Pauline had been enjoying so much before the rude interruption, so once they'd waved Gemma and Todd off to their party again she suggested they retire outdoors to the hot tub with a couple of cold beers to mull things over. Naturally she felt anxious about Matt, but that was as nothing compared to the effect Gemma's news had had on his father. In all their married life Pauline had never seen Mick look so utterly miserable, and though the wooden-sided tub in which they sat in chest-deep, warm bubbling water, was set in the most perfect of positions – jutting out from the sheer rock of the cliff face at the bottom of the garden on a cantilevered platform, with nothing above them but the stars and the moon, nothing below them but the silver-crested waves returning lazily to shore – they might just as well have been sitting in a small dark pit as far as Mick was concerned, for that was where his spirits now resided, somewhere deep deep deep inside his painfully constricted chest.

Pauline knew what was upsetting him, and was therefore unsurprised when he finally broke the silence with, 'My dad never encouraged me to improve myself, not ever, not once. I wanted to stay on and do A levels and go to university, but he wouldn't hear of it. I had to learn a trade, bring some money in, that was all that mattered to him. I just thought I was doing what was best for Matt, Poll. I didn't think I was forcing him into something he didn't want.'

Pauline's heart ached for him. He looked so vulnerable and filled with guilt about something which, until now, had been his pride and joy, the jewel in his crown, the pinnacle of his fatherly achievements: his son at university, studying for a profession. She leant forward to caress his cheek. 'We'll need to hear what he's got to say when he gets in touch,' she said. 'It's no good getting it from Gemma. There'll have been some-thing lost in translation, you know what she's like. I just wish we knew how to get in touch with him. Something must have happened to have sparked this. It didn't just come from out of nowhere. He seemed all right over the summer holidays, didn't he? He'd quite enjoyed his first year – so he said.'

Mick's look of guilt intensified and he couldn't meet her eyes. 'We did have a bit of a conversation when he came home for the summer,' he said eventually. 'He did start to tell me he wasn't sure he was doing the right thing.'

Pauline sat up straighter. This was news. 'Did he? What

did he say? He didn't say anything like that to me.'

'He . . .' Mick started, his eyes now sparkling with unshed tears in the darkness. 'We were round at your mum's, sorting out her washing machine. It was like in the old days, when he was a lad and he used to come out in the van with me at weekends and school holidays sometimes, to help with the repairs. He started saying how he really enjoyed tinkering with machines, and how he felt more at home with practical stuff like that than with his study books.'

'What did you say?'

Mick looked stricken. 'I contradicted him – turned it round to the positive side of him doing his degree,' he said. 'I went on about my dad never supporting me to get an education, and how important that is, how it sets the mould for your whole life. I just wanged on about *me*, Poll, about how much *I* regretted not having been able to go to university. And I went on about no pain, no gain, you know – studying's hard, but you had to motivate yourself and think of the longer-term benefits, kind of thing. He didn't say anything about it after that, so I thought I'd won him round.' He gave a bitter humourless laugh. 'Felt quite proud of myself at the time, as it happens. Thought, well, that's sorted that out then, had a good father-to-son chat like *I* never had with my old man – done my duty there!'

'Well, that's what you thought you were doing,' Pauline comforted him loyally. 'If he didn't agree with you he should have said, he should have dug his heels in, asserted himself.' But even as she said it, she knew how impossible that would have been for Matt. He was a good-hearted boy, always had been – always so very sensitive to others' moods and needs. After Mick's speech about his own father blighting his life, he would have felt that he had to stick it out for his dad's sake. Chalk and cheese were Gemma and Matt. The one thought the world owed her a living, the other couldn't do enough to please you, even if that meant sacrificing his own desires. She just wished he'd come to her about it. She'd probably have listened to him more closely than Mick, not having the same agenda. In fact, her own agenda would most likely have led her to support him if he'd wanted to leave Nottingham and come home. She missed him, and she didn't give a toss whether he got a bleddy degree. She just wanted him to be happy. But then, so did poor old Mick.

'You see, the irony is,' Mick now continued hollowly, 'I didn't *encourage* him in what he wanted. I thought I was being supportive, but all I was doing was enjoying the sound of my own voice – being as selfish as my own dad. Like I swore I'd never be with either of my kids!'

'Don't beat yourself up about it, Mick,' said Pauline, reaching over the side of the tub to provide him with another beer. 'It'll all come out in the wash. He's young yet, and we'll sort it when we see him. Maybe it's just some girl trouble. Or perhaps he was disappointed with a mark he got for an essay. It could be something really daft, and he just needs a bucking-up talk.'

Mick accepted the proffered can and morosely downed half its contents. 'He's already had one of those from me,' he said. 'And look what happened.'

Pauline sighed. She'd just been getting her husband out of his depression about his non-functioning willy, and now here he was plunging back into the depths over being a bad dad. Much as she loved Matt, she felt a sudden flash of resentment about his rotten bleddy timing. Not to mention Gemma's, crashing into their bedroom again like that, only hours after Busty's lecture about parental privacy. 'Kids, ay?' she offered, with a rueful smile to Mick. 'Who'd have 'em?'

'Idiots like us, apparently,' said Mick, making a valiant

attempt to smile back. He bit his lip and looked embarrassed. 'What did you say to Gem, by the way, about her catching us . . . messing about?'

'Wasn't much I could say,' Pauline told him. 'She'd already decided we were filthy kinky perverts. Told her to mind her own business and learn to bleddy knock! But, yeah, I reckon she's left with the impression that we're at it like rabbits most of our waking life, and that's the version that'll probably make it into family history.' She shrugged. 'As legends go, it could be worse I suppose. And I'm not prepared to get my knickers in a twist about it. Don't know about you, but I was really enjoying myself before she burst in.'

'Yes, it was – fun,' said Mick politely, although his introspective expression lent little enthusiasm to his words.

Pauline sighed again and leant back against the walls of the tub to gaze at the stars. She felt sure that this had completely put the kibosh on any chance of things improving in the bedroom now. How was she ever going to succeed in seducing him when he had Matt to worry about, not to mention Gemma's habit of interrupting them with her little melodramas every time things started to get hot? And it would be even worse now she'd finished with Stu, she'd be living with them full time at home till she went off to uni next year. Let alone if she decided to follow Matt's example and not go. It was hopeless. Mick would never be able to relax enough to get himself in the mood again. Maybe she should just try to reconcile herself to having a sexless life, to growing old gracefully at thirty-nine?

No. She just couldn't see it. But neither could she see herself leaving Mick, particularly when he was so vulnerable and upset. So what *was* she to do with her sodding sex-drive then, when all it did was drive her to distraction? Carry on carrying on with Asheem discreetly, behind Mick's back? Find another lover, a safer distance from home, and make it clear from the start that it was for just one thing? But that wasn't what she wanted at all. She wanted sex *and* love, not loveless sex, and preferably with her own husband. Was that really too much to ask?

'Think I might have a go in the gym,' she said suddenly, standing up, too restless and frustrated now to lie there dwelling on the same old insoluble problem which had already tormented her for a year.

'The weird thing is . . .' Mick began guiltily, locked in the worry of his own conundrum. Since becoming a student of Ed Neuberger MD he was developing the habit of trying to analyse his motives honestly, as the good doctor had prescribed, however unflattering that might be. 'The weird thing is, I think there's this kind of a – sense of relief as well.'

Pauline sat down again. 'How do you mean, relief? What about?'

Mick shifted uncomfortably. 'That's what I can't quite work out. It doesn't make any sense. I keep dwelling on the thought of Matt not getting a degree, and half of me is absolutely devastated about it, and the other half is . . .' His voice trailed off as he stared into the distance, before, shaking his head in disbelief, he continued, 'I mean, why would I feel relieved, unless I saw it as a competition?'

'Between you and Matt?' Pauline asked doubtfully. He'd lost her completely now. 'A competition between you and Matt?'

Mick nodded glumly. 'I think,' he said slowly, 'that if I'm absolutely honest . . .'

'Yes?' Pauline prompted him at last, breaking a long silence that she could have gone off and baked a cake in. 'If you're absolutely honest, what?'

'I'm even beginning to wonder if it doesn't go deeper than this,' Mick said elliptically, as if she'd never spoken.

Clearly he was wrestling with some internal demon, but Pauline was buggered if she knew what it was. She helped herself to another beer while she waited it out, and tried to calm her impatience.

'I mean, the timescale's a bit of a coincidence, isn't it?' he appealed to her, his eyes finally engaging hers. He looked wretched and shamefaced.

'Mick,' she said, utterly confounded as to where this was leading, 'either you're going to have to go slower, or you're going to have to go faster, one or the other. I can hear your mind whirring, but I can't make out the words.'

Mick cleared his throat. 'Do you think I've been stressed this past year?' he asked, anxious for a second opinion.

Pauline laughed humourlessly. 'I think you can safely say we've both been stressed this past year. But what's that got to do with the price of eggs?'

'It's one of the three main causes of . . . you know . . . apparently,' he informed her bashfully, glancing down. 'After drug addiction and alcoholism. I looked it up.'

Now he had Pauline's attention. 'Stress?' she mused. To her shame she realised that she hadn't given a thought to Mick's emotional state over the last twelve months, only her own. Reflecting on it now, she realised with a jolt that he *had* become progressively quieter, less light-hearted and easy-going than the Mick she knew of old, but she'd put it down to him growing middle-aged and boring. 'Well, I suppose there's been a lot of changes at work that you haven't liked,' she offered, sifting through the history of recent family events. 'And your mum dying was a shock. Even though that was quite some time ago now, I don't know that you've ever really come to terms with it, have you?'

Mick felt the old familiar tightening round his heart and throat, and his hand went automatically to his chest. 'That old bastard led her a dog's life anyway. She was probably better off out of it,' he said bitterly.

'Your dad?'

Mick nodded.

'Why are you clutching your chest like that?' Pauline demanded, suddenly made anxious by Mick's pinched and pale face.

'Well, that's another thing that makes me wonder if I've been suffering from stress,' he now confided. 'I sometimes get pains – more flutterings, really – like if you suddenly get panicked, and your heart races and you feel like you could pass out.'

'Oh my God, Mick!' Pauline cried in anguish. 'How long has this been going on? Why didn't you tell me? Your mum died of her heart! It could run in the family!' Tearing his hand from his chest, she replaced it with her ear in a frantic examination. 'It's racing!' she said in alarm, and leapt to her feet to pull him up. 'You shouldn't be lying in this hot water if you heart's bad – it could set off an attack! Oh my God, Mick! We should call an ambulance!'

'You see, this is one of the reasons I haven't said anything before,' said Mick mustering a smile and gently disengaging her to persuade her to sit once more. 'If I wasn't already having a heart attack, you'd give me one.'

'It's no joking matter,' Pauline remonstrated. 'You're just at the age now when this happens to men! We'll have to get you checked out. There's no way you can get on that plane without an examination.'

'I've had it checked out,' Mick told her unexpectedly. 'I saw Dr Khan and he said I'm as strong as an ox.'

Pauline was gobsmacked. 'Without telling me? You went to the doctor about your heart, and you didn't tell me?'

Mick blushed. 'I'd gone to see him about . . . It, actually,' he said quietly. 'Only I got nervous, I suppose, so my heart started racing when I was sitting in the waiting room and I chickened out when I got in to see him. Just told him about the chest pains. Come to think of it, though,' he continued after a moment's reflection, 'he asked me at the time if I thought I was suffering from stress. And since I've been hearing the voice in my head . . .'

'Hearing the voice in your *head*?' Pauline checked, her eyes widening in alarm. Was he having a breakdown then? Bleddy hell, he'd been falling apart in front of her and she hadn't even noticed! Some wife she was. 'What kind of voice? Like you read in the papers, when they say God told them to do something?'

'Well, it's certainly somebody who *thinks* he's God,' said Mick wryly. 'It's me dad.' His eyes glazed over again as he pondered this. 'You see, it does all seem to fit when you think about it, doesn't it? It's all father-and-son stuff.'

'Lost me again,' Pauline sniffed. She was beginning to feel very uncomfortable indeed. How could she have missed all this – hearing voices, having chest pains? She'd been so obsessed with her own side of things, she hadn't even considered how Mick had been feeling. And she'd misjudged him. Harshly. Thought he'd been ignoring the sex problem, but there he'd been, going to the doctor on his own, and – what had he said before? – looking it up somewhere. All she'd done was sulk and shag the boy next door. Very grown-up. Not.

'What does your dad say when he's in your head?' she asked, trying to get a handle on all this. 'And how's it fit in with Matt leaving uni and you not wanting sex?'

'He tells me I'm useless,' said Mick.

Pauline made a face. 'Oh, just the usual, then.' There was no love lost between Mick's dad and his daughter-in-law.

'Exactly. But it would be, wouldn't it? Because it's not really him saying that stuff, it's me. It's like the mind replaying tapes. Or me trying to tell myself something, using me dad's voice.'

'Why would you want to tell yourself you're useless? That's just daft. You're anything but!'

'I've been pretty useless in one department,' Mick reminded her ruefully.

'But you've been trying to do something about it,' she said, rising to his defence. If only he'd told her he'd been in a state like this, she wouldn't have felt so resentful all year. 'Honest, Mick, you and me should learn to talk more.'

'I know,' Mick admitted apologetically. 'It says that in the book as well. It's just – that's what I've been finding the hardest.'

Pauline was intrigued. 'What book? Have you been out and got a sex manual?'

'Not as such. It's about when a man can't – you know – and why that might be, and how to put it right.'

In the light of this confession, two and two finally made four on Pauline's mental abacus. 'Is that how come you've been saying not to try to go all the way, to take the pressure off, and why you've been a bit more adventurous of late?'

He nodded shyly.

'You are one bleddy dark horse, Mick Watkins,' she grinned, and kissed him, hugging his chest and nuzzling her head into his neck. She felt a sudden rush of love for him, a deep affection which she'd been in danger of forgetting. He cared. He hadn't been ignoring her agony, he'd been trying to do something about it. Relief swept through her like a muscle-relaxing drug, releasing her long-held tension. She had forgotten how light a thing her body was. It was like shedding a coat of armour. Her face wreathed in the happiest of smiles, she looked up at him coyly, her hand straying to squeeze his thigh. 'Shall we go up and have a look at your book together, then – have a bit of bedtime reading, now Gemma's safely out for the night?'

Mick's heart, which had just begun to settle into beating to a calmer rhythm, now put on its tap shoes and started to dance frenziedly up the walls of his chest. 'I – don't know, Poll,' he protested, as once more Pauline got to her feet and attempted to bring him to his. 'What with everything going on tonight, I don't think, you know, under the circumstances, that I'll . . .'

'We'll just look at the pictures together,' she cajoled giddily, while determinedly pulling on his arm. 'Have a bit of a laugh. Take your mind off things.'

Looking up at her womanly form framed against the night sky, the water running in rivulets down her breasts, the moonlight illuminating the soft swell of her hips, Mick knew in his bones that if gazing on this picture produced no reaction in him but panic, then nothing in Ed Neuberger's sparse and clinical line-drawings could possibly do the business. He could hardly believe that Pauline was even suggesting such a thing at a time like this. Couldn't she see what a state he was in? Hadn't she been listening to a word he'd been saying? What could he possibly do to make his mental torment any plainer? He felt as if he had been sending up a huge volley of smoking red distress flares, which surely must be visible to orbiting satellites in outer space, let alone to his overexcited wife at his side. Hadn't he been screaming his terror from every pore?

The real and tangible scream of horror which eerily interrupted this train of thought had a dramatic effect on both of them. Shock attacked Pauline at her knees, forcing her to splash back, wide-eyed with alarm, into a huddled sitting position in the water, while Mick's body seemed to spring to its feet of its own accord, every sense now alert to this new source of danger, scanning the darkness for clues.

'It's only Busty,' said Pauline dismissively, as her wits at last returned to her and she recognised the coloratura vibrato in the final falling notes. 'Probably just broken one of her finger-nails.'

But Mick, who had similarly deduced the source, but not the cause, of the blood-curdling shriek, sprang out of the hot tub like a rescuing knight. 'Can't ignore that!' he cried, racing away like a greyhound on steroids. 'Sounds like she's being attacked!'

Watching in open-mouthed disbelief as Mick hared off to another damsel in distress, Pauline slapped the surface of the water viciously with the flat of her hand, which gave her no relief, but some discomfort, as the resultant spray splashed into her eyes. Tearing the ring-pull off another can of beer, she glugged it down angrily. She was in no way tempted to follow him to see what was going on, certain as she was that, on Busty's scale of drama, a mere scream would register some trifling thing like smudging her eyeliner, or at worst perhaps, seeing a mouse.

God! Could they never get any peace or privacy, even when there wasn't an intrusive teenager in sight? What a fool she'd been, obviously, to think that coming all the way to Australia, where they knew nobody, would be the answer. She should have booked a fortnight for two on a small deserted island in the middle of a landless ocean. Even then, Mick would more than likely have discovered sodding footprints in the sand by this time, tracked down Man Friday and bonded with him rather than spend time with her. So near and yet so far they'd been. A curse on Busty-Chin! Draining the can, she crumpled it viciously and tossed it over the side of the hot tub in the rough direction of the sea. Message in a beer can - *Help! Send sex! Woman starving!*

Helping herself to another and chugging it down, she gave a bitter laugh. What a farce. Here she was, driven almost demented by whatever hormone it was that made you gag for it, and there was Mick, driving away as fast as he could. What was wrong with her? Was she really that repulsive? Well, Asheem didn't seem to think so. Her anger turning her thoughts to vengeance, she leant back to settle herself comfortably in the hot water again, and gazing drunkenly at the unfamiliar constellations of stars above her, gave herself over to the pleasant fantasy of what she'd be up to now if Ash was here in the tub with her.

Todd was feeling understandably confused. He'd been deeply disappointed earlier in the evening when Gemma had asked if she could use his mobile to text her boyfriend; had been heartened when Stu's response had been to dump her; sympathetic when Gemma had cracked up at this news and wanted to leave the party; overjoyed when she'd called him back to say she'd changed her mind; accommodating when she'd said she needed to pop back to the boat to retrieve a bracelet she'd left there; and solicitous when, on getting out of the car down at the marina, she was inexplicably hit on the head by a falling beer can that some tosser had chucked down the cliff.

Now that he was back on board the *Lovelorn*, however, with Gemma's arms around him and her tongue halfway down his throat, elated as he was, he felt that there were a couple of things he needed to get clear before he could return her ardour with the enthusiasm it deserved.

'This is pay-back time then, right?' he suggested, when Gemma came up for air. 'This is to get back at your bloke?'

'In a way,' Gemma admitted. 'But don't get me wrong, I do fancy you.'

Todd grinned. 'You do?'

'I fancied you right off, but I couldn't do anything about it cos I was already going out with somebody. Unlike some, I'm the faithful kind,' Gemma said darkly, before burying her tongue in his ear.

Caught between ecstasy and anxiety, Todd gently pulled her off him to hold her at arm's length. 'I'm glad about that, Gem,' he told her, looking meaningfully into her eyes. 'Cos that's what I'm like as well.'

Now Gemma was confused to. Though her actions had indeed been fuelled by revenge, locked now in the intensity of Todd's gaze, her heart gave a little flip. No boy had ever looked at her like this before, like she was the only thing worth looking at in the entire world. He had dead nice eyes, and there was no getting away from the fact that he was a wicked snog – much better than Stu. Gazing back, she sighed tragically. It would be just her luck if she was starting to fall for him when it was almost time to go back to Leicester. 'I really like you, Todd,' she whispered.

'Me too,' he murmured. 'I mean – *I* really like *you* – not . . .'

Gemma giggled, and they laughed like drains.

'I think you're really special, Gem,' he said, as they melted into another long, long kiss.

On top of the cliff above them, the disgruntled tosser of beer cans sprang suddenly awake, coughing and spluttering and in fear for her life. Her body jack-knifed, catapulting her head clear of the water and back into air. She clung to the sides of the hot tub, her mind reeling. Bloody Nora! Close call or what? What a fool! Drunk. She was drunk. Or rather, she had been. Clearly there was nothing like a near-death experience to sober a woman up bleddy quick sharp. Standing up carefully on shaking legs, she clambered out of what had so nearly been her final resting place and sat gingerly on the edge to recover and clear her lungs. What on earth had she been thinking? She didn't normally drink that much, and she must have had – how many glasses of champagne? How many beers? Stupid. Idiotic. Falling back into the old habit of blaming Mick for something he couldn't help and obviously felt bad about, wanting to punish him with Asheem. Well, this was a timely warning. A woman could drown in her own mardiness if she went down that road.

She shivered and pulled on her towelling gown. The night air had cooled. How long had she been lying there? She had no idea. Could have been five minutes or five hours as far as she knew. Staggering to her feet, she registered the thick dull headache which already presaged a corker of a hangover, and scooping up Mick's gown, she made her way carefully through the darkness towards the lights of Busty's granny annexe.

Poor old Mick. He deserved better. Most women would have given anything to have a man like him, who was caring enough and responsible enough to run towards the screams of a transvestite rather than away from them. Recovering her sense of humour, she chuckled softly as she neared the house. If she'd been right and the worst that had happened was that Busty had broken a nail, it wouldn't surprise her to find Mick helping to repair the damage right now, busy at work with an emery board and varnish.

What did surprise her, however, as she glanced casually in at the window on her way to Busty's front door – indeed, what welded her to that same window, open-mouthed and pop-eyed with unalloyed shock – was to see Mick in a bra, a blonde wig and make-up, arranging his whatsit in some kind of corset, while at his feet, Busty was strapping him into a pair of spike heels.

12

Lying in bed on that cold, wet, grey November morning in Leicester, Lorna couldn't remember when she had ever spent so much time alone, with only her thoughts for company. Back home she was always dashing about like a woman pursued, either hard at work, or doing stuff with Greg as a couple. Here in New Vistas there were no such distractions, and her sharp and busy mind had little else to occupy it than to worry away at why Greg still hadn't been in touch with her. There could be only one explanation, of course. Having arrived back in Melbourne, he had shacked up with Shitlipz; but that still left the question, why? Was it just, as Melissa had suggested, that her rival had bigger bazookas?

Tempting as it was to conclude that Greg was capable of being so pathetically shallow, reason dictated otherwise. She had scanned her memory for any sign that her husband was obsessed with large mammaries, and had come up with no evidence to support it. If anything, in fact, the reverse. She could still remember how scathing he'd been when one of his mates had booked his wife in for a breast enlargement a couple of Christmases ago – the same Christmas, she recalled wryly, that Greg had passed off the *Lovelorn* as his gift to her. Which surely led one to deduce that he was more impressed with different kinds of status symbols altogether?

So what else was it that Shitlipz had that she didn't? This was the question which was at the forefront of her mind when, with some reluctance, she finally forced herself out of bed at 11 a.m. in response to the sounds of lively conversation and shrieks of laughter downstairs, which clearly signalled that Aunties Mo and Jo had come round to visit her mum.

Entering the warm and cosy kitchen, however, in the hope that the three sisters' jocundity would dispel her gloomy mood, she found yet again that her presence froze the laughter on their lips and silenced their lively discourse. Indeed, they all looked caught out and shifty, including June, who sprang up to busy herself with the teapot. Did they think that mirth was inappropriate now that Greg had obviously deserted her, or was it just that she was such a killjoy that all merriment went out of the window as soon as she came through the door? Neither of these alternatives did anything to restore her self-confidence as she struggled to smile bravely and return their embarrassed hellos.

'Thought we'd let you lie in, love,' said June, still not meeting her eyes. 'Cup of tea.' She set it down on the small kitchen table while Mo and Jo shuffled their chairs to make room for Lorna to join them.

'Thanks.'

'How's the projectile vomit going?' asked Jo amicably enough as Lorna sat beside her, although perhaps she was merely finding out if she would need to take cover.

'Settled down a lot,' said Lorna. 'I think it was made worse that day at the hospital because of – everything that was going on. As much to do with nerves as the pregnancy, probably.'

'And have you heard from the bastard yet?' Mo enquired, with characteristic Hibbert bluntness.

Lorna shook her head, eyes lowered, to look steadfastly at her tea. Now it was her turn to be embarrassed. She wasn't used to this level of intimacy and everybody knowing her business. 'Not yet, no. Can't phone him, of course, because of—'

'Melissa,' Jo chuckled. 'She's a one, she is.'

'She's a one and a bleddy half,' complained her mother, but the smile lines around her eyes belied the harshness of her tone.

'Have you tried e-mailing him, love?' June asked, the idea suddenly occurring to her. 'He'd be checking into that wherever he was, wouldn't he? You know what he's like about work. And there's a computer upstairs you could use.'

'God, what an idiot!' Lorna exclaimed, slapping her forehead. 'I hadn't even thought of that. How stupid.'

Jo reached across the table to take her hand. 'You're not an idiot, love, you've just got a lot on your mind.'

Lorna smiled back gratefully and saw three smiling faces regarding her fondly. Perhaps she'd misjudged the situation when she'd first walked into the room, she mused. They certainly didn't seem to feel the need for circumspection in her company.

'So what were you three cackling about earlier?' she asked them cheerfully, trying to get the hang of this intimacy thing and hoping to be given entry to the gang. But at this enquiry the atmosphere changed immediately, as if a steel fence had shot up to keep her out. Eyes that had been smiling now became evasive, Mo suddenly becoming galvanised by an itch on her foot, Jo disappearing into her handbag to find a tissue, and June impulsively leaping up from the table to ask a puzzled but obliging Whiffy – who had been happily snoozing in her basket – if she didn't need to go outside.

'Nothing much,' said Mo. 'Ought to be going really.'

'Just popped round for a quick cuppa, say hello and that,' said Jo, standing to put on her coat.

'Sorry?' said June vacuously, returning indoors, as if she had never even heard the question. 'Want a biccy, love, or a piece of toast before I go?'

Lorna felt both baffled and paranoid by all the displacement activity that was going on around her. 'Go?' she asked. 'Where?' June had already left her to her own devices yesterday evening and she really didn't feel like being left in her own company again today.

'Er—' said June.

'Rehearsing,' said Mo. 'For our Melissa's wedding. Hibbert Sisters are doing a spot. New number. Got to practise.' She glanced at her watch and looked meaningfully at June. 'Are you right then, duck? Betty'll be waiting.'

'Just do me lipstick,' said June, and dived out of the room.

The two aunts, now buttoned into their coats, handbags on arms, smiled at Lorna. 'What you doing today then, chick?' asked Jo. 'Going out?'

'No,' said Lorna hollowly. What on earth were they up to? Was it just her imagination that they were cutting her out of their plans? Must be. After all, what would be their motive? At this thought, she brightened. 'In fact, if you could hang on just a minute,' she offered, 'I could get dressed and come with you?'

'Aah, that would have been nice,' said Mo, immovable as a rock. 'But you've got to go into Leicester to return these.' With her toe, she nudged the *Celebrate in Style!* bags on the floor which Lorna had hitherto failed to notice. 'I brung them round for you. May as well get your money back. Must have cost you a fortune.'

'Return them?' Lorna exclaimed. 'Why would I do that? Don't tell me the wedding's off?'

'Course not,' said Mo, aghast at the idea. 'It's just that we're having the do at the Social, so we don't need plates and glasses and that – they've got it all there.'

Lorna couldn't believe her ears. After all the trouble she'd had in the shop trying to get dozy Melissa to concentrate on numbers, counting out plastic cutlery, agonising over champagne flutes – had that all been in vain? 'Then why the *hell* did Mel—' she began.

'She only went in there to get the serviettes and balloons,' Mo explained quickly, cutting her off. 'She said it were you who were so keen on getting all this, and she didn't have the heart to stop you.'

'But she could have just said!' Lorna protested hotly. What a waste of bloody time. What an airhead of a cousin! And the last thing she felt like doing today was battling through the rain into town.

'Well, if you remember right,' said Melissa's mother, rising to her daughter's defence, 'she were just about to go into labour at the time, so she weren't in her right mind. You'll find that out when it's your turn.'

Lorna's cheeks coloured as she reran the scene in her head. She had been swift to surmise that Melissa was being more than normally stupid, but now, with hindsight . . . perhaps it was she who had been the idiot that day? Well, nothing new there, she concluded morosely. Everything she touched, it seemed, turned to dust in her hands.

'Ne'er mind, duck,' said Jo, moved to give her downcast niece a goodbye hug. 'You meant well, and now it gives you sommat to do today, don't it, while your mum's out with us?'

'Right then,' said June, arriving in the doorway, having apparently changed her entire costume and redone her face in a breathtakingly short time. 'Are we ready for the off?'

'*You* look nice,' Jo told her, and once again the three sisters were all wreathed in what looked to Lorna like secretive smiles.

'Lorn's going out, into town,' Mo said significantly.

'Oh,' said June, stopped in her tracks. 'What time you going, love? You going now, or later on, after you've had your bath and done your e-mailing?'

'I don't know,' said Lorna irritably, cross with herself, and annoyed at being organised by her mother as if she were still a child. 'Does it matter?'

'No,' June said, with what seemed a strangely false offhandedness. 'I'll take a key then, shall I, in case you're out? Don't know what time I'll be back, so you just stop out and enjoy yourself. Will you make sure to let Whiffy out before you go?'

'Yes,' Lorna replied shortly. 'See you later.'

'And our Melissa says to tell you to go round and see her and the baby when you're done in town,' Mo called back from the front door, before the trio disappeared, laughing and chattering their way down the street, and a lonely silence took their place.

It was hard not to feel paranoid about the speed at which she could empty a room merely by entering it, but after only a few moments of self-pitying introspection, Lorna rallied and rose to her feet. Thanks to her mother's bright idea about e-mailing she now had a method of contacting Greg, and she was eager to use it. Taking her tea upstairs to Gemma's room, therefore, she settled herself in front of the family computer and, creating a new mail in Outlook Express, began the process of filling the screen with her feelings.

For an hour and a half she sweated over the document, honing and refining her case. The first draft she rejected out of hand as being too accusatory and resentful; the second was deleted for its dry and legal tone; but by the third attempt, having marshalled her thoughts and sifted through her emotions, she finally felt that she'd managed to say everything she wanted to say in as good a way as she could say it. It was fair, it was reasoned, it admitted to faults on both sides, and it offered room for negotiation, forgiveness and rapprochement. All in all, she decided, as she read it back and corrected the last small typo, she was happy both with the finished result, and with the process which had produced it. In striving to make it more than a mere cataloguing of his faults, she had gone beyond her injured pride and feelings of rejection, and reminded herself of his good points and how much she would miss him if they parted. She wanted him back. She was clear on that now. But she wanted him back changed for the better. She congratulated herself on time well spent. It had been instructive and clarifying to write it all out, and she already felt lighter and calmer. When she clicked on Send, however, to commend her higher thoughts to the ether which would carry them to her husband on the other side of the world, she was greeted with a window inviting her to confide which Watkins she was, and to type in her secret password.

Some days, she concluded, as she thumped the blasted keyboard in frustration and stormed thwarted from the room, it just wasn't worth bloody getting up at all.

Had Lorna had the gift of omniscience, if she could have seen Greg at that precise moment in his pinny and his leg chains at the bootee camp to which he'd been committed by her cousin, she might have felt, as did his mentor Sheila Strict, that he was indeed changing for the better. Gone was the bombastic braggadocio who had screamed blue murder for the first few hours and had threatened to enlist all the forces of international law, and in his place was a quiet, compliant, courteous helpmeet who couldn't do enough to please. Only four days into his sentence and it was as if he had been born to serve.

That very morning, for example, he had risen at six thirty and uncomplainingly scrubbed the kitchen floor with the toothbrush he'd been allotted for the purpose, had changed baby Darren, washed and dressed little Marcus, cooked and served breakfast, boiled nappies (Miss Strict was a keen conservationist), cleaned the oven, defrosted the fridge, planned the day's menus, and by the time Lorna was aggressively shoving the *Celebrate in Style!* carrier bags into the back of the Watkins' Datsun, to drive with ill grace into town, he was hard at work studying the Jamie Oliver textbook his mistress had thoughtfully provided, and kneading dough for the home-made ravioli she had ordered for that evening's tea. He even whistled softly through his teeth as he worked, until he was informed how irritating that was and told to pack it in, at which point he apologised immediately and profusely, showing his contrition in the manner to which he had become accustomed: to wit, full prostration at his dominatrix's feet.

But then, today was a big day for Oy You (the new name to which Greg now responded), and he was more than eager to keep his mistress sweet. For today was the day that he would be left alone, on trust, in sole charge of the children, while Miss Strict attended to important business elsewhere. Hers was a simple but effective regime which initially required total abasement and humiliation of the recidivist, followed by a rigorously firm but fair system of punishment and reward. Though initially a recalcitrant and unwilling student, Oy You had quickly made the connection, as he was meant to do, between good behaviour and an easier life, and since then he had been working hard to please.

The major reward he had earned, once he had calmed down on the first day of his captivity, was to be unstrapped from the bed and allowed to change out of his wet trousers. It was true that he had then been forced to wear only a huge nappy made out of a bath towel in their stead, as punishment for his accident, and had been fitted with ankle chains and handcuffs, but at least he was at liberty to wander round the flat at will and stretch his aching back, once he had stripped and changed the sheets. The relief had been so huge he had almost wept again, and that had been when he had learnt his first lesson, that bullying got him nowhere, but begging brought results.

'I need pain killers,' he'd announced belligerently, after he'd shuffled down the hall with his soiled sheets, as instructed, and found Miss Strict doing some kind of paperwork at the kitchen table. It was the first time he'd had sight of her in the light, and now he could see that the full-sleeved cloak-like garment she was wearing was in fact a teacher's gown. Under this she wore a no-nonsense tailored suit, black stockings, and the kind of severe black high-heeled shoes once favoured by Mrs Thatcher. She also had a cane. Despite his desperate straits, schoolboy fantasies had immediately flooded Greg's befuddled brain.

'Hands,' she'd said automatically, her eyes reluctant to leave the page of her book as she rose to administer his punishment.

'What?' Greg had said.

'Don't say "what", say, "I beg your pardon, Miss Strict",' had been the swift reply, before his hands were grabbed each in turn, and the cane brought down sharply on both palms.

'Jeezuz H. Fucking Christ!' Greg had bellowed, all fantasy fleeing as he flapped his stinging hands. 'Are you mad?'

'Bed,' she'd said, and spinning him round by his shoulders, which almost toppled him in his leg chains, she had marched him back to his room and retied him to his cot.

'There are a few lessons you need to learn to survive life in this school,' she'd said, in a calm controlled voice as she was about to leave him. 'One: there is no swearing, ever – it sets a bad example to the younger pupils. Two: after I have been kind enough to punish you, you will thank me. Three: should you require anything, you will get down on your knees and beg. I had just rewarded you for your good behaviour, and allowed you some liberty, but you showed you couldn't be trusted, so that has now been taken from you again. Let's see if you can learn some manners before I return.' And with that, she had closed the door and plunged him back into darkness.

As his impotent rage gradually subsided over the next couple of hours, Greg did some serious thinking. As a businessman, he prided himself on getting the best possible deal. If he was operating from a strong power base, which was almost always the case these days, this was accomplished by stating his case firmly, and allowing no negotiation. If, however, he was starting from a weak position, as he often had been when he had first been building his business up, he had need to be more wily. Nod and smile, bite his tongue, pretend that he was going along with the flow, while setting subtle traps along the way, into which his opponent would eventually and inevitably fall. This, clearly, was one of those times. He still had absolutely no idea who this woman was, or who had hired her to torment him, but that could wait. First he'd work hard at earning her trust. Then, once she'd relaxed her guard – as she surely would under his subtle manipulation – then he would go in for the kill.

When Miss Strict had returned, he was duly penitent and polite. He had apologised for his bad behaviour, thanked her for taking time out of her busy schedule to teach him right from wrong, and promised her he would strive to be a better student. 'I think it was just that I was confused and in pain,' he'd offered, in a small and broken voice, trying his first experiment at wheedling. 'It's my back, you see, Miss Strict. I've got a condition, and it really hurts.'

'You've got a *condition*, have you?' Miss Strict had said imperiously, as she stalked around the room, tapping her cane against her hand. 'My, doesn't that sound grand? And what, pray, might this "condition" be?'

'If you please, Miss, I've put out two vertebrae in the lumbar region of my back,' Greg had whined. 'I'm sorry I can't kneel down to beg, Miss Strict, what with still being tied to the bed like this, but if I could, Miss, I would truly beg you really humbly for some pills.'

'We'll see if you are good enough to earn them,' she'd said, bending to untie him, and refitting his leg chains and hand-cuffs. 'But first there are potatoes to be peeled, pans to be scrubbed, and windows to be cleaned. Do you think you can do that?'

'Yes, Miss Strict,' he'd returned eagerly, and he had followed her, in his nappy, to his tasks.

That night, his contrition and obedience had brought him rewards he hadn't even dared to dream of. Having acquitted himself to his mistress's satisfaction with respect to his chores, he had been duly given two paracetamol, and then told to lie on his front on his cot. Miss Strict, it transpired, had a talent for massage, and with a surprising deftness and dexterity she had coaxed his muscles out of spasm, and his vertebrae back into their rightful place. Beneath his subservient demeanour, a lip-curling sense of his own cleverness and superiority had been growing in Greg as he'd prepared vegetables and polished glass, but having been given the astonishing gift of an absence of pain for the first time in days, together with the unexpectedly reassuring sense of comfort he'd experienced from the physical contact this had entailed, he was filled with an overwhelming surge of gratitude and humility.

'Do you see now how well things go for good boys, and how terribly they go for the bad?' Miss Strict had asked him, as she allowed him to sleep without his restraints.

'Yes, Miss Strict. Thank you, Miss Strict,' he'd said. Released at last from his agony, he had felt an almost post-coital affection for her at that moment, but as he'd heard her locking his door from the outside and her footsteps retreating back down the corridor, he'd reminded himself sharply that he mustn't fall prey to the hostage mentality which he'd read about in the true-crime books he favoured. Bonding with your captor was the first step on the slippery slope of total sub-mission, and he needed above all to guard against that. Nevertheless, his dreams that night had been of sitting on her knee, thumb in mouth, and being allowed to remove her hair pins one by one, to watch her tresses fall.

There followed several days of similar emotional confusion. All the time, while outwardly appearing to be biddable, he secretly plotted and connived. But even as he did so, he found he was often disarmed by her charms. Clearly she was an intelligent woman. He knew better than to ask her direct ques-tions about herself, but once he managed to sneak a look at the books she habitually had her nose in, and he'd been astonished to discover they were some kind of medical texts, full of arcane tables and diagrams and footnotes. From this he surmised that, whoever was her mysterious current employer, she had undertaken this job of Greg's correction in order to fund her studies. Since, in Greg's mind, he had already pigeon-holed her as a sex worker, this came as quite a surprise.

It was late into the second day of his imprisonment that he earned the right, by his continued good behaviour, to meet her kids, and he could see at once from the fierce maternal look in her eye that if he dared to put just one toe out of line in their company, he'd be dead. By this time he had also been rewarded with the return of his clothes, with the addition of a flowered apron, and though his leg chains were still firmly in place, he was allowed the mercy of being handcuff free. He was taught how to change baby Darren's nappy, to wash him and dust him with talcum powder, and though bile rose in Greg's throat as he did it, he swallowed it down manfully, and even managed a bit of baby talk along the way. He'd never held an infant before, let alone had to deal with the gunk you had to put in one end and the muck that came out the other, but once he'd got the hang of it and mastered his disgust, he found it was quite nice to hold him afterwards, all bathed and clean and sweet-smelling, and tell him how handsome he looked. The first time that Darren had rewarded him with a smile he had been cock-a-hoop, and had even remembered some long-forgotten nursery rhymes, in an attempt to elicit more.

No such great efforts were required for Marcus's approval, however – in less than no time the little chap was all over him like a rash and, unwilling captive though Greg was, he had to admit that playing with the kid was one of the high points of his sentence. The rest of the time, it was drudge drudge drudge – he was assigned his chores for the day and pretty much left to get on with them while Sheila studied. Alone with his thoughts for much of the day, then, he found himself worrying about Lorna, and what she would be thinking about why he hadn't been in touch. At first he had comforted himself that she would be alarmed by his silence, that she would call him in as a missing person to the police, but the more he thought about it, the more he became convinced that it must have been she who had arranged for him to be here, albeit with Melissa's local knowledge of where to find a dominatrix at short notice, and Elroy's assistance in getting him here.

Despite this, or perhaps because of it, he found that his heart ached for his wife, and that his ardour for his lover had grown so cold it was a wonder to him now that he had ever thought to stray. When, or if, he got out of his prison, he vowed, he would make it up to Lorna with every means at his disposal. Maybe take her away on a proper holiday after this disaster, somewhere exotic and warm. A five-star hotel with a private beach and white-coated flunkies. Pamper her rotten. If she'd let him.

It was while he was in this reflective and remorseful mood, on what later proved to be his last evening in the house of correction, that Miss Strict allowed him to sit with her after dinner with a small glass of wine. She eyed him shrewdly.

'You look like a person who is regretting his past actions,' she offered.

Greg nodded, too tired from his tasks and too low in spirits to play the game. 'I am,' he said simply.

'Oy You, manners!'

'I am, Miss Strict,' he amended. Anything for a quiet life. Jesus.

'Would you say you have deserved this punishment?'

He shrugged. 'Yeah, I guess.'

'I am inviting you to reflect, not to guess,' Miss Strict admonished him. 'Sit up straight! Feet together! Hands on head! Do not mistake this formal occasion,' she continued as, sighing, he put down his glass to follow her instructions, 'for a casual drink with one of your mates.'

'Formal occasion, Miss Strict?' he ventured warily. He might have known there was no such thing as time off for good behaviour with her.

'One of these days you will walk out of here,' she ventured. 'It depends on you and your behaviour as to how soon that will be. But before that can happen, I must be satisfied that you will never, ever need to return.'

Greg brightened visibly. 'Oh no, I'd never need to do that, Miss Strict. I've learnt my lesson, and I did deserve my punishment. It's been very kind of you to take such trouble over my education,' he added, mindful of his manners.

'There was wild talk when you first arrived here of police and lawyers, and having me punished for punishing you,' she said sternly, an arched eyebrow inviting his response.

'Oh! Yeah, well, that *was* wild talk,' Greg blustered. 'I'd never do that. That would be ungrateful.' And besides which, he had already acknowledged to himself, it would implicate his wife in a kidnapping plot which would entail a custodial sentence. That would never do. He wanted rapprochement, not revenge. 'I think it was the shock of waking up here, in captivity,' he suggested, eager to impress his jailer of his desire to reform. 'And the pain I was in with my back. Made me tetchy. Unreasonable.'

The eyebrow arched higher.

'Badly behaved,' he conceded, raising the stakes. 'Angry. Totally out of order. Mad with rage. Very rude indeed.'

Miss Strict nodded her agreement sagely. 'And what would you say you would do differently in future to prevent a recurrence of this punishment?'

'Play with a straight bat,' said Greg with feeling. 'Never stray again.'

'Will you?' mused Miss Strict. 'There are some boys who will agree to anything while the pain of chastisement is still fresh in their minds. Once the memory has faded, however, those same boys re-offend again and again.'

'Not me, Miss Strict. I've learnt my lesson,' Greg was quick to aver.

'And what is that?' probed his instructor.

'If you're married then you're married, and you don't bugger about. 'Scuse my language,' he amended hastily. 'You make a commitment, and you stick to it.'

'So you blame your affair entirely, do you, for the sorry state you're in?' Miss Strict tested.

'Absolutely. One hundred per cent,' Greg agreed eagerly.

'Oh dear,' said Miss Strict, putting down her glass and rising. 'And I had hoped you were beginning to show signs of improvement. Dismissed,' she told him, glancing at her watch. 'Time for bed. I shall come to inspect you presently. Make sure to clean under your nails.'

Hands still on head, his mouth now hanging open in confusion, Greg stayed sitting exactly where he was. No matter how much time he spent in this wretched woman's company, he could never seem to second guess her motives. Hadn't she just been holding out the prospect of freedom, and hadn't he, surely to God, just given the magic answer to pass the test? 'Please, Miss, I don't understand,' he said uncertainly, striving to banish any irritation from his tone. 'I want to learn, Miss, really I do, but I can't seem to quite grasp the lesson? I thought you'd be pleased that I held myself solely responsible for getting myself in this mess?'

Miss Strict regarded him minutely, clearly weighing up whether this pupil's education was worth her precious time. 'Are you familiar with the phrase, "It takes two to tango"?' she posed thoughtfully at length.

'Ye-es,' Greg answered slowly, painfully aware that one foot put wrong now might dash his hopes of an early parole. 'But are you saying that *Lorna*'s as much to blame as I am for me having an affair? That doesn't seem entirely—'

'Of course not, boy!' Miss Strict snapped. 'You really are trying my patience! Out of my sight! Get to your room at once.'

Puzzled and defeated, Greg rose to his feet and left her reluctantly, head bowed. What the hell kind of game was she playing, he asked himself bitterly, as he brushed his teeth and prepared for another night in his cell. It was either his fault or it wasn't, surely, and she'd made it pretty plain that it was. So what the heck had he been supposed to say, and what was with the 'two to tango' business, for Pete's sake? Exchanging his pinny and shirt for his striped pyjama top, he shuffled back to his room to sit on the narrow single bed to wait for Miss Strict to come and release him temporarily from his ankle chains, so he could change out of his trousers. His mind roved over the koan-like poser she'd set him. Takes *two* to tango . . . Could she have meant that Diane was as guilty as him, then? No – Diane was neither here nor there. He knew that, and so did his teacher. If it hadn't been her, it would have been some other girl – had been in fact, times a hundred. Well, times half a dozen, at least. No, she definitely must have meant him and Lorna. So how was she culpable, in any respect?

'What if you take blame out of the equation?' prompted Miss Strict from the doorway, and Greg jumped, having been so lost in his thoughts as to have been unaware of her presence. 'What is the main cause of two sides going to war?'

'Differences of opinion?' he ventured hopefully, scanning the shared properties of all the conflicts he could remember. 'Your God versus my God, capitalism versus communism, you say eether and I say either – bang, you're dead and I'm right?'

'And that is a failure of . . . ?' asked Miss Strict, as she bent to unlock his chains.

'Politics? Human nature? Religious leaders?' Greg offered desperately, wildly grasping at straws as he obediently completed his night attire and slipped into bed.

'You are a disappointment to me, Mackenzie,' said Miss Strict severely. 'I had hoped to see the back of you soon. More specifically, I had thought you would be ready for your final test tomorrow. Sadly I was mistaken, it seems.' Crossing the room, she switched off the light and made to leave, at which point Greg's frustration finally got the better of him.

'What the bloody hell do you want me to ruddy well say, then?' he demanded venomously, adding sarcastically, 'Sorry for the language, love, but for crying out fucking loud! I'm a grown man, a man of some importance where I come from actually, not some snot-nosed kid who deserves your contempt! All right, so I've been a bit of an idiot, everybody's had a bit of fun at my expense, but enough's enough! I want out, and I want out now. I can't solve your bastard riddles! Jesus! It's like being trapped in some kind of kid's bloody fairy tale! Rumpelstiltskin! There! How's that for an answer? Hey? Did I get it bloody right?' But he was shouting at the blank face of the closed door, and the sound of the key turning in the lock was his only reply. Exhausted, he lay in the darkness, and as his anger slowly ebbed he started to regret the haste with which he had blown all his hard work. This was exactly what he had sworn he wouldn't do. Of course the bitch wouldn't trust him if he blew his cool so easily. All that scrubbing and cleaning, all that changing of shitty nappies, all that endless kowtowing, for nothing. There was no way she was going to let him out now. He could have wept.

But, despite all his faults, despair was not a vice which Greg Mackenzie often fell foul of, and before too long his mind was busy again with the conundrum with which he'd been left: war was a failure of . . . what? And what the hell had military engagement got to do with his infidelity and the breakdown of his marriage? Come to that, where the fuck did the tango come into it? Cursing, he berated himself again for his outburst. He should have played along with her. He should have tried harder and more calmly to understand what the irritating bitch was getting at, made a bigger effort to please her, to negotiate his release. Now he'd cocked up completely, set himself right back at square bloody one. She hadn't even bothered to censure him as she'd left, evidently regarding him now as such a lost bloody cause.

Well, stuff her. He'd tried playing the nice guy and that had got him nowhere. Tomorrow he would look for an opportunity to overpower her, force her to give him the front door key. Preferably when the kids were out of the room, of course.

He wouldn't want them growing up scarred with the memory of when the madman in the leg chains and pinny grabbed hold of their mother and grappled her to the floor. It didn't sit well with him, he wasn't a man of violence, but for Christ's sake, she'd left him with no other bloody alternative if she wasn't willing to . . . Shit. So that was the answer. It was that bloody simple.

'A failure of communication, please, Miss Strict?' he offered penitently the next morning, standing by his bed to be inspected as she unlocked his door. He had thought long and hard into the night, re-examining his failing marriage in the light of this new revelation, and realising by degrees how little he and Lorna were used to talking about important things. Some of her words from the last evening they'd spent together had come floating into his head: 'How would *you* like it if the boot was on the other foot?' she'd asked him. 'How would you feel if you knew I was lying to you and having affairs?' Bloody awful was how he'd feel. Enraged. Diminished. Rejected. He knew that Lorna had always found it difficult to discuss the personal, to expose how she really felt and to discuss it, but instead of encouraging her to feel safe enough to do that, he'd taken advantage of it. Well, he'd walked a mile in her moccasins now, all right, she'd made sure of that with this incarceration. It was horrible when the power base was weighted unfairly to favour one party at the expense of the other, he knew that now. Though it was an extreme example of the form, being on the receiving end of this sub/dom relationship with Miss Strict (or whatever the bloody woman was really called) had been a salutary experience. It made him feel rather uncomfortable and ashamed now, to realise that he had been so blithely domineering and selfish, and he had a sneaking suspicion that, were he to catch himself attempting the same thing again in the future, he would involuntarily picture himself wearing a teacher's gown, high-heeled shoes and brandishing a cane at his baby self in nappies. It was no image for a man – at least, not for the kind of man that he would like to be. His cheeks had coloured in the darkness as he had recalled his infantile reaction when Lorna had told him she was pregnant. It was disconcertingly reminiscent of little Marcus when he couldn't have his way. *His* wife, bearing *his* baby – a woman's finest hour, the kind of miraculous good news that a real man would bust a gut to hear – you only had to look at idiot Elroy to see that. But what had been his own response? Said he needed to think it over because it might interfere with his lifestyle. What a bloody . . .

'I realise I've been an absolute arsehole,' he continued with difficulty, under Miss Strict's sceptical scrutiny. 'But all that's going to change if I'm given the chance. And I'd like to apologise to you, Miss, about losing my temper like that last night. Very childish. I sincerely beg your pardon, and though I know I don't deserve it, I beg you to reconsider my eligibility to take my final test today.'

'We'll have to see to what extent your behaviour has really improved,' was all she said, glancing at her wristwatch. 'But already we're off to a bad start this morning. That little speech has put you behind with your chores by ten minutes.'

Jesus, she was a tough nut to crack. But for the next four hours, Greg slaved away at proving his fitness for the ultimate test – whatever that might prove to be. He just wanted to be allowed to get back to Lorna, to comfort her and hold her, to tell her how much he cared, and yes, damn it, to tell her how much he was looking forward to having this baby. After all, being around Strict's two kids hadn't proved to be quite as much of a drag as he might have expected, and with Lorn's and his combined salaries, for Pete's sake, they could easily afford to hire a nanny for the messy bits. Thus it was that he put his whole heart into cleaning the kitchen floor with his toothbrush that morning, was uncomplaining as he boiled Darren's nappies, took pride in cleaning the oven and defrosting the fridge thoroughly, and thanked Miss Strict with enthusiasm and humility for the learning opportunity she was affording him when she opened the Jamie Oliver book at 'blinding pasta recipe', and told him to get kneading.

It was then that she finally rewarded him with the announcement that he would indeed sit his final test that very afternoon, and that test would be one of trust. He would be left in sole charge of her children while she went out, and he must prove by his actions that he was worthy of this privilege, that he took his responsibilities seriously, and by his correct execution of this ultimate exam, that he was fit to be released back into the community. Hence he began to whistle happily while he worked, and thus it was that he came to be in full prostration at his mistress's feet, nose pressed against the vinyl tiles which he had scrubbed, his breath held anxiously, hoping for forgiveness and permission to rise.

Later yet, after they had overcome this hiccup in relations caused by his whistling, and he had acquitted himself uncomplainingly during his punishment of scrubbing the lavatory pan with his trusty toothbrush, he began to entertain real hope that these really would be his final hours in captivity. Sure enough, as the big hand on the kitchen clock swept up to its zenith, and the little hand trembled on the brink of two (he was teaching Marcus to tell the time), Miss Strict reappeared in her outdoor coat, a briefcase tucked under her arm.

'I shall be gone for an hour. I don't need to tell you what would happen to a boy in your position who let me down,' she said, with meanly narrowed eyes.

'No, ma'am,' he replied honestly, trying to dampen any sign

of his feelings of mounting exuberance. For frankly, what did it matter, and what did he care? Once she was out of the way and he'd made his escape, he'd be safely out of her clutches for ever – they'd never capture him a second time. Once bitten, twice bloody shy of ever accepting another bloody lift from Elroy, or of taking somebody else's prescription bloody drugs come to that. No, he'd learnt his lesson, but now it was over. No more. The gloves were off. He couldn't count on the quixotic Strict to honour her side of the bargain – she'd be just as likely to shift the bloody goalposts again when she got back, and he'd be buggered if he'd let this chance of freedom pass him by. He'd wait half an hour after she'd gone, make sure baby Darren was snug in his cot, plonk Marcus in front of the box with his favourite video, close the door on them safely, and he'd be gone. They'd be fine till their mother got back – they'd only be alone for thirty minutes or so, probably wouldn't even notice they were on their own.

There was one small bugbear to this plan, of course, and that was the matter of his fetters. It was going to be difficult enough just to find his way back to New Vistas once he got outside, let alone with his ankles shackled. A man asking his way in leg chains was bound to cause a stir, and he didn't want the police involved. 'Miss Strict,' he ventured, heart in mouth, as she drew on her gloves and at last made to leave. 'I feel a bit anxious about wearing these leg chains while you're out.'

Her answering look could only be described as old-fashioned. 'Indeed?' she remarked acerbically. 'And why would that be?'

'If there was a fire?' he offered. 'Or some other kind of emergency where I might need to run? Like if I suddenly spotted Marcus playing with the electric sockets again, or if he got too close to the stove and I was on the other side of the room, changing Darren, let's say? I just worry that I might not be in a good position to do my job effectively, being hobbled, and I wouldn't want to let you down, as you said yourself, Miss. I really do appreciate this opportunity you're giving me to prove myself, and I'm frightened of anything which might threaten that, or worse, might compromise the safety of your children.'

He could see the flicker of fear in her eyes as he said that, and he had to bite his lip against the self-congratulatory smile which threatened to give his devious plan away.

'You're right,' she said at last, and to his dismay, began to peel off her gloves. 'I shouldn't go.'

'But Miss, you must!' he insisted with feeling. 'I know that, wherever it is you're going, it must be very important, and I swear to you that I won't abuse your trust.' He lowered his eyes diffidently, praying that he hadn't fallen foul of his own trap. 'I just want to be in the very best position to undertake my duties responsibly, to the best of my abilities. I wouldn't want anything to compromise that, Miss Strict. Nor would I want to be the cause of messing up your plans.'

Clearly torn, she gave him a searching surveillance, crossing the room to lift his chin between finger and thumb, the better to look deeply into his eyes. 'So you won't abuse my trust?' she echoed eventually, satisfied, it seemed, by the look of wide-eyed innocence he'd mustered.

'Absolutely no way,' he vowed passionately. 'Frankly I'd sooner cut my own throat.'

'Believe me, boy, that would be the very least of your punishments if you should fail me,' she said trenchantly, and in a momentary reversal of their relative status, she bent down at his feet to unlock his chains.

'Disappoint me, and you're dead,' were her last words as, rising to cross to the door once more, she was gone with no looking back.

For some minutes Greg stood stock-still, his ears straining to listen as she turned the key in the lock, and her footsteps receded across the hallway and out into the world. Free – he was free! Or he soon would be, once he'd settled the kids down, scoured the flat for his wallet, changed his accursed pinny for his coat, and smashed his way out through one of the front windows – the only ones not barred – which he'd identified as his escape route when he'd been set the task of cleaning them with cotton buds.

He could hardly believe his luck, or Miss Strict's stupidity. Was she mad? Did she really believe that her power was so awesome that he would obey her even when she wasn't there to crack the whip? Ha ha! Well, her foolishness was his good fortune. Soon he'd be back with Lorna and they'd have a good old laugh about all this. He wouldn't whinge or bear a grudge, she'd see at a glance that he had already changed for the better.

Yes, things were definitely on the up, he decided, returning baby Darren's delighted smile while jiggling him in his arms. 'Who's a good little fella, then?' he whispered to him fondly as he gently put him back in his cot. 'Darren is. Yes, he is. Now off you go to bye-byes, so Uncle Greg can bugger off.'

With uncanny synchronicity, the last four words of her husband's soft entreaty formed themselves as a muttered imprecation on Lorna's lips almost simultaneously. Already out of sorts after having been unable to e-mail the marital peace proposal she had sweated blood over, she had driven irritably into town to return Melissa's unwanted wedding breakfast place settings to *Celebrate in Style!*, where her temper was unimproved by the implacable response of the manager. 'It's company policy, me duck,' he told her, in an aggravatingly familiar tone. 'Look, it's writ up there on that poster – "Goods may be exchanged only, no refunds will be given."'

'But that's outrageous!' she spat, the lawyer in her rolling up her sleeves for a spirited legal debate. 'What happened to my statutory rights?'

'I wouldn't know anything about that, chick,' he returned, with a disingenuously consumer-friendly smile. 'I don't make the rules, I just stick to 'em. Go on, no need to hurry – have a good look round. I bet you'll find sommat you didn't think you needed.'

Ain't that the truth, Lorna thought bitterly as, forced to accept defeat by the restive queue behind her, she roved enraged through shelves of plastic Yuletide holly wreaths and Rudolph the reindeer headbands with illuminating antlers (*Needs only 1 x AA battery!*). At last, turning a corner and coming literally face to face with the life-sized inflatable bride and groom which had so entranced Melissa, and noting that the exorbitant price matched almost exactly what she was being forced to trade, she finally and reluctantly decided to let her cousin have her way. Softened by her earlier bout of critical self-examination, she even smiled at the prospect of witnessing the inevitable childlike joy which would be evoked by its receipt. She had vowed to cultivate a lighter side to her personality, had promised Greg in the unsent mail that she would learn to be less stuffy and more spontaneous, and here was an opportunity to put her good intentions into practice straight away. If she wanted him to change, she had acknowledged, then she must prove her willingness to change too.

She felt quite saintly at her ability to convert so quickly and effortlessly into being more of a fun-loving animal. Her mother and her aunts would be proud of her – indeed, if she had demonstrated earlier that she was the kind of person who could give a blow-up nuptial sculpture as a wedding present, they would probably have *insisted* on her accompanying them to their rehearsal, rather than leaving her to her own devices. Yes, it was an ill wind, she thought indulgently as she queued for an assistant's attention, a silver lining to her dark and angry cloud.

But that was before she had been informed that they had no more of this item in stock, and that if she wanted to buy one, then she must take this pre-inflated display model.

'Well, at least it'll save your puff,' the girl at the cash desk called after her cheerfully, as Lorna struggled out of the door in a bizarre *pas de trois*.

Her new-found spontaneity already a source of regret, as the large target she now made was buffeted down the street at speed by wind and rain, her recent sea change of good humour similarly ebbed, and even before she had to face the challenge of how to cram the connubial couple into the back of the Watkins' Datsun, her mood had turned from sunny to thunderous. The subject of why Greg had not called her had come venomously to mind as she battled to maintain her hold on the bloated bride and groom through windswept streets. How *dare* he leave her here all alone like this and slip back between the sheets with Shitlipz? What kind of a man abandoned his newly pregnant wife for the bed of his mistress? And what wife in her right mind would want such a selfish and cowardly man back?

Few would have blamed her if it had been then, when she was blown precipitately across a busy street into hooting oncoming traffic, that she had cursed her spouse to buggery, but it was not. Even then she still maintained her desire for a reconciliation with the man who had given her so much, and who had taken so much away. This hope sustained her, despite her rising rage, while she sandwiched the tumescent twosome between herself and the side of the car to stop them eloping on the wings of the wind and frantically searched her handbag for the keys. It maintained its glow, deep within her breast, as she tore the bungs out of the back of their necks and attempted (unsuccessfully) to squeeze somebody else's breath out of them; and it was still there when, with tears of vexation, she finally slammed the door on the tangle of limbs which now filled the Datsun's interior.

No, it was not then that she ceased to care about her husband, crying out in frustration the manner in which he might go; nor was it when she was swallowed up by the open maw of a waiting flyover and was swept, weeping, to the wrong side of Leicester. It wasn't during the anxious moments when at last she found her way, and promptly lost it again, amongst the identical streets of New Vistas. And it was most certainly not at the moment when the nice chap from next door, seeing her struggle to evict the demonically distended duo from the back seat, jumped over the fence to appear at her side with a disarming smile and an offer of aid.

Indeed, once inside the safe haven of Pauline Watkins's semi-detached, this dusky Adonis improved her mood a hundredfold as, propping the happy couple in the hall, he shared his mirth at their flaccidity. 'Downhill all the way for them now, innit?' he suggested, his cheeks dimpling in a grin. Turning his liquid gaze on Lorna, he offered her his hand. 'Hi. I'm Asheem, by the way.'

'Lorna,' she said, her frost-bitten fingers, clasped in his warmth, already finding comfort. 'Thanks so much for your help. It's been one of those days.' She laughed lightly, her brow completely clearing of frown lines with the unexpected tonic of his company. Returning his smiling gaze, she noted that his eyes were as big and brown as chocolates, his lashes long enough to whip any woman into envy, his lips . . .

The dog, whose cheerful bark of greeting had been easily

ignored, as had her whining and howling, was now using her body as a battering ram against the kitchen door. 'I'd better let the mutt out,' she said, briskly breaking their digital embrace and preceding him into the kitchen. 'Cup of tea?'

'That'd be nice. Hiya, Whiff!' he said, bending to return the pet's enthusiastic greeting. 'Come on then, girl! I'll let her out while you get the kettle on,' he told Lorna.

Was there no end to his friendly helpfulness, she mused, watching his winning way with animals through the back door window. It was enough to make one hum a happy tune while measuring out tea leaves; enough to lift a woman's spirits in what had been her darkest hour; it was enough – yes, even enough – to restore her faith in the better side of human nature. She smiled brightly at his return. 'Sugar?' she offered.

'No, I'm sweet enough,' was his light-hearted rejoinder as he settled himself at the table as if this were home from home. 'So, Lorna, by the looks of that dirigible out in the hall, you've come over for a family wedding?' he asked, lifting his mug and regarding her through the fragrant steam of his tea.

'That's right,' she agreed. 'You probably know that we've done a house swap with the Watkins. They're at our place in Australia.'

'I was sitting with Pauline upstairs at the computer when your e-mail first came through,' Ash confirmed. 'She was over the moon.'

Hope for her marriage, even then, quickened Lorna's heart-beat. 'You were? I don't suppose you know her password?'

'Course I do. I set it up for her. Taught her everything she knows,' he said immodestly. 'Why, did you want to send a mail?'

'Oh, God, yes,' she breathed, a sense of giddy anticipation sweeping over her at the thought of finally being able to dispatch her olive branch to Greg.

Asheem at once rose gallantly. 'No time like the present,' he said, taking her mug with an accommodating smile. 'Shall we have our tea upstairs?'

Settling Lorna at Gemma's computer, he stood behind and leant over her shoulder to work his magic with the mouse. 'You've already written it, have you? Did you store it in Drafts?'

'Yes.'

'This one here, to Greg Mackenzie?'

'That's right.'

A few deft clicks, and it was gone. 'There we are,' he said cheerfully. 'On its way. Pretty important, was it?' he asked, noting how relief had changed her posture at the desk. He put his warm hands reassuringly on her shoulder muscles and squeezed them. 'Wow,' he said, 'you're tense.'

'Ohhh,' she said, her head dropping forward involuntarily in response to the comfort of his touch. 'That's so good. I hadn't realised how – ooohhh.'

'Sshhh,' he murmured softly. 'Just relax and enjoy. Here, lean forward, rest your head on your arms, and I'll give your back a go. I've done a course in massage. There – that nice?'

'So-o nice.' So nice she was practically drooling, slack-mouthed, on the keyboard.

'So who's this Greg Mackenzie?' Asheem enquired companionably as he coaxed her aching muscles to unwind. 'And what's he done to get you into such a state?'

'He's my husband,' she said, lulled by this intimacy with such a friendly stranger into uncharacteristic candour. 'And he's flown home to his mistress.'

'What an idiot,' said Asheem levelly. 'No wonder you're upset.' His hands went back to her shoulders and he lifted her gently to an upright position again. 'You know what? This'd be so much better if you were lying down, Lorna. I've often helped Pauline like this. She's got some massage oil in her bedroom. Let's go there and give this back of yours a proper seeing-to, shall we? You'll feel so much better afterwards. It'll help put things in perspective.'

With apparently no effort at all on her part, she found she was already on her feet and being helped next door to sit on the double bed. 'Just slip your top off,' he said, turning away from her discreetly to close the curtains and search the dressing table for the oil. 'Don't mind me, I'm a trained professional. Might as well pop your jeans off too – you'd be amazed how much tension we carry in our calves. I'll just fetch a towel from the bathroom while you make yourself nice and comfy.'

Left alone, far from home, in the bedroom of a woman she had never met, taking her clothes off for a man she didn't know, though she was dazed as she began to unbutton her blouse, Lorna was fully aware of where this massage might lead her. Was this wise, she stopped to ask herself soberly, having just told Greg in an e-mail how much she loved him and wanted him back? And how would he feel if he knew? But after the briefest of pauses for this introspective caution, she shrugged her shoulders in a gesture of dismissal.

For it was then that she finally and unwittingly echoed the words her husband had crooned to baby Darren only moments before.

'Greg can bugger off,' she muttered to the empty room, and defiantly she shimmied out of her jeans.

With Darren gurgling at the mobile over his cot and Thomas the Tank Engine tooting in the living room where Marcus sat entranced, Greg was free to roam milady's flat at will, and opening the closet in her normally out-of-bounds bedchamber, he at last espied his cashmere coat. Pushing his arms through the sleeves, he already felt more like himself in its soft embrace – high status, independent, and in control. He checked the pockets anxiously for his gloves, his scarf and – ah! – his pigskin wallet, as full of cash and credit as when he'd last held its reassuring bulk in his hands. The woman was an absolute fool! He stifled a giggle out of recently acquired habit. This was going to be so ruddy easy, he thought with a wicked grin, his eyes alight with mischief as he spotted his case on the top of the wardrobe; this was like taking candy from a bloody baby.

Yes, unbelievable though it seemed, the last day of term had finally come for little Greg Mackenzie at the house of correction. He felt as euphoric as he had been as a lad going out through the gates of Melbourne Grammar at the beginning of summer. Goodbye to all this! No more Strict, no more punishments, no more mindless shitty chores! Hello freedom, hello autonomy, hello independence! Now all he needed to do was to take his case through to the living-room window, and – Crash! Smash! – look out world, here comes Greggie boy!

Sauntering down the corridor he stopped briefly outside the children's bedroom. Wouldn't hurt to sneak a quick peek at baby Darren, make sure the little chap was safely in the Land of Nod. He opened the door a crack and peered in. Yup, there he was, lying quiet as an angel in his cot. So quiet, in fact, you'd hardly think the young fella was breathing. Despite his urgent desire to make his escape, Greg tiptoed quietly to the crib and bent down fearfully to check, his own breath put on hold. Whooh! Thank Christ for that! There was the tiny chest going up and down in perfect working order. Little bit of crusty snot on the young bloke's nose, which was easily removed with a soft wipe from Uncle Greg's silk hanky. Nappy dry. Covers in place. Sleep tight and fare thee well.

Next on the agenda was the potentially knotty problem, which he now acknowledged he had not thought through, of smashing the window in the room where young Master Marcus was watching the telly, but hell – what could the lad do to stop him? He may be his mother's son, but standing at less than a metre in stockinged feet, the little ankle nipper was hardly a match for a full-grown and desperate escapee. As relaxed as he could muster, Greg entered the lounge quietly, careful to keep himself behind the sofa and out of sight, his tell-tale suitcase carried casually in one hand.

'Oy You,' said Marcus, aware of Greg's presence, but his eyes never leaving his hero on the screen. 'Can I hab a dink of duice?'

Oy You sighed with irritation, reluctantly putting down his weapon in the recess of the bay window. So near and yet so far. 'What do we say?' he asked automatically, as was the custom in this house.

'Pease,' said Marcus.

'That's right,' said Oy You, and glancing at his watch, he made for the kitchen. Strict had been gone for forty minutes, which meant she'd be back in another twenty. He was behind schedule, having dallied too long with baby Darren, but maybe that was for the best after all. It was a little bit of a worry, leaving Marcus in a room which would inevitably have broken glass on the carpet and a gaping hole where the window had been, but it couldn't be helped, and in twenty tiny minutes, what could the boy really do to harm himself? Probably wouldn't even notice over the noise of Tommy Tank and Cranky Crane, especially if he told him he could turn the volume up as a special treat. Course, that might wake the baby, but – Jesus! Greg admonished himself crossly as he poured juice into the Bob the Builder plastic mug – it isn't my responsibility, for Christ's sake, it's his bloody mother's, the slag! Going off God knows where, leaving her kids in the charge of a man she's been imprisoning for money – what did the silly cow expect?

He slammed the fridge door shut and marched back to the living room. Teach her a bloody lesson if she came back to find Darren crying and Marcus bawling over a cut knee. Wasn't nice to think that the kids might have to suffer, but hell's teeth, you couldn't make an omelette without cracking a few bloody eggs.

'Here you are, Markie,' he said, putting the mug in the little boy's hands and picking up the television's remote. 'What do we say?'

'No turning off!' Marcus answered passionately at once. 'Me watchin it, Oy You!'

'I'm not turning it off, I'm turning it up,' Oy You said affably, false excitement colouring his voice with collusion. 'We can be naughty while Mummy's out. Hee hee! We're bad!'

'Bad boy,' agreed Marcus, his attention now returned to the screen, juice dribbling down his chin.

Greg inched towards the window and looked out. No sign of passing pedestrians, no nosy neighbours loitering nearby, just a couple of empty cars parked across the street and the swish of traffic speeding through the rain. Perfect. Or was it? Could a little kid of Marcus's size climb up on the sill and get out onto the road where he could be mown down? He assessed the height with a critical eye. Unlikely. Particularly if he shunted the sofa a bit further away from the window.

Okay, so it was now or never, with fifteen minutes left to go on the ticking clock of fate. Courage, Mackenzie, he said to himself, and aiming carefully, he resolutely swung his case to make his break for freedom.

The inevitable was about to happen, and still Lorna had not

demurred. Under Asheem's deft and intuitive hands her habitually clenched muscles had unwound so much that she wondered if they would ever find the will to move again. 'Let me do all the work,' he had gently admonished her right at the start when she had helpfully attempted to adjust her position, and since then she had been more than happy for him to decide which of her limbs should be moved and when. Without doubt he had the gift of healing in his touch – he seemed to have an uncanny ability to *listen* to her body's silent language through his hands; to go over her head, as it were, and speak directly to her flesh, her bones, her sinews, to coax and reassure that all were worthy of his best attention, that there was not one cell whose tale of secret sadness failed to fascinate him, or arouse his ready compassion.

This was certainly like no other massage she had ever had. It made Lorraine at the *Body Clinic* look like a rank amateur by comparison, her weekly fifteen-minute session at the *Neck and Shoulders Pit Stop Check for the Hectic Professional* a vulgar insult to this ancient, mystic art. For it was not just to her body that Asheem spoke, but also to her spirit. 'There's a place you know, where you feel safe,' he'd murmured softly, when his oiled hands had first begun to smooth her back with long firm strokes. 'Maybe a beach, a forest, a glade, where the sun is shining, where you can perhaps hear birds singing, the tinkling sound of water, the light rustle of a warm breeze kissing leaves and grasses – aah, you can breathe out with it. So relaxed. Utter contentment, total peace. Imagine yourself there now . . .'

After an initial flap of panic, a mental dash around the whole of the state of Victoria in search of the perfect remembered oasis of calm – a lake in Daylesford, selected then rejected on account of the blood-sucking whine of the mozzies which her imagination also provided; a particularly peaceful corner of the Botanical Gardens where she'd sat beneath trees as a student on long sun-dappled afternoons, but which now became unaccountably desecrated by the imagined cries of hyperactive children and their screeching mothers' complaints; the gently undulating deck of the *Lovelorn*, where she settled herself to sunbake as the boat skipped across the glistening waters of Port Philip Bay, became a similarly no-go area when Greg swaggered into view – but at last, lulled by Asheem's persuasive and sensitive touch, she found that her mind had returned her to the broad hammock in her own back garden, a flock of galahs flashing pink-winged across the blue, blue sky, the soft soughing of the sea, the comforting fragrance of gum trees, of jasmine, the lazy warmth of the sun, and nothing to do in all the world but just lie there and enjoy.

'So much sadness,' Asheem crooned, his voice aching with empathy, 'so much old sadness, just melting away.' And it was. It did. Like a primeval glacier at the end of the ice age, Lorna Mackenzie melted: layers of long-held tension shifted and groaned, sparkling crystals of rock-like rigidity swooned into liquid to escape through her eyes. 'So brave you've been,' he whispered gently. 'So brave and unhappy for so long. All gone now, Lorna, all washed away with your tears. Clean and new and happy to be you, just exactly as you are. Beautiful. Perfect. Serene.'

So serene, indeed, that, some time later, nestled skin-to-skin in his naked embrace, there were parts of the session she could barely remember. A vague recollection of him casually re-assuring her that he was removing his clothes to avoid getting them oily; a barely heard ringing telephone downstairs which hardly impinged on the fringes of her consciousness before it stopped; an old, now ridiculously out-dated notion that once she had known where her body ended and his began. There was nothing whatever to trouble her thoughts in any of this, though, here in the sanctuary of this cocoon, in the safe harbour of his arms where she lay cradled to his chest in this comfortingly autumn-darkened room, his warm hands caressing her back, her belly, her breasts – oohhh – slipping down between her thighs where her body was opening like a flower, petal by petal, to his touch. No, here she felt so safe and warm that danger seemed far, far away, on a different continent, in another world, as distant as the sound of a key in the front door lock, of a woman's laughter floating lightly up the stairs, of a kettle striking the kitchen hob . . .

'Bloody hell, it's my mother!' she exclaimed in a frantic whisper, as she threw herself out of bed with muscles rewound like tightened springs and began to fling on her clothes. 'She must have brought my aunties back. Quick, get dressed! Oh my God, what am I going to say to her? How am I going to explain this away?'

'I was helping you with the computer,' Asheem answered easily, being, as we know, no stranger to this same scenario in this very room. 'Helping you work out the e-mail. You go down first. I'll follow in a while.' He caught her by the hand as she was about to leave, smoothing her hair for her and sighing. 'Such a shame, Lorna. Maybe we can finish this tomorrow?'

'Doubtful,' she said brusquely, her body stiff as a board in his arms. 'I've got a wedding to go to.' The magic spell broken, now back in her right mind, she was free to remember that, not only did she disapprove of marital infidelity (and her marriage was not over until the fat lady served the divorce papers), but also she was pregnant. Good grief, she shuddered. That she had been about to introduce her unborn baby to the world of men in the most intrusive and inelegant fashion – the very thought! 'Maybe you could print off my e-mail to my husband and bring it down with you in a few moments,' she said, her legal mind now back in working order as she made to leave the room again. 'It's circumstantial evidence, but it might help weight our case downstairs.'

Asheem shrugged, clearly able to recognise a line drawn under an event when he saw one. 'Sure,' he said graciously. 'Not a problem.'

Going downstairs still adjusting her clothes, flushed, she was quite sure, with guilt, Lorna rehearsed her opening remarks to her mother and aunts. 'Took your advice, Mum,' seemed to her to be a good start, 'wrote Greg a mail, then couldn't send it. Bit of luck – bumped into the next-door neighbour outside, and he's up there sorting it now.' Sounding casual would be the key. Offhand. It wasn't that she thought they'd disapprove – on the contrary, the sisters Hibbert would be more likely to cheer her on if they knew what she'd been up to with Asheem. But that was just the point – she didn't *want* them knowing her business, particularly unfinished business which she had no intention of concluding. She could do without the ribaldry and the elbow digs, and she could certainly do without having to watch their inevitable high-spirited re-enactment of 'Confessions of a Computerman', complete with tortured puns about his hard drive.

The kitchen door was closed, she was relieved to see, which gave her a blessed moment longer to check her blouse and her features in the downstairs mirror. Reassured that both were nicely buttoned up, she adopted a brightly welcoming smile and made her entrance. The effect on her mother was explosive.

'I—!' June exclaimed, propelling herself speedily backwards out of her passionate clinch with a tall and grey-haired stranger. 'We—!' She laughed manically, her turn to adjust her hair and her clothing. With an effort she calmed herself, eyes lowered in embarrassment. 'Bert, this is Lorna. Lorna' – and now the eyes swept up in a direct appeal for her daughter's approval – 'this is Bert.'

'How do you do,' Lorna offered with stiff formality, both bemused at the speed with which she had regained the high moral ground, and in shock to see her mother as an enthusiastically sexual being. She'd never been like this with Dad! 'You've just come from rehearsals, then?' she put to Bert politely. No wonder Mum hadn't wanted her there if this was what she got up to under the influence of music! 'Do you play keyboard?'

'Er—' said Bert, shooting a look of lost helplessness at June. 'Not so's you'd notice, me duck. Spoons is about my limit.' To demonstrate this ability, or perhaps merely to break the current mood of inquisition, he grabbed a couple off the table now, and knocked himself viciously about the arms and legs in a syncopated rhythm. Actually he wasn't bad, thought Lorna abstractedly, though this was no time for musical appreciation. The silence, when he had finished, held them all in its thrall like flies trapped in amber.

'The thing is, Lorna,' June began slowly at last with a gesture which ceded, *Fair cop, we've been rumbled*, 'Bert is – is— My God! Who's that?' Clutching her heart, hand over mouth, she pointed towards the young man in the doorway.

'Asheem, next-door neighbour, been helping me out with the computer,' Lorna blustered without turning round, now similarly copped and rumbled.

'No – I'm Matt Watkins,' said the youth in a sleep-furred voice. 'Got here earlier. Crashed out in my room. Hope you don't mind. Bit knackered. Was somebody making tea?'

Behind him, the sound of Ash's jaunty skip down the stairs presaged his arrival, printed page proffered in his outstretched hand. 'Hi all,' he said with an amicable smile. 'Here's your e-mail, Lorna – any more trouble, just let me know. Got to shoot. Don't worry – I can see myself out.'

'*That* was Asheem,' Lorna felt bound to clarify while, with everybody having too much to explain and nobody wanting to be the one to begin, the assembled company gave their full and grateful attention to his progress down the hall.

It was to their collective surprise, therefore, when Ash dodged round the detumescent bride and groom and opened the front door of 236 New Vistas Boulevard to make his exit, that he was swept aside by the staggering entrance of a euphoric-looking man in a cashmere coat, swinging his suitcase and crying, '*Home*, darl, I'm home! I'm bloody home, at last!'

13

There was no shadow of a doubt whatsoever that Mick Watkins now wished fervently that he had never said yes to Busty. Not just because it had put Pauline in such a strop, nor because (despite his recent resolve to become less hide-bound) he felt daft wearing heels, but because of the one thing that he hadn't even dreamed of in this whole epic saga – that he would suffer so badly from stage-fright.

But how else could he have responded – as he had challenged Polly to consider in his own defence – when Busty had seized on him as being her last hope, her only salvation? Having dashed from the hot tub the night before in response to her blood-curdling scream, crashing through her front door, there had been no time for him to collect his scrambled wits as he stood there, fists clenched, prepared to fight an intruder who appeared to be nowhere in evidence, and Busty had swooned on his chest. Her co-star Linda Loveless, it turned out, had just called from Sydney to say that she would be delayed by one more day – she couldn't bring herself to leave her new lover on his birthday, so the show must go on without her or not go on at all. 'So unprofessional!' Busty had sobbed. 'Tomorrow is opening night – we've spent a fortune on publicity! And if I don't perform, the club will never ever book me again – my career will be over!'

Volunteering himself had been the last thing on Mick's mind when he'd tried to comfort her by suggesting that, even at this short notice, she might yet find somebody else to step into the breach for just one night. 'Didn't you tell me that Linda didn't have to do much except stand there and look beautiful?' he reminded her, as she paced round the room throwing cushions. 'Surely that can't be so very hard, there must be somebody you know who could—'

'She has to change from a man to a woman over the course of the show,' Busty had snapped irritably. 'Linda is unique in that respect, damn her eyes – she can look luscious as both. All the queens I know look like they're in drag when you put them in trousers . . .'

It was then that the pacing had slowed, and then stopped altogether, a new light appearing in her eye as she surveyed him critically, standing there in only his swimming trunks, water dripping down his tanned body and onto the living-room carpet. 'Dorothy!' she'd sighed at last. 'You are the answer to my prayers!'

Everything thereafter had gone by in a dizzying whirl of frantic activity. There had been the immediate trying on of ladies' clothes right then and there, despite Mick's protestations that he'd look a right dork in a skirt; there had been Pauline's gobsmacked entrance in the middle of all this, followed almost immediately by her storming off to bed; there had been his attempts to run after her – his first time in high heels – which had resulted in a very nasty tumble, a badly bruised knee, and a stern admonishment from Busty that on no account now must he damage the goods. So when he had finally been allowed to go back to the big house to wash off his mascara in the en suite mirror and slip gratefully between the damask sheets for a cuddle with Poll, it was to find that he had been sent to Coventry, and try as he might, with her here in Melbourne wearing earplugs, he just couldn't make himself heard.

Lying there beside her, her implacable back turned coldly towards him, his life flashed before his sleepless eyes for hour after hour, his worries about the show now forgotten. He could understand entirely why she was so miffed, and he couldn't say he blamed her. What had started out as a make-or-break night of romance at the opera had turned into an angst-ridden drama about his tortured relationship with his father and his son. It was enough to try the patience of a saint – particularly one who had already been deprived of nooky for a whole year. He desperately wanted to be able to reach out to reassure her that things would get better between them in bed, but how could he, when they were currently lying on opposite sides of it, his own confidence as shaken as hers? He was a washout, a failure: a disappointing son, a horrible father, a worse than useless husband. How much plainer could Pauline have been that she was at the end of her marital tether? And what had he done by way of response? Dashed off to sort out somebody else's distress, that's what. Avoidance, Dr Neuberger called it. Cowardice, by any other name. His dreams, when finally he fell into a light and troubled sleep, were of him eking out his days in a bed-sit, reviled, rejected and alone.

He awoke depressed, unsurprised to find that, as far as his wife was concerned, he was still where she had sent him, eleven thousand miles away, to that small West Midlands city which had been flattened by Nazi bombs in the Second World War. Even now, he noted with a sense of helpless self-disgust, when he should have been finding the courage to appease her, his butterfly mind sought refuge in facts. *Coventry, to send to: to ostracise, in the manner of the people of that city, during the Great Rebellion (1702–4); so great was their hatred of soldiers that any woman caught talking to one was instantly outlawed, hence a soldier being sent there was cut off from all social contact . . .* Fat lot of use that was to him now, his ability to remember etymological trivia. Bleddy hopeless. She hadn't even ended her silence to comment on the complimentary ticket he left for her on the kitchen table. Nor did she tell him to break a leg as he stood in the doorway to say goodbye, with Busty tugging at his sleeve like a terrier.

Thus it was, with his marriage in tatters, his guilty feelings towards his son as yet unresolved, and having been kept so busy all morning – being drilled by Busty about the finer nuances of his parts while dashing between an excruciatingly embarrassing make-up session with Shirlee in the very public arena of the cosmetics department of David Jones, a costume fitting with Sukie, hair and wig appointments with Jean-Pierre of Prahran – that he hadn't had a moment to stop and think about how he'd actually feel about being up on stage in front of a paying audience. Indeed, so far was stage-fright outside the realm of his experience that he was completely unaware that he might fall prey to it until mid-afternoon when, arriving hot-foot outside the club for the walk-through and full dress rehearsal, he looked up and saw his name spelt out in day-glo pink on a twenty-foot banner. *Busty Springboard-A-Go-Go Goes Ga-Ga In: The Seven Ages of Wo/Man*, it read, though that was really neither here nor there. It was the terrifying words that followed: *Introducing The Lovely Mick Watkins*, which caused the first nauseating wave of panic to seize him in its grip.

'Wahh!' he choked gormlessly, pointing up, his progress impeded by the trembling muscles which, hitherto, had always managed to propel his legs so efficiently and so effortlessly, but which now refused to take him one step closer towards his certain doom. Mistaking this reaction for one of unalloyed excitement, Busty was modestly pleased. 'I know,' she said. 'I called the club first thing this morning to repaint the poster. Queen Linda is dead-*lah*. Long live Queen Dorothy!' And with a gay laugh, she pushed him through the darkened foyer and towards the bright lights of the stage.

Left to enjoy her silent sulk solo, Pauline had sat alone at the kitchen table for some long time after Mick had gone that morning, imagining her life without him. For now there was no question in her mind that her marriage was over. When she had stormed off the night before, having seen him in drag (still pretty tipsy – and, lest we forget, having just survived death by drowning) she had been convinced that her earlier wild fears about him having turned gay had now been proved true. Returning to their bedroom alone, enraged and unloved, her eyes had settled on the remnants of her thwarted hopes – the silk scarves still tied to the bedposts, the accursed Ann Summers teddy making a lewd display of itself on the floor – and with a bitter laugh, she had vowed then and there to abandon all hope.

Even so, she had still half-expected him to come chasing after her, to appear in the doorway at any moment, breathless, his blonde wig askew, to try to explain it away, and when he didn't, her heart at last admitted to what her mind had already decided – that her husband was away with the fairies.

Unknotting the silk scarves, kicking the red and black teddy viciously in its crotchless behind, yanking the passion-tossed sheets straight (*Huh!* on two counts), she had rediscovered the half-drunk bottle of champagne, and had got into bed to swig from its neck. Was it possible for somebody to turn gay overnight, out of the blue, without any warning, she asked herself again. She was no expert in these matters, but she doubted it. So if Mick had known all along that he'd had these . . . urges – why the bleddy hell had he married her? As a defence against what he couldn't accept about himself as a youth, as a last-ditch stand against his true nature? And if so, how insulting was that to her? How ruthless? How selfish! How cynical!

Staring at the empty bottle in her hand she was surprised to see there were two of them, and was forced to conclude (the swaying floor helped in this) that she was now as drunk as a skunk. Was this to be her life then, she asked herself woozily as she pulled the covers over her ears – a sad divorcée who drank herself incapable, alone in her cold double bed? And how was she going to hold her head up back home, when the news hit New Vistas that the reason they'd split was that Mick Watkins was now called Michèle?

She was out for the count when Mick slid into bed, and when she awoke in the morning, was aware of his presence beside her as a consideration of secondary importance to the more pressing matter of where the bleddy hell she'd put the Nurofen. Swaying at the bathroom sink, gulping down water, she had met her own swollen-eyed gaze in the mirrored cabinet and sworn not to let herself go. Pushing Mick's moisturiser brutally out of the way, she saw with dispassionate coldness that her commitment had to be to herself now: with only one year left of her thirties to find a new partner, she couldn't afford the luxury of ruining her complexion with booze and tears.

Slipping into Lorna's silk kimono, she sighed at the wasted opportunity of this posh holiday. Soon it would be back to terry towelling in Leicester, back to the cold winter and gloomy grey skies, back to her cubicle in the call centre (if her job hadn't already gone to somebody in Bangalore), and back to a single life, which she could hardly remember, having married so young. Well, she'd be buggered if she didn't enjoy the time she'd got left here, with Mick or without him. Without him, she concluded viciously, as she swept out through the bedroom, ignoring his pathetic call of 'Polly? Pauline . . . ?'

and went down to the kitchen to make coffee for one. I'm supposed to take his little life-change in my stride, she thought, in white-hot rage as she slammed cupboard after cupboard in her hunt for a cup, but he can't even be bothered to remember what I've repeatedly asked him to call me! Well, that's it. No more Mrs Nice Guy. From now on, Pauline Watkins is her own woman. Passionate. Red in tooth and claw. A wild gypsy.

She was blind to his presence when he eventually joined her, shamefaced; deaf to his crappy, stuttering explanation about how he *had* to help Busty out for just this one night; mute on the subject of how, in so doing, he had turned his back on her, in her own hour of need. Let him work it out for himself, if he was capable of it. Let *him* feel rejected for a change. She was just going to sit here and enjoy her breakfast in silence (though her stomach felt queasy at the mere thought of how it would cope if she ever did manage to swallow the dry ball of toast her teeth were attempting to beat into submission). Humming might help to show her insouciance, she considered; shoving her nose in this magazine, surely to God, would leave him in no doubt that he was dead to her.

And sure enough, after a while, his girlfriend called for him and led him away to his new life as a drag queen – she could hardly believe that he actually had the front to leave her a ticket for the sodding show! – and she was left alone with the silence which she thought that she'd craved. Huge tears rolled out of her eyes and plopped in fat splashes on the table before she was even aware that she was crying. He was gone. It was over. Life as she had known it would never be the same again.

When she heard the car arrive outside in the driveway, her heart surprised her with its little pitter-patter of relief. He'd come back. He'd reconsidered. He too had realised that what they had in their good times was too good to throw away. But looking out of the kitchen window she saw it was Gemma and

Todd walking up to the house, back for breakfast as they'd promised. God, how awful! She'd been so busy being a rejected wife, she'd forgotten completely about being a worried mother whose daughter had been out all night. Dashing her tears away under the cold tap, she was drying her face on a tea towel as they came in.

'Hi, Mum,' said Gemma cheerfully, coming up behind her at the sink to squeeze her waist and plant a kiss on the side of her neck. Now this was something new. 'Sorry we're a bit later than we said.' And this!

'My fault, Mrs W,' Todd said staunchly. 'I know it sounds a pathetic excuse, but it turns out my watch had stopped. I hope I didn't have you worried about Gem?'

'No, no,' Pauline demurred, busying herself with some dishes, deferring the moment when she would have to turn round and expose her swollen eyes. Worried about Gemma being half an hour late? Luxury! She'd been worried in the past when she'd disappeared for three days at a time with no phone call. Worried when she'd first clapped eyes on Stu. But worried when she was out with Todd? The thought hadn't even occurred. 'You said you'd be here for breakfast and look – I'm still eating my toast. Help yourselves. Put the kettle on, Gemma. I'll just go upstairs and—'

'Actually, Mum, I've just come for my swimming cossie and stuff, if that's all right?' Gemma told her with uncharacteristic deference. 'Todd's going to teach me to windsurf today.'

Something in her daughter's tone made Pauline forget her reluctance to show her tear-ravaged face, and she turned to peek first at Gemma, and then over at Todd. She could tell at a glance that she was safe from their scrutiny, for both pairs of eyes were shining with the myopia of love. 'Yes, that's fine. Great!' she said warmly, her distress about her own affair of the heart now put temporarily on hold. Of all things –

Gemma, in love with a decent, wholesome, handsome boy!

'If that's okay with you and Mr W?' Todd enquired politely. 'I don't know if you were thinking of taking out the boat today?'

'No, that's all right, Todd,' Pauline quickly assured him. 'So – good party?' she continued, as she bustled to the fridge to take out juice and eggs. This was something to be celebrated! A proper breakfast must be served, due ceremony accorded to this occasion.

'The party . . .' Todd faltered. 'Well now—'

'We never got there,' Gemma supplied blithely. 'We went down to our boat, and just sat on the deck and talked, and looked at the stars all night. Did you know they're different here, Mum? I mean, I know it should be obvious, but I hadn't even thought about it!' She sounded as touchingly and inno-cently enthusiastic as she had as a little girl, coming back from school with her first new-learnt facts. 'And now, of course, the Aussie flag makes sense to me – those stars on it are the Southern Cross. Todd knows loads about the constellations.'

'Well, you know,' Todd said modestly, his whole face suffused with a celestial radiance all its own. 'Not much more than the next bloke. You have to know a bit as a sailor, in case your nav gear goes bung.'

'Eggs,' said Pauline brightly, a party air colouring her tone. 'Scrambled, boiled or fried?'

'Nothing, thanks,' said Gemma. 'We've already stuffed ourselves on mangoes and papayas. We went and got them from a market, and ate them straight out the bag on the beach. God, Mum, it's brilliant here! Could you ever have imagined all this in a thousand million years?'

No, Pauline could not, but she was still too wary of her daughter's instant change of personality to dare to say so. 'Yeah, it's great,' she concurred.

'Mum organised it all, you know, Todd,' Gemma told him, with a warmth in her voice Pauline had rarely heard her daughter associate with her name. 'She went on a computer course, and – whoa! – there she was, surfing the web in minutes, like she'd been doing it all her life! I'm dead proud of you,' she concluded, and gave her mum a hug.

Could essence of Todd be bottled, Pauline wondered, as she blinked her sparkling eyes and returned her daughter's embrace. Could it be supplied on demand to other mothers worried witless by the company their teenage girl was keeping?

Icing on her cake came again in a big sweet scoop, with angelica and glacé cherries on the top when, releasing her, Gemma checked, 'You don't mind me going out again, do you, Mum?'

'Of course not,' Pauline assured her, smiling giddily. 'I'm just glad you're having fun.'

Gemma turned and grinned at Todd. 'Mum and Dad'll probably be glad to be rid of me. I've been a bit of a pain recently. Cramping their style, if you know what I mean.'

Todd laughed good-naturedly. Clearly this was something they had already discussed, and Gemma had mentioned it now more for her mother's benefit, to show that her view had been recently changed. 'Well, as I said before,' he said, 'it's nice to know that your parents still love each other enough to want you out of the way, occasionally, after all these years of marriage. My mum and dad are divorced, Mrs W,' he added, as if he were bravely admitting to his worst credentials first, in the role of her daughter's would-be suitor. 'Pretty messy on both sides. So I've got a lot of respect for couples who stick with it, richer or poorer, through thick and thin.'

Feeling her smile slide off her face and onto the floor, Pauline also became aware of the complimentary ticket winking luminously on the kitchen table, which would give the lie to this fantasy of Todd's. 'Well, you know,' she said carefully, busying herself with returning eggs and juice to the fridge, hoping that both sets of eyes would follow her, if she waved her arms round enough, rather than settle on the evidence before them. 'There's nothing wrong, necessarily, with divorce. Sometimes people change too much to stay together, and the best thing they can do is to call it a day.'

'Mm,' said Gemma contentedly, with a happy dismissiveness which, Pauline realised with a stab of guilt, she and Mick would soon be responsible for destroying. 'Where is Dad? Is he upstairs?' she asked, already on her way out of the kitchen in search of her swimming things and her father.

'No,' said Pauline. 'He's – gone out with Busty. He's had to help with her show.'

Gemma stopped in the doorway. 'God, yeah, that opens tonight, doesn't it? Shall we go, Todd? It'll be a real laugh! I watched her rehearsing when I was over there staying with her. She's dead funny, and it's a really clever script – she wrote it herself.'

'I don't know . . .' said Pauline in alarm, at the same time as Todd answered, 'Yeah, great!' and Gemma continued, 'So what's Dad doing? Driving her round for last-minute props, or has she nabbed him to do something backstage?'

'Your dad,' said Pauline evenly, striving to keep her bitterness at bay, 'has had to step in for Linda Loveless tonight, who's been unavoidably detained in Sydney, apparently, on account of her boyfriend's birthday. Or some such twaddle.'

Caught off-guard, Gemma's immediate reaction was a return to her old ways, a sarcastic explosion of mirth. 'What? Dad, wearing drag? Old Mick, in high heels? Bleddy hell fire, Mum! We thought he'd gone a bit poofy with his new shirts and shorts, but – wearing a skirt?' She clutched at the door frame for support as she bent double, the better to cackle. 'This I have got to see!'

'Well, you know, Gem,' Pauline said in a discouraging tone, her nervous smile flickering with the effort of hiding her husband's secret from his child, 'I don't know that he'd like that. He'd be very embarrassed if he thought you were there. Even *I'm* not going!' she called after her, but Gemma was already skipping up the stairs and shouting back, 'Tough, he'll have to suffer! There's no way I'm going to miss it!'

Turning back to face Todd, Pauline saw, to her horror, his eyes flicking up, puzzled, from the invitation on the table, saw him process this piece of contradictory information with what she'd just said, catching her out in her deception about Mick not wanting her to go to the show. His young face showed a maturity she was yet to see in either of her own kids, put there perhaps, she mused, during the time he'd had to try to make sense of his own parents' messy divorce. 'You're okay, Mrs W?' he asked her seriously, searching her expression with a directness born of concern.

'Fine, Todd!' she blustered, now remembering her swollen eyes, her hands going automatically to rub them. 'Bit too much to drink last night!' she laughed with high-pitched gaiety. 'I must look like something the cat's brought in!'

'If you wanted to come with us to the beach . . .' he began.

'No, no . . . !' she demurred, in a frenzy of activity, wishing to God she was in her own Leicester kitchen, where there would be far more to fiddle and faff with and tidy into drawers.

'. . . you'd be more than welcome, for sure.'

'Thought I'd just chill by the pool,' she shrilled hotly.

'He's a great bloke, Mr W,' Todd continued, watching her carefully, his recent tunnel vision now corrected, it seemed, by the absence of his love object from the room. 'A lot of blokes – my own dad, as an example – would never be man enough to take on board a person like Busty, befriend her like your husband has, and treat her with exactly the same respect he'd have for anybody else. I admire that. Sure enough of his own masculinity not to feel threatened by diversity. Takes guts – and balls, if you'll pardon the vernacular – for a straight guy like him to go on stage in a dress to help out a mate.'

Pauline could have kissed him. She had been emboldened enough during his gracious and educative speech to abandon her frantic tidying and to turn her attention towards him. Something about him reminded her of the young Mick she'd fallen in love with – the thoughtfulness, the seemingly effortless sense of taking responsibility seriously, the dependability which had 'perfect father material' stamped all through, like a stick of seaside rock. 'Your mother is either very lucky, or very clever to have had you,' she told him warmly.

He grinned. 'So she thinks. But then, she hasn't met Gem yet. You're pretty clever yourself, if you don't mind me saying.'

Was there no end to this boy's charm? 'What is it that you do when you're not sailing, Todd?' she asked him fondly, already imagining her prideful boasts back home (and as yet unmindful of the wrench it would be to have Gemma living so far away).

'I'm training to be a primary schoolteacher,' he said, squaring his shoulders to the task of impressing this mother whom he already had ambitions to one day call his own. 'Two more years to go. Can't wait. It's what I've always wanted, ever since I was a kid.'

My son-in-law the teacher. Pauline could imagine herself saying it, as she handed round photos at work.

'Hmm. Don't you wish you'd had him to teach you the alphabet?' Gemma asked, as the bounced back into the room to claim him by the hand.

How was it that love could come so quickly, Pauline mused with wide-eyed wonder, could blossom and transform the prickly cactus that her daughter had been, into this sweet and luscious, tender flower? Perhaps she had been as clever a parent as Todd had said – her and Mick both, of course, she hastily amended, credit where credit was due. This was a Gemma they hadn't seen since Stu had got his grubby hands on her and turned her into a creature of the night. It was nothing short of a miracle to see her now, all scrubbed up and smiling, and as Pauline waved them off to their day at the beach, she silently wished Todd all the luck he would need to keep that softness growing.

Left alone again, she had much to think about, and this was best done, she decided, cleaving through the turquoise waters of the pool she'd soon be forsaking, the sun on her back, hope for her marriage again in her heart. For surely Todd had been right in suggesting that Mick's acquiescence to Busty's demands was merely proof of both his mature masculinity and his friendly, helpful nature? Would she prefer a macho idiot who was so insecure about his own sexuality, she asked herself, as she racked up twenty lengths, that he couldn't bear any grey areas outside his own narrow field of experience? Of course not, she concluded breathlessly, spreading herself on a lounger to dry in the sun, her fears about her husband's gender-bending now banished to a small file at the back of her mind marked *Innocent until proven guilty*.

She was the first to admit she hadn't exactly had the kind of experiences (barring recently, with Asheem) that would qualify her to be called a woman of the world, but she was a citizen of a developed nation in the twenty-first century, and open to the influences of its popular culture. People thought nothing of girls kissing girls now, of boys wearing skirts – it didn't even mean, apparently, that they were necessarily gay.

Look at Madonna, how she chopped and changed. Or that chap who threw pots while wearing a dress, who'd won the art prize – he had a daughter, though he called himself Claire. Good God, she thought feistily, though she personally had never had a lezzie inclination in the whole of her life, she could easily get her head around snogging Mick in a frock, if that's what it took to get laid. Let *him* wear the teddy – it was all one with her.

No, it wasn't so much his willingness to wear make-up, as his keenness to rush off to help somebody else rather than her. That was what still rankled. Mick's inability to face his own problems – and hers.

The deleterious effects of the previous evening's surfeit of alcohol having somewhat receded, due to two quarts of water having been imbibed, two Nurofen taken, and a glass of freshly squeezed orange juice now being savoured, she tried to recall in detail the events which had led up to the discovery of her husband in heels. She reviewed the opera, so far so fabulous; the touchy-feely drive back with her hand on his thigh – hadn't seemed like he'd had any objection to that. She spent some long and enjoyable moments recalling the rollicking good time they'd been having in the bedroom before Gemma had arrived to deliver the kiss of death. It had been the wildest session they'd ever had together, and look at the results: all Mick's 'Stop' signs had turned to 'Go'; he'd been gagging for it when she'd had him parcelled up on the bed; it had stuck out a mile that he'd been up for it.

Reluctantly she forced her thoughts away from the excitement of this memory, this milestone in their marital history, and now she listened again to the effect Gemma's tale of Matt leaving university had had on his dad. (Matt! God, so wrapped up in her own misery she'd been, she'd even pushed her son's drama to the back of her mind! Where the hell was he, and what was he up to? No use worrying about that, now, she counselled herself calmly, catching herself before she went off into a worried mother spin. He was twenty, a sensible lad normally, and Gemma was right, there was nothing they could do until he called them, or they got back home and tracked him down through his mates.)

Her mind now took her back to the hot tub, and Mick's stumbling attempt to explain . . . something – which evidently had huge importance for him. By that time, of course, she'd been well on the way to being nissed as a pewt, so there were some frustratingly blank spots in her memory this morning. But at last she forced herself to focus on the bit where Mick had lost her completely – something about feeling a sense of relief over Matt not finishing his degree, some guilt he was feeling about – competitiveness, was it? – and the timescale being too much of a coincidence. Then stuff about his own dad, hearing voices in his head . . .

Pauline shook her own head here. Nope. It was hopeless. She couldn't untangle that one any better now, stone-cold sober, than she'd been able to while under the influence of champagne and lager. She should have pressed him harder to explain in words of one syllable, she ruefully admitted, instead of being drunkenly obsessed about how soon she could get him back into bed. She couldn't even remember how that part of the conversation had ended, or if indeed it had ended. Had there been some talk of stress? The subject of a sex manual had next grabbed her attention, she seemed to remember, and shamelessly, lustfully (she cringed now at the recollected image of her lascivious leer) she'd tried to persuade him to go upstairs with her and look at the pictures.

She sat up suddenly, orange juice spilling down her chest. Might there be some clue in that? If she could find the book he'd been reading, would it answer her questions?

Running back into the house, leaping the stairs like a steeple-chaser, she ransacked their bedroom thoroughly and settled down in a fever of anticipation with Dr Ed. Several pages, she discovered, had been dog-eared, so she devoured them first, but though they gave her a fresh and touching insight into Mick's attempts to put theory into practice, it was the passage he'd highlighted in Chapter Eight, *Some Successful Case Histories*, that at last illuminated the dark corners of Mick's mind, and the truth about the black hole of their marital bed slowly dawned on her, as it must surely have dawned on him.

Mr X's experience is not uncommon and certainly not new, Dr Neuberger confided, *having its roots in Greek mythology. We are all familiar with Oedipus's side of the ancient story* ('Are we?' muttered Pauline churlishly. 'Seems to have passed me by, clever clogs.' Dr N, however, conscious that not all his readers were classics scholars, went on to explain): *the idea of the new generation replacing the old, here depicted in the archetypal instinct of the son to slay his father and impregnate his mother* ('Filth!' she cried in outrage. 'Not my Matt!' But still the good doctor was ahead of her), *which must, of course, be seen in its allegorical context – the struggle of the human mind to comprehend the everyday tragedy that all life must end in death.* ('Fair point,' she conceded.)

Which brings us to consider the no less archetypal instinct of the father to avoid this fate. Just as Laius, forewarned by Apollo that he would be killed at the hands of his own son, tried to escape his destiny by giving away his first-born, Oedipus, at birth, so did Mr X, and many other fathers like him, struggle to maintain his dominance by diminishing his son (here, Mick had underscored the last three words and written in the margin 'Dad!'). *When that failed and, despite Mr X's constant criticism, his son continued to enjoy success, gaining his first-class honours degree and going on to a career in research, Mr X's only option was to diminish himself instead. (Remember, this was all in his uncon-scious,* Dr Neuberger counselled. *If he had ever managed to reflect on this [see Chapter Three:* Facing your Fears Fairly and Squarely*], he might have understood why it was that his peter had lost its perkiness.) Comparing himself unfavourably to his progeny, however, he began to see himself as a failure, his life as a skilled worker a futile waste, and the more he accepted this skewed vision of himself, the less he could rise to the challenge between his own sheets.*

When his marriage started to fail as a result of this, Mr X saw it as further proof of his inadequacy . . .

It was the phone ringing so insistently which finally prompted Pauline to realise that she had been sitting with the book abandoned in her lap for almost half an hour, staring into space, full of sadness and regret, shedding tears over her own stupidity, her treacherous infidelity, and poor Mick's endless struggle to come to terms with his life. Of course he must have been envious of Matt. She knew full well that he had longed to go on to university when he was at school. But had he ever sunk as low as Mr X, or his own father come to that, and undermined his children? Never. Not once. He'd been as good a father as you could ever wish for, offering encouragement and support all along the way, pushing them off their lazy behinds to do their homework, taking them on trips to museums, trying to get them all excited about the challenge and stimulation of an education that he'd been deprived of. He, whom she had written off as such a coward – and yes, yes, as a failure too – had been fighting his own demons while she'd been diddling with the dildo next door. Because that, she now realised with red-faced shame, was all Ash had ever been for her.

For some annoying reason (Gemma forgetting to reset it,

probably, Pauline thought tetchily) the Mackenzies' answer-phone was not kicking in, and whoever was calling was refusing to give up. Heaving herself off the bed to give short shrift to whichever of Lorna and Greg's friends had forgotten they were away, her heart leapt in recognition of the voice she heard instead, and shortly thereafter she was behind the wheel of the Beemer on a rescue mission, driving like a maniac to a certain gay venue downtown.

The Seven Ages of Wo/Man was elegantly simple in its conceit, but a breathless backstage flurry of complexity in its execution. For while Miss Busty Springboard-A-Go-Go had to transform herself from woman to man in seven lightning-quick changes between monologues and songs, her co-star had simultaneously to work his way across the gender spectrum in reverse, from man to woman, thus providing the audience with a contrapuntal leitmotif, or, for the theatrically illiterate, with eye candy, until the diva returned. In this way, the stage would never be empty: while one artiste was on stage, the other would be in the wings having their costume changed by Sukie, their hair teased by Jean-Pierre, and their make-up amended by Shirlee.

Thus it was that when Pauline – who had prepared herself stoically to take the sight of her husband in false boobs and stilettos in her stride – burst through the auditorium doors and ran towards the handsome figure currently caught in the bright lights of the stage, her first confused thought was, *Am I in the wrong club?* Pursued as she was, however, by the two rather large and very butch lady bouncers wearing headsets whom she'd dodged round outside in the foyer, she continued on her course stage-ward none the less, although her strides became more laboured, it is true, her lower jaw slacker, her eyes ever wider, as she came finally to realise that the muscled hunk strutting his stuff in the sequinned posing pouch was none other than The Lovely Mick Watkins.

It perhaps goes without saying that Miss Springboard-A-Go-Go was not best pleased, as she sprang out of the wings, mid-change, in response to the ruckus, to witness the mêlée of mayhem on stage. But once Mick had stopped hyper-ventilating and Pauline had fought her way out from under the impressive Aussie Rules tackle of the two leather-jacketed dykes to announce, wild-eyed, that she had to talk to Mick in private and that afterwards he would need to make a long-distance phone call, Busty rose to the occasion and told everyone to take five. The bouncers withdrew with muttered apologies, smoothing their hair and explaining that they'd only been doing their job, Jean-Pierre tore off his nicotine patch and gratefully lit up a fag, Shirlee embraced Pauline as a heroine before running out to buy sandwiches all round, and Sukie put the kettle on: they all had tea.

Left tactfully alone in the manager's office, then, Pauline at last debriefed herself to the anxious man in the bejewelled jock-strap. She told him that she loved him, never more than now; she assured him of his pricelessness to her as a husband, as the father of her children, and as an all-round wonderful human being; she convinced him that she now fully under-stood that he had been locked this last year in an archetypal struggle (although she lost him at first with her allusions to what she reckoned the Greeks got up to, since their last family holiday had been taken in Corfu); and finally she told him of his son's story, and the central role for him contained therein.

'He wants to give up law to be a *plumber*?' Mick queried, feeling sick.

'Like his dad,' smiled Mum.

'But why?'

For answer, she dialled three handfuls of digits and passed

the phone to him, and after a lengthy conversation between father and son, the Watkins family's fate was sealed. For what could Mick do but concede that he had long since hated his job with the big firm who treated him worse and worse each passing year, with their new management initiatives involving longer hours, shorter pay, and no respect for him at all; how could he argue that he knew better than Matt, at twenty, what made the lad happy; what could he say, in short, to the proposal that, while his son studied plumbing part-time at college, he himself would head up the business they would go into together, and which, in the fullness of time, Pauline would gleefully give up her job to administrate?

Hence it came to pass that on that night, *Watkins Washers (Leicester) – Family Plumbers* was born during a break in the dress rehearsal of a transgender cabaret in a Melbourne club, where its senior partner was about to make his debut.

14

Returning the receiver to its cradle, young Matt Watkins turned back to smile at the assembled party in the kitchen of New Vistas, whose own agenda had perforce been put on temporary hold. 'Sorted,' he said. 'Cheers for that. So, I'll let you guys get on. Mum says I'm to go and stay with Gran till they get back. She says it was bad enough saddling you with Whiff, without having me to put up with as well.'

June, who had been the one sensible enough, even in extremis, to make Matt call his parents and tell them he was safe, now looked from her daughter to the man she was embracing, and from him to the man whom she wished she was embracing herself. 'Normally, love,' she said regretfully, 'I'd like nothing better than to have the pleasure of your company, but just at the minute, we've got a couple of bits of family business that we need to take care of ourselves.'

'Sure,' said Matt easily, ambling upstairs to get his rucksack. 'No sweat.'

When he was gone, and Greg's earlier, sketchy explanation of his recent imprisonment was being made fuller over several glasses of wine, the two women dried their tears of hysterical laughter to turn as one against him, stern, judgemental and cold.

'You smashed your way out of the window, leaving a toddler and a baby all on their own to fend for themselves?' his wife accused him, disgust and disbelief discolouring her tone.

'No, I didn't,' Greg assured them hotly. 'I couldn't do it in the end. And that was when Miss Strict knew I'd learnt my lesson. She'd been hiding outside, staked out in her car the whole time – I'd misjudged her about that – misjudged her about a few things, actually. I thought I'd been really clever, duping her into taking off my leg-chains, but the whole thing was a set-up. It was my final test. She knew full well it'd be a temptation for me to escape, but if I had've done, she'd have been down on me like a ton of bricks – I'd be there now, back chained to the bed, and most likely having pins stuck down my fingernails. No,' he concluded, his eyes softening with the memory, 'what happened to bring me to my senses was that Darren started crying – me turning up the volume on the telly saw to that – and when I didn't go to see him right off, cos I was still dithering at the window, dreaming of my freedom, little Markie starts to trot off there himself. I was shamed by a three-year-old. Suddenly hit me that this little fella, toddling off to look after his baby brother, was more grown-up than I've ever been.'

'God,' said Lorna, leaning back in her chair with a sigh of relief and awe. 'What a woman Sheila Strict is. I'd like to shake her by the hand.'

'I think she's expecting a bit more than that,' Greg chuckled. 'Turns out she was doing it all on a kiss and a promise. Your dear cousin Melissa had told her that she couldn't afford to pay her, but if the experiment was a success, you'd be so grateful you'd make it more than worth her while. You'll see her tomorrow at the wedding, so you better go tooled up with cash!'

'You'll see her later today,' June corrected him briskly, glancing at the kitchen clock, and clearing away their empty glasses. 'Will you look at the time!'

If she had hoped by this to escape having to tell her own tale, however, she would have done well not to have ended as she did with, 'High time we were all in our beds!' for this drew her daughter's attention back to the as yet unasked question, 'Who is this spoon-playing mother-snogger, and why exactly is he still here?' Wresting the glasses from her mother's grasp, therefore, she refilled them with reckless abandon, and glittered a steel-eyed smile. 'So, Mum,' she invited. 'Your story now, I think.'

June blushed. Bert grinned. They both sought the comfort of each other's hand underneath the table. 'Well, love,' June began at last, after nervously draining half her glass. 'A long time ago, I was a very, very silly girl. I'd been going out for ages with a truly wonderful man,' (here Bert's grin grew broader and his answering look more fond) 'and we were even engaged to be married.'

'For two year,' Bert supplied helpfully. 'Engagements were long in them days. Well, we had to save up.'

'That's right,' said June, and as she reached again for her wine glass, Lorna saw with astonishment that her late father's wedding and engagement rings had been recently replaced with a small solitaire diamond on a platinum band, which she had never clapped eyes on before. 'Anyway,' June continued, 'as I said at the beginning, I was very silly. Because along came your dad, Lorna, who I met one night after a Hibbert Sisters' session in a pub, and I got swept off my feet with all his exciting talk of making a new life out in Australia. It was all over the news at that time that the Australian government had decided it needed more people out there, and in order to get them, they were offering passage across for only a tenner. Your dad had made up his mind to go, you see, and he was looking for a girl to marry and take with him. So – I did a dreadful thing. I left Bert without a backward glance, and I let that girl be me.'

Lorna swallowed hard. 'Are you saying you didn't really love

Dad?' she asked querulously, he whole existence now coming
into question.

'Oh, she did, chick,' Bert cheerfully assured her. 'He were a
handsome bugger, weren't he, June? And he were quite a good
bloke, I thought, as it turned out. I didn't have half his
gumption. I could quite see why she went off with him.'

'I grew to love him,' June said apologetically. 'At first I was
just bowled over by the idea of adventure abroad. Then when
I got there I realised just what I'd left behind. Like Princess Di
said, there were three people in our marriage, but for me, one
of them was eleven thousand miles away. But yes, Lorna, your
dad and I had a very happy marriage for the most part. Hurtful
for Bert as that was.'

'No hard feelings though, duck, ay?' Bert murmured, slipping a supportive arm around her shoulders. 'You had your
happy married life, and I had mine in the end, and now,
maybe, we can have another one together.'

An awful lot of information had come Lorna Mackenzie's
way in a very brief time, and you might think she would have
been so busy digesting it all that it was this which kept her
awake for the rest of that night. But as it transpired, after
her mother and her step-father-to-be had repaired to their
room to rekindle their romance, and after she had asked Greg
the burning question, 'So, do you want this baby?' and found
his answer to be, 'More than anything – if you can overlook
me having behaved like such a prat,' she was kept extremely
active in another pursuit altogether.

For what could she do but rejoice in her mother's happiness
at last, in her third year of widowhood; how could she argue,
after Greg's education at the hands of Sheila Strict, that he had
not learnt his lesson, nor already been punished enough; what
could she say, in short, about her mum finally marrying the
man she'd been engaged to, and her own husband's avowed

intent to make up for his bad behaviour as best he could for the rest of his natural life, which included (at Lorna's behest) a promise to go on a sensual massage course as soon as they got home?

Hence it came to pass that on that night, the Mackenzie family of Black Rock, Melbourne, was reunited in the back bedroom of a council house in Leicester, where its first baby was already beginning to grow, preparing herself for her debut.

15

It was tribute to Busty's enormous popularity with the excited first-night crowd in the packed club that, when they were plunged into darkness and a single spot came up to illuminate nothing more than the split in the velvet drapes upstage centre, the applause and the whistles were deafening: the mere thought that it would soon be filled by their hilarious heroine was enough to drive them wild. It was well known that she was a consummate performer, her new shows always eagerly awaited, for she never failed to surprise them with her innovation and wit.

Watching from the wings, her hands on her husband's naked waist, ready to launch him out on his brief stage career on cue, even Pauline, who had already seen most of the dress rehearsal, felt a frisson of excitement bordering on hysteria.

Once she and Mick had finished their family conference after his phone call with Matt, and the cast and crew had polished off their tea and sandwiches, she had been pressed by Busty and Sukie to stay behind and help backstage.

'Maybe you'll be able to calm him down-*lah*,' Busty had said, with desperation in her voice. 'I've never seen a pair of legs vibrate like that with fear – usually when a man turns to jelly in my company, it's for a different reason altogether.'

'Oh go on, Pauline – he might be okay if it's his wife helping him on with it,' Sukie had added, holding up the elasticated contraption at which Mick had drawn the line. 'He won't let me anywhere near him with this.'

'It hurts!' Mick had protested. 'It's unnatural to parcel your package away like that! It could do irreversible damage!'

'Darl,' Busty had said firmly, 'if it did, do you think I would risk my own magnificent equipment? Do you think I would risk my friend Pauline's future happiness? No-*lah*. Such a fuss about a tiny little bit of discomfort. A girl must suffer for her art.'

'I'm not a girl,' Mick had sniffed petulantly, but with everybody looking at him like that, drumming their fingers and tapping their toes, he'd known that his cause was lost.

Pauline, who had been temporarily lost in admiration of her husband's current makeover as a man – the bleached highlights in his sharp new haircut, courtesy of Jean-Pierre; the way his eyebrows had been waxed into that wonderful shape by Shirlee; the muscles of his bare buttocks so taut and firm around the rear portion of his posing pouch, where a thousand sequins sparkled, sewn on by Sukie's hand – had shaken herself and come at him resolutely. 'That's right,' she'd told him in a no-nonsense tone. 'You're not a girl. Yet. But you soon will be.' Grabbing the 'man-trap', as Mick had dubbed it, she'd pushed him firmly back to the quick-change area with a cheeky twinkle in her eye and a devil-may-care shrug. 'Might as well be hung for a sheep as a lamb,' she'd told the relieved company, and had grinned broadly at their cheers.

From her ringside position now that the show had begun, pressed up against Mick's back in the wings, she didn't need to feel the trembling of his knocking knees to know that he was terrified. 'You're going to be fabulous,' she whispered loudly in his ear, striving to make herself heard over the crowd's roar of approval as Busty took the stage, arms held aloft, graciously inclining her head to acknowledge their adulation before bursting joyfully into her opening song. It was now or never for The Lovely Mick Watkins to make his entrance, and with a final admonishment to 'Just enjoy it,' and a reassurance that she would be waiting for him right here when he returned, Pauline gave him the last little push, without which he would never have gone on. Peeking round the black curtain which hid her from the audience, she felt as proud as a mother at her child's first nativity play as she basked vicariously in the wolf whistles which greeted her husband's appearance. Indeed, so enthralled was she by his performance as he swaggered on, flexing his biceps and pecs as taught by Busty, despite his desire to crumple and flee, that he was almost upon her again before she remembered her own role as dresser, and she flew to help Sukie to denude him and dress him again.

'There now, that wasn't so bad was it, love?' Shirlee murmured encouragingly as she subtly adjusted his make-up on the first of its seven steps towards the feminine. 'And you even remembered your twirl.'

At the back of the auditorium as the crowd hushed themselves to listen to Busty's monologue about the fluidity of gender, Gemma was reeling from shock. 'I can't believe it,' she said, gobsmacked, to Todd. 'He is so bleddy gorgeous! I've never seen it before.'

'Hands off,' a cute queen beside her hissed in warning, turning to eye Todd enviously. 'You've already got yours, sweetie. That one's for me.'

'He's my dad, actually,' Gemma confided proudly.

'And virile too!' groaned her neighbour, before they were both shushed into silence from all sides.

*

By the end of the show, when Gemma's father had been fully transformed into a beautiful woman, and Chin, in suit and tie, had finally reclaimed Busty's body to deliver the last line, '*You're* confused!' it was clear to everybody on both sides of the footlights that Mick had finally relaxed enough to enjoy his once-only performance thoroughly. For it was exactly as Jean-Pierre commented drily at the backstage party afterwards – if they hadn't dimmed the spots and brought the curtain down, he would still be standing there now, bowing and blowing kisses from his satin-gloved fingertips.

Pauline, still awed by this curvaceous, buxom stranger, despite the fact that she had helped in her creation, edged towards her through the congratulatory crowd. As he saw her coming, her husband's eyes were just recognisable to her – powdered lilac as they were, and fringed with false lashes – and the discomfort expressed in them unmistakable. 'Polly,' he said, through smiling but clenched teeth, 'I've been looking for you everywhere! Can you help me out of this crippling bleddy nut-cracker?' And taking her by the arm, he led her gratefully to his dressing room.

Kneeling at his feet, her hands up inside his long dress, Pauline wrestled him free from what ailed him. 'You were brilliant,' she said, as she tugged the tight offending article down his thighs and he gave a groan of relief. 'You've made me proud today, on every count.'

'Did I?' asked Mick, suddenly serious. 'Cos I haven't made me very proud. I had time to think, once I'd settled down out there, about what Ed Neuberger says about Laius. It isn't very nice to think that I stopped being able to – you know – how's-your-father – just because I was scared of my own son outshining me.'

'It wasn't just that, and besides, that happens to a lot of men – he says so in the book – it's unconscious and archetypal,'

Pauline corrected him, glad to have learnt some new technical terms with which to support her argument. 'It was the damage your own dad had done to you earlier, and you not having the self-confidence to tell him to go to hell – even in your own mind, and even now you're grown up. Plus you're at a difficult age – just look at what turning thirty-nine has been doing to me, made me grumpy and horrible and—'

She left the sentence hanging, stopping herself short of a full confession about Asheem. Knowing about her past affair wouldn't do Mick any good now, and it certainly wouldn't help their relationship get better in the how's-your-father department. Besides, it was over as far as Pauline was concerned, and therefore irrelevant. 'It makes you realise that you're growing older,' she continued instead, 'that your best years are behind you, and that makes you question what you've achieved with your life.'

Mick grinned, trying out a bit of recently learnt camp badinage. 'I'll have to take that on trust, darl,' he said in a womanly tone. 'You may remember that some of us are still a youthful thirty-eight.'

Hitting him with the sweaty nut-cracker, Pauline laughed and took him in her arms to kiss him. 'This feels strange,' she said with a voice thickened by lust, as she inspected his unfamiliar face and cleaned his smudged lipstick with her finger.

'*You're* confused,' Mick riposted with a smile. 'What about me? I swear to God the blood's stopped flowing to me whatsit – I've got no feeling left there at all!'

'No?' Pauline queried, pressing her loins against his and wriggling them appreciatively. 'So what's this? Scotch mist?' And so saying, she took his feminine face in both her hands and snogged him again assertively.

It was typical of Gemma that she chose this moment to track her parents down, but this time, emboldened by the theatricality of the event, Pauline didn't even bother to blush, let alone leave off her shenanigans. Inviting her daughter and her new boyfriend to take a seat, she sat down herself and patted her knee for Mick to join her. 'Now then,' she told Gemma, holding her husband on her lap and stroking his stockinged thigh absent-mindedly, 'I think I know what you're going to say, Gem, but you'd better put me out of my misery.'

'I'm going to stay on after you've gone,' Gemma said, eschewing a chair of her own and similarly sitting on her own lover's knee, all smiles. 'It seems daft to come all this way and then go back home after a fortnight, and this was always going to be my gap year for travel.'

'Blimey,' said Mick, who hadn't had his wife's advantage of seeing this coming earlier in the day. 'But where will you stay, and what will you live on?'

'I've already found myself a couple of jobs, today,' she told her father proudly. 'Sales assistant in a bookshop in Acland Street, and two nights a week in the bar where Todd works.'

'When he's not at college studying to be a teacher,' Pauline supplied, for Mick's benefit.

'As for where Gemma'll live, Mr W,' Todd offered, 'if it's okay with you, she'll be staying with me and my mum. And by the way, Mum's invited you round tomorrow for tea, so's you can check us out and give our place the once-over.'

'Blimey,' said Mick again, blinking his long mascaraed lashes. 'Right. Well, then.'

'You don't mind, do you, Dad?' Gemma asked, which was as much a surprise to him as the rest of her revelations had been.

'No, no,' he said. 'It's just – well, it's all happened so quick. I'm a bit—'

A huge grin suddenly split Gemma's face from ear to ear. '*You're* confused, Mother,' she told him, bending forward to brush back a lock of his wig. 'Just think what it's like from where I'm sitting!'

They were all still laughing when Chin arrived to round them up and herd them back to the festivities. 'It's your finest hour, Dorothy,' he complained as he chivvied them to their feet. 'We can't have you missing your first first-night party.'

'It's The Lovely Mick Watkins to you,' Mick corrected him grandly. 'And I can tell you this, I shan't be sorry to stop being called Dorothy. I'm going to burn those bleddy red trainers when I get back home.'

'What's in a name?' his wife teased him, as she took his arm to help him totter along in his heels.

'You're right, Pauline,' he admitted ruefully. 'I've been really bad about that. From now on I'll make sure I remember not to call you Polly.'

'From now on, darl,' she said flirtatiously, her hand straying to caress his bottom through his dress, 'I'm expecting you to keep me feeling young enough to answer to the name of my youth.'

Mick grinned, stopping in the corridor to kiss her. 'We'll certainly try,' he said, 'me and my Scotch mist together.'

'By the way, you don't have to worry about me bursting in on the two of you again later,' Gemma said flippantly as she and Todd passed them by. 'We're thinking of sleeping over on the *Lovelorn* again tonight, if that's okay?'

'Yes, that'll be fine,' her mother assured her, and safely alone again for a moment, she returned her attention to exploring the contours of her husband's new breasts. 'You'll never guess what,' she challenged him, feeling more confident about what his reaction would be since the Scotch mist was already beginning to rise again, but nevertheless examining his face for any signs of evasion, 'but I'd started to wonder if you were gay.'

'Darl,' laughed Shirlee, who appeared at that moment to squeeze past them in the corridor on her way back from a visit to the Ladies, 'you should have asked me! My gaydar is infallible – or should I say "inphallicable"? – and, believe me, sister, that man of yours is as straight as they come. That daggy old shell suit still haunts me.'

'I was just being supportive to Busty,' Mick added when she'd gone. 'Trying to be less narrow-minded about gender-bending. I mean, it's not as if we come across much of this in New Vistas, is it? And I'd caught myself being a bit uncomfortable to be seen out with her when we were shopping in town. Made me feel a bit of a Judas.'

Pauline smiled and pulled him to her again. 'For a good man, you make a damned fine figure of a woman,' she said rakishly, brushing back an imaginary moustache from her lips. 'I'm beginning to wonder if I'm not a little bit susceptible to this gender-bendering myself.'

'I don't think we'll stay too long at this party, Polly,' Mick offered huskily, some time later, when they came up for air from a full-blooded snog. 'What do you think?'

'I'm thinking, young lady,' Pauline returned boldly, eyeing him with heavy-lidded passion. 'That if we were to promise Sukie we'd bring it back first thing in the morning – would she let us borrow this costume of yours, just for one night?'

Mick groaned. 'Let's be realistic here, Polly,' he said breathlessly, as his wife stroked the naked flesh around his suspenders through the high split in his frock. 'We shouldn't make a promise that we know we can't keep. Second thing in the morning'd be all the same to her, wouldn't it?'

16

Though both *Hello!* and *OK!* were conspicuous by their absence, having evidently decided it was not worth getting into a bidding war for exclusive photos, it was unanimously agreed by all who did attend the civil ceremony at the Leicester registry office and who afterwards repaired for baked meats at the New Vistas Working Men's Social Club, that it was most definitely the wedding of the year. For who amongst them had ever seen so tiny a newborn baby tricked out in a hand-sewn bridesmaid's dress before? Where else could they have danced the night away to the Sensational Swinging Sixties Hibbert Sisters, reunited after all these years? And who would have guessed that some chap from Australia would suddenly get up after the toasts to announce that, in honour of his wife's cousin's wedding to one of the best mates a bloke could ever have, and in honour of his mother-in-law's upcoming marriage, and last but not least, in honour of his lovely wife Lorna being pregnant with their first child, picking up the tab at the bar would be his pleasure, and that the more they drank, the greater that pleasure would be?

Well, for one, it was certainly not Elroy.

'See?' said his new wife, digging him jovially in the ribs. 'What did I say? It all worked out right in the end. I told you Sheila'd sort him.'

'Bleddy risky, though,' Elroy complained, as he was dragged

off by Parveen to dance. 'What if she hadn't? You and me would've been dead meat.'

'Not with Lornie here to protect me,' the bride purred, pulling her cousin into a lung-crushing hug.

'That's right,' Lorna agreed, with what little breath was left at her disposal, and freeing herself from the embrace, she returned her gaze to what she'd been watching before: Greg with a baby in his arms, a toddler hanging off his leg, deep in conversation with a woman who, to Lorna's surprise, looked as normal as any of the other guests at the wedding. She didn't know what she'd been expecting Sheila Strict to look like – tight black leather with loads of straps and patent thigh-length boots? – but she was astonished now to realise that she could have passed her in the street and never had an inkling of her profession.

'I need to sort out a bit of business, Mel,' she said now, leaving her cousin to the attentions of other well-wishers. 'I'll get you another drink, shall I, on my way back?'

'Cheers – love you, Lornie,' Melissa beamed, and handing baby Lornetta to a goo-ing relative, she swept Elroy's mum and gran out onto the dance floor for a bit of disco fever round their handbags.

When Lorna self-consciously approached Greg's group, it was baby Darren who received her first big smile, then little Marcus, before, shyly, she raised her eyes to her rescuer. 'Sheila, is it?' she asked, extending her hand. 'I'm Lorna, Greg's wife.'

'Make myself scarce for a bit, let you girls chat on,' Greg said amiably, handing Darren back to his mother and taking Marcus by the hand. 'Okay if the two of us boys go off for a dance, Mum?' he asked Sheila, who nodded her assent.

'So – thank you,' said Lorna, at a loss to know quite how to start this conversation with her husband's teacher, once they were alone. 'I know I owe you a huge debt of gratitude, but I believe there's the matter of settling a bill too?'

'That's right,' said Sheila, a little uncomfortable herself to be doing this transaction with another woman.

Lorna took an envelope out of her handbag and handed it over. 'Couldn't be a cheque, or it'd be in Aussie dollars,' she explained. 'So I hit the ATM with Greg's and my cards. If there's not enough in there, I'll have to see you again to pay you the balance.'

'I'd thought three hundred pounds, if you can afford it,' Sheila told her, feeling the weight of the packet and striving for some of the authority that she wielded with such ease over her charges.

'In that case,' Lorna smiled, 'think of the balance as a tip. Cheap at the price, in my view – by rights, you should have your own weight in gold.'

'Well, you know, Lorna,' said Sheila, returning the smile, 'we try to be of service.'

Their business concluded, Lorna was still reluctant to leave, curious to know quite how it had ever occurred to this woman to come up with her business plan. 'Melissa tells me you're training to be a – radiographer, is it? Radiologist?'

'-ographer,' Sheila supplied. 'Radiologists are doctors, and studying for that'd be a bit beyond my purse, even with my . . . little job on the side. Still means doing a three-year BSc Honours, though, but I'm nearly there, thank God.'

'So how did you . . . if you don't think I'm being too much of a stickybeak . . . how was it that you . . . hit on your idea for self-support? I think Melissa mentioned a circuit judge?'

Sheila nodded. A loud and boisterous group of men had formed itself beside them, and taking Lorna's arm, she edged them both away. 'I needed a job I could do from home after I had Marcus, so I did the phone chat lines for a while.' She gave a short sarcastic laugh. 'Can't tell you how weird that is, to be breast-feeding a baby while you're talking daft smut down the receiver to some sad bugger. I tell you, if some of those blokes could have seen me, they'd have been quite put off their stroke.'

'But what about the babies' father?' asked Lorna. 'Wasn't he offering you any financial support?'

'Which one?' Sheila said flatly. 'No, love, in my experience they sod off after they've shot their bolt. Did you know that in this country, forty per cent of kids grow up never knowing their dads? I certainly didn't see either one of them for dust after I gave them the glad tidings. Which is partly why I took on this job of yours – I've got a personal interest in retraining men, you see. Well, that, and because the judge was away and I needed the money – and the help with the housework, if I'm honest. But, God, I can tell you, this one was tough. I've never had one live-in before – the judge just comes for a few hours to do my lav and the floors. Never wants anything else, mind, if that's what you're thinking. Just likes to be on his knees cleaning, and for me to tell him he isn't doing it well enough.' She shook her head. 'There's nowt so queer as folks, duck. Anyway, I'd got a reading week from uni, so the timing was good and I took it on. With your hubby looking after the kids, I could get on studying for my finals. Credit where credit's due, he's learnt fast – at least, I hope so for your sake.'

Looking over at Greg dancing with Marcus on his shoulders across the floor, Lorna smiled again. 'I'll keep him up to scratch with his homework,' she assured his teacher. 'No need to worry on that score.'

Scores were what were exercising the members of the strident group next to them, whose conversation, having become heated, had become reduced to a series of numbers:

'. . . 3–2 in '97 . . .'

'. . . Bollocks! What about the 5–nil result in 2002?'

'Noisy buggers,' said Sheila crossly, moving Lorna away again so they could hear themselves think. 'You know, I reckon that if men could just learn to talk about their feelings, instead of battering everybody round the bonce with numbers, half the world's ills would be solved. Not that I mean to sound retro-feminist or anything,' she joked with some irony, and fixed Lorna with a beady look. 'Obviously that goes for some women too.'

Confirmed now in her suspicion that Greg had had a full and frank conversation about his marriage with Miss Strict before leaving school, Lorna blushed and bit her lip. 'Yes, I know,' she said, feeling quite the chastised pupil, 'I'm going to be tackling that. I've found it quite hard in the past, but I see now how important it is to tidy things up as you go. Anyway,' she concluded briskly, seeing Greg and Marcus approaching in the distance, and offering Sheila her hand in a formal salute. 'I wish you all the very best for the future, and once again, thank you for all you've done for Greg.'

'You're more than welcome, Lorna,' Sheila grinned back, juggling Darren and her packet of cash to return the hand-shake. 'Any time, I'm sure.'

Aware of the bizarreness of this encounter with a woman to whom she owed so much, and whom she would most likely never meet again, Lorna suddenly, and quite unlike her old self, let down her guard to hug her and kiss her on the cheek. 'I owe you so much that I'd seriously consider naming this baby after you if it's a girl,' she said, chancing her arm at a joke. 'But back home in Oz, we've already got quite a few Sheilas.'

Working her way back to the bar for the drink she'd promised Melissa, Lorna spotted her mother enjoying a passionate embrace with Bert, in between Hibbert Sisters' spots. As resolved as she was to become less rigid in her outlook, Lorna was still undecided over her feelings about this. It seemed somehow to be a betrayal of her father to welcome this old flame into the family, and yet, she reminded herself, what right did she have to stand in her mother's way? At least Mum had stayed with Dad all those years, and grown to love him, as she'd said. This rediscovery of her ex-fiancé must be pure serendipity for her.

Swapping her anxious frown for a smile of blessing, therefore, Lorna squared her shoulders to advance and break up the clinch. 'Great singing, Mum,' she said warmly, 'and – terrific support on the spoons, Bert. Quite a talent you've got there.'

'And that's not his only talent,' June answered buoyantly, but with her look turning more serious, Bert took his cue to leave.

'I'm pretty talented at getting drinks and all,' he said. 'Another gin and It coming up. Anything for you, Lorna, love?'

'Not just now, thanks.'

Turning back to her daughter, her look of seriousness back in place, June seemed unsure of how to broach the subject of what was clearly on her mind. 'Well then,' she began awkwardly, 'soon be going back to Melbourne—'

This issue had been in Lorna's thoughts too, and taking her mother gently by the shoulders, she bravely put her new theories about expressing her feelings into practice. 'I think I know what you're going to say, Mum,' she said, 'and yes, I'm sure it'll feel a little bit strange for us all at first. But of *course* Bert must come and live with you in the cottage when we get back home. I just think it's great that you've found each other again, and that things are still the same between you.'

'Actually, love,' June admitted, after a brief internal struggle, 'what I was going to say was that I'll be staying on here. For a while,' she added quickly, seeing her daughter's face fall. 'I've been having the time of my life catching up with all my folks, and I just feel a fortnight's not long enough after all these years. And to be honest,' she confided, drawing Lorna closer, 'I want to be a hundred per cent sure that me and Bert are a goer, before he uproots himself from all his friends and family, and packs up to go over to Oz. It's early days, and we're still at the mushy stage at present. We could just be kidding ourselves.' Her mushy look, however, belied her belief in the probability of this sentiment.

'But you *are* coming back to live in Melbourne eventually?' Lorna checked, panic kicking at her heart. 'You'll be back in time for the baby?'

'Oh, love, I'll be back long before that,' her mother assured her. 'A girl needs her mum when her time's coming due, no mistake. 'Sides, try keeping me away from my first go at being a proud grannie – are you kidding? As for settling back in Melbourne, with Bert or without him, I'm pretty sure I will, yes. I mean, we complain enough about the changeable weather over there, but let's face it, who could put up with this kind of cold and wet, once they know different?'

Lorna laughed with relief. 'And you can come back on regular visits,' she reminded her. 'We could even help Aunty Mo and Aunty Jo out with the airfare, if they'd like to come over and see us.'

'I think you'll find your cousin'll be the first one in that queue,' June joked, turning to see Melissa doubled up at one of Greg's jokes. 'But, love, as to *where* I'll live in Melbourne in the future,' she continued rather more carefully, fearful as she had always been of seeming ungrateful for her daughter's concern, 'well now, that might be another story. It's not as if

I'm in my dotage yet, and I'm certainly not incapable of looking after myself. Don't get me wrong, I really appreciate you and Greg wanting to have me close by, but I've missed St Kilda real bad, and it isn't so far on the bus to come and visit you – every blessed day, if you like. Anyway, there's life in this old dog yet – might even bite the bullet and learn to drive a car at last. Or Bert can drive me, if things go as well as I hope in that direction.'

'Whatever you want, Mum,' Lorna said, hugging her, moist-eyed. 'I just want to see you being happy.'

'No more nor less than what I want for you, darl,' June assured her, as they shared the tissue she fished from her sleeve.

Coming up behind them, Greg circled Lorna's waist with his arms. 'Okay with you if I take my wife and kiddie off for a dance, Mum?' he asked June, and watching them go, she felt for the first time that her daughter's future happiness was more or less assured.

Out on the dance floor, Greg breathed deeply of his wife's scent and sighed with contentment. 'You're the most precious and important thing in all the world to me, Lorna,' he said, swaying with her to Bert Kaempfert. 'I've done nothing to deserve you, but from now on I'm going to make sure that I do.'

Lorna freed herself a little in his embrace and looked into his eyes. 'There's been faults on both sides, Greg,' she admitted. 'I hope we've both learnt some valuable lessons about what's really important in our lives. I've been – rather cold and distant. I can see that's how I've been coming across. To tell you the truth,' she continued with difficulty, 'I think I've always been scared of losing you. I never really understood why you picked me, of all the girls who were hanging around.

We're so different, you and me. You're so out-going, and I'm . . . I've *been*,' she amended with a grin, 'so tight-buttoned. I don't know how that's possible, with a mother like mine.'

'Well, she's a hard act to follow, is Junie. But if *I'd* helped you to feel more confident of me—' Greg began.

'I just didn't want to scare you off by seeming to be too clingy,' Lorna confessed at the same moment. 'I suppose I've been trying to appear independent, keep my worries to myself.'

Tightening his embrace again, Greg swung her happily round the floor. 'I quite like being clung to, if it feel like this,' he assured her. 'Otherwise, I start to feel I'm surplus to requirements. Or to put it another way,' he joked, taking in the assembled company of family and new friends, 'a bit like a spare prick at a wedding.'

17

The send-off party at Tullamarine airport was small in number, but big in turning heads, since Chin had come as Busty yet again.

'So did we show you a good time?' she asked rhetorically of Mick and Pauline Watkins, as they were about to disappear, hand-in-hand, through the door marked Departures.

'Utterly brilliant,' said Mick happily.

'I'd never have believed it,' Pauline smiled smugly.

The group fractured for a moment, mother clinging tearfully to the daughter she was going to leave behind, father having his last few words with the young man who had caused this.

'You'll look after her for us, then?' he instructed Todd anxiously, gripping his hand.

'Course I will, Mr W, don't you worry about a thing,' said Todd, and putting his arm round the older man's shoulders, he drew him closer. 'And in the unlikely event that things didn't work out between me and Gem, sir,' he confided in a low tone, 'I'd stick around to see her right till she was either back home with you, or settled somewhere safely here. Not that I think that will ever happen, mind,' he said, relinquishing his grasp to return his shining smile to Gemma. 'Far as I'm concerned, the girl's Christmas on a stick!'

She who had been thus favourably compared to a Yuletide kebab was similarly comforting her mother. 'I'm going to be right, Mum, no worries,' she assured Pauline, already almost fluent in the language of her adopted country.

'But if you weren't, Gem, you'd call us?' Pauline worried.

'Course I would.'

'And I want you to know, duck,' her mother said, in a voice trembling with unshed tears, 'that as soon as we've paid off the card for this trip, I'm going to start saving for your emergency airfare – just in case you ever did need to come back sudden.'

'Big girl now,' Gemma told her firmly. 'I'll save for my flight home, and you two start saving up for yours to come back. Now go on, you'll miss the one you've already paid for!'

'Everybody snuggle up, arms round each other, closer!' cried Busty, organising the family group into the last holiday snap with Mick's camera. 'Lovely! Big cheesy smiles, all say "Lesbian" . . .'

'Lesbian!' they chorused, making heads turn towards the unlikely recipient of this soubriquet, before, laughing, Mick and Pauline reluctantly went through the gate.

'See you soon, Dorothy and Polly!' Busty called after them, making a Gemma sandwich between herself and Todd. 'You'll have to come back, now we've kidnapped your daughter!'

'Great folks,' said Todd smiling, as they watched Mick and Pauline, arms round each other's waists, disappear from their view.

'They are, you know,' said Gemma, with a tear in her eye and something like surprise in her voice. 'They're well wicked, as it happens.'

The flight back seemed much shorter now its duration was a known quantity, and particularly since Polly and Mick had exhausted themselves in the last few days, trying to cram in all they could in what remained of their stay, ever since Mick had gratefully given up his evening job to Linda Loveless. They both slept well till Kuala Lumpur, where they sat side by side in the air-conditioned transfer lounge, feeding coins into the slots of their all-over massage chairs.

'See what I mean?' Pauline groaned to her drooling husband, holding his hand across the small divide.

'Not half,' he smiled, eyes closed for maximum enjoyment. 'We'll have to get a couple of these, Mother, when we make our first million with *Watkins Washers*.'

Matt was there to meet them at Heathrow airport, having driven down in the Datsun as a surprise. It was the first time he could remember his old man kissing him in public, and he grinned as he rubbed his cheek afterwards. 'Somebody could do with a shave,' he admonished his father. 'No wonder women complain!'

'It's only cos he packed his moisturiser in his suitcase, and he couldn't get to it on the plane,' Matt's mother explained rather puzzlingly as she grabbed him out of his father's arms and into hers. 'Anyway, come here – see what you make of my five o'clock shadow!'

Back home, at 236 New Vistas Boulevard, Mick and Pauline sank with relief into their comfy settee, while Whiff tried to lick them both at once.

'Shan't be long out of me bed, Dad, even though it is still only afternoon,' Pauline said happily, as Matt returned with mugs of tea.

'That's right,' said Mick, and yawned in an exaggerated fashion, stretching his arms and letting one fall back around Pauline's shoulders. 'Might even take this tea up.'

'So you had a great time, then, did you?' Matt pressed them, as they got up as one to go up the stairs.

'Out of this world,' said Mick. 'Leave the suitcases, Poll, I'll bring them.'

'I had thought you might want to talk about setting up the new business,' Matt said faintly, sounding disappointed.

'I do, duck,' his dad said. 'But I'll be more alert in the morning. You're staying here, aren't you?'

'If that's okay? Till I sort myself out with a flat.'

'No, that'll be great,' Mick assured him, but his footstep faltered on his way out, and he turned in the doorway to eyeball his son. 'Just one thing, though, Matt. Your sister had a very bad habit of bursting into other people's bedrooms . . .'

'Yeah, well, that's where she and I differ,' Matt said firmly. 'So, see you in the kitchen at breakfast, whatever time you're up.'

Having turned back the covers of their lovely soft double bed, Pauline crossed the room to close the curtains. It was already almost dark outside, despite the earliness of the hour. This time yesterday (or was it the day before?), Mick and she had been sunbathing on the beach and swimming in the sea.

A figure caught her attention outside in the street, scuttling out of Dolly and Dinesh's gate next door. Hiding behind the curtain, Pauline peered out and recognised Lizzie Greer from round the corner, being waved off by Asheem, all smiles.

But as she turned back from the window to acknowledge her husband's arrival, Pauline knew whose smile was bigger. It was her, the cat who'd got the cream, right here.

18

The send-off party at Heathrow airport was large in number, and larger than life in its make-up, comprising as it did representatives from most of England's old colonies, including a small half-Indian girl who might have been disguised as a floral tribute (or else she was holding one as big as herself), a young woman wearing either a very short skirt or a very deep belt, three generations of a Jamaican family, and a trio of sexagenarian singers, whose rendition of 'We'll meet again', in close three-part harmony with support from the spoons, caused a complete traffic jam at the door marked Departures.

'Bye then, darl,' said the group's lead vocalist, as she hugged her daughter while everyone whistled and cheered.

'Bye, Mum. Don't be too long following us,' Lorna told her. 'You'll take care of her for me, won't you, Bert?'

'Course I will. See you soon, duck,' Bert said, tucking his percussion instruments back in his top pocket to give her a kiss.

'If he don't, he'll get what for from me,' warned Aunty Mo, taking her turn to squeeze Lorna.

'Don't worry – he's already getting what for from her!' screeched Melissa, pointing a frosted nail extension at her Aunty June.

'Thanks for everything, mate,' Greg told Elroy warmly. 'I never thought I'd hear myself saying it, but I'm grateful for your part in teaching me a lesson.'

'It was against my will, man, that I drove you to that place,' Elroy protested, easing baby Lornetta onto his other arm, and looking down with embarrassment at his Nikes.

'I don't mean just that, El – I mean being such an all-round beaut of a bloke,' Greg qualified generously. 'Great role model in the fathering arena. Something for me to try to match up to. Be about the last time you bloody Pom buggers ever beat us Aussies at something!' he joked, unable to sustain his seriousness for long.

'Ay – who you calling a Pom?' Elroy's mum riposted. 'This 'ere a fine Jamaican boy, even though he born in Leicester!'

'Yeah, fair enough, Bev,' Greg conceded, adding cheekily, 'But you'll accept I got the "bugger" bit right?'

'Come on, then, let's be having the coach party back on board, so these folks can catch their plane,' said Uncle Vince, who'd hired the minibus for the outing.

'I don't want you to go, Lorn,' Melissa started wailing, clinging to her favourite cousin, which was being captured on video by her mother's sister-in-law's second husband's son. 'Now I've found you, I want to keep you!' she adjured.

'I'll send you a postcard from sunny Melbourne soon as we get there,' Lorna promised her, returning her fervid embrace.

'And a boomerang earring?'

'I'll keep adding to your collection, every year at Christmas,' Lorna laughed. 'Koala, possum, wallaby – everything under the Australian sun. If you really think you've got any room left in your ears for any more.'

'Love you, Lornie.'

'Love you, Mel.'

'Love you, Lorn.'

'Love you, Mum.'

'Love you, love you, see you soon,' the tribe from Leicester chorused, as the well-dressed couple from Black Rock,

Melbourne, picked up their YSL cabin bags, on the first leg of their first-class flight back home.

'Champagne?' asked the Singaporean flight attendant, as they cruised at thirty thousand feet.

'Why not?' said Lorna with a self-indulgent smile. 'Thanks.'

'Do you think you should darl, in your condition?' her husband cautioned.

'A sip or two won't hurt, love,' Lorna protested. 'And we're still on holiday after all.'

'Great bunch of folks you've got there,' Greg complimented her, as he bit into a tiny foie gras brioche. 'But I can't say I'll be sorry to get back home.'

Lorna turned to him with softened eyes. 'Did you know that that's what you said when you burst into 236 New Vistas Boulevard?' she reminded him. 'After you'd escaped from the prison camp? "I'm home at last," you said.'

'Well, love, by then I'd learnt that home is where the heart is,' Greg told her, brushing her cheek with his lips. 'So I am home, wherever I am, if I'm with you.'

Thus, he came home again in Changi airport, when they were reunited after their brief spell apart in the showers; he was already home as they were driving in the limo down the Tullamarine toll road, and he was home from home as they stretched out together in their large double hammock under the trees at the house at Black Rock, to watch the last of that day's sun. 'Missing your mum already?' he asked Lorna sympathetically, as he caught her gazing wistfully over at the granny annexe.

She nodded. 'It's going to be strange having that place empty,' she admitted.

'Well, if June really doesn't want to come back here to live,'

Greg suggested, 'it'll make a great place for the nanny.'

'You're right,' Lorna agreed pragmatically. 'I guess we'll have to start interviewing for one soon.'

Greg shifted himself to put his arm under her head. 'What qualities shall we say we're after, in the ad?' he mused. 'She'll need to be someone we can both feel comfortable living near, as well as being great with kids and fully trained, of course.'

'And quiet,' joked Lorna, listening to a bird sing and the far-off swish of the sea. 'I mean, don't get me wrong, they were all lovely people back there, but isn't it just bliss to be on our own again, away from all that overexcited hysteria?'

The thrum of an arriving moped drowned out her husband's reply, and sitting bolt upright sharply at the intrusion, they both very nearly fell out of the hammock as they witnessed the blonde bombshell who dismounted and took off her helmet, plumping out her tresses as she advanced towards them on platform heels.

'Lorna, daughter, you're back!' she trilled in gay welcome. 'And this gorgeous spunk must be hubby Greg. Busty Springboard-A-Go-Go-*lah*, star of the stage, and feeder of June's pussy. I am so *delighted* to welcome you home!'